Parties

Girls Weekend Book 2

C.M. Nascosta

a MonsterBait romance

xoxo

Cover & Interior Art: Ilustrariane

MEDUAS
EDITORIALE

Dedicated to the Patrons who
patiently waited for this book when real life got really real.
Thank you for sticking with the girls

An enormous amount of gratitude from this Christine to the
other Christine
— thank you for your boundless enthusiasm and eagle eyes!

Author's Note:

Don't let the illustrated cover fool you! This is a work intended for adult consumption.

In case you're new around here and the green hand wasn't a clue: this is a work of monster romance; there are no human characters. This is a *series* and there is another book forthcoming. No, I'm not saying when, that's just a cue for the universe to fuck with my best intentions.

CW include:

SIZE DIFFERENCE and all the yum that comes with it, negative body image, external fatphobia, pegging, public sex/threesome, light blood play, and just a stupid amount of angst from these idiots.

No plot/just horny vibes has been my mantra on this book, but a decent bit of plot probably snuck its way in too, my apologies.

Autumn

The Foreshadowing-Laden Beginning

Tate

"I don't want to hear from any of you. At all, for *any* reason. Do you understand? If everything in the freezers goes, figure out a new menu. Don't call me. If the glassware comes together and conspires with it itself to simultaneously shatter, you all know where the brooms are. Start sweeping. Don't call me. If the bleedin' building catches on fire, call the fucking fire brigade and let me fend for myself. Do *not* call me."

Cymbeline nodded with wide eyes, sitting up straight at attention, her hands clasped tightly in her lap with small fangs worrying her lower lip. *At least someone was listening*, he thought. It was unsurprising, for the mothwoman was always the first and quickest to take direction, always eager to please, to prove her worth. Seated directly behind was her diametric opposite. Elshona rolled her eyes dramatically at his words, and Tate felt the muscle behind his own eye jump; a tic that had gradually worsened over the last several weeks that he was certain made him look positively homicidal, which was truthful, in any case. The orc met his glower defiantly, pursing her lips, and his teeth slipped several centimeters in response.

The dining room beyond the service hallway hummed with voices despite the lateness of the season, and he could easily envision the hulking bodies within, testing the weight of his chairs, their giggling guests leaning over the tabletops to show off their best, barely covered assets. The resort's bonfire party was planned for the following night, one that would spill over to parties within the commune in an orgiastic bacchanal — excellent news for his brunch business as the bleary-eyed tourists awoke beside suddenly sheepish orcs, all eager to display a measure of civility they'd forgotten the night before. It was the last resort event before the cold winds of late autumn blew in the year's first snowflakes, sending the tourists scuttling along with the last leaves clinging to the trees.

He ought to be there that weekend, ought to be present to oversee the last burst of business, to keep things humming smoothly at the bistro and prevent any unwary tourists from being overserved at the bar. Ought to be . . . but if he had to be on his feet for one more day, if he had to hear Cym's non-stop chatter or 'Shona's sullen barbs, if he had to drag himself up the Pixie's back staircase at the end of the night stinking of stout and sweat and orc *one more* bleedin' night, he'd likely burn down the entire town, regardless of the weekend's profitability. *Burn it down and spit in the ashes.* The time of year was contributing to his mood, a fact he knew all too well, to the thrumming in his veins and the hint of fiddles and drums that teased at his ear; an irritability that itched beneath his skin and the desire to hit something or someone until they were nothing but messy pulp beneath his fist .... but he hadn't had a proper day off in nearly two months, a fact his back reminded him of with every step. The only thing he wanted to do that weekend was crawl directly into his bed and perhaps die.

"I don't want to hear your chirping wee voices or see your precious fucking faces. Do you understand? If I have to see any of your faces at *any* point in the next seventy-two hours, I'm cutting them off."

Thessa grinned at his completely sincere words, and Elshona's head dropped back, throwing her hands in the air. "Will you just hurry up and go then? No one told you to be here every fucking moment of the day, Tate. You chose that all on your own."

He watched Cymbeline open her mouth, raising a long, velvety finger in protest — clearly wanting to remind Elshona of the server who'd abruptly quit mid-shift the previous month and the part-time hostess who'd hidden her pregnancy so effectively that she'd gone into labor in the small employee break room only two weeks after the server had quit, splashing the tiles in a gush of liquid he'd been unfortunate enough to witness as he paced in the next shift change, bile rising in his throat as he left the girl with her shrieking coworker, locking himself into his office to stare in dismay at his no longer relevant schedule — but Cym's words never drew breath, her eyes darting between the air beside her head and Tate, wanting to speak, but not wanting to talk out of turn.

"Let's see if you can manage to actually stay away for more than twenty-four fecking hours," Elshona plowed on, undeterred. "My money's on 'no.' You'll be back by tomorrow night to rewrite a schedule that doesn't need to be meddled with or to clean the bar, or whatever other shite excuse you'll come up with. Go *home*, Tate. Better still, why don't you go straight to the hospital and have them put you in traction, because I'm not sure how you're even bloody standing at this point. When they tell you your back is broken, I'll visit with some bleedin' 'I told you so' flowers. Or just fuck off home. Take a whole heap of drugs all weekend and pretend you're fine. But *leave* is the fucking point. We're as tired of hearing you as you are of us."

His eye jumped, muscles spasming just beneath the skin, and his fingers twitched, desperately wanting to fasten around the orc's neck and squeeze for all he was worth, but settled on clenching into fists. "D'you remember that one time, 'Shona — and I know it can be hard because we've shared so many memories together over the years — but do you remember that one time when we were together, it happened about three and half minutes ago, when I said I didn't want to hear your fucking voice?"

Somewhere on the dining room floor, the crash of broken glass shattered through the voices of patrons, and his eye fluttered again, threatening to bulge from its socket.

"It's fine, I've got it," Cym leapt to her feet, wings folding gracefully at her back, pausing in her exit to wrap his wrist in a velutinous grip. "*Please* go home and get some rest. It'll be fine, and we'll see you next week!" The mothwoman straightened her skirt, forced her painted lips into a bright smile, and pushed out the door in a flutter of pink and green and the sweet smell of lilacs, leaving Thessa still sitting before him, Elshona having made good her escape the moment his attention was pulled by the crash.

"You know it pains me to the core to agree with Elshona about literally anything," the tiefling began, pushing to her feet and retying the black apron which swung slack around her neck, "but maybe she's right. You probably *do* need to see a doctor. But seriously, go home. Now. Who cares if we're short-handed? Big fucking deal, it's the last weekend of the season." She shrugged, her numerous piercings catching the overhead light, gesturing to the dining room floor beyond the hallway. "What are they gonna do if ticket times are slow, not come back next week when the resort shuts down and they don't have any other options? It's not like any of them know how to fend for themselves. Go. Cym and I have everything under control. I'm closing up tonight, she's on tomorrow. Everything will be spick and span when you come back on Monday, and you should come in late anyway. We're just going to be inventorying, I can do that in my sleep."

It was a busy night, the last busy Friday of the season, and he'd absolutely be leaving them short-handed . . . but the lure of his bed was too great. "Fine then, I'm cracking off . . . push that veal, I don't know why she ordered so much. Veal and the swordfish, and guilt them into bottles. There's a lot of that—"

"Tate. I know. *Go.*"

His back protested the step he took out the back door, feeling the tiefling's eyes following as she leaned on the jamb, making sure he actually left. The prospect of climbing the steps to his apartment was agonizing to contemplate, but his bed was calling and he'd gladly spill the blood of anyone who kept him from its confines that weekend. *Spill it. Drink it. Bathe in it. All of the above.* Pipes had joined the sound of the faraway flute, the tempo upbeat and merry and familiar, but his back hissed at his toes to ignore the sound and keep moving, and he continued to stagger through the dimly-lit alley.

"Go home, turn your phone off," Thessa called out, her voice bouncing between the buildings to his retreating form, the prospect of absolute silence for the next three days making him hasten his step as much as he was able. "It's the last weekend, what could possibly happen? Everything will be fine!"

♥ ♥ ♥

Ris

She hadn't planned on returning to the nudist resort.

After all, the first trip she'd taken with her friends at the start of the summer had yielded the exact results she'd hoped for. She'd gone back to Cambric Creek having crossed several lines off her bucket list, with a trove of only slightly embellished stories of her experiences at the bonfire orgy to covertly tell Dynah over their lunch breaks, and she was more than satisfied to allow time and distance to color the experience with rosier hues than it had actually comprised. *Time to find someone real,* she'd told herself in the weeks and months afterward, *someone interesting and fun.*

"I play the market," her date explained with a cocky smile, leaning over the small table, several inches into her own space, "I guess you could say I'm a bit of a stock jockey." Ris pulled back, unable to keep her nose from wrinkling at the smell of the wheat beer his breath carried.

"And it never ends, let me tell you. I have to be plugged in morning, noon, and night, twenty-four seven. I probably shouldn't even have my phone put away now, but I promised myself I'd get one night to focus on me . . . and my beautiful companion, of course."

She was meant to be impressed, she understood. Impressed and fawning, but unfortunately for her date, understanding did not equal acquiescence. His particular brand of braggadocio may have been attractive to other women, but, alas, he wasn't out with one of them. The gastropub was bustling and busy that night, buzzing with the voices of the after-work crowd spilling into the dinner crowd, and she was glad for the press of bodies and distractions, for the elf across the table wasn't giving her much to work with.

"That doesn't sound like it leaves room for much else. What about hobbies?"

She didn't bother holding in her huff of irritation when he laughed as if she'd told a fantastically funny joke. She had perfected the art of fitting in over the years; of being pretty, popular Ris, chameleon-like in her ability to slip into whatever role was required of her, but these days she found herself less and less inclined to be anyone but herself. *And we're not impressed.* She rarely matched the criteria most elves her age were looking for, and it had been a surprise when she had with this one. She'd tried to be positive when the evening started, but her optimism, as well as her drink, had just about run out.

"Who has time for that?" he laughed. "I can take up coin collecting when I get to my jubilee. Until then, *making* coin is more important."

If he noticed she didn't join in as he chuckled again at his own words, he didn't let on, draining the drink in front of him and glancing down to the glittering watch face on his wrist. "I was thinking we could head over to the Pickled Pig. Better crowd than this place."

He glanced around swiftly, raising a hand to catch the attention of the server, and Ris patted her lips with her cocktail napkin before slipping her wrist through the strap of her clutch, more than content to call it an early night. Gildersnood & Ives had become the girls' preferred happy hour spot over the last few months, always bustling, always packed with the office dwellers of the commerce parkways and employees of the local businesses, the same people who were her neighbors and friends. The crowd at Gildersnood was good enough for her, and if it wasn't for her date, that meant she wasn't either. Besides, Ris reminded herself, she'd somehow managed to get a large splotch of ink on the sleeve of one of her work dresses, glad she'd noticed it before tossing it into the wash the previous morning. She'd set it aside for a spot treatment she'd not yet done, plus there was a documentary she'd borrowed from the local library and a new video up from a yoga studio she supported on Benefactoring. *All preferable options to this date.*

"I think we should probably call it a night, actually." A slender troll arrived at their table, familiar and harried-looking, and Ris gave her a broad smile. "Put mine on my tab, Ruby. Zeig will close it out at the end of the night."

There was a bit of a breeze that night, a sign of the waning summer, and she was glad it would only be a quick dash across the street to the municipal lot where her car was parked.

"Do you want to follow me? I'm over in Lindë Terrace, on the other side of Oldetowne. I valeted, where are you parked?"

She turned up in confusion at his words, unsure of why he thought she'd be following him anywhere. "I'm not sure what—like I said, I think we should call it a night. It was great meeting you, though! Good luck with making that coin, right?"

The elf's smooth brow furrowed, and his sapphire eyes narrowed, nose wrinkling.

"Wait, that's . . . that's it? We're not going to — you're just leaving?!"

She raised an eyebrow, glad for the presence of the ogre at her back, a security guard she knew well. "Yes? Look, you're a nice guy, but I don't think we really have anything in common. It was nice meeting—"

"Your profile said you weren't looking for a relationship," he interrupted, a scowl marring his handsome features. "And now you're just leaving? You shouldn't be wasting people's time like this."

She stepped back, her mouth dropping open in shock. *What a fucking prick.* "And what? You thought that meant a sure thing? My profile didn't say 'adventurous 34f, DTF', but if you interpreted it that way, that's your problem, not mine." She glared, ears heating in outrage. "I take it back, it wasn't that great meeting you, actually. Try spending some of that coin on buying yourself an actual personality." The chill in the air was bracing as she strode across the street, exchanging a knowing nod with the ogre before crossing the street in front of him, gratified to see the way he glowered at the elf she left on the sidewalk, confident that she could cross to her car and exit the vicinity without worry that he might follow. One more bad date from the app, one more reason to delete it from her phone altogether. *Jokes on him*, she thought sardonically, pulling through town. *You **might** have been down to fuck, if he'd actually been interesting.*

She hadn't planned on returning to the nudist resort . . . but then Dynah's relationship with the arrogant Dragonborn had fizzled. It had been Dynah's idea to come back to the orc resort, Dynah who'd whined about missing out the first time, Dynah who'd insisted she wanted to be the filling in her own orc orgy sandwich. Even though she hadn't felt a pressing need to go back and repeat her experience of the first trip, the lack of luck on the dating app was enough to make Ris restless, and Dynah's whining pleas were wearing her down.

Restlessness was only a part of the problem, she contemplated, a symptom of a larger cause. Ris felt as if she were stuck in place, like she was spinning in mud, sinking a bit further with every day, every week that passed . . . but worse than desperately wanting something just out of her reach, she didn't *know* what she wanted, a far worse affliction, she'd determined. She had a job she liked well enough, one that kept her comfortable that she was able to leave at the office each day, and one that supported her love of museum and theater visits . . . but she tired of making said visits alone. She didn't want a husband, she barely wanted a boyfriend. Despite her community's obsession with babies, she had no desire to have children. She was selfish and settled and entirely unwilling to give up her freedom and quirks — but that didn't mean it wouldn't be nice to have someone to spend time with. *A friend with benefits. Someone you'll have things in common with. Someone good in bed who will go with you to the art museum and actually have fun. A friend with benefits who won't decide they want to get married after a month, that's what you need. Funny. Articulate. Well-hung would be a plus.*

She felt better, she'd decided, articulating exactly what it was she was looking for. She still had no idea how to find such a partner, but putting her wish out into the universe was the first step in manifesting it, wasn't it? She gave the ideal FWB a considerable amount of thought, wrote down a list of personality traits and hobbies and non-negotiables, feeling like a child writing her list of wishes to burn at the solstice oracle fire, taking her yoga mat to the roof of her condo to breathe out her wants to the sunrise, stretching into her salutation, feeling as if she were taking up the reins of control for the first time in months. *Months? Years?* One last wild weekend of debauchery felt like a fitting way to close out the past year of discontented ennui, she decided jovially.

The resort had been, unsurprisingly, booked solid when Dynah had pled her case, the late-summer festivities too great a draw and the balmy nights too licentious a setting at the nudist resort for other sight-seers to resist. The end of the season was the best they could do, a full five months after the first trip she'd taken with Lurielle and

Silva. It hadn't felt like that long a span, but she'd determined that time passed differently on the other side of thirty. Already she could feel her existence starting to slow, the milestones celebrated by her peers at work seeming somewhat trivial, nearly half a year passing in what felt like a handful of weeks. She wondered what seventy-five would feel like and if two hundred would be upon her before she could blink; if this restlessness would still live in her bones, like grains of sand, chafing just beneath the skin.

Reservations were made, bags were packed, and orc-sized condoms were purchased.

And then Dynah, flippy-floppy, wishy-washy Dynah, met some oily-voiced kitsune through the stupid app and canceled at the last minute — again. *"I really think he's the one! I know I've said that before, but this time is different, I know it!"* It had been so unsurprising, she'd hardly been angry. It wasn't the first time Dynah had broken plans the instant some guy sniffed in her direction and it likely wouldn't be the last, she thought tiredly. It was a condition of being her friend, and Ris had begun thinking of it as a medical affliction Dynah simply couldn't control.

In any case, Lurielle had been furious on her behalf, and that had been enough.

"Are you fucking kidding me? She's doing this again?!" Lurielle's face scrunched across the breakroom table, shaking her head in disgust. "What is *wrong* with her? How many times are we going to let her do this? Are you able to get your money back for the room?"

She shrugged, helping herself to one of Lurielle's veggie crisps. "She was raised to think that her self-worth is based on male attention and fucking of course I can't get the money back. Seventy-two-hour cancellation policy, same as last time. It's not her fault. I mean, it *is* her fault, but . . . you know. Peak Dynah. Soooo, whatcha doing this weekend? Big plans with Mr. Perfect or do you wanna play wingwoman?"

"I can't," Lurielle sighed. "He has a mudball match on Saturday afternoon and Sunday we're picking up landscaping stuff before the weather turns. I don't like the idea of you going back there alone, what if something happens? I can't believe Dynah. I don't understand how you're not raging."

"What are we raging over? Ooo, is it the cider thief? I have some choice words if you caught them." Silva appeared in the doorway, prim and perfect in an a-line dress several shades darker than her lavender skin, topped by a snug, coral-hued cardigan with dainty pearl buttons.

Ris snorted as their younger co-worker pulled her apple cider jug from the fridge, carefully pouring several glugs into her half-full water bottle. Silva had been cheerfully hauling a half-gallon jug back and forth every day since the local farms began advertising the fresh-pressed beverage with a bevy of roadside signs. In the beginning, she'd been leaving it in the communal refrigerator, until the day she'd come in to find the empty jug sitting on the countertop, drained down to the last drop. They had witnessed her smooth lavender skin darken, the tips of her ears turning purple in anger as tiny, indistinct yips and squeaks came from her throat like an adorably furious bunny, her movements tight and jerky, stabbing her salad in the same way, Ris assumed, that she might drive her fork into the ribs of the unknown juice thief, were they to materialize before the table. Since then, her precious apple cider commuted with her, cut with water several times a day at the break room counter.

"No, we're mad at Dynah. You know, I'd be concerned you were going to turn into an apple at this rate if you weren't pouring that into water."

"It's too much sugar on its own," Silva chirped cheerfully, sipping from her bottle with a hum of contentment, taking a seat at the table. "And you can't be mad at Dynah. Dynah's just Dynah. You know what to expect going in. Let me guess, you were supposed to go to the fair together this weekend and now she's going with some guy she met three minutes ago?"

Lurielle nearly choked on a forkful of her lunch, laughing at Silva's words, and Ris sighed. Everyone had Dynah's number, it seemed, except Dynah herself.

"Basically. We had out-of-town weekend plans and she dumped me. Do you want to take her place? All the fresh-pressed cider you can drink, on me. The room is already paid for and I'll bet the leaves are beautiful in the valley right now."

Silva's rosebud mouth opened, but her words never had a chance to draw breath. Tannar appeared in the door, his face lighting up at the sight of the girls, beelining to where they sat and pulling a chair from the neighboring table, straddling the seat and giving them a bright smile as he rested his arms across its back. The break room was mostly empty that afternoon . . . mostly empty, but not entirely. Ris watched Puldra, a troll from accounting, return to the neighboring table from the microwave, only to find the chair — in front of which she'd placed her lunch only several minutes earlier — missing. The troll scowled at Tannar's back, forcefully yanking another from the other side of the table to her now-empty spot, not that he paid any mind. Ris sighed, shooting Puldra an apologetic look, hoping she'd not blame the entire table for the transgressions of one, for it wasn't a good idea to make enemies with anyone in accounting.

The elf was new to their little work friend group, having elbowed his way in with the self-assuredness seemingly possessed by all men of their species: an assumption that the entire world was theirs for the taking and that they'd receive a thank you from anyone they might step on in their climb. Tannar's pushiness was somewhat tempered by his dazzling smile and gregarious nature, and he'd unsurprisingly set his sights on Silva practically since his first day.

"An official meeting of the Lunch Bunch and I wasn't invited?! Ladies, I'm wounded. Are we making weekend plans? Fallfest, right? Whaddaya say, Silva? Fancy a spiced cider and a spin on the haunted hayride on Saturday?"

Tannar's interest in Silva was as unsurprising as Dynah's eleventh-hour cancellation, but what *was* surprising was Silva's lukewarm reaction to his attentions, considering Tannar was exactly the sort of match Ris thought Silva would be gaga over. He was a Summerland elf, like Lurielle, with a creamy ivory complexion and caramel-colored hair, a sharp contrast to their Silmë co-workers. His blue eyes sparkled and his bright smile was likely the result of pricey whitening treatments; his aftershave smelled expensive and the watch on his wrist probably cost more than her car — all the makings of a good catch in the Elvish community. He was friendlier than most privileged men of their kind tended to be though, and although Luielle disliked him on principle, Ris thought he seemed like a genuinely nice guy. As pushy and arrogant as one could expect from the upper echelons of Elvish society, but friendly with bright, kind eyes. She didn't understand Silva's seeming apathy, but didn't want to add to the lectures she knew her younger co-worker regularly received from her family.

"Oh, that-that sounds so fun! I wish I could . . . but I have plans for the weekend. Are you and Khash going, Lurielle?"

"We might drop in to get some food and walk around for a bit, after mudball, as long as the rain holds out. We'll see . . . I don't want to put on real pants all weekend, that's the only real goal."

"Not even for fried cheese on a stick?" Silva asked, taking another sip from her bottle before carefully capping it. "That's my favorite fair food, I'm kind of sad I'll be missing it. Well, that and the cider, but I don't need the fair for that."

"You don't need to wear pants to get fried cheese on a stick, Silva. That's the beauty of fried cheese. Pants aren't required to enjoy it."

Silva's laughter tinkled like a delicate crystal bell, Tannar's nostrils flaring at the sound as if he were memorizing the pitch and frequency before her attention turned back to Ris.

"Hopefully you can find someone to go with you? If I hadn't already made plans, I would . . . I should get back before anyone notices I'm gone. Not that they ever do, but today will be the day."

Tannar's bright blue eyes dimmed momentarily as Silva rose, brushing non-existent crumbs from her skirt, smoothing over the fabric in a graceful movement. "Something at the club?"

"Mmhm," Silva hummed, keeping her eyes downcast as she pushed in her chair. "No way out of it. I'm really sorry, Ris. See you all later!"

The click of her heels competed with the tinny voice of the video Puldra watched on her phone, and Ris watched Lurielle's narrowed eyes follow Silva from the room before they turned to Tannar.

"So you haven't joined the club here yet? I'm not sure you should even be talking to her without a membership. You're just the help without it, you know."

She winced at Lurielle's unnecessary barb, casting a quick glance at their co-worker. His long, ivory ears reddened, but Tannar straightened in his seat at the less-than-subtle dig.

"I belong to my parent's club, obviously. I was going to wait until the end of the season and transfer my renewal, but maybe you're right. Maybe if I apply this weekend, I can get a pass to whatever event they're holding. Well, I'm supposed to be heading up to legal .

. . have fun this weekend on your adventures, ladies. I want to hear all about them on Monday." He straightened out of the chair, returning it to Puldra's table and earning another scowl from the troll before leaving the break room without a backward glance.

"Like there's actually something going on," Lurielle muttered to herself once he'd left, and Ris turned to her friend in exasperation.

"You need to stop being so mean to him, he's *actually* nice."

"I can't help it. He looks like every asshole who tormented me growing up. And besides, he's only nice because he thinks he's sniffed out a sure thing. The second she tells him to take a walk, he's going to ignore us, just wait."

"Yeah, well, *you're* going to feel like the asshole when we're bridesmaids at their wedding. He's literally everything she's looking for, so be nicer."

Lurielle mumbled something Ris didn't catch before shifting back to the Dynah-caused conundrum at hand. "What are you going to do? I *really* don't like the idea of you going alone."

"Nothing's going to happen, I'll be fine. I might not even do anything but shop, to be honest. One trip to the buffet was enough for me. *Or* maybe this time I'll order off the menu. Find my own tasty weekend entrée."

Lurielle laughed, stretching her legs at the now unoccupied table. "Please be careful, okay? I don't care what you 'order,' just don't wind up in someone's trunk. Look, if something happens . . . call Silva, okay? Just . . . please don't ask me why. I don't know what game she's playing, just . . . just trust me. Promise me if something goes wrong, you'll call her first. *And* weekend entrées sometimes come home with you, you know. Don't discount a doggy bag, just sayin'." She reached out for the top file in the stack Ris had set on the table, before the latter smacked her hand away.

"Don't touch, these are confidential."

"Then why do you have them in the break room?!"

Ris smiled with a shrug, gathering up her stack of files before rising from the table.

"I'm not on break, I was looking for you."

"Am I the only sap in this building who takes a break when she's supposed to?"

"I'm pretty sure you are," she agreed with a laugh, ignoring the dirty look from Puldra. "Don't worry about me this weekend, I'll be fine. I promise to call Silva if something happens, she can make bunny squeaks through the phone at whoever is threatening me, I'm sure that will work. Have fun at mudball."

She left the breakroom to the sound of Lurielle's snort, turning over her friend's words. *A weekend entrée is exactly what you need. And if you can't find one, then you just relax. And then on Monday, we start the fuck buddy plus search. It's a perfect plan.*

♥ ♥ ♥

Silva

"**F**uckmmmmgggghhh"

Silva paused at the unintelligible curse he yelped into the pillow, easing up the pressure of her elbow as it ground into the base of his neck. The long, gentle strokes she'd made against his skin with her oil-slickened hands had not pulled any reaction from him, while the application of her thumbs had at least shed some clarity on the topography of knots and bunched muscles she was working with, the physical evidence of the appalling care he took of himself Monday through Friday when she wasn't around.. Her hands weren't strong enough to dig into his knotted muscles and she knew better than to tell him he ought to see a professional, so she'd stripped off the sorority hoodie she'd worn on her drive and dug into his back with knuckles and elbows, pressing her weight into each target until he'd begun to curse in both Elvish and Common, which she decided was a sign her efforts were yielding the necessary result. She'd discovered that pressing into the vertebrae at the base of his neck at an angle, as she'd just done, made his entire body twitch, and she was certain it was the source of a significant amount of his pain.

"Too much pressure? Are you okay?"

Tate weakly lifted his head from the pillow, squinting in the lamplight.

"Oh, I'm grand, dove. You can get one of the heavy-duty bin bags from the stockroom tomorrow morning. Just push me down the stairs and drag me to the alley. Trash pick-up is Tuesday." He settled his face into the pillow once more as she laughed, his voice muffled as he continued. "Do that bit again, I felt that in my toes."

Silva huffed, leaning forward to press her lips to the back of his long neck, inhaling a deep lungful of the wild forest smell of his skin, still warm from the scalding hot shower he'd stood under a short while earlier. He groaned when she dug her elbow into the same spot, digging in from the side with a firm, rolling pressure, and was unable to hold back her self-satisfied grin. Despite the weekend's inauspicious start, everything was going exactly to plan, the makings of her very own perfect romance unfolding in the apartment above the Plundered Pixie.

There had been a panicked moment shortly after her arrival that evening, when she'd beamed down from the landing at the top of the stairs where she'd been sitting, her smile freezing and fading at Tate's stricken look. *He forgot you were coming. He doesn't want you here.*

He probably already made plans. It had been a little over two months since the weekend she'd rode shotgun with Lurielle, returning to the resort town for the first time since the girls' weekend trip. Silva knew that she was likely in the way on the weekends she came to visit him, feared her presence was a hindrance to his productivity and that he probably breathed a sigh of relief when she left on Sunday afternoons. Even if her suspicions were true, Tate did a quality job of hiding it week after week.

His mischievous smile would stretch the moment she met his gaze from across the bar, a long-fingered hand dragging down her spine when she would raise up on her toes to kiss him in greeting after she'd pushed through the press of huge patrons. More than that, Silva had noted over the past weeks, his eyes would light like a child's on solstice morning, a shine they would hold until she departed, kissing her softly at her car window, urging her to drive carefully and have a good week. "Fly away, little dove," he would whisper against her lips; would stand in the alley and watch her departure, his silhouette shrinking in her rearview mirror until she turned back onto the road. He was *happy* to see her on the weeks she made the drive to the resort town, even if she was in his way, she was certain of it.

The look on his face that evening, as he'd gazed up from the bottom of the Pixie's staircase, had been anything but happy. His expression had been pinched, his posture tight and uncharacteristically inelegant, and his eyes, rather than lighting at the sight of her, only looked tired.

24

"Dove." His voice was a croak, absent the lilting ring it normally held, and he'd hesitated, glancing back at something she was unable to see, his body seeming to fight with itself on which direction it wanted to move. For the briefest moment, she'd thought he was going to turn his back on her, choosing whatever was behind. The moment passed and he groaned, beginning the ascent up the narrow staircase with a wince. Silva struggled to her feet, her self-pitying internal monologue halting as she remembered her raison d'être for the weekend. He'd not had a day off in ages, was exhausted and aggravated and in desperate need of rest, even though the words *weekend off* had initially conjured images of romantic candlelit dinners and nights spent panting and tangled in his sheets, the notion of playing nursemaid for the weekend made her positively giddy. *Caretaker trope!*

"I'm not going to be particularly good company this weekend, Silva." Another grunt once he'd reached the top of the landing, swaying as he fished for his keys, not protesting when she pulled them from his clumsy hands.

"You don't need to be good company because all we're doing is resting, remember? Jammies. Breakfast in bed. Bad television. That's it, mister. I brought dinner from the club for tonight and tomorrow, and I'll pick up take-out for lunch. You're not doing anything but getting into bed. Are you sick?" He grunted in response, an unintelligible grumble in response to her question, hardly the warm response she'd been hoping for.

"Not sick, I never get sick . . . but my cunting spine has the fucking audacity to be *Orcish*." He raised an accusing finger, glaring down at her with another wince as she unlocked the door. "Do *not* tell me to go see a doctor. I've always had a bad back, this isn't anything new. There's nothing some know-nothing troll scoff out of med school three minutes will be able to tell me I don't already know. I just need to be off my feet for more than a few hours. Resting sounds perfect." He staggered over the threshold as she gathered up her bags, raising her head to see his wrinkled nose as he considered her words. "But no eating in bed, that's disgusting. Crumbs will get in the sheets, that's how you wind up with brownies."

So far, everything had gone exactly to plan. It had been a risk, ordering food from the club — too many questions could have been asked, too many lies she'd need to tell. It would have been far safer to have patronized one of Cambric Creek's many restaurants, but she was eager for Tate to sample the Elvish cuisine from the club, could close her eyes and easily envision him there, having brunch with her family and taking tea at her side, across from the approving eyes of her grandmother. It was her favorite fantasy: one that involved no dramatic confrontations with her parents, no compromises on her lifestyle, and no shift in her social circle. Tate would simply appear at her side, welcomed by her family and accepted by the elves in her community; accepted because it was clear he and Silva belonged together, embodying her most favorite storyline — *fated mates*.

She had recently joined a book club with Ris, and while the

monthly wine-soaked meetings were an enormous amount of fun, outside the parameters of the club, Silva found herself falling back into a hobby she'd not indulged in since undergrad — burning through romance novels. Reading at her desk when the projects requiring anything more than busywork were given to her more assertive coworkers; reading in the evenings during the week, alone in her small, tastefully decorated apartment. Reading in waiting rooms and on her break when her friends weren't around. She'd bought herself a brand-new e-reader in a dusty mauve with a rose-printed sleeve, and had taken to carrying it around in her handbag, saving herself from unkind comments over the pulpy covers of the sweeping historicals she preferred, needing to force herself to push through whatever book had been chosen as the group's book of the month.

Unlike those university afternoons spent binge-reading in the sunny window nook of her sorority house, she now avoided Elvish romances. When she'd been younger, she couldn't get enough of the starry-eyed tales: always formulaic, always featuring a devastatingly handsome, supercilious male lead whose icy heart was melted by the polished Elvish lady, the story ending in marriage and babies. Now she sought out novels from authors of other species, reveling in the variety of the storylines and appealing love interests. She liked to imagine herself in the role of the female leads, regardless of the species portrayed: harpy businesswomen and dryad ingenues, all braver than she was; Scottish duchesses who managed to live happily ever after with their rakish selkie lovers, regardless of who their families wanted them to marry. The shifter who hosted the monthly book club would engage the group in serious discussion of how cathartic finding oneself in the pages of a book could be, and she was right. Silva loved escaping into the pages of stories about women who weren't afraid to pursue their happily ever afters, who allowed love to conquer all and found comfort in her preferred genre's reliability that the couple would always wind up together despite all of the obstacles in their path, no matter how prim the princess or how much of a scoundrel her rake seemed at the beginning.

"Are you hungry? Did you already have dinner?" She turned, having pulled each of the takeaway boxes from the bag, separating that night's meal into a pyramid of plastic containers, only to find him slumped against the wall with his eyes closed.

"Dinner?" He squinted blearily, as if his mind couldn't quite grasp the meaning of the word. "No . . . Cym puts water in my hand and I drink it, that's it today."

"What?! Tate, that's so bad! You shouldn't be working so hard, this is why your back hurts! You need to make sure you're taking breaks like everyone el—"

She cut off when he pushed off the wall, lurching across the room to where she stood, pinning her against the counter. Tilting her chin with a massive hand, Silva bit her lip to hide her small smile as he squinted down at her.

"Dove, I've been at work since six o'clock this morning moving cases of veal in the walk-in, of which there is *so* fucking much, I'm a bit concerned it came from a minotaur nursery and we're going to be raided at any moment. I opened every case to make sure there weren't any wee blankets forgotten inside. Last night I had to bar back in my own bleedin' pub because the shite-for-brains langer Rukh hired decided he's going to fuck off to be an actor. The boggart in the cellar chewed through the wiring on the conveyor, so I had to drag the kegs up the staircase myself, and *then* the cunty little bastard grabbed at my foot through the steps and nearly pulled me through. My shoe is still down there somewhere. I had a biscuit with my tea yesterday afternoon, and I'm relatively certain I haven't eaten since. Just in case you're keeping score, Silva, this is just the last twenty-four hours. My back feels like it's broken in no less than three different spots. I'm in pain and, *yes*, dove, I'm fucking starving. I also smell like swordfish and sweat, so all I want to do right now is get in a shower and burn at least three layers of skin off my body, eat something, and go to bed to die. I seem to remember mentioning I wouldn't be very good company this weekend."

Silva couldn't help the smile that stretched across her face, any more than she was able to swallow down her small bubble of laughter at the visual of him struggling on the staircase, limping into the Pixie's bar floor with only one of his scuffed boots. Tate scowled, and that only caused her giggle to escape. Everything was funnier in his accent, she had decided weeks earlier, and that included his dramatic recitation of the previous day's tale of woe. He was adorable with his face screwed up that way, and she couldn't resist stretching up to kiss the tip of his scrunched-up nose, noting that he *did*, in fact, smell a bit fishy.

"Go then, go take a shower while I get things heated. Jammies. Dinner. Then bed. That's it. Good company is not required, but no one is dying on my watch."

She found the grey joggers in one of the dresser drawers, laying them out on the bed with one of his ubiquitous black tees while he stood beneath a scalding hot shower, steam billowing out of the partially open bathroom door as she moved down the hallway to the bedroom. She already knew he possessed a closet full of clothes, discovered during a previous thorough snooping session. There was a full wardrobe of black and grey with the occasional pop of oxblood and royal purple, at least a hundred of the same snug-fitting, black v-neck t-shirt; half a dozen pairs of jeans that showed more of his long, green legs than they concealed, a shelf of finely-crafted brogues and oxfords, scuffed Chelsea boots and motorcycle boots, a garment bag that contained several suits . . . but *nothing* in his closet would ever be able to compare with the thin grey joggers, she decided — turning from the kitchen counter to watch as he crossed the room, winding his long, wet hair into a loose topknot. The grey sweats sat low on his narrow hips and hugged the round curve of his ass, accentuating his long, muscular thighs . . . . Silva felt her pulse quicken, trying and failing for several seconds to pull her eyes from the long, thick bulge resting against his thigh, the pants seeming to go out of their way to highlight its heft.

"Shower. *Jammies*," he mimicked her voice, pulling her attention away from the delectable sight. "I hope you took dinner out of the boxes, because I might just eat the styrofoam."

If he'd found the club's food unsatisfactory, it hadn't stopped him from devouring everything she'd artfully plated, inhaling the food as she nudged her bare foot against his leg, testing the softness of the material. She wondered if he would go to tea with her at the club, a favorite pastime since she was a little elf, putting on her prettiest dresses and begging her grandmother for a tiny dab of perfume behind her long ears. Tea in the formal day room was often thought of as a ladies-only event, but Silva had spied couples sitting together at the small tables, sampling the menu before announcing their engagement in an afternoon affair, hosted in the club's outdoor dining garden. Working in a pub might not be a desirable profession for the match her mother and grandmother planned for her, but *owning* a pub was a different story; a pub *and* a bistro, both successful, from what she could tell. He might use coarse language, but Tate possessed refined manners, a sign of a good upbringing, she thought. They might be resistant to his appearance at first, but Silva could too easily envision him at her side in the tea room, sampling tiny cakes and petit fours, quietly planning their big announcement to the community.

"It's good, right?"

"Delicious," he assured her, grunting when he pulled himself up from the table, pinning her against the counter once more where she rinsed the plates, burying his face in her hair.

"Hmm . . . I feel like you would say that about anything at this point, even minotaur veal."

The rumble of his laughter vibrated against her back, and Silva grinned unseen in satisfaction, vindicated in her decision to come and take care of him for the weekend. *See? He needs you here. He **wants** you here.* She turned in his arms, pressing her lips to the base of his throat before her eyes dropped to his waistband, hoping to catch a glimpse of the sweats from a different angle.

"I don't think I'm going to last long on my feet, dove."

The joggers were well-worn and soft, and as he staggered back a step, releasing his hold on her, Silva decided they were the only article of clothing she ever wanted to see him wear again. *What—what did he say? Something about your feet? Using your feet?* She imagined herself sinking into the sofa cushions with her legs stretched across him, her toes caressing the tantalizing, cotton-encased shape of him until he was thick and straining, moisture darkening the material as her toes worked their magic. *He wants you to use your feet?*

"Okay, yes!" she'd blurted excitedly, cheeks coloring, imagination working overtime, blood pounding in her ears at the thought.

"What?" Tate's dark brows drew together in confusion, and Silva realized it was possible she'd not accurately deciphered his words.

"Oh! Oh, um . . . what?"

His fire-lit eyes had narrowed, examining her suspiciously before limping around her to reach for the bottle of painkillers beside the sink with a wince. Silva shook her head, knocking the lust-addled cobwebs the grey joggers had caused away. *Another time. You're supposed to be taking care of him! Maybe you can do that tomorrow after he's slept . . .*

"My poor Tate! C'mon, right to bed. Let me rub your back, I have oil in my makeup bag."

He'd not argued when she pulled him down the hall, dropping to the bed in an exhausted heap; hadn't protested when her ineffectual hands had skated over his skin. Now though, *now* she was making a difference, and as she kneaded and pressed, his muffled curses subsided and he grew boneless beneath her.

"Dove . . ."

It would be different when they were *official*, she thought, when she was around more to mind him and not let him work so hard. She'd make sure he took days off and fed himself, would plan outings and date nights and lazy Sunday mornings in bed that were *not* spent waking at the crack of dawn to set up the dining room ahead of the brunch rush.

"Silva . . ."

A cozy love story with a guaranteed happily ever after.

"Silva, I'm going to fall asleep and it's going to hurt your feelings, so here I am, making my apologies in advance. Mark it down."

His voice shook her out of her daydream and she slid off his back, quickly finding the pulled back duvet to draw over them.

"Oh no, it's not. C'mon, head right here, mister. You need to rest."

"It's too early for you," he grumbled, his eyes already closed.

Despite the protestation, he did as she asked, and the heat of his body radiated against hers as he puddled into the mattress. She thought he felt a touch feverish, his always-warm skin hotter than normal, and decided she'd search his bathroom for a thermometer later.

"Is my tablet going to bother you? If not then I'm fine right where I am."

His hair was silky-smooth as she sunk her fingers into it, dragging her nails down the back of his neck once he'd settled against her, his head pillowed on her breast. The soft, sandalwood smell she was accustomed to had been completely overtaken by something wilder — pine needles and black earth and crunchy leaves, the swirl of bonfire smoke weaving through his hair and the brightness of plump red berries, so sharp and juicy she could almost taste them bursting on her tongue. Her brow wrinkled as she inhaled deeply, wondering how it was possible for him to so thoroughly smell as if he'd just come from a party in the woods when he'd taken such a scalding hot shower. *Tomorrow you can take a shower together, and you can use your rosewater shampoo on him. For now, just finish your book, that's all you'd be doing at home anyway.* The highborn nereid in her book hadn't yet realized the grouchy centaur horse trainer she verbally sparred with each day was the laird of the neighboring clan, but she would soon, and the tension between the two was delicious.

Tate's breath was a hot, steady huff against her skin, just above the low neckline of her tank top, and Silva closed her eyes, trying to imagine him as the secret prince of some faraway highland castle and herself as the unwitting highborn lady. It was silly and stupid to have fallen this fast she reminded herself for the hundredth time, the tips of her nails just barely grazing his skin. Stupid and silly and she'd lied to her family and friends more in the past two months than she had in her entire life, a habit in which she was becoming quite adept as she invented reasons to be away from her life and responsibilities. *And for what? It's all going to catch up with you eventually and you don't even know what kind of a relationship he's looking for. You're probably just in the way. Real-life isn't a romance novel.*

"I'm glad you're here, dove."

Her breath caught and her heart tripped in an uneven cadence at his soft exhalation, just on the edge of sleep, as he was able to hear her thoughts as clearly as if she'd spoken them, and she was unable to answer for a long moment. Stupid and silly which meant *she* was stupid and silly, but at that moment, she didn't care. She was exactly where she was meant to be.

"I am too."

♥ ♥ ♥

Lurielle

"I don't think half the orcs on the field were this muddy. You're soaked to the skin!"

Lurielle winced at the amount of rainwater dripping from the hem of her boyfriend's soiled jersey, collecting on her laundry room floor as she pulled it up his body. The tight, white shorts he wore were caked in mud and similarly dripping, their original color completely hidden beneath the wet muck. "Just hold still and don't touch anything. You're getting mud everywhere, you're as bad as the dogs!"

"The half that kept their shorts clean were relying on the rest of us to win the match," Khash huffed, ignoring her and pulling the jersey over his head, his long braid swinging free to drip even more water down his body. "You don't win Grumsh'vargh by keepin' clean, darlin'. This isn't one of your croquet matches."

"I don't even like croquet," she muttered, sinking to her knees on the towel she'd dropped on the ground. "*This* is why I call it mudball."

The clutch of orcish wives and girlfriends who populated the sidelines at the bi-monthly matches had thawed to her presence amongst them, but as she sat at the edge of the supporters week after week with only Ordo for company, listening to the women chatter and laugh in Orcish, she wondered if there would ever be a stage in her life when she actually fit in with her peers. She'd downloaded a language lesson app on her phone and diligently studied her Orcish in fifteen-minute bursts several times a day, the app's benevolent but slightly bullying bat mascot reminding her periodically through the day to complete her lessons, but she was still completely unable to decipher a single guttural word during spoken conversations. *You need to sign up for classes at the school, or see if the community center offers anything*, she'd thought that afternoon, listening to the laughter of the group.

It had rained that morning, leaving the field a muddy mess. Ordo had been left behind, and as she'd shifted in her seat, tucking her hands up into the sleeves of the oversized hoodie she wore, a small part of her wished that she too had been left at home. *He's going to want your kids to speak Orcish, so you need to learn it now.* Perhaps she'd fit in then, Lurielle thought, dipping her nose beneath the hoodie's neckline and inhaling, when she was a room mother at the Cambric Creek elementary school. The hoodie was Khash's and still held the subtle smell of him — amber-touched leather and a hint of warm musk — and she'd taken to wearing it to the matches like a security blanket, insulating her from the unkind words probably being spoken about her by the group. *Don't be stupid, they probably didn't even notice you're here.*

"These are going to need to soak until next week if you want them to actually be white again." She loved the sight of him in the tiny uniform shorts; loved the way his thick thighs filled out the legs and the curve of his generous ass strained the stitching on the backside, and even darkened with mud and dripping wet, the bulge of his thighs against the snug fabric made her weak. His thighs weren't the only bulge, she observed appreciatively once she was eye-level with his waistband. The only thing surprising about the story he'd once told her about splitting his pants while walking the dog, Lurielle had decided over the course of the past five and half months, was that it didn't happen to him on a weekly basis. The structural integrity of every pair of pants he owned was in danger each time he put them on, strained in every direction—his muscular thighs, the considerable bulge at his crotch, and the twinned globes of his ass, somehow managing to be solid with muscle and deliciously soft all at once, protruding enough to be used as an emergency end table if the need were ever to arise and threatening to burst free like a particularly rambunctious juicy peach. She had never considered herself an ass aficionado, but she was proven wrong every Saturday at the sight of him in the tight, white shorts, no matter their state of cleanliness.

"That's what bleach is for," he chuckled as she drew down the short zipper, hooking her fingers beneath the waistband and pulling the soiled shorts down. They had casual plans for the night, to visit the fairgrounds where the community Fallfest carnival was taking place, at which Khash would announce they ought to get chickens for her backyard, a proclamation he would somehow manage to voice with a straight face, regardless of the fact that he lived in a luxury highrise in the city most of the week. Lurielle would buy goats-milk soap scented with rosemary and mint, made from a local vendor and carried at every single street fair, maker's mart, and community sale the town boasted, yet she always sniffed it like it was the very first time she'd ever heard of something as fanciful as homemade soap. They would eat terrible fair food that would have had her hating herself just a few years ago, but these days she attempted to simply not think about it. It wasn't as if there were a fair every weekend, after all. Fried cheese on a stick was calling her name, but the shorts had other ideas, it seemed. Lurielle tugged again, and the soaked fabric refused to budge.

The full curve of that juicy peach was the culprit, she realized, the wet fabric molding around it and settling beneath each cheek's double handful like cement. The shorts were a size too small, likely purchased when he joined the league, before years of city living and rich, high-end restaurant food, which hadn't helped the situation. Hooking her thumbs beneath the waistband, she pulled with all her might, to little avail.

"Mmm, you know, I could get used to this. All this pawing and pulling . . . it's almost like you want to stay in tonight."

"Why is it like a shelf?!" she yelped, her nails scrabbling against the wet fabric for purchase. All movement ceased once the end table of his ass was reached, progress halting as the shorts held fast.

"Bluebell, don't pretend you don't love butterin' this big ol' biscuit. You think I'd be able to keep your side of the bed warm with a flat ass? This space heater does all the heavy lifting."

"This space heater is going to get a slap once these shorts are off."

Lurielle looked up to see a lascivious smile stretching his broad features, chocolate eyes sparkling, and drew her hand back in warning.

"You're just threatening me with a good time now."

The shelf of his ass was no longer the only obstacle, she realized. The bulge at the front of his shorts had thickened and solidified, preventing her from being able to yank the fabric straight down, even if his big ol' biscuit was removed from the equation.

"You're making this extremely difficult." A rumble moved up his chest as she cupped the growing shape of him, using it as a hand-hold as she hauled herself to unsteady feet. "Keep it up and this biscuit will be getting more than a slap."

"Promises, promises, darlin'."

Despite the mud, the thick outline of his cock was clearly visible, fat and curving. The wet material had so completely molded to his shape that the flare of his head stood out in relief, and she knew the meat of his balls were tightly constricted in the snug encasement, her determination to free them and his big biscuit increasing tenfold.

The rumble opened up to a groan as she squeezed him, grazing her nails over the shape of his shaft, pressed flush to his body in the snug shorts.

"I thought we were going to the fair."

Lurielle wrapped her arms around his waist and plunged her hand into the soaked waistband of the shorts, forcing into the tight space, her hand sliding over the swell of his ass until the wet fabric released its hold on his skin with a squelch.

"We need to get you clean," she said sternly, "and then this big ol' biscuit is getting buttered. And *then* you're going to buy me fried cheese *and* a candy apple."

She would never tire of the heft of his hair in her hands as she worked the shampoo into a thick lather, nor would she ever be completely used to the sensation of his lips moving over every inch of her skin, every imperfect bump and ripple she flattened with shapewear during the workweek, imperfections he didn't even seem to notice. *Not an imperfection*, she reminded herself as his nose moved over the well of her stomach. *Perfect doesn't exist.*

She still sweated her ass off at dance aerobics every Monday, still met the girls for happy hour on Thursdays, and now on Tuesdays, she saw a therapist — a sphinx with severe bangs and a laugh like a goose, who had put her instantly at ease from her first appointment. There wasn't anything wrong with her body because it was *her* body — strong enough to carry her through each day, just as worthy as love as those smaller, slimmer versions belonging to her elvish peers.

There was nothing wrong with *her*, only the mixed messages she had received growing up — that her body was too much, that she took up too much space in her own life, which somehow made her less. Too much, and made smaller as a consequence.

Lurielle didn't know if she would ever be able to look in the mirror and love the individual pieces and parts staring back at her, but she was trying to change her own thinking, to quiet the voices of her mother and her ex in her head, to *stop* seeing herself as a collection of parts. Tev's voice was nearly gone, replaced with her favorite therapy exercise — thinking of the voice of someone who loved her in its place and what they might say. The original assignment was to replace the voice with her own, to compliment herself as she would someone she loved, but despite the fact that she had no problem speaking up for herself in her daily life, she'd been left silent in the mirror the first time she'd tried it, eyes filling with tears.

She wasn't sure *how* to love herself, she'd admitted haltingly in her next appointment, and so the exercise was modified. Every time Tev's haughty condescension questioned the groceries she placed in her cart or the clothes she wore, it was replaced with a syrupy drawl. Khash's appreciation for her curves and intelligence and Lurielle-ness slowly obliterating the internal insults she'd been making herself live with for years. She acknowledged it wasn't *quite* what she needed to accomplish, but she'd be lying if she tried to pretend that having a partner who loved every inch of her didn't help the way she saw herself in the mirror.

"Bluebell, if my hair gets any cleaner, it's gonna whistle you a song."

She stamped her foot in the tub, hand swiping playfully in his direction, palm sliding down a thick swathe of his black hair, squeaking in cleanliness, all traces of mud gone.

"I'm trying to have deep thoughts!"

Lurielle squealed when he surged unexpectedly to his feet, more sure-footed in the tub than she would be, scooping her up and out, striding to the bedroom, heedless of the water they tracked as he bounced her to the center of the bed.

"You're not supposed to be having 'deep thoughts,' and you know it. Changing the terms of the agreement, that's what you're doing. Is this biscuit supposed to butter itself now?"

Her breath caught as he tented himself over her, braced on his hands, giving her his very best glower. Full lips curled in an approximation of a snarl around his tusks, thick eyebrows drawing together, but his eyes sparkled with mischief, and she couldn't help laughing. He was the most handsome orc in the world, and she had him all to herself. Pushing herself up to her elbows, she caught his lips, her heart thrumming when he hummed in satisfaction, his broad tongue licking into her mouth.

He'd settled himself on his knees between her legs, the heft of his cock laying against her cleft. Drawing back his hips, he slid the thick rod of his shaft against her slick folds, his back arching slightly as he did so with a groan. Back and forth, back and forth, he slid through the lips of her sex. the fat head of his cock bumping into her clit repeatedly. Pushing down gently on the top of his shaft with the pad of his thumb caused his foreskin to move and retract, providing a friction similar to what it felt like when he was inside of her, and he groaned again. His other hand cupped first one breast and then the other, rolling them, kneading them, pinching her nipples into hard buds, the slow drag of his cock against her never ceasing. She was sopping from the treatment, but it wasn't enough, wasn't *nearly* enough. She needed to feel him inside of her, filing her and stretching her; wanted to feel that same drag of his foreskin against her inner walls, wanted his sensitive cockhead to be squeezed by the tightness of her channel and the oxygen knocked from her lungs on every eye-watering pump into her, so big her belly would bulge with the shape of him . . . but he seemed perfectly content in the rhythm he'd established, much to her consternation.

"I'm not going to pretend this isn't enjoyable, but I'm not sure if this is foreplay or if you're trying to buy fruit."

"Now darlin', you know what a connoisseur I am of the sweetest melons in the patch. You need to tap and squeeze, become intimately familiar with its weight and all of its sensitivities. It takes a certain amount of *finesse*," his sticky voice clinging to the word, extending it like a hiss, huge hand squeezing the globe of her breast, "and this is the sweetest pair I've ever come across. You can't blame a man for lingering over a meal so fine."

"He's gonna linger so long, he misses the main course."

He huffed, pinching her nipples between his thumb and forefinger. "Now I promise you, there is no danger of that. You've worked up my full appetite, and a itty-bitty bowl of fruit just isn't gonna cut it." The dome-like head of his cock pushed into her then, as if to underscore his hunger. Pushed in and immediately pulled out, sliding across her clit once more. Lurielle knew the extent of his appetite for pleasure, both carnal and other worldly luxuries, and knew he wasn't lying. He was an orc of indulgence and excess, and although she hardly qualified as a bowl of fruit, itty-bitty or otherwise, she knew his appetite would not be satisfied until his fat, full balls had been drained, either in her or on her, and she was eager for his appetite to be satiated.

"Is this what you want, Bluebell?" He pushed his head into her again, his eyes closing as he groaned. "You want this big ol' dragon to go dragging through your garden?"

She nearly choked on her laughter, head dropping as he pressed into her once more, withdrawing on a slow drag. "This dragon is going to grow wings and fly away if you keep *teasing* him with all these metaphors. He knows what he wants, let him have it." Her breath left her in a whoosh when he covered her completely, head pushing into place again."

"I'm going to fill this pretty little pussy up, Lurielle, is that what you want?"

Her back arched when he sunk into her, the tight press of his thick cock making her toes curl like every single time was the first, seating himself to the hilt in one slow glide.

Aside from the significant size difference, orcish anatomy was identical to Elvish, not the only similarity the two species shared, she'd determined. Stubborn and prideful, insular, and under the impression that their species was best among all others. Khash had much to say about orcs being physically superior to similarly-sized ogres and minotaurs, lauded orcish clan unity, and the way they unfailingly took care of their own. Lurielle didn't have much of an opinion when conversations about her mixed-species neighborhood arose and admonished Khash every time he engaged in what she called "dick waggling competitions" with her minotaur neighbor. Privately, she couldn't help heaping praise on her foremothers for having the sense to have lain with orcs and ogres centuries ago, ensuring that she was able to take her boyfriend's giant cock with ease. *They fucked for the betterment of Elvish kind, and for that we thank them.*

Every slow, deep thrust made her vision go spotty, his shaft dragging back and forth against that spongy spot within her, against *every* spot within her, as three thick fingers made lazy, slow circles against her clit, his deep groans vibrating up her core. She imagined that the base of her spine possessed an indentation in the shape of his cockhead, for on every backslide he withdrew to the tip, pushing in until the heft of his balls kissed the curve of her ass, emitting another groan every time he did so. There were perks to mudball, she was forced to admit. He was always horny afterward, and if having to clean up the laundry room was the payment for *this*, Lurielle would happily see her towels a muddy mess every week.

When he hitched her legs over his elbows and angled his hips in such a way that his pubic bone rocked into her clit in a constant motion, the aid of his fingers against it no longer required, Lurielle knew she was done for. She never lasted long in this position, a fact he knew well, and his eagerness for her to come only telegraphed his own need. *You're perfect the way you are. He loves you exactly the way you are. You're smart and successful and you have a gorgeous boyfriend who's going to fuck you into next week.*

"Are you ready to come for me, Bluebell? I'm ready for you to squeeze this cock. This dragon is ready for a hug."

His low voice was enough to complete the affirmation and her composure broke, her muscles clenching around him convulsively as the room spun and she shook, pulsing pleasure thudding through her until her heartbeat matched the cadence, the orgasm deep enough that the clench of her muscles was nearly a cramp. Khash slowed long enough to enjoy the squeeze, pumping shallowly through her peak until she lay weakly beneath him.

"Mmmm, that's my good girl. We might get *two* candy apples." Lurielle laughed in outrage as he began to rut in earnest, chasing his own release with shallow, piston-like pumps. "I'm going to fill you up, darlin'."

She had no doubt that he was. His balls slapped her skin on every thrust, and his eyes had fluttered shut in concentration. She almost felt guilty when his brow furrowed as she pushed against his chest, slowing him.

"No. Roll over. You're not finishing like this."

He wanted to complain. She could see the shape of it in his warm brown eyes, narrowed in confusion, a protest sitting unspoken in his mouth, but he allowed her to push him off of her, propping himself up on his elbows when she forced him to his back, face screwing up when she slid off the bed.

"Darlin', I'm going to sue for broken promises. You got this squirrel ready to bury his nut, and now you want to have a fashion show? I'll see that cute little tush in court, you keep this up."

She stumbled as she crossed the room, her shoulders shaking in laughter over his utter ridiculousness. "I'm not breaking any promises! This is exactly what you asked for."

He hooted when she turned from the dresser with the harness and squat dildo in hand, dropping back against the mattress and bending his knees until his feet were flat.

"Bluebell, I thought you wanted to go to the fair."

Lurielle wrinkled her nose, tightening the straps around her thighs.

"What does that mean?! Are you going to need to take a nap or something? I thought that big ol' biscuit wasn't going to butter itself?"

The harness had been purchased online, saving her from the mortification of needing to return it to a physical store if it didn't fit. The first one she'd purchased had fit like a belt, swinging haphazardly around her waist and offering no control, leading her first down a rabbit hole of research into different models and accessories, and then to further research on choosing and installing a VPN that would protect the sanctity of her late-night web browsing. Her research paid off with the second model: a snug but not uncomfortable fit around her thighs and straps that curved around her ample cheeks, that she could tighten to increase her control, if necessary.

She thought she'd feel ridiculous the first time she'd tried the harness on, standing in her dimly lit bedroom after work with the shades tightly drawn, lest her minotaur neighbor glance in the direction of her bedroom window while he did lawn work. She thought she'd feel ridiculous — that she'd focus on the unflattering way the straps highlighted the jiggle of her ass or cut across her thick thighs, that she'd feel foolish and embarrassed and humiliated . . . instead the opposite had happened. The harness spanned snugly across her pubic mound like a piece of armor, a curiously powerful feeling. Her cheeks had flushed at the sight of her rear end in the bedroom mirror, cupped by the straps in a way that seemed to emphasize its roundness and the curve of her hips, as if she were some softly-painted fertility goddess, the shadows of room casting her in gold and pink. She'd wondered, bouncing on her toes giddily, if *this* was how Khash saw her, feeling nothing but beautiful at the thought.

The first dildo had not gone over as well. Khash had stared at it on the bedspread, his square jaw working, but no sound emitting from his throat, a condition of speechlessness from which he rarely suffered. Lurielle had just begun to worry he was suffering from apoplexy when he, at last, managed to choke out words.

"It-it's so . . . so . . . *big!*"

"I got the orc size!" she exclaimed defensively as he gestured wildly at the silicone behemoth on the bed. It was as long as his own cock and nearly as thick, textured with snaking veins and ridged where the molded foreskin bunched at the base of the pink-tinged head. She'd been impressed with the likeness when she'd first opened it, and didn't understand his reaction.

"You're an orc! What was I supposed to buy, the pixie?!"

"Bluebell, there is a *difference* . . . I can't just . . . it's too big!"

"Well how was I supposed to know that?! I've never done this before!" She'd collapsed into giggles at that point at the stricken look on his face, screaming with laughter when he caught her around the waist, throwing her to the bed with a bounce. "So there's a difference between what *you* put in *me*, but not the other way around."

"Darlin', that is above my paygrade," he'd scowled. "And requires conditioning that, one, I'm not invested enough to undertake, and two, you are not experienced enough to administer. That's like offering me an ice cream cone on the other side of a dung heap and then setting the dung on fire. I don't need the ice cream that badly."

"But you love ice cream," she reminded him, kissing his throat as he harrumphed.

"Yeah, well, I love cake too, and there's a sexy lil' cake in the kitchen that I can help myself to any time the cake desires. I can live happily with cake. You can keep your ice cream."

"I feel like I'm both the cake *and* the ice cream in this metaphor, and if I have to be a food, I'd rather be cheese. You're making this very confusing."

When he'd pressed into her a short while later, Lurielle paid attention to every inch, every ripple of texture and press against her walls, the pressure and fullness of his enormous girth leaving her breathless. He fed his cock into her in such a way that she felt the drag of his foreskin on every slow thrust of his hips, felt the press and stretch of him as he slid in slowly, the same way he always did, moving with care until he was seated within her fully, his fat testicles kissing her skin. She had never been especially well-coordinated; had never excelled at dance or liltenu or any other activity that required any degree of agility. She conceded that she was not, in fact, skilled enough to wield a cock of that size and take as excruciating care of him as he took of her. Much like the harness, her second purchase was made after copious amounts of research and browser clearing, with similar success. The goblin model was short and squat, tightly riddled with veins and possessing a bulbous head that never failed to make Khash grunt, small enough for her to control and for him to take with ease, and it got the job done every time.

He groaned then, as she slowly pressed into him, always a bit hesitant on the first press. Their height difference made taking him on his knees untenable, and she wasn't coordinated enough for any position requiring balance or stamina, but him laying on his back with her in between his legs did the trick. "Is this okay? Do I have enough lube?" His hitching breath was her only answer for a long moment as she slid into place, grunting again when she bottomed out within him.

"You're perfect, Bluebell." Warmth suffused her face as she began to move, his words curling around her earlier affirmation in a way that made her stomach swoop, and she began to rock against him determinedly. He was close, after all, had nearly finished inside her before, and she didn't want to keep him suffering. The benefits of this position, she'd discovered, was the unfettered access to the acres of his rich green skin — thick thighs and straining cock, slapping against his belly; his solid abdomen and the dips above his hips, the deep cavern of his navel and the way his muscles jumped when she pressed her finger into it. The broad valley of his chest beckoned to her fingertips and she stretched, keeping up the pumping of his hips as she reached out to drag her nails through the dark hair dusting his sculpted pectorals, catching his nipples and tugging.

"Darlin, you're tryn'a kill me now."

"Oh, I am *not*, you big baby." The rhythm required to thrust her hips in an even cadence was not one she possessed naturally, she'd discovered in the beginning, but her proficiency had improved since those early, unskilled forays into pleasuring her boyfriend this way. His heavy balls lifted as she pumped into him, the wrinkled skin of his sac stretching as she pulled it, cupping and squeezing his fat testicles, ensuring each of them received her attention; his deep rumble as she did so letting her know the action was appreciated.

His cock was thick and heavy when she lifted it, at last, earning

52

a throaty groan as she did so. It took both hands to span his girth, the pre-come he was steadily oozing slickening her fingers as she began to pump him, doing her best to match the rhythm against his prostate with the rhythm she used to stroke his cock. Every pull of his foreskin exposed the shiny, pink-edged glans of his head, and Lurielle wished she boasted even a tenth of Ris's flexibility, wanting nothing more than to bend in half and suck the domed mushroom cap into her mouth. She loved the exquisite feeling of fullness that came when he erupted inside of her — the way his hips would jerk with every pulse of his release, the way he instinctively buried himself to the hilt when he did so. She loved it, but she loved making him come like *this* as well. His entire body would shiver and then stiffen, and then his legs would begin to shake, a tremble that tightened his big thighs and made his hips jerk. When his cock released, at last, it was like a geyser — thick ropes spattering his belly and chest, and the accompanying groan would nearly sound pained, but she knew better. Or at least, she did now.

It wasn't long before Lurielle felt that tell-tale shiver move through him, redoubling her efforts as his spine stiffened. The tremors moved up his body in a wave, nearly dislodging her as his hips jumped, and she pressed forward, kissing his prostate with the goblin model as she stroked his cock, tightening her hands when he began to throb.

"C'mon, baby. Come for me," she whispered, unsure if he was even able to hear her. Khash said the most ridiculous things, but also the most deliciously filthy things to her, groaned against her hair and her skin, hissed in her ear, syrupy sweet and sinful in his sticky drawl, but being able to reciprocate was a work in progress. *Expressing your love for others is easier when you know how to love yourself,* the sphinx had said, and she was working on it. For now, her practically inaudible murmurings were all she could muster.

She told herself that her whispered encouragement had worked, for he moaned immediately after, cock erupting. The first shot hit his shoulder, white release spilling over her knuckles before a thick rope let loose over his stomach, another over his chest, another, then another. *So much for that shower.* Khash let out a throaty groan as he came, and she fought to retain control over his erupting cock, feeling as though she were indeed wrestling a particularly porcine dragon as it jerked and thrashed in her grip with every thick rope it released.

He sucked in a shuddering breath when she pulled out slowly, moving off the bed and beelining to the bathroom, unbuckling the harness and dropping it into the tub. Clean up would be taken care of later, and Lurielle liked to occasionally entertain herself with thoughts of her mother dropping by unexpectedly, opening the dishwasher to find the two dildos in the top rack — the oversized orc version, dark green and veiny, which she availed herself of on the nights Khash slept in his own apartment in the city, and the squat goblin version she used on him. She was certain her mother would simply will herself out of existence at that point, a thought that always brought a smile to Lurielle's face, which was most definitely something she needed to bring up in therapy.

"You made a giant mess," she accused, returning with a towel to find him slumped in the exact same position as when she'd left him — covered in his own cum, cock deflated and spent, looking exhausted against his thigh, his face turned against the pillows, his dark hair spread over it like a thundercloud. "Your huge load, one; scalding hot shower, zero."

"Bluebell, *you* are the one who made this mess. This big load was for you, by you. So much for being clean enough to whistle you a song."

There was *so much* of it, and she bit her lip as she toweled him clean, unable to pretend the sight wasn't hotter than anything she would have been able to imagine a year ago. *Drop-dead sexy orc, exhausted and covered in a gallon of his own cum because you fucked him so well.* Her lips twitched at the thought, heat pinkening her cheeks as she wiped the last bit of evidence away.

"I don't know what evil thoughts are causing that little grin, but you sure are beautiful when you blush."

The heat that suffused her face then had the unexpected tug of tears, and she dropped the towel, scrambling onto the bed to bury her face against his neck and breathe him in, pushing the tears that wanted to fall away. She still had *so much* work to do, needed to learn to love the reflection in the mirror and the elf attached to it, but pretending that it wasn't made easier hearing it vocalized would have been disingenuous.

"I thought you wanted to go to the fair, darlin'," he pointed out as she tugged the folded quilt over them, tucking under his arm.

"I do, and now I've been promised *two* candy apples. Don't think I forgot that. But we can take a little nap first." He chuckled, pulling her tighter against him. He was an inferno, warming her skin, and Lurielle pressed herself into him, peppering his neck in tiny kisses. She needed to be the voice in her own head quieting the insults, stopping the negative thoughts, and turning them around. She would get there, she reminded herself, closing her eyes, refusing to cry.

She would get there, but in the meantime, if she had to live with another voice, one that would work to silence those belonging to her mother and her ex, one to be kind to her when she could not, she could think of no other syrupy drawl in the world she would have picked to live in her head.

Ris

There had been nothing appetizing on the menu at the resort's bonfire party. Oh, there had been handsome orcs aplenty, in snug designer tees and button-downs unbuttoned to the middle of their broad, hair-covered chests, mingling around the resort grounds where pop-up beverage stations were serving an Orcish beer and cups of spiced rum and cider; mingling and cuddling up to the sightseers around the edge of the blazing fire. They were all seeking the same thing — a tourist like her, someone looking for the temporary carnality the resort town was known for . . . but they moved and mingled relentlessly, playing a numbers game she simply didn't have the appetite for this time around.

When the guests began to drift away to seek out the more straightforward entertainment on the commune grounds, Ris found her feet taking her in the opposite direction, heading to the small business district with its restaurants and shops. After all, she'd experienced what the commune had to offer, had sampled the local buffet and found the experience . . . somewhat wanting. Not that she regretted the first trip, not in the slightest, but it hadn't scratched the itch under her skin, and she'd discovered that the *thought* of anonymous public sex was far more exciting than the impersonal reality, for her at least. *No kink shame, boys and girls, just not for me.* The buffet of manly bodies that would pack the commune parties held little attraction for her, but there were other options for the night.

It was with that thought that she'd made her way to the black-bricked pub in town, tugging her cropped jacket a bit tighter as she walked against the breeze. Silva was the one who had mentioned the bar, when Dynah asked their straight-laced co-worker what she'd done in lieu of the more carnal activities the little town boasted. Silva had blushed prettily, mumbling about there being a nice little pub where everyone kept their clothes on, before hurriedly changing the subject. *A nice little pub* was a bit of a candy-coating, Ris scoffed as she approached. It looked like a dive bar from the sidewalk, and she'd paused, attempting to make out the curious creature depicted on the wrought iron sign above the doorway as it creaked in the wind.

Before she'd been able to make sense of the sign, the door pushed open, a tall orc on a cell phone exiting the bar. As it slowly swung shut behind him, she was able to hear raucous laughter and music spilling from inside, and quickly reached out, catching the handle and squaring her shoulders before stepping over the threshold. The bar was *bursting* with orcs. She stepped through the doorway with raised eyebrows, surprised by just how many burly green bodies were packed into the space; the last place in the world she could imagine demure Silva feeling comfortable. *Definitely a dive bar*, Ris thought, albeit a surprisingly spacious and clean one. The place felt positively ancient, all hardwood and exposed beams with a mix of hightops and lower tables lining the perimeter, and beyond the pool tables at the back of the room, she could see a doorway, leading to yet another section of the pub. *Maybe that's where Silva hid the whole weekend.* The pool tables were clearly the center of the action, and she'd wondered if anyone would even notice her presence as she moved to the tall bar. It was not hard to see that wagers were being placed, money changing hands for sport with a ring of loud, laughing spectators. Two large clusters of women, other sightseers, sat at a group of high-top tables in the center of the floor, attempting to woo the few orcs who were not thoroughly absorbed by the noisy action taking place at the green felted tables.

"What'll it be, lovely?"

The orc behind the bar was a good bit older than the other others in the room, with at least a dozen heavy silver rings in his long ears, the weight of which dragged them towards his neck. Bands of copper adorned his left tusk, while the right had been broken off just above the first circlet and filed smooth. Ris beamed up at his endearment, sliding onto a stool.

"Ginblossom and tonic with rosemary, if you've got it, and a shot of Lysträe."

The orc turned with a smile, the wide set of his shoulders completely blocking her view of the bottles on the wall behind him, the overhead light catching on the steel copiously threaded through his dark hair before he turned, expertly assembling the drink and setting it on a napkin before her. She watched as his head raised, his attention caught by something over her head for the space of a heartbeat before he gave a short nod, lips tugging around his thick tusks as he refocused on her drinks once more, lifting the bottle of Lysträe.

It started with a prickle at her neck, a whisper of attention that hadn't existed only a moment before. The weight of eyes bore into her back as the grizzled bartender placed the shot glass beside her drink, turning away without another word to take the order of the next person who'd sidled up to the bar. Ris kept her gaze trained on the drinks, listening to the *chink!* of pool cues glancing off polished stripes and solids, and waited for the feeling of observance to pass. When it persisted, she threw back the shot. The silver-white burn of the alcohol flared her nostrils as it went down, and she sucked in a deep breath, counting to ten before turning.

It was an audience of one, she saw immediately: one of the orcs, sitting in a low chair along the bar's front wall, looking completely out of place amongst the other bar patrons, his hair fashioned into gleaming black points and his long legs stretched before him. He gave the impression of having just stepped off a stage somewhere, a far cry from the orcs crowded around the pool tables with their thick braids and broad backs. He was bare-chested beneath the studded leather jacket he wore, and half a dozen piercings gleamed and swung from his long ears. The smile he fixed on her was brilliant and knowing, and Ris felt the corner of her own mouth curve up in response. Coming to this little bar had been a good plan after all.

Even from the way he lounged in the shadows she could tell he was built differently than the others of his kind from the pool deck the previous night — great, hulking brutes with deliciously muscled arms and straining cocks, eager for the small collection of tourists present to stoke them and suck them, taking their pleasure before moving on to the next mouth. She'd gone up to the pool bar shortly after her arrival, retreading her familiar steps from the previous trip on a quest for a single partner with whom she might enjoy the night. It was too cold to go around naked, at least for her, and the throngs of other sightseers who'd clogged up the decks and restaurants the last trip were mostly absent now. Despite the better odds, she'd left the pool the night before more than a little aggravated with the lack of reciprocity from the crowd of orcs. The guys there that night were all horny and eager to get off, but they'd been spoiled by the plethora of easy sex all summer, and she witnessed very little effort in return. *This* orc, by contrast, was focused intently and solely on her. *A nice little pub where everyone kept their clothes on.* The orc did indeed have his clothes on, although Ris had the distinct impression he was envisioning her without the same modesty.

"Excuse me . . . did someone pay for my drinks?"

"Aye." The old orc didn't bother looking up from where he wiped down the polished surface of the bar, and Ris pursed her painted lips.

"Am I allowed to know who?"

"Guess that's part of the game, lovely . . . the findin' out." This time he did look up, giving her a silver-toothed grin. Her punkish watcher may not have been her normal type, she considered, turning to flash him a brilliant smile, earning one in return, but she'd already lost one night of the weekend to the buffet. *He won't be any different. They're all looking for the same thing, but you may as well have fun.* She watched him drain the glass that had been sitting on the table, pulling his endless legs back and straightening in his chair, pocketing his cellphone and pushing the chair back . . . *Showtime, baby. Time to order off the menu.*

She had just turned back to respond to the barkeep's quip and give her audience the chance to make his move when a sudden shout made her jump. An angry, accusing voice at one of the pool tables was quickly joined by a second, and then a third. Her stomach clenched in panic when the old bartender added his own gruff shout to the mix, limping to the corner of the bar, threatening the orcs behind her to take it outside, but his voice was ignored.

The orcs at the center of the noise were enormous, one wearing a white t-shirt that looked nearly painted on, the fabric straining around his thickly muscled arms. A heavy-linked gold chain sat around his bulging neck, and his black hair glistened with product beneath the overhead lights, his braid a long, fat snake down his back. A preening peacock, she thought, he was the exact sort of orc who probably spent time nightly around the pool bar, she thought, enjoying anonymous blowjobs from the steady stream of tourists before heading back up to town for a different sort of entertainment at the bar. By contrast, the orc he quarreled with seemed like a rougher sort. Two long braids hung down his back beneath the bandana wrapped around his head, the emblem of a motorcycle club on the back of the leather vest he wore.

A satyress sitting at a hightop with her friends shrieked, high and shrill, as the men began to point and push accusingly, the bystanders egging on the confrontation until the two huge orcs in the center of the circle were nose-to-nose, the angry shouts not subsiding. Ris watched as the two tables of women quickly cleared out, the satyress and friends disappearing through the metal door, wondering if she'd be able to skate past the tables to do the same when one of the orcs shoved the other, and the crack of a barstool hit the floor beside her. In an instant, there was a buffeting presence at her back, pressed to her tightly, his hands at her shoulders.

"You don't want to get caught in the middle if they start tussling, Nanaya. Just stay right where you are."

She could tell it was the mohawked orc without even needing to crane her neck back, and could feel the heat rolling off him as the shouts behind her increased. His big hands squeezed her shoulders reassuringly before lowering to the bar on either side of her, the leather of his jacket pressing to her sides. She was trapped, but Ris recognized his action as one of chivalry. He'd tented himself around her, preventing her from being hit by any flying objects or orcs.

"Rukh, you planning on stopping this?"

The grizzled bartender had backed up behind the bar once more, had killed the music that spilled from the speakers upon her arrival, still shouting at the orcs around the pool tables, but at the punk orc's words, he glared.

"You see how many of 'em are standin' now? I've got arthritis in both hips, boy. Don't see you sailing in to save the day."

"*Me*? I don't work here. Fuck, I don't even get a friends and family discount! But I'd like to see the old girl still standing tomorrow. These are your customers, they listen to you!"

"Well, they're not listening to anything right now."

"Then you need to call him."

The old orc grunted unwillingly in response, raising his voice again, calling out to several of the orcs by name, to no avail. His face reminded her of a bulldog, even more so when he scrunched it up, as he did then.

"He won't be happy . . . got his little beauty in, said not to disturb him..."

From her limited vantage point beneath the punk orc's arm, she watched as the peacock raised a thick finger to jab in the other's face; one that was hit away roughly, several other orcs wearing leather vests bearing the same emblem surging behind their fellow, the ring of bystanders continuing to goad the agitators in the center. Ris tried to envision what might happen if they erupted into violence — huge, colliding bodies, toppling bar stools and tables as though they were nothing; shattering the glass bottles behind the bar, the shards of which they'd use as weapons along with snapped pool cues and broken chairs, heedless of anyone who might get caught up in their rage . . .

"You let them start swinging and they'll tear through this place like a herd of rhinos." She whimpered, her fears confirmed by her protector. "Do you mean to tell me you've never had to break up a bar fight?"

"We don't *have* fights," the old barkeep growled, his words nearly being lost as glass shattered against the floor to her back, and Ris tucked up her feet with a squeal.

Another shatter, the green gleam of shards sliding beneath her stool where her feet had been only a moment before.

"Rukh, it's going to be *so* much worse for you if *I* have to come around the counter and call him."

The barkeep lifted a heavy-looking wooden club from somewhere beneath the bar, moving to the edge of the bar to add his voice once more to the din. Ris yelped when the club struck the base of the bar, several sharp thumps that seemed to rattle down the heavy wood, but the orcs intent on brawling paid no mind. The shouting had coalesced into a chant, it seemed, and she squealed again at the unmistakable sound of large bodies colliding. Although she was not able to see anything, Ris felt the moment when a huge body slammed into them, feeling the jolt against her back, hearing the grunt of the orc braced around her as she was pressed painfully to the bar. If he hadn't been there, she would have been badly hurt, she realized, her heartbeat thudding in her throat. *Silva, I'm supposed to call Silva.* She didn't understand Lurielle's admonition, but it was all she could think of as they were slammed into once more, her phone too far out of reach to be able to do so. The arm around her tightened as her punkish protector shouted at the bartender, but the old orc had already hobbled a foot away, picking up the receiver of a cordless phone tucked unseen under the bar.

"We need some assistance down here . . . aye, I know . . . I *know*, wouldn't have done so if it weren't an emergency." He grimaced, face screwing up as the person on the other end of the line continued to speak, nodding in agreement with the unheard words. "At the tables. . . Aye," he gritted out, replacing the receiver in its cradle with a grimace after a brief moment. "Well, there'll be blood to pay now, that's for fucking certain."

Ris gripped the leather jacket of her orcish shield when another glass smashed, the fragments bouncing across the scuffed floor under her feet. The sound of huge fists connecting with flesh punctuated the shouts of the surrounding crowd, and she wondered how anyone but the police would be able to stop the brawl the group of giant men seemed intent on having. She had just tucked her legs up further when a lilting, musical voice cut through the din.

"What seems to be the problem, gentlemen?" In an instant, the room fell silent. The sound of her panicked breath was clamorous in her ears as the noise in the room ceased, her fingers still tightly clutching the arm of the orc pressed to her back. Ris felt the tiny hairs on her neck stand on end as the air chilled, all warmth leached away, leaving a heavy, tangible sense of dread hanging in the suddenly silenced pub. Lowering her head, she peeked again around the arm surrounding her to see this newcomer who'd ended the fight with a few mildly spoken words. She recognized him immediately.

The handsome server from the little bistro up the block, where she and the girls had eaten several times during their first visit. He'd been working each time they'd been there, had seated them the very first night, and slid a magnum of champagne into their ice bucket with a cocky smile when they'd come for brunch. He was smaller than the group of burly orcs he stood before, slimmer and shorter than everyone in the room but her, and the sight of him there was incongruous, standing in the doorway with his hands on his hips and a wide, toothy grin, in what appeared to be pajama bottoms and a thin, v-necked t-shirt. Bare, pale green feet peeked from the pant legs, as though he'd been pulled directly from bed to materialize before the fight. *Where did he come from?!*

"Is that glass on the floor? *My* glasses? Or did you bring your own for the occasion? Is there a reason those stools are tipped?"

His head was cocked slightly, as though he were greatly amused by the scene before him, and he continued to smile at the cluster of larger orcs. She gaped at the silent group, the men who'd been fighting only moments ago, now standing shoulder-to-shoulder in silence; watched, to her amazement, as one quickly bent to right one of the felled barstools.

"I'm not in the business tonight, gentlemen. It's my weekend off. I'd thought you'd be able to carry on as usual . . . enjoy a pint, have a laugh with your mates, maybe show one of the tourists a billiard shot or two. But ins*tead*," he paused, glancing to the floor and nudging a shard of glass with his bare toe before beaming beatifically at the group of subdued orcs, "instead you poxy, gobshite fucks have proven me right yet again — you're as stupid as you are ugly, and you've forgotten whose hospitality you're enjoying under this roof." His smile abruptly dropped as he advanced several steps, one of the orcs in the motorcycle vests hastily backing away until his legs hit the pool table behind him. "I haven't had a single night away from you cunts in fucking months."

Ris watched, spellbound as the smaller man continued to advance, enunciating every word, all trace of the false levity he'd displayed only a moment ago gone, the bigger orcs before him seeming to shrink.

"I have to listen to your pissing and your moaning every fucking day like a bunch of bleating old women, and I take *one* bleedin' weekend off to wash the stink of you from my skin, and this is what you get up to. You've forgotten your manners, gentlemen. But fear not — I'm here to remind you."

One of the agitators grumbled something then, the peacock at the center of the trouble. Almost as if it were choreographed, the two orcs on either side of him edged away, lest they be blamed for his words, but the damage, it seemed, was done.

"D'you have something to say there, Matuk? I'd take care to make sure it's something you're willing to bleed for, because it might just be the last words that fall out of that gash in your face."

"And you'll do what?" the big orc sneered, puffing his chest out to tower over the smaller man. "You think you're going to just prance in and threaten all of—"

The peacock, Matuk, never had a chance to finish his words, for at that moment something cracked, a *pop!* that left her ears ringing, and the very air seemed to jolt, nearly rocking her off the barstool. The orc tented over her stumbled, gripping the bar to keep his balance and position behind her.

"Don't look," the punk orc hissed into her hair, the arms around her tightening, steadying her on her seat. "Just take a deep breath and don't look."

Before them, the older barkeep had hunched, his eyes squeezed shut and his head turning away from the pool tables. She ought to have listened, Ris thought after she'd sucked in a lungful of air, peeking around her protector's arm again to see the handsome server again; ought to have followed the old orc's example and squeezed her eyes shut. Instead, she stared open-mouthed, unable to look away.

It was his jaw bone that had cracked, Ris realized, unable to pull her eyes away from the smaller orc, his jaws separating like a python's, giving room for long, jagged teeth the length of daggers to descend, a gruesome smile stretching back to his pointed ears. The number of his teeth was unfathomable, reminding her of some horrifying creature from the depths of the ocean, and the space between them where his jaw had opened was black as pitch — a void of screaming emptiness so sharp and shrill that she thought her eardrums might pop, a great maw that would swallow the room whole, she was certain. His hand had pulled back as if he were holding something in his grasp, and the room had frozen . . . except for the strutting, cocky orc before him who was being pulled forward, his big body fighting against the grasp to little avail. He was more than an orc, Ris realized, was something sinister and dark, some malevolent fae creature of the nighttime, like the ones from the stories her grandmother would tell her, terrifying her when she was a child. The sharp cold that filled the room carried the smell of pine and black earth, slicing through her and freezing the air in her lungs until an unseen weight pressed against her chest, leaving her unable to draw breath, her hands clawing at the leather-clad arms around her. *You never should have come here. You should have stayed at the pool, you should never have listened to stupid Silva!*

As soon as the thought crossed her mind, his flame-colored eyes met hers. She was unable to blink, trapped like some unfortunate animal who'd wandered onto the highway, held spellbound by the leaping fire of the smaller orc's wild eyes. He recognized her, of that she was certain. He kept her trapped in his gaze for interminable minutes, ample time for her to see the jumping flames in his eyes, the smell of bonfire smoke curling around her, the spell broken when he shook his head as if he were shaking off a gnat. Tight fury colored his features when his head raised again, replacing the manic bloodlust that had been there, and the hand he'd drawn back opened, releasing the room from whatever airless thrall in which he'd held it. Ris gasped, sucking in a lungful of the air she'd been deprived of, the staggering orcs around her doing the same.

"We've a lady in our midst," he bit out, swinging his attention back to the orcs.

His jaws had begun to knit themselves back together, she realized as his face contorted, still unable to look away. The black void between his teeth began to shrink, air and warmth returning to the room, and Ris was positive she was the only reason why. "One of my guests, and this is how you've chosen to act in her presence. She could have been hurt."

"A whole table of 'em," the old bartender rasped helpfully, his breath labored from the deprivation, earning the smaller orc's attention. "Left screamin' when the trouble started. Can't imagine they'll be back."

"Frightening away my customers. Smashing glasses, breaking barstools—"

"Ay now, nothing's broken," interrupted one of the biker orcs, only to be interrupted in turn by the handsome server once more.

"It's broken if I say it's broken," he snapped, advancing on the group again, his bare foot coming down on one of the tipped stools, cracking the leg. "And if there's so much as a ripple in that cloth, you'll be replacing the whole bleedin' table. Destruction of property and now you're costing me business. You'll all be making amends, and this'll not happen again, you understand? Time to wind your necks in, gentlemen. Since you've had so much to say, you can start us off, Matuk." That unnatural, dagger-toothed smile stretched once more, further than any mouth should be able to stretch, lit with mania, and she shuddered. "You'll all be payin' the Piper, or I'll see to it your grandchildren will wish you had."

The threat seemed to rattle off the exposed beams above her head, the old building doing her part to amplify the voice of her apparent proprietor, and for a long moment, the room was silent. The bandana-wearing orc moved first, pushing past the peacock and reaching into his back pocket, depositing a roll of bills on the pool table. Each of his motorcycle-vested brethren quickly followed suit before the orc called Matuk moved, still trembling, dropping his own roll of cash. Warmth slowly began to seep back into her bones as each of the huge orcs pulled out fistfuls of bills, dropping the money in a mounting pile on the pool table before hastily exiting the bar.

Ris was suddenly very aware of the enticingly spicy smell wrapped around her. Her mohawked protector had relaxed his stance, and now his big hand rubbed soothing circles at her back as they watched the procession of exiting orcs. Once the door swung shut behind the last huge body, the only sound left in the room was the labored breath of the slender orc, who looked as if he still might decide to kill them all. His mouth no longer resembled something from a horror story, Ris was relieved to note, but his eyes were wild and his breath hard and sharp, trembling as if he were standing outside in a snowstorm, his delicate features not *entirely* restored.

"Lock her up," he bit out, the barkeep jumping to obey. "Call down the street, have Cymbeline send you one of the boys to clean this mess up." He picked his way across the glass-strewn floor carefully, stepping around the bar to remove a bottle from the shelf along with a rocks glass, pouring himself several fingers with a shaking hand before leaning on the polished surface with a grunt, reaching back to rub at his neck.

"H've you seen a doctor for that back yet?"

The smaller orc's eyes popped open, scowling at the old man's words, and she was certain he'd change his mind on allowing them to leave. "That's some nerve on you, lad," he spat. "Drag me from bed just because you let your man there flap his gums until those Ghul'nag boys were ready to knock you all arseways. Get this glass cleaned up, pitch that stool. We'll be raising the price of all the drafts to buy a new set, and you can remind them of that every time they want to give out over it."

As he snapped out orders, Ris took the opportunity to look him over. Half of his dark hair was pulled into a haphazard topknot on the side of his head, while the other half had been fashioned into an intricate plait, the sort she herself might get for a special occasion, requiring a salon visit to accomplish. The effect, coupled with the way he was dressed, was the least intimidating thing she could imagine, a far cry from the way he'd looked standing before the group of towering orcs only minutes earlier. *Still*, she thought, averting her eyes lest he meet them again, he was still vibrating in fury and Ris had no doubt that he yet might decide to swallow them all whole.

"Ains, are you on my payroll?" Ris realized her protector was the target of the snapped question, felt the hand that had dropped to her hip squeeze lightly before nudging her gently. "Oh, abso*lute*ly not."

"Then take her," he gritted out, fists balling again, "and *go*."

"Tate," her punkish protector paused, nodding meaningfully at her drink, and she quickly tipped it back, "you sure you're okay? Because you don't really seem okay."

The slim orc dragged a hand over his face, huffing out a hard breath. "Just *go*, Ains."

The alcohol burned and her head spun as the tall orc scooped her up like a bride. Ris threw her arms around his neck, holding on for dear life as he swung her away from the bar, feeling like she was several stories in the air, not having appreciated his height or the way he'd been bent over until that moment.

"Thank you for protecting my customers, Ainsley. I appreciate you helping to prevent a lawsuit, Ainsley. I'm sorry I blew you off and ignored all of your texts, Ainley. You're a good friend, Ainsley."

"Good*bye*, Ainsley." The slim orc rolled his eyes dramatically before turning away, carefully stepping around the broken glass that glittered across the floor to disappear through the doorway once more as the barkeep let two young goblins in, armed with brooms and dustpans, quickly setting to work on the mess of the floor.

The breeze had a chilly bite as they stepped out into the black night, and she was thankful for the heat his body provided her. If the fight hadn't broken out, he would have had to work quite a bit harder to get this close, she thought, as he smirked down at her. *Guess that's part of the game, lovely . . . the finding out.* She wondered if it *was* the same orc from the first trip, and her stomach swooped at the thought. The roar of motorcycle engines moving up the block, the sound reverberating between the buildings on the narrow street made conversation impossible, and they had made it all the way to the corner before the night had quieted once more. She was still held aloft in his arms, her own arms wrapped around his neck, and the curve of his lips was tantalizingly close as he paused before the building on the corner. There were people milling about, strolling beneath the twinkle lights strung across the lane, but all Ris could focus on was the devilish sparkle in his eyes; the overhead streetlight catching on the silver bands around his tusks as he grinned. Coming to the little bar had been a good plan after all. *Ainsley.*

"The night is young, Nanaya. Fancy a proper drink?"

♥ ♥ ♥

Silva

She woke that morning to his nose bumping her own, wide awake as she blinked blearily. Silva wasn't sure how they always managed to wind up sharing the same pillow when the bed was heaped with them, but she'd not found a reason to complain — she would unfailingly be pressed to the long line of his body, his knee pushed through her legs and his arm around her, warm and close, exactly the way she liked. She suspected it was her own nocturnal doing anyway, as it was usually his pillow she shared. Her body would be in the middle of the bed, crowding him on his side, but he'd never once disentangled them, forcing her to wake up cold and lonely in her own far corner, and when she woke up in the middle of the night to tiptoe to the bathroom, which she always did, his arm would open for her return, his eyes never even opening. The fact that she even had a *her side* of his bed thrilled her, one of the tiny, insignificant things she had begun counting.

When she'd woken sometime the night before to find herself pinned beneath his arm, her pea-sized bladder demanding she get up, his breath was a steady exhalation on the pillow beside her. Detangling herself carefully so as not to wake him, tiptoeing to the kitchen after using the restroom to refill her water glass, she'd discovered the unopened gallon of apple cider, pressed by one of the shops in the resort hamlet.

She'd told him about the cider thief in her office several weeks earlier, sitting across his lap with her arms around his neck, lamenting that she counted on the half-gallon jug she purchased from a local farm to last the whole week, and he'd clucked his tongue in annoyance on her behalf. His eyes had lit as he told her about the end-of-season press made by the local shop, one made from bitter apples, insisting it was delicious when she'd pulled a face.

"You *would* like something made from sour apples. Those are the garbage apples! That's probably why they press it at the very end of the season when all the delicious sweet ones are gone."

"What's wrong with sour apples? Garbage apples deserve to have their cider dreams realized, same as the perfect little pageant apples, dove. Didn't realize I'd been bewitched by a fruit snob. Didn't you just say you pour it into water? I don't think you get to have an opinion on the worthiness of any apple, sour or not."

She'd called him a garbage fruit apologist, pealing in laughter when he'd surged to his feet, throwing her over his shoulder as if she herself was a sack of apples, striding down the hallway and flipping her down to the bed. She'd continued to shriek when her panties were pulled down her legs and discarded, squealed when he'd elbowed her legs open, hitching her knees over his shoulders.

"I'll be the judge of sweetness around here, thank you very much."

The first stroke of his tongue was slow and savoring, the subsequent laps opening her folds and tightening her stomach as she gripped his hair tightly. He kissed the exposed bud of her clit the same way he kissed her lips — with gentle suction and a seeking tongue, pulling a breathy moan from her throat and a tremor down her spine, one that made her toes curl. When she'd unspooled beneath his ministrations, coming against his mouth with a wheeze, her thighs tightening and shaking, he continued to lick her, his greedy tongue lapping up her release before he kissed his way up to her mouth.

"Sweetest thing I've ever tasted." He'd sent her home that week with two gallons of the local press nestled into her backseat and a slow kiss at her car window, and a tiny bubble of warmth had floated within her all week long, thinking of that afternoon in his bed with every sip.

She'd stood in the dark kitchen the night before, hugging herself at the sight of the cider, bouncing on her toes and smiling so hard her muscles ached from the stretch. He'd been not feeling well, was tired and aggravated and in desperate need of rest, probably wished he was spending his weekend off alone . . . but he'd still thought of her, *had*, in fact, remembered that she was coming for the weekend. She'd scampered back down the hallway, sliding into bed and threading her fingers into his hair when his head once again found her shoulder, renewed in her determination to take care of him for the duration of the weekend.

"You're supposed to be sleeping in," she accused him with a yawn, smiling in spite of herself when he bumped her nose again.

"I can't help it. Internal clock." His voice was a murmur into the pillow as the wide span of his fingers cupped the curve of her bottom, tilting and pulling her flush against him. Her breath fluttered, coming out in a small sigh at the hard press against her, the thin grey cotton doing nothing to disguise the thick shape of him, nestled against the front of her panties.

"Is this part of your internal clock setting?" she giggled, shifting until she was able to trap his erection against her body, grinding herself against him until he groaned. *He's never allowed to wear anything else ever again.* "I don't know if you should be doing any physical activity though, you could barely walk last night."

"I don't usually wake up with the loveliest lass in all the land sleeping on top of me," he countered, holding her against him as he rolled to his back. His fingers felt endless as they dragged up her body, pushing up the thin material of her pink cami until he could cup the globe of her breast in his palm, kneading her skin gently, catching the stiffened peak of her nipple, and tugging until she gasped. "And it's a good thing she's capable of being athletic for the both of us."

His thumbs caught under the sides of her panties, forcing her

79

to rise up on her knees to drag them down her hips, an action she mirrored on him with the grey joggers until he was bare beneath her as she straddled his hips. Slowly dragging herself over his straining shaft, coating him in her own increasingly slick arousal, Silva whimpered every time the pink-edged tip of his head bumped into her clit.

It was rare she got to feel the drag of his bare cock against the lips of her sex, for Tate possessed the speed and talent of the most in-demand backyard magician, managing to produce a foil-wrapped condom seemingly out of thin air every time she mistakenly thought was going to enjoy taking him without the thin membrane separating their skin, as though he were producing a coin from behind her long, pointed ear, as her grandfather had done when she was a very small child. It was, she thought, one of his most annoying traits. She didn't know why the thought of having unprotected sex with him excited her to the degree it did, maybe because it was another thing he withheld, she thought, much like his every inner thought and secret, all of the trivial things she wanted. Silva knew she ought to be grateful he was protecting her from an infection or an unwanted pregnancy, and with the way her imagination supplied her with unwanted suppositions of him with a variety of different species of women, she knew she should be glad . . . but the thought of there being no barrier between the most intimate parts of them thrilled her, the thought of being filled by him, flooded with his heat . . . she had *seen* the evidence in the condoms he filled, tied and discarded instead of dripping from her, and it made her twist in regret. It was easy to insert herself in half a dozen different fantasy scenarios involving animal heat and an utter lack of planning, all of them ending with him coming inside of her, leaving her sopping and sticky, each one more exciting than the next. *Historical setting, forced proximity, primal lover, surprise baby!* It was ridiculous, especially when she considered how much she actively disliked the touch of any liquid that wasn't directly from the tap. She'd fallen over herself to run to the restroom and wash her hands after her palm accidentally grazed an unnoticed puddle on the table at her favorite coffee shop, and the time she'd been changing the wastebasket in the office break room and some unknown liquid dripped on her ankle, she'd nearly expired. But, she told herself, she couldn't help her kinks.

Gripping him snugly, she pushed back his foreskin to expose his shiny head, pulling the sheath up and down until a bead of moisture welled from the tip, her small fist moving down the entire length of his shaft before returning to the tip, bringing his foreskin up in a pucker. Her small fingers were never able to fully span his thick girth, but this morning he seemed even more engorged than normal, the tips of her fingers rolling over an unexpected texture.

"Silva, it's called a morning stiff," he groaned, attempting to prod her hips, "not a 'you've got me fully bricked during pre-dinner drinks and we have until second dessert to do something about it' all-night event."

She nearly lost her balance atop him as she shook in laughter, slapping at his chest. "Don't be so impatient, Mr. Bossy, or I'll fall off!" Feeding the pink of him into her with a breathy sigh, her back arched as his girth stretched her walls. He *felt* different, she noticed immediately. Maybe it was the press of his bare skin, or perhaps it was the position — not one they indulged in particularly often, as he was too much of a bossy control freak — but there was something foreign about the drag of his length that made her head drop back, whimpering when it moved over the spot within her that made her writhe. When she rocked her hips, Silva was unable to hold back a small cry, a lightning bolt of pleasure quivering up her spine. His cock *always* felt good, filling her in a way no partner ever had in the past, and she loved his gentle dominance, holding her down and directing her pleasure . . . but it had never felt like *this*. She was meant to be taking care of *him*, and she was sure that probably included letting him come first, but there was something about the way he dragged against her that had her leaning forward, all thoughts of his pleasure lost as she rocked in small, quick movements, chasing the sparks that lit at the corners of the room with every pass over that sensitive spot within her.

"You're going to be the bleedin' end of me, dove," he laughed unsteadily, realizing what she was doing. Silva cried out when he cupped her ass, angling her in a way that made the press of him feel snugger, the drag of him against her g-spot even more pronounced. "Is this what you want to do?"

It was a ridge, she decided, head lolling. It felt as if she were scraping against a deliciously textured ridge, and with every rock against it, her breath hitched, chasing her peak faster and faster. He'd pushed up to a near-sitting position by then, his thumb brushing over her clit in the same steady rhythm in which her hips rocked against him.

"Are you going to come on my cock, Silva?" She keened, about to do exactly that, and when he began to rub circles against her clit as she rocked, Silva knew she was lost. "You are the most selfish," his teeth grazed her throat, "greedy," a nip at her ear, one of his sharp canines catching on her lobe, making her cry out, "*cheeky* little minx I've ever known. I want to feel this perfect little cunt squeeze my cock, dove. I want to be dripping with you."

She came with a shudder and a wheeze, shaking in his arms until she thought she just might shake apart, clenching around him until she sagged. Silva couldn't account for the speed in which he reversed their positions, flipping her to her stomach before she'd managed to even catch her breath. "But your back!"

"I suppose you should have thought about that before," he grunted, pressing into her from behind, the hand he'd pressed to the small of her back keeping her flat to the mattress. "You'll just have to walk on it after breakfast."

She *was* greedy and selfish, she admitted as he pistoned into her, hard and deep, moving his hand from her back to grip her hips tightly. Greedy and selfish and impossibly bratty, but she could still feel that delicious friction dragging against her, and was unable to apologize for her reaction. She pushed back against him, crying out every time he hilted, the slap of their skin competing with her panting, the pressure within her tightening. She could tell the moment he came — hips stuttering in their rhythm, surging against her once, twice, a prolonged shudder on the third, a hard exhalation against her neck — but no rush of heat, no pressure to indicate she was being filled by an erupting orc cock, no gush of hot seed leaking from her to run down her thighs. Tate pushed her forward on the mattress, covering her with his weight and snaking a hand between her and the mattress. The roll of his fingers over her clit in tight, quick circles, coupled with the thick press of him still within her was enough to finish her off. Silva gasped as she clenched around him again, pushing her face into the duvet cover as he groaned into her hair.

"The bleedin' fucking end of me, dove," he repeated, chuckling. When she turned her head, his mouth was waiting, sucking her lower lip in between each of his, his teeth biting down gently before pushing himself off her.

The condom he carefully eased off, expertly knotting the end, was full; bobbing and heavy with his milky-white release. Silva fisted the sheets in frustration, cursing his magician's ability to produce condoms from thin air, but she'd not had time to dwell on her annoyance. He'd scooped her up and carried her to a hot shower, where she had washed his hair with her rosewater-scented shampoo and rubbed something called "dragon's breath balm" into the damp skin of his back afterward, squealing when her fingers had begun to tingle from the heat. Despite her proclamation that she would make him breakfast, she'd been served delicate, strawberry-filled crepes, dusted with powdered sugar and garnished with a sprig of mint from the small pot on the kitchen windowsill.

When she'd asked his opinion on a movie to watch that afternoon, he'd had none. When she'd mentioned the hot new horror series that everyone at work had already binge-watched, he'd only given her a non-committal "whatever you'd like, dove." She disliked horror normally. Humans were bad enough on their own and the thought of *undead* humans terrorizing a town of helpless goblins sounded positively ghastly, but she decided she'd be brave enough to watch cuddled to his side. She'd been fiddling with the unfamiliar remote, searching for the function that would load the streaming service when she discovered several seasons' worth of a saved and unwatched program called *Attic Wanderers*, all thoughts of the undead human series vanishing as she whirled in triumph.

Now it was hours later. She'd emptied the dishwasher and thrown a load of laundry in for him, including the grey joggers, which she'd pressed into his arms straight from the dryer, insisting he ought to change immediately to enjoy the maximum snugliness.

"There's no way this is real, that has to be a counterfeit. Watch this gowl's face when they break the news, dove." Tate was stretched across the slate-colored sofa like a giant, contented cat, his head in her lap and his breath warm on her thigh as she plaited half his silky locks into the sort of elaborate braid it took hours to manage on her own hair. Silva had no idea how many episodes of the antique appraisal show they'd binged at that point, but she'd happily spend the rest of her life watching nothing else if they could remain suspended in the comfortable, complacent bubble of the previous twenty-four hours. *Maybe there will be a storm or a flood and we'll be trapped here for weeks. Forced proximity trope!*

"If that's authentic, we're finding where this jammy hoor lives and we're stealing it. But it's not going to be, just wait."

She giggled as the bespectacled presenter examined the ancient-looking knife, finishing the hand-over-hand plait design at last. Tate's hair was too sleek and silky for the braid to hold on its own, but she had no intention of dislodging him just to retrieve a hairpin.

"Do they tell you where these people are from? I'll bet we could find him. Roadtrip." Tucking the end of the braid up, she threaded it through one of the plaits to secure it, sitting back to admire her handiwork. *There.* Elves of both genders had worn their hair in elaborate ceremonial braids on their wedding days, when long hair had still been in fashion for men. Tate had been raised in a conservative household, he'd said, and his long Orcish hair would be easily explained away as a conservative Elvish convention.

"What you have here is a rather excellent example of what mermish craftsmanship looked like at the turn of the century . . . . but do you see the etching on the handle? Every master carver would include a signature of some sort, using symbolry distinct to both oceanic region and tribe. These hash marks represent numbers that

86

denote a production series. From the design and the discoloration of the whalebone, we can tell this is a reproduction of—"

The boom from below sounded like a muffled explosion, shaking up the wall and rattling the triangle of polished balls in their rack upon the green felted surface of the pool table on the far side of the room, swallowing up Tate's triumphant exclamation at the television, and she jolted in alarm at the noise.

"What was that?"

He didn't answer, but his eyes narrowed into amber slits as his head lifted, his wide mouth pressing into a flat line, her hands falling away from his hair. When another thud rattled the pool table, he struggled to sit up, his shoulders returning to their tight position of the previous evening, despite the hours she'd spent kneading through the collection of knots.

"You're supposed to be relaxing," she objected as he rose from the sofa with a slight wince, crossing to the wide windows that lined the far wall to peer down to the street. "Can't they handle whatever it is?"

"Hard to relax when it sounds like the walls are about to come down. Rukh is alone down there." He'd already been crossing the apartment, tugging his previously discarded t-shirt over his head when his phone buzzed across the coffee table's smooth mahogany surface. Silva listened as he exchanged tense, terse words with whoever was on the other end of the line, his voice sharp and clipped, tight fury replacing the serenity that had softened his brow only moments earlier; watched their relaxing weekend die as he flung the phone on the sofa, striding across the room and out the door without even pausing to put shoes on.

"Silva, stay upstairs." His short bark echoed up the narrow stairwell as he disappeared into the blackness, almost as if he knew she stood at the top, slipping on her flip-flops to follow him. She kicked the shoes off in frustration before slamming the door, adding to the clearly heard commotion coming from below, stomping back to the sofa and flouncing down in what even she admitted was a childish, petulant way. *So much for a nice, relaxing weekend out of the business.*

She would never voice her opinion aloud, lest she hurt his feelings, but Silva was convinced Tate never actually *needed* to be at the restaurant or the bar. He was exacting and regimented and his staff was cross-trained in nearly every operation — a credit to his experience and business savvy and management style, to be sure — but it left him very little to actually do, from what she could tell. Cymbeline and Thessa were both full-time, as was Rukh, and Elshona had her own staff in the kitchen . . . there was no reason he couldn't spend more time with her, no reason these weekends together couldn't be a more regular occurrence, an opinion she knew was shared by members of his staff.

"I'm so happy to see you again," Cymbeline had squealed several weeks earlier on a Sunday morning, just a few hours before she returned to Cambric Creek and her life of heavy expectation for another week. Silva felt like a drab mouse next to the beautiful mothwoman and had tortured herself in the very beginning, wondering what kind of relationship she and Tate had shared before her hiring, but Cym was sunny and friendly and impossible to dislike. "Things are getting serious then?"

Silva had no idea how she was meant to respond, feeling her neck heat at the question. They'd never discussed their relationship in any way and it had only been a handful of weeks at that point, and she had convinced herself that was for the best — they needed time to get to know one another, time to decide if this was anything more than an extended weekend hook-up, and she wasn't any closer to deciphering Tate's feelings towards her than she had been the day she'd first returned to the resort with Lurielle. She'd been saved from answering, for Cymbeline was nothing if not a chatterbox.

"You know, Thessa thinks he needs a girlfriend." The mothwoman beamed before bending to pull her tablet from its charging station behind her hostess stand, and Silva knew she'd been flushed purple. The empty bistro would be packed with bodies within the next fifteen minutes, the brunch crowd already humming on the sidewalk beyond the ornate doorway, but Clover's hostess was undeterred. "But I disagree." Cymbeline had turned to face her fully, crowding her against the wall, with no escape. Tate occasionally grumbled about the way Cym and Thessa had a tendency to "trap him," and she'd never fully appreciated what he'd meant until that moment. "He doesn't need a girlfriend, Silva. He needs a wife. A wife and at least three children, close enough in age that there's *never* any downtime. You can't threaten an infant, and a toddler isn't going to care how many color-coded checklists he makes. He's really good with kids, did you know that? He's been my kids' favorite babysitter since I started here. A hobby that's not this place, one he can only do on Sunday mornings, that too. *That's* what he needs. I've never in my entire life known anyone more tightly wound than that man. He needs someone to unwind him. You'd be a perfect unwinder, Silva, I'm just saying."

She'd burned with embarrassment at the time, but the mothwoman's words had stayed with her and she'd revisited the conversation in her head numerous times since then, their fantasy binding ceremony growing more detailed with each passing week she spent in his company. The grounds of Applethorpe Manor would provide the perfect wooded backdrop for a twilight ring ceremony, in spring when the gardens would be in full bloom, their lush scent perfuming the air. She would wear flowers in her hair, and his would be plaited in a traditional old Elvish style . . . their children would have her wide eyes and his mischievous smile, her lavender skin and his glossy dark hair. It was stupid and silly and they'd never discussed where things were going. It was still early days, but it had become her favorite daydream, and she simply couldn't help herself. But just maybe, Silva reminded herself, pushing up from the sofa to peer down at the line of bikes parked in front of the pub, her feelings weren't so entirely one-sided after all.

The presence of the cider in his refrigerator was a little thing; a meaningless, insignificant thing . . . but it was one of many little, insignificant things she'd noticed over the last two months. When he'd learned the eucalyptus diffuser in the ladies' room at Clover made her sneeze, it had been replaced with one in a crisp cotton scent by her next visit. She liked having a glass of water on the bedside table every night, and she made due on the weekends she visited, despite the fact that his glasses were too big for her to comfortably grip . . . and then one weekend she'd opened the cupboard in his kitchen to find a line of smaller, daintier glasses on the bottom shelf, easily within her reach, one he'd filled from a filtered water pitcher in his refrigerator, another new purchase, setting it on a cut-glass coaster that had been placed on her side of the bed. When she inevitably woke in the middle of the night, slipping out of bed to tiptoe across the room, her path would be lit with moonlight, the blackout curtains on his wide windows left open, knowing that she disliked the dark. Tate wasn't as big and bulky as other orcs, but he still towered over her, and would do the same to every elf at her club, she was certain. He had no need for a stepstool in his kitchen, yet one had appeared — a pop of mint green, her favorite color, neatly fastened on a hook beside the sink. He kept his apartment at a near arctic temperature, and one weekend a cashmere throw had appeared on the back of the sofa, kitten-soft and wonderful to snuggle into, despite the fact that he was always warm.

A heap of little, meaningless things he did and never mentioned, never making a point to draw her attention to his actions, never mentioning them at all until they had accumulated into a whole pile of insignificant little things that made her giddy. It was early days and they'd not discussed the future of their relationship or their differing expectations . . . but it seemed to her that he'd wasted no time making a space for her and catering to her unspoken needs. Little, insignificant things that were never mentioned, that she noticed all the same — tiny adjustments to his life to make her more comfortable in it, signs that he listened when she talked and paid attention to her comfort, despite the fact that she still wasn't sure where she fit.

Silva had lost track of the tears she'd shed during the numerous drives back to Cambric Creek — for reasons that had very little to do with Tate, yet were entirely about him and the way he treated her. It was more than just feeling desired, she had decided, more than the intoxication of his independent life — she felt *seen* when she was with him, seen in a way she'd never before experienced. It didn't matter if she was bratty and over-privileged, or too naive and trusting and foolish; didn't matter if she felt invisible in her life ninety percent of the time, positive that she could be replaced with an automaton and no one would notice, because she was *seen* when she was with him. There was nothing about herself she needed to change because he saw it all and accepted her exactly as she was, and Silva was certain she would never feel this way again with anyone else. A pile of small, insignificant things, but they mattered greatly to her.

Saw her, but saw her through a wall of his own making, one she was determined to dismantle. She'd begun to dwell on the mothwoman's words, when she wasn't daydreaming about wedding flowers, parsing and dissecting each one, paying attention to his facial tics and subtle vocal inflections, memorizing the moments when he slipped on a mask of impassiveness and feigned disinterest, and she'd come to the conclusion that Cymbeline was wrong. Tate didn't need to be unwound, Silva thought. He needed to be *rewound*. Somewhere along the line, his coil of existence had twisted; twisted and kinked, and the rest of the spool had tightened around his heart. She needed to rewind him, she was certain; unspool his closely guarded emotions, untwist the flaw that kept him holding himself from her at arm's length, and rewind their threads together.

Her reverie was broken when the air around her jolted; an almost visible ripple in the atmosphere that nearly knocked her off her feet. For the first time since he'd disappeared down the black stairwell, it occurred to her that the commotion from below was coming from with*in* the bar, and that the street beyond the loft's wide windows was empty. A frisson of panic shivered up her neck at the thought of there being real trouble downstairs, for even though he was tall and strong to her, the Pixie's regulars dwarfed Tate, in addition to vastly outnumbering him. *What if he's in trouble?* He'd not hesitated to go charging down the steps, hadn't ascertained what sort of danger might wait beyond . . . *he's not even wearing shoes!* She knelt on the sofa in panic, certain at one point that she was able to hear the sharp ring of his voice. She ought to call someone, ought to do *something* . . . but before long, she heard the sound of him dragging up the steps once more. Vaulting from the sofa, she'd made it halfway across the room before he came through the door, freezing when she saw him.

Something was wrong, very wrong. Although he didn't appear to be injured in any way she could see, his eyes were lit with a manic and feral energy, as if he were some wild creature, panicking at finding itself trapped indoors for the first time. His wide mouth seemed slightly off-kilter, as if it were tilted on his face, and she realized, feeling her stomach flip as she approached him, that his eyes reflected the leaping flames of a fire that wasn't actually present. "Tate? Are-are you okay?" His gaze shifted to hers, as if noticing her for the first time, and she sucked in a breath, closing the distance between them in several strides to fist the material of his shirt, a rattling panic gripping her at how far away he seemed, despite being directly in front of her. "Tate?"

". . . Silva." Her name sat in his mouth as if he were tasting it for the very first time, and her hand tightened around the black cotton, pulling him closer, the panic licking up her neck. "Do you hear that music, dove?" The only sound was the distant rumble of a motorcycle engine and a car alarm going off somewhere down the street, and the rasp of his breath, his chest rising and falling beneath her hand in short, sharp heaves.

"Tate." She repeated his name, her voice finding a bit more strength as she gripped his shoulder, giving him a small shake. She had no idea what was wrong, nor what she could do, how she could help, if there was someone she ought to call . . . rising on her toes, she pressed her lips to his jaw, feeling utterly useless. Silva gasped when his hand pressed to the small of her back, nearly lifting her off her feet so that he could bury his face into her hair and inhale deeply.

"Sweet Silva," he murmured into her hair. "You smell like the summer, dove. Summer rain."

He sounded so far away, so far from her, despite being right there, and her heart began to pound in her throat. His hand shifted and her balance slipped, the soft press of her lips turning into a drag of her teeth down the side of his neck as she floundered, the sound rumbling from his throat very nearly a growl when his hand pressed into her once again, trapping her in place. She didn't know what was wrong and she didn't know how to help, not truly . . . but she could distract him, she decided, distract him away from whatever sucking morass had trapped him, distract the only way she knew how. Someday she would know his heart well enough to do so without the use of her body, but today was not that day and she needed to work with what she had.

His chest heaved when she bit at the tender skin of his throat, stretching up to trap his earlobe between her teeth, slipping her hand beneath the t-shirt's hem and scraping her nails down his chest until his mouth caught hers in a bruising kiss. She felt him inhaling her, his own sharp teeth catching her lips, needle pricks that didn't hurt as much as she thought they should, until she gasped against him. She had tightened her hand in his hair, squeezing until she felt his skin pull, pushing off his chest until she could drop from her toes, dragging her small canines against his clavicle.

The grey joggers were a perfect canvas for the thick swell of his erection when she lowered to her knees before him, pressing her lips against the fabric, tracing the shape of him until his cock jumped. She'd wanted to do this anyway, Silva reminded herself, heat curling through her as she kissed down his shaft. The trail of her tongue left dark patches of moisture as she worked him through the cotton — down to the root where the thick length jutted from his body, tracing back up a snaking vein until he jerked again. Silva opened her mouth wide, wide enough to take the meat of him, wide enough to bite down on the girth of his shaft with her unsharp teeth. Hard enough to feel; hard enough to hurt. Excitement flared through her when he hissed, dark moisture seeping through the cotton from the puddle of precum he released, just beyond the fat outline in the fabric of his cockhead. She loved how careful he was with her, she reminded herself, stroking him through the cotton, the heat of her breath warming the wet fabric as her tongue laved over him. She loved his gentled teeth against her thighs, loved the way he held her in his arms at night and how considerate and thoughtful he'd been . . . but her heart was racing, exhilaration thumping in her chest when he groaned, his pre-come and her saliva darkening the material as she swallowed him through the cotton barrier, trying to find and work her tongue into his slit.

When she finally pulled down the waistband, his cock released with a bounce, slapping into her cheek. *Wind him back to you*, she reminded herself, squaring her shoulders when he gripped his shaft, tracing the head over her mouth, leaving a smear of pre-come coating her already glossed lips. His eyes were less wild already, less distant, and as she caught him in her lips, licking a slow stripe over his head, holding his eyes with her own, Silva was relieved to be able to see her reflection there.

"Do you feel better?" she asked innocently, pulling her cami up her body, letting her breasts swing free, knowing he liked to palm the curve of them and roll the dark purple buds of her nipples between his fingers until they were painfully peaked, relief only provided from the heat of his sucking mouth.

"You're going to be the end of me, dove." His voice was still rough, still slightly ragged, but the echo of that morning's words set her at ease, almost as much as the sight of herself reflected in his eyes did. The cozy simplicity of that morning seemed like it had happened in another lifetime, but she was close, so close to winding him back to her from wherever it was that he'd unspooled.

When she took him in hand at last, as she'd done more than a dozen times before at that point, she realized something was wrong. Not wrong, she corrected, holding her breath as she gave him a slow pump. He was thick in her hand, her fingers not quite meeting as she stroked him, but that was normal . . . longer than anyone she'd ever been with, deep green edged in pink around the shiny dome of his head, the concave of his slit bubblegum pink, all traces of green left behind, all normal . . . It was the ripple beneath his skin that was decidedly *not* what she was used to, forming a ridged line up the underside of his shaft, a small squeak escaping her when she realized *this* was what she'd been feeling as she rode atop him that morning. She couldn't explain what would cause such a change, what *happened*?! — but as she remembered the drag of him within her, Silva whimpered, deciding it didn't matter, as long as he was okay.

She held his gaze as she sucked him into her mouth, pushing his foreskin back with her lips, humming as she did so, pumping him slowly with her hand, those newly-discovered ridges rippling beneath the sheath of his foreskin. She'd been good at this once, and she'd become good at it again over the course of the last several months, for she'd learned he loved the sight of her with her lips wrapped around his cock nearly as much as she enjoyed the bump of his nose and the slide of his tongue when she sat astride his face, her thighs pressing into his long ears and her ass bouncing on his chest as she moaned. It didn't take long for his fingers to thread through her hair and hold the back of her head as she sucked him, pumping lightly against her mouth as her hand pumped him in long strokes, sucking in a quick breath to take him as deeply as possible.

She wanted to make him explode, wanted him to shoot down her throat and fill her mouth, wanted her lips to overflow, a river of his release to run down her chest and over her breasts, felt herself dripping at the thought, wondering if he'd notice if she slipped her hand beneath the waist of her panties to find relief . ... but before she had a chance to live out the debauched image in her head, he was

pulling his cock from her mouth, hissing when she deliberately let
him feel the scrape of her teeth in retaliation. Silva pushed the shirt
up his body once he'd pulled her to stand before him; her kicked-
off panties joining the grey joggers in a heap on the floor when he
scooped her up, the felt of the pool table rough at her back when
she was laid atop it.

She was used to sitting on the smooth wooden edge of the
table, her legs stretched wide as he licked her, a prelude to the push
of his cock, her legs wrapped around his waist as she balanced at the
table's edge . . . but she'd never been placed in the center in such a
way, the triangle-shaped rack of balls pushed away to make room
for her. She squeaked in surprise when he pulled himself to the felt,
pulling her legs open to kneel between her thighs, feeding his cock
into her immediately. He normally teased her, sliding his head against
her slickness and stroking her with his long fingers, but there was no
time for gentleness and play right then; no time for anything other
than heat and desperation, and little need for more, for as he pulled
back to the tip, thrusting fully in, she felt the drag of those ridges and
cried out. She could already see reddened welts rising on his chest
from her nails, and scraped down his arms to give him a matching
set. When his thumb began to circle her clit in tight, urgent circles,
her back arched, feeling the rasp of the table as pleasure coiled in her
core, the drag of his cock already making her see stars.

She didn't know what happened downstairs; didn't know what
had caused his abrupt mood change or the wild look in his eyes and

she had a feeling he'd not actually tell her . . . but she was absolutely positive he'd not be able to produce a condom from their position on the table. She could tell from the relentless hammer of his hips that he was close, a good thing, as the angle of her hips coupled with the friction of his cock and roll of his thumb were doing her in. There was no way for him to pull out and disappear to the bedroom — no way she was going to let him reach behind her ear for *anything!* — when her body seized, clenching around him in a wave of tremors, crying out in annoyance as he pulled out, just in time for his cock to erupt.

The first long rope of his release landed across her belly, while the second pulse of his cock managed to reach the underside of her breast. She'd never had the opportunity to fully appreciate the sheer volume he came, not with his obsessive zeal for the *miserable* condoms, causing her to huff in frustration once during happy hour when Lurielle had groused about having to wash the sheets constantly. She wanted to feel him emptying into her like a geyser; wanted to be filled and overflowed . . . but she would settle for being painted in stripes of white across her stomach and chest.

Silva waited for him to say something in explanation when he backed off the table — an explanation for his crazed mood, for the apparent calamity in the pub, for the magical, unexplainable, *delicious* change to his anatomy . . . but all he did was hold his back and twist, testing his mobility. Silva waited for him to wince, or exclaim in pain, her mouth dropping open when he began to laugh, his shoulders shaking.

"I've cracked myself back into place," he exclaimed in wonder, nearly doubling over in musical laughter as she gaped, the puddles across her stomach beginning to cool uncomfortably. *A possible kink downside.* "If I'd known all I needed to do was have a row with those miserable cunts, I'd have done it a month ago. You're a sight, dove, let's get you into a bath."

A sharp gust of cold air woke her later that night, and she found him standing before the open window down the hall, his eyes far away once more.

"What are you doing? It's the middle of the night."

"It's always night in her majesty's forest," he answered dreamily, a completely nonsensical response. "Can you hear that music, Silva? Can you hear them dancing?" Beyond the window, the night was silent. "The bonfires have started. The veil is getting thinner every day." His eyes were fixed on the middle distance, at a point she was unable to see, and she shivered from more than just the cold.

"Come back to bed with me," she insisted, reaching around him to push down the window lift, locking the sash for good measure before threading her fingers with his. "Tate? Come back to bed with me, I'm cold without you."

To her relief, he did not argue. She pulled him against her in the sea of fluffy white bedding, with his head on her shoulder and her fingers in his hair, flattening herself beneath his heat. She wound her legs with his, so that she'd wake if he got up again, her stomach tightening at the inexplicably smokey smell of his hair, finding his hand

in the sheets and lacing their fingers once more. *Caretaker trope it is.*
Keeping him close, she told herself, winding him back to her heart.

♥ ♥ ♥

Ris

He was a programmer.

It was a shockingly mundane profession for someone like him, she thought, hunching over the table in laughter at the thought of him sitting in the tech department in her office, wearing the department's green polo, the peaks of his mohawk visible over the top of a cubicle. He specialized in a specific programming language, one she knew ran on her office computer, furthering the amusing vision until she was breathless and wheezing, her composure a thing of the past. His name was Ainsley, an improbable-sounding name for an orc, and he lived in Starling Heights, the suburb on the other side of the resort hamlet. The town was larger and older than Cambric Creek, a bit more urban in feel, and its business district teemed with every chain store under the sun, in addition to a tight press of bars and restaurants. She'd had fun the few times she'd met dates and friends there, but it was too far to visit regularly, not when Cambric Creek had its own thriving nightlife and the main city was only a short drive away.

"I thought for sure you were going to say a musician. Is that super stereotypical of me? I'm trying to picture you in the tech uniform at my office . . ." The warmth from the heater above flushing her cheeks when he laughed, eyes still sparkling, reaching across the table for her glass.

"Well, I do play in a band, so you're not completely wrong," he chuckled, topping off her champagne flute. "We don't have a uniform, thank the stars, but I *do* have to wear a lanyard, and that's bad enough. My work ID makes me look like it's my first day of prison and no one told me I shouldn't actually smile when they took our pictures."

She'd already laughed more in the short time they'd been together then she had on her last several dates combined, Ris thought, her shoulders shaking again, her face beginning to ache for how long she'd been smiling. He shrugged with a grin, leaning back in his seat, looking incredibly pleased with himself, the glow from the overhead strand of twinkle lights glinting off his numerous piercings.

After leaving the disaster at the bar, he'd set her carefully on the sidewalk, weaving his fingers with her own before tugging her down the street. They wound up at the little bistro on the corner where the terrifying server worked. Ainsley relayed the story of the bar fight to a beautiful mothwoman, the same hostess Ris remembered from her last visit.

"You're supposed to be sending down one of the boys to help clean up, and we get a bottle of the house bubbly."

The lovely moth frowned, her delicate brows drawing together. "Rukh didn't say anything about a bottle..."

"It's Rukh, are you surprised? This lovely lady was trapped amidst the melee and I kept her safe. Better not call Tate, he's indisposed tonight."

The hostess snorted, shaking her head. "Indisposed the rest of the weekend, actually. He's been on for two months straight. I'm not calling and getting my head bitten off . . . fine, a bottle of the house, but you have to sit on the patio so we can start shutting down the dining room."

The patio had several torchiere-style heaters, and they'd chosen a table beneath one. She'd sipped the champagne he'd poured as Ainsley fired the heater up, and the effect—sitting with him at the small bistro table with the heat radiating down, surrounded by the tiny white lights—was surprisingly cozy. He'd asked her about her job, about the meaning of her name, what books she'd read and movies she loved. Ris hadn't had a date pay quite this much attention to her in recent memory, embarrassing considering how many she'd been on, but she quite enjoyed the nonchalant way he shrugged and his easy smile.

"So a weekend trip alone? Mental recharge from the office grind? And why exactly is it herd resources? I've always hated that. It makes us sound like a bunch of hippos fighting over the only working copy machine."

"Because it's called 'human resources' in human-majority companies. It's important to keep the acronym, so when you're doing business with a human company they know what's going on. You can't imagine how much time is wasted on inter-office red tape because the all-human firms pretend they don't understand what an office pupation suite is or why we work from home on the full moon. And I wasn't *supposed* to be alone, but my friend blew me off at the last minute and it was too late to cancel. But I guess if she hadn't I wouldn't have been almost killed in a bar fight, right?"

"Always look on the bright side," he agreed cheerfully, leaning forward on his elbows. Unlike her most recent date with the elf, Ris found herself leaning in, rather than away from this charismatic orc, so unlike any other she'd met at this resort. "And how serendipitous, for I too was blown off this weekend. Here's to friends breaking plans." He raised his glass to hers with the same guileless cheer, giving her no choice but to clink her flute to his, chuckling as she shook her head.

"I don't know if that's something I want to toast!" she laughed protestingly. "This isn't the first time she's done it, and it probably won't be the last. Did your friend cost you money on a hotel room?"

"He did not," he conceded, raising his hand in defeat, "and I guess we didn't *technically* have plans, but in my defense, he's not someone you can make plans with, because he'll always say no. He used to be a lot of fun, but I've come to realize in the past few years that he was fun out of necessity. Now he's only interested in pursuing his life goal of being a hunched old cat lady who never leaves his apartment.

But it's his first weekend off in months, and I had *thought* he might be willing to come hang out with his very charming friend, which was clearly a delusion."

"What happened? I can't believe your charm failed you."

He huffed in mock offense, smoothing the studded lapels of his leather jacket in a preening fashion, making her laugh again.

"Ah well, I forgot about the new girlfriend, gorgeous little thing. She rates much higher than me, I didn't even get a text back."

"Oh, in *that* case," she raised her glass again, clinking to the side of his, "we're birds of a feather. That's Dynah all day long. It doesn't matter what sort of plans she's made with any of us or how long they've been made. If a guy blinks at her from across the street, she'll leave the rest of us standing there on the corner without a moment of hesitation. This is the second time she's bailed on this trip! She'd miss her own funeral if the grave digger expressed any interest. And all the guys are terrible! That's the only thing any of them have in common, and that makes it *so much harder* to not be mad about it. Do you at least like your friend's girlfriend?"

"Oof. Yeah, that's rough. Shame on you, Dynah." His eyes dropped to the diminishing contents of his glass, as though the champagne bubbles held the answer to some secret, hesitating a long moment before answering. "Do I like the girlfriend . . . jury's still out, to be honest. She's an elf, like you," his eyes raised, flashing her that bright smile once more. "She seems lovely, but she's got 'heartbreaker' written all over her. She's not what I would deem terrible though, so you win this round, Nanaya."

"That's an awful trophy," she laughingly protested. "And the worst part is I'm not really surprised it happened, so I'm not mad about it. I *should* be, but it's not worth the energy to be mad. It's just how she is, you have to know that going in. Peak Dynah."

"Same, I'm not mad." His sharp jaw cut a stunning profile in the warm golden glow of the twinkle lights, the silver gleam of the cuff around his tusk sparkling. "This isn't how he is, not normally, but he seems happy-ish, so I can't be mad. Tate doesn't really *do* happy, he . . . endures. So, if he's happy and I'm his friend, I guess I should be happy that he's happy."

"Tate? With the teeth? *That's* your friend?"

He grimaced, rubbing his neck with an uncomfortable chuckle. "Things we accept as the cost of entry, right? *Allegedly* I talk a lot, that's my cost of entry, I guess. Dynah's cost of entry is she's going to leave you high and dry for a date. His cost of entry is . . . you don't ask questions you don't actually want to hear the answer to. If the question is how far can you fuck around, the finding out is not worth the fuckery that precedes it, and the boys at the bar learned that tonight. But he's a good friend. His bark is sharp, but he bends over backwards for his people, and I consider myself one of the lucky few who get to claim membership to that club. Bailed me out of jail once, used to be a lot of fun. So . . . it's fine, I'll live, and so will all the troublemakers in the Pixie tonight. *And* they've learned the answer to just how far they can fuck around. I wouldn't have had the opportunity to play the gallant and rescue a distressingly lovely damsel if I'd been across town, so it's more than fine. Like I said, serendipitous. What's your cost of entry, I wonder, Nanaya?"

There was something about the name he called her, something foreign and sultry-sounding that made her stomach flip and her neck heat. She wasn't sure what it meant, but she intended on finding out before the night was done.

"Wait, wait. Rewind. You were in *jail*?!"

He laughed sheepishly, dropping his head back. "It wasn't for anything bad, honest."

"*What*?!"

He explained that he'd been arrested with other labor protestors at a Starling Heights industrial factory, after the workers had been locked out of the factory floor. "They said we were on private property, but that was just something to say to shut things down before the local news stations arrived. You can blame my mother for that," he laughed. "'Fuck the man' is Shu'la's motto."

The warmth she felt in her chest definitely had nothing to do with the champagne, she decided as she giggled. He had lovely, high cheekbones and a long jaw, a straight nose and sharply pointed ears. His endless legs were stretched to the side of the table, and she could easily imagine her own, long and plum-colored, entwined with his green ones. Ris shook her head, chasing away the champagne bubbles and chastised herself, feeling her ears heat. The image in her head was far more intimate than any encounter she'd experienced with the orcs here, after all. *Everyone here is easy meat, and they're all the same.* It was unwise to hope for some storybook relationship like Lurielle's, and she didn't really want that, in any case. *Ainsley.*

"You don't have a very Orcish name," she blurted, letting her internal thoughts bubble to the surface with a blush. *Ainsley.* Every orc she'd ever known had rough, guttural-sounding names, like Gruvush and Viggu, the two orcs in her office. By contrast, Ainsley was delicate, almost poetic sounding, matching his unconventional appearance.

"That's also my mom's fault," he laughed. "She'd already picked the name out, thought she was having a girl . . . then I showed up and she decided it was too late. She'd been calling me Ainsley for months, figured I'd already be answering to it."

She smiled at the thought of his mother being shocked when she gave birth to a strapping son, and not the little girl she'd been expecting. "Every orc I know at home is either named for their grandfather or for some mountain god. How did she not get bullied by your grandparents?"

"None around to do so, otherwise you're right, I'd probably be named Yarg. My dad died when I was a baby and they had already moved pretty far away from the clan before I was born. It was just the two of us, and no one tells Shu'la what to do. I suppose she couldn't give up the freedom at that point."

He smiled widely at the grin she gave him, her cheeks heating again. It was more than she'd learned about any of her recent dates, she realized wryly, eyeing the chipped black nail polish on his pinky nail. *You can actually tell Lurielle you met an orc at the resort and found out his name.*

"Are you still close to your mom?"

"Oh, I'm what is scientifically known as a mama's boy," he chuckled, and she was unable to hold in her own laughter once again. "I go home to visit at least once a month." His eyes sparkled, and Ris felt her own mouth stretching to match his bright smile. "She's the coolest mom I know, and we have a lot of fun together. She raised me on her own, no clan support or anything like that, but she's happy I'm still just an afternoon's drive away, and I'm happy to be near enough if there's an emergency. And you never really grow out of needing your mother, right? I haven't at least."

"I'm close to my parents too," she quickly agreed. Her relationship with her family was something she rarely discussed, even with her friends. Too many years of pretending, of molding herself into the sort of elf that fit in seamlessly with her better-heeled peers, of blurring the edges of who she was and who they thought she was, and even though she no longer felt the need to be anyone other than herself, letting others peek behind the curtain of her confident facade was not a skill she possessed in any quantity. There was something about his easy smile, though; his sparkling eyes and self-effacing laughter that set her at ease. "I still go on vacation with them every year. My mom and I go thrifting and we eat completely unfancy beach food, and it's my favorite week of the year; has been since I was little. And," she added with a wry smile, "it's a relief getting away from the herd."

"Herd Resources! It's such a terrible name! You can't make me believe they couldn't come up with something better than *herd resources*, it's like they weren't even trying. Who does that even apply to?!"

"Minotaurs, cervitaurs, centaurs," she ticked off on her fingers. "All the 'taurs,' I guess? Don't ask me, HR Generalist isn't my dream job, but it pays the bills."

He leaned forward in his seat, smile stretching. "And what did Ris want to be when she was just a little elf?"

"Little Ris wanted to be a ballerina. She didn't know then that most of the big companies are almost exclusively nymphs. Also, she's never taken a single lesson in her life, so it's a good thing she went to school for something sensible. Now big Ris can afford to go see the ballet in Bridgeton and go to the art museum whenever she wants."

"Oh, same, totally. Well, not the ballet part. I absolutely did *not* have aspirations to be a tech bro growing up. We had one computer, a big, clunky, second-hand desktop, and if I was on it for more than an hour or two, the motor would run so hard it sounded like a plane was taking off. It was in our living room, two feet away from my mom's chair, so it wasn't like I was even able to do anything fun on it, you know? No horny lagomorph hot tub chatrooms I could creep in pretending to be a thirty-two-year-old werewolf doctor. She was right there, so it was homework and pre-teen cock-blocking and nothing else."

She doubled over in laughter again, her breath hitching each time she tried and failed to speak. "That is a *very* specific example," she wheezed. "I, uh, have *doubts* that you weren't doing exactly that every time she left the room."

"Yeah, maybe that was too specific of an example," he grinned, "I learned the importance of clearing the web browser and cache very early. But, my point is, it was just something that happened. But I like the company I'm with, I like my co-workers, and more importantly, it pays well enough to support the stuff I am passionate about."

"Like playing in four different bands," she suggested, smiling broadly as he tipped his glass in her direction in agreement. "I totally get that though, I'm the same way. When I leave the office, I don't need to take it with me. I like the company, I love the people I work with, I've made really good friends there." She smiled wryly, imagining Lurielle and Silva, and even Dynah, with all her faults. "They're just work friends, and I know that's supposed to mean less, and we're not super close, but . . . I don't know," she shrugged, sipping her champagne. "I don't really know how to make friends as an adult."

"Right?" he agreed animatedly, making her laugh again. "How in Hades are you supposed to make friends as an adult?! We lived in an apartment when I was a kid, and I was friends with everyone. The old troll down the hall with all the cats, the building super, every kid in the building. If they lived there, I would be friends with them. And apparently I got into my head that that's how you make friends? And then you go off to school and it's the same. I was friends with all the guys I shared a house with, we were friends with the girls next-door, the house behind ours. Everyone in the vicinity, we were friends."

"Same," she agreed. "Proximity-based relationships, hence why all I have now is work friends."

"Right! Flash forward to adulthood, I'm living in an apartment in Bridgeton, and at the end of the hall there's a guy who looks like he's around my age, another orc. So of course my friend-meter goes off. I can admit now, all these years later, that the events that followed were tantamount to harassment."

Ris could barely breathe, she was laughing so hard, *again!* she thought, trying and failing to imagine anyone not wanting to be friends with the funny, verbose orc.

"You know, here he is, just being a normal adult, and then here's me, popping out from behind the dumpster with pizza every time he comes home from work and trapping him in conversation in the hallway. I literally harassed Tate into being my friend. But," he paused to wink at her devilishly, "again—serendipity. Otherwise, I'd not have been in the Pixie tonight."

"So . . . four bands."

He nodded earnestly, eyes crinkling. "Mhm, four different genres of music."

"So music is your main passion then?"

His brow furrowed and lips curled around his tusks as his face scrunched in consideration.

"It's definitely a passion, but I don't know if I can call it my main passion? I love anthropology and cultural studies. I could spend *weeks* in the museums that cover ancient civilizations. Oh! I took a class in sumi-e painting last summer, the oni who taught it was incredible, and I've been collecting little postcards with that style of art since. Reading? Reading is probably my main passion, I guess? I would rather spend money on books than food. I've been collecting books my whole life . . . I've also gotten into astronomy in the last few months? I-I have a lot of hobbies." He chortled nervously, rubbing his neck in what she decided was an adorably self-deprecating way. "I guess that's probably weird."

"Not weird," she corrected, smiling broadly as she shook her head, excitement thrumming through her veins. It was as if her FWB list had taken on sentiency in the form of the handsome orc across the table. "You know, you're not like *any* of the other orcs I know," she grinned, giving him her best twinkle over the rim of her champagne flute. "Especially the ones around here."

A black brow raised and his head cocked curiously. "Hmm. I suppose I could say the same thing about you? You're not what I'd normally expect from an elf. You're right, I'm probably not a 'typical' orc, I didn't grow up with a clan or speaking orcish. To be honest, almost everything I know about Orcish culture is from books or second hand, it's not really my lived experience. But orcs aren't a monolith. Are elves? Does that mean you're busy playing the harp and croquet on weekends when you're not sightseeing?"

Her cheeks heated at his words, uncomfortable in the knowledge that he was right, her stomach flipping at the assumption that she was just another tourist, there for anonymous sex with the local nudists, maybe a bit of shopping between. *Aren't you though?* He wasn't wrong, she admitted to herself before squaring her shoulders. She'd come to the resort to get laid, and she didn't have anything to be ashamed of, not really. Everyone came here for the same thing, after all, and the orcs benefitted from the relationship just as much as the tourists. *He's not wrong though.*

"Hardly. My folks didn't have a lot of money when I was growing up." She shrugged, swallowing the rest of her glass. She didn't need to be ashamed of that either. "They sent me to a good school, but there wasn't a lot of money for extras. I guess I didn't grow up like most elves."

"Well, there you go," he hummed, refilling her glass. "We're not what people expect us to be. Two of my closest friends are orcs who don't belong to clans either. And I know folks have a lot of assumptions about what elves are like, but how much of it is true? I don't know, I just think maybe those expectations aren't really fair. My mom worked at the museum when I was growing up. Always loved ancient history and civilizations. She wanted to be a docent, but they wouldn't hire orcs for anything other than security at the time. A friend of a friend eventually got her a job in the gift shop, and she made sure I was in every kid's program they offered, but it was never what she wanted to be doing, and she knew those exhibits inside and out."

She nodded, heat moving up her long ears. "You're right, that's not fair of me. My mom and I are professional thrifters. When I was in school we would drive two hours away to hit the consignment shops, far enough away from home that no one would see us. I had designer shoes and bags just like all my friends, and it never occurred to them to wonder why I wasn't playing croquet at the club on weekends. I guess I meant . . . you're different from the orcs I've met here. Most of these guys treat everyone like meat."

"Okay, that *is* probably fair to a degree," he chuckled, shrugging. "But everyone is here for the same thing, aren't they? So how much of that is a self-fulfilling prophecy? I could tell myself all elves are just looking to get laid, right? Then I come to a resort party and find a drop-dead gorgeous elf like yourself, and we both go home satisfied. Is that all you are, or did we both find what we were looking for?"

He'd leaned over the table again, and without realizing it, she had as well, until his face was nearly touching hers. He was right, and she *hated* admitting it . . . but he was right. She'd gone looking for a weekend of anonymous sex, and she'd found it in ready supply. The exact experience she'd been hoping for. *And you don't have anything to be ashamed of.*

"So I guess the question," he murmured, near enough that she could feel his heat, "is if you had such a terrible time before, Nanaya, why did you come back?"

Ris blinked. There was a hint of knowing in the question that she didn't like, playing at the corners of his easy smile. "Who said I had a bad time? I had the time I went looking for. Don't recall ever saying

I regret it. And how would *you* know?" A bit of fire flared in her veins at his presumption. "Were you there? Were you at . . . the pool bar?" She felt an uncomfortable prickle move up her spine as she asked the question, knowing he hadn't been. She'd seen him the morning she went jogging, she was positive, but she hadn't gone to the little black-bricked bar on the last visit, and if he hadn't been at the pool, then he must have been . . . "You were at the bonfire?"

She thought of what he must have seen—her, on her knees in the grass, being taken roughly by the two huge orcs, used and discarded before they moved onto the next tourist. When she looked up, Ainsley was grinning with that same broad, knowing smile, and her chest folded in on itself in embarrassed disappointment. She knew she was blushing all the way up to the tips of her long, pointed ears, her normal bravado failing her as her stomach twisted. She didn't care about a single one of the nameless orcs who'd used her for their pleasure the night before, or on the last trip, but she didn't like the thought of *this* orc thinking of her poorly. *Who cares if he does? If he was there, he was looking to get laid, like everyone else. You had fun, and you don't have anything to be ashamed of.*

"You were beautiful," he interrupted her whirling thoughts. "So confident. You knew exactly what you wanted...like I said, refreshing."

Fire flooded her face, even as his words mollified her embarrassment, slightly. "I don't remember seeing you," she shot back. "You just like to watch? Were you jerking off behind a tree or something?" His laughter echoed around the small terrace, his shoulders shaking beneath the black jacket he wore. Ris pursed her lips, waiting.

"No! I was walking back to my car from the Pixie," he shrugged with another cocky grin. "Knew there was some sort of party going on, cut through the field to see if it was my scene. It wasn't, but you certainly were."

Her stomach flipped again, wondering if he was sincere. His gaze had been locked onto her from the moment she'd walked into the bar that night, despite the fact that the satyress and her friends had been right there . . .

"I don't believe you. You were jerking off in the bushes like some creeper."

This time, her own laughter joined his as his shoulders shook, and that curious warmth curled through her once more. "I wasn't! I swear!I barely slowed down, just enough to see you taking control, making those orcs do what you wanted...back arched, that confident smile . . . *but* I'd be lying if I said that's not a vision I've revisited many times since then, Nanaya. "

The notion of him pleasuring himself to thoughts of her being taken on her knees was very appealing, she decided, but still...she was slightly embarrassed that he'd seen her that way, had seen her been so thoroughly used. She suddenly had the desire to pick a fight with him, wanted to raise her voice and have him do the same, wanted to feel her face flame and her pulse race. A shouting match to whet the appetite...then rip his clothes off right here.

"What does that mean? I did tell you my name, didn't I?"

His laugh was a deep rasp, a steel guitar pick, scraping over stone, and she shifted impatiently in her seat. Ainsley leaned forward, propping a leather-clad elbow on the table, tightening the space between them. She watched the chain attached to the piercings in his ear swing as he lowered his head conspiratorially.

"Nanaya was an ancient goddess," he explained with an arched eyebrow, "of sexuality and pleasure and war. She was worshiped under many names . . . Inanna, Ishtar, Tašmetu . . . I thought it was a fitting sobriquet. That's what I've been calling you in my head all this time." He paused, tipping back the remains of his glass before re-fixing her with a heavy, hooded look that caused a tingle between her thighs when she squeezed them. "Her followers celebrated with ritual sex for days and days, a bacchanal at her temple, that she would bless them with pleasure and fertility."

Ris leaned forward on her own elbows, closing the distance from him across the table. "And what does that make you? High priest? Acolyte? Creeper in the bushes?"

"Devotee?" Heat pooled low in her belly, a quiver of excitement ran down her spine and rippled in her blood, igniting the tingle between her thighs to a bright spark of need as Ainsley leaned further in, close enough to kiss her, if she only inclined her mouth. "A worshiper, prostrate before your altar. You know, you never answered the question."

"You've asked me about two hundred questions already. Which

one did I miss?"

He smiled with his whole face, she thought, watching his eyes brighten and crinkle, his nose scrunching slightly as his mouth split. She'd always heard the expression 'a sparkling smile,' but she'd never understood what it meant, not truly, she realized then. It had nothing to do with attractiveness or intelligence, both of which he had in spades. It was an inner warmth, Ris decided, one that radiated out of the person possessing it, and he shone as warm and bright as the sun.

"What's your cost of entry, Nanaya?"

The whole world seemed to slow, and the only thing that existed was the closeness of his mouth, the twinkle lights reflected in his shining eyes, and the certainty that she was standing at the precipice of change, the opportunity to pull herself from the grasping pit of inertia which had mired her, all she had to do was take the step . . .

"I'm not looking for a serious, monogamous relationship. I don't want kids and I don't want a husband. I just want someone to have fun with, without all the pressure of what's supposed to come next."

She tilted her head, able to feel the heat of him nearing her lips, her stomach clenching in anticipation . . . when the moment was broken abruptly, the lights above them flickering out. Ris jumped at the sudden darkness, as the light in the dining room was also extinguished.

"Ains, I still need to make my kid's lunches and do laundry. Are you planning on observing our business hours at any point tonight?" The willowy, beautiful moth leaned in the doorway, her arms crossed resolutely in front of her.

"You know, Tate needs to leave you in charge more often, Cym. You're a natural leader. A+ focus on customer experience."

The lovely moth scowled as Ainsley rose, giving Ris a conspiratorial wink as he did so. "Yeah well, you're not a customer. You tricked me into giving you free champagne and you're preventing us from going home. No!" she cried, blocking the door when Ainsley scooped up the empty bottle and glasses. "You can't come through this way, I finally got the floor perfect. You know he's probably going to pop in at the crack of dawn just to check up on me. Just leave it on the table and go out the gate."

Once more, Ris found herself easily scooped up by the tall orc, as Ainsley stepped over the black spikes of the terrace fence. He carried her that way until they'd reached the intersection, and she tightened her arms around his neck before he had a chance to set her down. It was easy to reach his mouth, easy to kiss him the way she'd wanted to at the table, and so she did, aloft in his arms on the empty, darkened street corner. His breath caught against her mouth, groaning as she nipped his lower lip with her teeth, sliding her tongue against his slowly.

"Where to, Nanaya?" His voice was slightly breathless as the kiss broke off, his eyes crinkled with mischief and desire. She released her grip on his neck so that he was able to lower her to the ground. He was going to need his energy, she reckoned. *Time to order off the menu.*

"To the resort hotel."

♥ ♥ ♥

The journey to the resort from the little downtown was a fast flight, full of laughter and groping kisses in the dark, until they burst into her rented room. If she'd thought the length of time they'd spent talking on the bistro's terrace was indicative of what they'd do once they arrived at her bedside, she would have been disappointed. Her jacket was dropped in a heap, and Ainsley had wasted no time before slowly peeling her tank up her body, his hot tongue licking across her collarbone and down the valley between her small, firm breasts. His leather jacket joined hers on the floor, once her skirt had been eased down her hips, and she'd paused undressing him, taking a moment to enjoy the slow glide of her palms across his leanly muscled chest. It was completely different than any other experience she'd had, here at the resort, with any other orc she'd encountered. Ris considered, as he caught her wrists, meeting her mouth with his own once more before quickly reversing their positions, laying her out on the bed and dropping to his knees before her, that perhaps he was right, and she'd been the one who was wrong all this time. They might have all been cruising for the same thing, but maybe they weren't all the same.

"A disciple at your altar, Nanaya," he murmured into the skin behind her knee, kissing his way up her leg, grazing her with his teeth.

The smooth hotel coverlet bunched in her fists as he reached the juncture of her spread-open thighs, licking a broad stripe over her hot flesh. If she had thought it was going to be a fast prelude before he climbed over her, intent on his own pleasure, she would have been wrong. Ainsley seemed intent on showing her his devotion, groaning against her heat as he licked, slipping his tongue inside her before dragging the moisture up her flesh, pausing to suck and nibble at her aching clit. He teased her relentlessly, changing his pattern, never staying in one spot for long, caressing with a tantalizing fingertip until she was lifting her hips, attempting to buck against his face.

"I-I don't know if I'm going to be a benevolent goddess if you keep this up," she panted, gasping when his deep chuckle vibrated against her.

"Your namesake is not, so that tracks. It's the journey, not the destination, laughing girl."

She was panting, crying out in pleasure and frustration every time he suckled at her clit before pulling away, knew that she was drenching his face, simultaneously wanting him to continue this game indefinitely, and hurry up and give her what she wanted. The great spikes of his hair were handy to grab onto, she decided, directing his head and holding him in place as her hips bucked beneath his attentive tongue, daring him to pull away. When he finally settled into a pattern, licking her steadily, it was an embarrassingly short amount of time before she reached her peak. She could feel his deep chuckle as she came against his tongue, shuddering as he continued to lap at her pulsing flesh. When the pressure at her clit became too much, she stilled him with a hand to the side of his shaved head. He pulled back immediately, transferring his attention to her quivering thighs, kissing up her hip, over her stomach, crawling up the bed until he met her mouth.

Curling his fingers with hers, he caged himself around her, as he'd done at the bar. Ris was able to taste herself on his mouth as he kissed her, deep and slow, kissing *her*, not just the next mouth in line. It seemed, she thought, almost impossible that she was in the same place. He rolled to his back with a laugh when she pushed him, folding his hands behind his head, letting her struggle with removing his tight, black jeans. Peeling the uncooperative material down his endlessly long legs at last, she crawled back onto the bed with a devilish smile, pulling back the waistband of his boxer briefs, releasing his swollen cock with a bounce. A deeper shade than his fern green skin, thick with a slight curve, he seemed completely at ease with her eyeing his cock as if it were a tasty meal. The wrinkled skin of his scrotum was yet a darker shade of green, the heavy balls it held hanging like a piece of juicy fruit. He was just as well-endowed as his fellows at the tiki bar from the previous evening, and a million times more interesting than any date she'd recently been on. *Well hung and a better conversationalist*, she thought, pulling back his foreskin to lick a broad stripe over his shiny head; circling with her tongue once, twice, closing her lips around it on the third, hearing his groan.

"I take it back. She's a benevolent goddess," he grunted when she sucked him deeply, relaxing her throat as best she could until she gagged. He flipped them deftly when she'd finally released him with a pop, laughing again when she'd tugged her purse strap, still sitting on the edge of the bed, spilling out the orc-sized condoms across the mattress. "Altar tools," he grinned down, raising her ankles to his shoulders.

She wanted him closer than he was, wanted to be able to feel his heat and grip his arms for leverage, but he towered over her, a million miles in the air, leaving her gasping as he rubbed himself against her, coating himself in her slick, teasing her once more. When he finally pushed his cock into her, she cried out in relief, exasperated by his maddeningly slow pace.

"The high priestess and the king would act out the divine roles of the goddess and her consort every year to ensure a good harvest," he murmured, lowering himself over her at last, giving her the chance to rake her nails down his long back as he pumped into her, writhing beneath his weight.

"And is this how they did it?" she gasped, arching as the thick head of his cock dragged over the spongy spot within that made her toes curl. "Are you fucking me the way the king fucked the goddess?"

Ainsley growled against her shoulder, his hips picking up speed until her moans came out as a high *yip!* every time his cock slammed into her, pressing her legs back until every thrust dragged against her g-spot, his pelvic bone rubbing her clit, hurtling her towards another spine-shaking climax. When he abruptly pulled out, she nearly sobbed.

"Up on your knees, Nanaya," he rasped against her ear, a flinty strike against stone, igniting her blood as he flipped her to her stomach, "if you want to be fucked like a goddess."

When he pressed back into her, the angle was deeper and Ris keened, fisting the sheets. His mouth was at her back, hot tongue licking up her spine until his skin was flush against hers, his thrusting hips the only part of them not fused together. She moved her small, plum-colored hand over his large green one where it was braced against the mattress, threading their fingers to make up for space. When his free hand dragged up her thigh to press between her legs, long fingers circling her clit, her vision went white. Ainsley's hips surged against hers, his rhythm erratic as he came with a hiss, his circling fingers not ceasing their movement until she joined him, only a few moments later. Her back arched, her muscles clenching around his cock, and he groaned again, pumping against her weakly to prolong the pleasure as she shook beneath him, her legs no longer able to support her.

When she dropped, he caught her, easing them both to their sides as his softened cock slipped from her. For several endless moments, nothing existed except for the thudding of her heartbeat, thundering behind her eyes and in her mouth, and the echo of his beneath her ear. She'd never heard of the goddess the humans had once worshiped, but as his long, leanly muscled arm closed around her, Ris thought she would surely be happy with their performance in her name.

The sharp peaks of his hair came apart with surprising ease under the rich lather of her shampoo in the shower they shared afterward, leaving his hair dripping over one side of his head. When they repaired back to the big orc-sized bed, he pulled her tightly to him, pressing into her once more. She was used to his languid pace at that point, grinding against each other as they lay on their sides, her breasts pressed tight to his chest as their mouths met and parted, over and over.

It had been more intimate than any sexual experience she could remember.

When he'd rolled to his back, keeping her pressed to him until she was astride his hips, impaled on his thick length, she was certain she really was the goddess he'd claimed, rolling her hips and letting her head drop back as his huge hands moved over her neck and breasts, stroking her thighs, circling against her clit once more. When she shook apart atop him, he gripped her hips tightly, murmuring about how beautiful she was before flipping them once more, rolling on another one of her condoms before chasing his own release with a thunderous pace.

Her head was impossibly heavy, once she was curled at his side, her cheek pillowed against his broad shoulder, the warmth of his skin radiating through her. Ainsley's long body spanned the entire length of the mattress, his long legs tangled with hers, his damp black hair a swooping swirl on the coverlet beside his head. She idly wondered how much higher an orc's core temperature was, compared to an elf, an amusing thought, as she drifted between sleep and wakefulness. The night had been like nothing she could have imagined, when she'd left Cambric Creek the previous afternoon.

"I need to get going." His voice was warm at her ear, his arm heavy across her waist. Ris stirred, realizing she'd fallen asleep after all, the warmth of his skin and the evenness of his heartbeat lulling her into unconsciousness. Impossibly, sunlight was already beginning to lighten the resort grounds, brightening the small room around the unopened blinds. "Tate probably already had my car towed," he grumbled against her neck, untangling their legs. Ris felt him stretch, groaning when his back popped beneath her, and then he was pulling away.

"This was fun," she blurted, watching as he slowly dressed, carefully laying her own clothes at the foot of the bed instead of leaving them in a heap on the hotel room floor. She remembered the night she'd needed to go hunting for her red dress in the dark, finding it in a tangle at the base of a tree. Her face heated as she swallowed at the stark difference of this weekend. "This was...really nice."

"It was," he agreed, zipping his jeans, flashing her a wide smile. She jumped when he leaned across the narrow space, kneeling on the bed once more. "It was *really* nice." His hair was a thick, black curtain that she fisted tightly as he kissed her again, feeling warth curl through her. *Not a piece of meat at all.*

Room service brought up the grapefruit and croissant she ordered after he left, which she ate on her small terrace, as she programmed his number into her phone. Ainsley had been scratched out on a piece of the resort stationary, along with his phone number, and she tucked it into her bag. By the time she checked out of the resort that morning, a jug of cider in the backseat for Silva, Ris decided to head home to Cambric Creek. There was laundry waiting for her, and a book she wanted to finish reading. Besides, she thought: she wasn't interested in anything else the little town had to offer. She would send him the name of the book, she thought, once she finished. He'd already sent her two messages by the time she loaded her bag into her car, and she couldn't help the way warmth bloomed through her belly each time his name appeared in her notifications.

Do you have ChitterChat on your work laptop? I'll walk you through the install so that your tech dept won't see it

A squirrel turned to glare at her burst of laughter. The thought of spending her afternoons chatting with him in between her work, instead of swiping left on an endless parade of guys on Dynah's dating app made her bite her lip to keep her smile in check. Nothing serious would come of it, but he was smart, and he was funny, and she was looking forward to seeing him again.

Drive safe, Nanaya

She owed Dynah lunch, she thought, pulling onto the road that would take her back to Cambric Creek, and Silva too. Her elevation from a piece of meat to an ancient goddess would have never happened without flippy-floppy Dynah and Silva's recommendation, after all, although she wouldn't share the details of this particular evening.

Some things, she thought as a golden autumn sun lit the sky behind her, were best kept sacred.

♥ ♥ ♥

Winter

Ris

It had been several months at that point, and thus far, she had no regrets.

She'd not expected Ainsley to be as responsive as he was, as enthusiastic as he'd proven to be, and never in her dizziest daydreams had she ever expected to meet someone so fun. As promised, he'd walked her through the installation of a chat app on her work laptop, and instantly her days had become more amusing, sometimes needing to stifle her laughter at her desk as she read his messages. Lighthearted banter and easy conversation that never felt forced or strained, and always unfailingly funny. Two weeks had passed since the weekend she met him, and as the third weekend approached, Ris found herself chewing her cuticle in indecision, wondering if it would be weird to invite him to do something that weekend. She was just about to lean over her laptop to open the chat app when her cell phone buzzed on the edge of her desk.

Do you like jazz? I don't think I ever asked. I play upright bass in a jazz quartet, did I mention that? Anyway, there's a concert this weekend I was planning on going to in Bridgeton tonight and I thought you might be interested? I can pick you up in CC on the way.

She'd stared, open-mouthed at her phone screen. She wasn't sure she'd ever had a date make the plans all on their own, for both the time and location of the event *and* her transportation. There was no game involved, no guessing to wonder his ulterior motives. He was refreshingly straightforward, and she'd enthusiastically responded yes.

She'd enjoyed the concert, enjoyed the time they'd spent in a wine bar up the block afterward, sharing a cheese plate and each other's desserts; and she most definitely enjoyed having him back in her condo, testing the strength of her bed frame as he fucked her like a goddess. She was nearly embarrassed when the old-fashioned brass headboard began to strike the wall, a solid *thump, thump, thump* that matched the percussive thrust of his hips, echoing the small groans that emitted from his throat as he did so.

She'd been up on her knees, her fingers curled over the inside rung of the headboard, and like the first time she'd slept with him at the resort, it had been one of the most intimate experiences of her life. He'd knelt behind her on the bed, and rather than just holding her hips and pulling her back onto his cock like a toy, he'd pressed flush against her, curled over her body. One of his broad hands had wrapped gently around the base of her neck, leaving the other hand free to caress down her body and play with her clit. She'd felt fused to him, every part of their bodies touching, the press of his chest against her back no less intimate than the squeeze of his thrusting cock within her. When her legs had begun to shake, she wasn't sure how she'd managed to stay upright, the orgasm shivering through her and radiating out from the fingers he'd pressed to her, rolling the bud of nerves in such a way that had made speech impossible and her whole body seize. All she'd been able to do was gasp and quiver until it was over, boneless in his arms. He'd groaned into her hair as she clenched around him convulsively, holding her steady until she'd come down from her peak.

"If you squeeze my cock like that every time, Nanaya, we're both going to need to find work-from-home jobs, because I'll never be able to stop fucking you."

His hips picked up speed afterward, teeth catching at her ear, tusks dragging against her skin, and she'd never in her life wanted a mirrored bedroom more, regretting her inability to see his back, the round globes of his ass and his strong thighs, the relentless way he hammered into her. When he'd released into her, not long after, she'd felt the contraction of his stomach muscles and the way his lungs hitched, the involuntary jerk of his hips and the hot pant of his breath in her hair, his lips pressing to the back of her neck.

"You made me work for that one," he groaned against her skin, flattening her against the headboard. "I think I just ejaculated part of my spine."

"If your spine and your balls have been negotiating space with each other, that has nothing to do with me."

He groaned again as she laughed, his tusks pressing into her shoulder.

"Note to self: jerk off twice before a Ris Rendezvous," he grunted before he withdrew himself slowly, the condom he'd filled pulling out of her with a pop. Despite the carnality of the night they'd spent together, she never found herself feeling like a piece of meat.

When the local university's film festival began in the middle of the following week, she texted him on a Wednesday, asking if he was interested in seeing the foreign film she was planning on attending, about a beleaguered Kikimora housewife and her dreams of emancipation from a cruel husband.

"This place is fun, what a good vibe," he remarked jovially, clinking their bottles together after Ruby left their table, the normal hum and buzz of Gildersnood and Ives providing a white noise backdrop to their conversation, making her beam. They'd spent the evening debating the hidden meaning of the film, whether it was indeed a domestic treatise on the way women were treated as household slaves even in a modern age, or else whether the Kikimora herself was a stand-in for the war-torn region where the film was set. He'd not stayed the night, citing an early work morning, but then she'd received a text from him mid-morning, as he looked up the film festival from his work laptop.

There are like three things on this list I want to see! Do we want to make a weekend of it? We can wear skinny scarves and horn-rimmed glasses and pretend to be very serious film aficionados. I'll park in town so your neighbors don't vote to kick you out of the development.

She'd grinned, quickly responding that she would pick him up at the municipal lot on Main Street so he wouldn't need to hitchhike like a vagrant. He drove an enormous vintage muscle car, all shiny black and silver chrome, which had been a result of "Tate and Rukh shopping with my money," so he'd claimed, but the car fit his aesthetic. What it *hadn't* fit was any of the parking spaces in her pixies-and-goblins tract condo complex, and he probably wasn't wrong in his assessment of the situation if he stayed the weekend. She'd taken him to her favorite sushi place after his Friday evening arrival, to the Black Sheep Beanery on Saturday morning to people-watch as the whole of Cambric Creek came through the establishment's doors, and to the best greasy spoon the town had to offer for breakfast on Sunday, which was neither greasy nor uncrowded, but completely worth the wait for a table.

The day that she'd left work early and visited Cambric Creek's small art museum to look at a visiting collection of ancient Elvish artifacts, she'd sent him a selfie in front of the display and was unsurprised when her phone rang a moment later. She'd *not* been expecting it to be a video call, however.

"You can't just tease me like that! I want to see everything!"

The sound of his voice, deep and smiling, sent a thrill of warmth through her skin, every single time. They'd toured the exhibit together, him on the phone, oohing and ahhing over delicate bits of jewelry and examples of fine Elvish bladecraft.

"This is what I want you to do with me when I die," he said cheerfully as they stood before a row of carved columns from the first age. "Put my brain in a jar and upload my consciousness onto a server. You can wear me around like a Go-Pro and we'll tour every museum in the unification after you retire."

Talking to him through the week — trading pictures and texts, playing games and discussing their respective days — didn't compare to hearing his rich laugh in her ear. She'd begun snapping photos of things and places she thought he would find interesting, sending him smiling, cocktail-accompanied selfies of herself at happy hour with Dynah and Silva, receiving snaps of him backstage in various small clubs where his bands were playing or his sly smile and towering mohawk, crowded around a bar table with a heavily-tattooed orc woman and his terrifying friend from the black-bricked pub. They kept each other up-to-date on movies they'd seen and places they'd gone and books they'd read; were engaged in a non-stop game of what he called "deathmatch scrabble," and Ris had begun to wonder if she'd ever had as much fun with any of the other guys she'd been involved with over the years, already knowing the answer was no.

She'd gone to the roof of her condo after returning home that afternoon from the museum, clutching a mug of hot tea, wrapped in her thickest cardigan. It was already too cold to spend any length of time out of doors, and she mourned the inability to do her sunrise yoga from the rooftop, but that afternoon she wanted to feel the sun on her face, even for only a few minutes. The sun was already beginning to set, earlier and earlier as the winter solstice approached, and it sat in a raspberry smear at the roofline of Cambric Creek's downtown, the encroaching indigo sky spreading overhead. She wasn't entirely sure why her eyes pricked with tears, because she was certain she was happy, and then she thought that perhaps *that* was why — because she *was* happy. She wasn't sure if she had fully realized how *un*happy she had become until that moment. Unhappy with herself, unhappy with the rut she had allowed herself to settle in. She couldn't make him responsible for her happiness, she already knew that, but he was a good reminder that she liked herself — she was smart and interesting, and wasn't afraid to do things on her own. She thought maybe she would sign up for a ballet class at the new studio that had opened next to her nail salon, and would treat herself to days like this more often. Her eyes were puffy by the time the cold drove her indoors, and she cut razor-thin slices of cucumber to lay on her closed eyelids as she settled on her sofa with a fresh mug of chamomile, content in the direction she was now moving.

She'd been invited to meet him at a little jazz club one evening, where they'd been joined by a tall Orcish woman with short, colorful hair and even more colorful tattoos.

"I'm going to order a bunch of the small plates," the orc woman announced. "I want to have a tapas menu ready to go by spring, so I'm sampling everyone else's." Her name was Elshona, and her eyes sparkled in mischief as she ordered half a dozen items from the club's small menu, winking at the server before the girl left their table.

"Please don't tell me the crux of this latest knock-down-drag-out is something as petty as menu aggression."

The other woman scowled at Ainsley. "Is that your way of taking sides then?"

"I'm not taking anyone's side, because this argument doesn't actually have anything to do with me. I'm simply pointing out, *yet again*, that I don't enjoy being put in the middle."

"Well I don't see him here tonight, now do I?"

"You don't, Shona, but rather than insist on that being a personal slight, which is the way you seem determined to see everything lately, I'm able to recognize it for what it is, which is depression. If you refuse to see that, at this point, I think that says more about you than it does about him."

Ris watched the exchange with wide eyes, staying as silent as a church mouse, biting her lip when the orc woman rose, pushing away from the table to stalk across the dimly lit space in the direction of the restrooms. Ainsley sighed, rolling his eyes dramatically at her exit before knitting his fingers with Ris's beneath the table.

"Sorry about that. Sometimes it's not easy being the filling in a friend sandwich, especially when one of the pieces of bread is determined to pick fights with the other. In this case, the piece of bread doing the picking is a piece of bread. And the piece of bread she's picking on is actually a switchblade. I am just an innocent pickle, trying not to get knifed."

Ris laughed at his analogy, having a feeling she knew exactly who the switchblade was in this scenario. "I happen to be very fond of pickles," she smiled, leaning up to press her lips to the side of his jaw. "But I'm sorry you're being put in the middle. I'm sure that sucks."

"It sucks less with you here. You're like a tasty, tasty milkshake, reminding me of all of the other fun things there are to be had in the diner."

When she wound up back at his apartment that night, he'd pulled her to kneel upright on the center of the bed, flush against his chest once more, the tight press of him within her feeling even more pronounced at the angle, the mirror on the other side of the room giving her the opportunity to be a voyeur to her own pleasure at last. His hands had wandered over the long expanse of her plum-colored skin, cupping each of her breasts and rolling her nipples between forefinger and thumbs, tugging them as his hips pumped into her, deep and slow. Ris had watched spellbound in the mirror when he released one of her breasts, hand moving down her body until he stroked into her heat, using all four fingers to rub at her clit. She watched Ris in the mirror shudder and moan, gasping when the doppelgänger's nipple was pulled, reaching her own hand down to scrape her nails gently against the thick snake of his cock as it disappeared into her over and over again, watching her twin in the mirror do the same. It felt decadent, giving him access to her entire body — his tongue in her mouth, his hand at her breast, his other fingering her to orgasm, watching her own reaction in wonder when she shook apart in his arms. The next morning, she'd learned the endurance of his tongue as he laid back on the long, orc-sized bed, insisting she straddle his face. She discovered she had the best traction against his tongue when she was facing the wall behind his head, although that left precious little opportunity to stroke her nails down the endless expanse of his green chest and grip his thick, pink-edged cock.

"It's not a pickle at all. I've been with pickles, and *this* beast is not a pickle. It's like a giant anaconda made of watermelon candy," she insisted once she switched positions, marveling over the color gradient from root to tip.

"If it tastes like watermelon, I need to visit the clinic." His chuckle broke off on a groan when she pulled back his foreskin teasingly to lick over the shiny, pink head of his cock. She watched herself suck him into her mouth; watched herself kneading his big balls, swallowing him as deeply as she was able. Watching her mirror twin suck him was exhilarating, nearly as much as watching herself come on his face, against his tongue, and when she stroked him to an eruption, she was able to see the way he pulsed, how exactly how the thick, white ropes of his release coated her small breasts, running down her stomach to pool against her thighs.

She'd never imagined coming home to Cambric Creek after that last solo resort visit with her FWB list accomplished, but he seemed to check every box, including some she hadn't even thought to include.

She was so incredibly satisfied with the way things had turned out, that when the dating app on her phone pinged one night with a match, she found herself agreeing to and getting ready for the outing in high spirits, knowing that the outcome didn't really matter, only that she had a good time.

He was handsome, she thought as soon as she spotted him across the pub floor. Platinum silver hair with long sideburns and expressive eyebrows, his eyes dark with a liquid sheen, and a bright white smile. The dress she'd worn borderlined on inappropriate for the icy weather, but she liked the way the dark denim corset hugged her figure, the pencil skirt elongating her slender frame. Her date grinned as she approached, never rising from his seat to greet her or pull out her chair, but rather than feel frustrated, she only smiled. It didn't matter at all.

He asked her about her favorite clubs, favorite DJ, favorite after-party spots. She asked him if he'd ever been to the jewel-eyed hummingbird gardens and if he knew the history of their exportation to the unified states. It was clear they had nothing in common, but she enjoyed the amusing anecdote he'd told about his little niece, and he had the good grace to not pull out his cell phone at any point when she was talking. *It doesn't matter, it doesn't matter, it doesn't matter.* It was certainly not the worst date she'd been on, and she couldn't even say that she disliked the demonborn's company, when his next words left her speechless.

"You know, you really shouldn't wear corsets, you're too flat-chested. It doesn't do anything for you. I figured since it's our first date, I'd tell you nicely now."

She was so stunned by his casual words that she actually looked over her shoulder to make sure there wasn't some unseen presence behind her to whom the words were directed. When she realized she was, in fact, the intended recipient, she couldn't help her shocked, indifferent laughter. *Un-fucking-believable.*

"You don't say," she choked out, nearly wheezing. "I'm sorry, are you *negging* me?! What century is this? Is that even a thing real people do?" She dissolved into giggles, draining the rest of her glass, and then reaching across the table for his. "Just so you don't go home confused, I just want to say that we don't have anything in common, so this wouldn't have gone anywhere anyway." He'd ordered something that tasted vaguely sooty, smokiness floating over a base of gin, and she wrinkled her nose as she drained it. "But the problem with your strategy," she continued, "is that it only works on women with no self-esteem. So you should probably specify that's what you're looking for? It would be a good warning if nothing else. I hope you have a great night," she beamed at him, fishing the cherry out of her own glass to cleanse the taste of smoke from her mouth.

She didn't look back to see him sputtering as she left the table, fresh laughter shaking her shoulders, confident that it didn't matter at all. Relocating to the bar, she soon engaged in conversation with a sleek-scaled lizardman. He was there drinking away his heartbreak, he told her, having recently split up with a longtime girlfriend. It was a shame, she thought, because he was charming and witty, with a self-deprecating sense of humor. *See? There are good guys out there too.*

"That guy is crazy because you are stunning," he scoffed when she told him about the demonborn she had just abandoned. She wasn't drunk enough to be unaware that alcohol was definitely lubricating her good sense when she left the bar with him a short while later, and alcohol was *certainly* responsible for the way she scraped her nails over the twinned bulges at the front of his pants. His cocks were identical — dark pink, with several vertical lines of nubs running from base to tip that she thought might feel exquisite inside of her, each shaft leaving the slit in his skin to balloon into a huge swell that tapered to a narrow tip.

She was not so far gone, however, to act recklessly. "Do you have any condoms?" she asked, knowing all she had in her wristlet were one or two orc-sized prophylactics that certainly would not work on him. He gaped at her, cocks bobbing.

"I . . . I don't. I haven't had to buy them in years. I . . . . What am I supposed to do without her?" Alcohol had directed her feet out the door to follow him, but she was not so far gone to do something she'd regret. She had the uncomfortable certainty that the intoxicated lizardman was very close to drunken tears, but she also knew that his broken heart wouldn't be any less broken come morning, regardless of what he did or didn't do with her.

Ris sighed, cursing her big heart. "You should call her this week. Give it a few days, don't call her tomorrow, and *definitely* don't call her tonight.

Sober up, get some perspective. You're a nice guy. Just tell her exactly what you told me." She gave the despondent lizardman a double hand job on the side of his car, an act of goodwill, she thought, despairing that his nubbed texture would have indeed felt amazing.

When she'd arrived home, her fingers keyed open her phone, tapping on Ainsley's devilish grin practically without her approval, but she didn't disconnect.

"Nanaya, I was just thinking about how beautiful the moon is tonight, and here you are calling. I don't think that's a coincidence."

The sound of his voice, deep and smiling, sent a thrill of warmth through her skin. Talking to him through the week—trading pictures and texts, playing games and discussing their respective days—didn't compare to hearing his rich laugh in her ear.

"I had the *worst* date tonight," she admitted, gratified by his noises of disgust as she told her story, grumbling at the demonborn's tactics, cheering her leaving with the lizardman, and nearly choking in laughter when she relayed the sad conclusion to the night.

"I hope he appreciates your commitment to making the world a better place, one pity handy at a time," he wheezed, interrupting himself with a coughing fit. "Fucking stars, you have me choking. You win the bad date Olympics tonight, Nanaya, I hope you're happy."

"Why are you always trying to give me the worst trophies? You know what I like? Flowers. Not trophies. Whatever, jerk. What about you? Do anything fun?"

"Actually," he'd chuckled, "I'm walking home from my own

questionable date. It wasn't as bad as yours, although if that bar were any lower, I might trip on it. We didn't click, nothing in common. I spent half the night rambling about seventeenth-century rakshasa invaders in Turkmenistan before I realized she was texting under the table."

Ris nearly dropped the phone as she hunched in laughter, pausing before hanging up her dress, thinking better of it, and tossing it into her bathroom hamper. "You've never once rambled at me, I refuse to believe this is true."

"That's because *we* have conversations, Nanaya." Her cheeks flushed at his words, listening to the echo of his boots thudding up the staircase to his apartment. "I'm sure if we'd gone out tonight, you wouldn't have left me solely in charge of doing the talking for the whole night."

"Well . . . you're getting home awfully late. It couldn't have been *that* bad."

"Like I said, not as bad as yours. Still not great though? I could tell she was bored the whole time, she might have been texting at one point then too. Didn't want me finishing anywhere near her and she had the *weakest* grip, so it took me forever. It was like jerking off with a fish. I don't think I even had an orgasm, it was like, a little dribble and that was the end. *Oh* . . . oh wow. Did I get a pity handjob too?!"

It was a good thing she was sitting, for she dropped back on her bed, convulsing in laughter. "I have witnessed a gallon of cum in your condoms, so if all you managed was a little dribble, you might want to take back your trophy. Sounds like you need it more than me."

She had never laughed this much with anyone else she'd ever known, she was absolutely certain. "Would you like to tell *me* about the seventeenth-century rakshasa invaders in Turkmenistan? Wait, is this that documentary about stolen artifacts?"

"*Yes!*" he bellowed in her ear as she laughed again. "I'm dying to talk about it, so tuck into bed, Nanaya, and let me tell you a story. I'm calling you back on video, give me two seconds to brush my teeth, and then I'll start my recitation. Please hold applause until the end of the lecture."

She curled into her sheets, leaning back on her pillow and propping the phone up against the folds of the comforter, wearing nothing but a thin cotton camisole. She was not particularly good at being vulnerable, she reflected as she watched him peeling off his shirt and shucking off his jeans. The thick skin she'd developed in childhood had developed into a brash brazenness with age, one that served her well and kept her heart protected. She wondered if he even owned pajamas as he slipped into his own bed a few minutes later, long and leanly muscled and completely nude.

"So this whole thing blew open because those scrolls were found out to be forgeries, right?"

She couldn't imagine being bored by anything he had to say, couldn't imagine not finding every minute in his presence to be interesting and amusing and rife with humor. She wasn't good at being vulnerable, and so she had a hard time explaining why being curled into her sheets with him on the phone seemed far more intimate than the hand job she'd given the lizardman earlier that night; intimate and personal in a way that made her stomach flip and her heart hum happily.

"Tell me if I'm boring you, my ego can't take much more abuse tonight."

She giggled as he paused, motioning for him to continue. "The land treaties. I'm riveted, professor. Keep going."

She could not explain why her heart seemed to have shed a layer of its protective armor, nor why the time spent in his company, even when it was just through texting or phone conversations, had become the highlights of her week. She wasn't good at vulnerability and didn't want to be pinned down to one person forever, for she could barely manage her own happiness, and the thought of having to be responsible for another person's made her itch, but as he gesticulated wildly, barely coming up for a breath, Ris considered that she'd never actually been happier. She didn't have to be anyone but herself for him, and he didn't ask her for anything more than she was willing to give, and she wouldn't have it any other way.

Lurielle

They're going to throw a party in your honor, the whole clan

will be there

Now don't get yourself all worked up, it'll be great, I promise

We'll talk more about it this week

Call me when you get home

Love you

The lines of text replayed behind her eyelids on a continuous loop, despite the fact that her phone now rested face down on the table before her. Across the sea of empty glasses, Dynah was relaying the latest tale of woe from her relationship with a ne'er-do-well kitsune she'd been seeing, as Ris snorted into her drink. Lurielle was only listening with half an ear, the text message from her boyfriend obliterating her concentration on anything else.

A party in your honor. Happy hour with her friends was supposed to be a way to destress after work; to replace her worries with fruity, two-dollar house cocktails, and trade away her insecurities for handfuls of the addictive crisps in the basket at the center of the table. *The whole clan will be there.* Happy hour was *not* meant to be an exercise in controlling her face or bottling her emotions, but right then it felt like a mighty effort to keep from crawling beneath the table to cry. *The whole clan. It'll be great.* There were few things in this world of which she was certain —and that being forced to endure the hospitality of Khash's entire Orcish clan for a long weekend out of town would *not* be great was one of them.

"And *then* he said he wanted to stay friends! Can you believe it? I drive halfway across the state to bring you to visit *your* brother in prison and you break up with me over BOGO appetizers in a Bartleby's off the highway?! *And* think I'll want to stay friends with you?!"

"And just think, you could have been with me having an actual good time. Sunrise yoga, champagne brunch . . . maybe it's time to give the app a break, Dy," Ris offered, draining the last of her glass before flashing their server a beaming smile from halfway across the dining room floor. The pub was a press of bodies, popular with the nine-to-five crowd to rub elbows and network over drinks before going home to families and obligations. Beside their table, two trolls and a wide-set minotaur crowded around a two-top, belly-laughing over a video on one of the troll's phones, and the slender satyr taking care of their wedge of the pub's floor had to flatten himself sideways to press around their hulking bodies.

"... It's not like you're meeting any winners from it. You should come back to yoga with me, get yourself centered. We doing one more round, ladies?"

Yoga. Maybe that's what I need. Ris had been a picture of serenity since she'd returned from her solo trip to the orc resort, after all ... although Lurielle didn't completely believe her friend's assertion that she'd spent the weekend reading and working on her advanced poses in the sunlight.

"Not me. I need to get going." *The whole clan. It'll be great.* Happy hour with her friends was meant to be fun, but she couldn't focus on anything other than the message waiting on her overturned phone, and the sooner she left, the sooner she could have her breakdown in private.

"That's easy for the two of you to say," Dynah moaned, as the satyr gathered up the collection of glasses littered across their table. "*You* get to go home to Mr. Perfect," she directed at Lurielle, before turning to jut her chin out in Ris's direction, "and you don't *want* a relationship!"

A red mist seemed to settle over the room as heat climbed up the back of her neck. She loved her boyfriend, loved the life they were building together, even if their differing cultures sometimes made things difficult. She wouldn't do anything to trade away the previous seven months and she was excited over what their future together held ... but the assumption that her being in a relationship had somehow magically transformed her life into one of stress-free ease set her teeth on edge. The same person with the same insecurities still stared back at her in the mirror every morning, with the same fucked up family and hair she didn't actually know how to style.

Having a boyfriend didn't suddenly make her less self-conscious over her weight, especially when he had a fondness for pricey takeout and rich desserts; being in love didn't magically negate the hard gazes they occasionally received when out together. It didn't mean she was suddenly a different person, and the sometimes less than subtle implications that it *should* was frying her very last nerve. *You get to go home to Mr. Perfect, who cares if you're stressed. You don't need to worry about your weight now that you have a boyfriend. Your problems don't matter anymore now that you're off the market,* **you** *don't matter because you're in a relationship*. Lurielle's lips pressed together in a hard line, a sharp retort forming, before Dynah's next words softened her tongue.

"You don't understand what my mom is putting me through. Every day. Every *single* day. 'Have you met anyone yet? You're not getting any younger, mele. Did you hear that so-and-so just had a baby? I'm sure *her* parents are over the moon.'

It was an impossible situation they were put in by their families and communities, one Lurielle knew by heart. Marry well, carry on the family bloodline, halt the population decline — lessons drummed into their heads starting in primary school. She had vivid memories of burning in mortification alongside her fidgeting classmates every year during the *family education* section of their school year, as the girls were sequestered in their own room, away from their male classmates, to be given The Talk. A yearly classroom lecture on the fertility issues they would encounter in adulthood, the fortitude they must display in the face of such challenges, the importance of doing their part to contribute to the dwindling Elvish population.

It is not enough to be satisfied with a long-lived life, híni. The gift of longevity sours with no kin to call our own. To live long enough to see the bloodlines of our mothers die is a cruel fate . . . which is why each of you must remember your duty to our community. To bear a child is the greatest gift you can give back to all those who have come before you, ensuring our traditions will continue on. The difficulty in conceiving only makes richer the reward of holding your own elvish child in your arms.

If she'd not already gone no contact with her mother, the reaction to hearing her only daughter was in a serious relationship with an orc would have been enough to prompt the same end decision.

"How could you do this to us?" her mother had moaned, wailing and carrying on as though Lurielle had announced she had just gone on a multi-state killing spree and was, in fact, calling from the scene of her most recent crime, the phone still dripping the blood of her victims. "After everything your father and I have done for you and your brother, *this* is the slap in the face we get . . . Is this how little you care about your family?"

She'd hung up the phone at that point, cutting off her mother's shrill wail in a way that made it hang in the air as she stared up at the rapidly darkening sky. Tears she felt betrayed at producing pricked the corner of her eyes, and she'd sucked in a long breath of the cold, autumn air of her backyard before going back inside, trying to remember how little her mother's opinion mattered.

It had been a mistake to call her, but Lurielle already knew that. She'd been placating Khash, who couldn't fathom parents not being thrilled for their children in any and every instance, who'd been making doleful puppy dog eyes at her across the pillow every time he asked if she'd talked to her family recently. She'd called to make him happy, and the call had gone exactly as well as she'd known it would, regardless of how that made *her* feel . . .

Dynah, she reminded herself, lived several states away from her family and didn't belong to the club in town. Lurielle had no doubt she was dealing with pressure from her parents, but if the string of trolls and Dragonborn and weres Dynah had dated over the past year was an indication that her family wouldn't care about her finding a non-Elvish partner, that her situation wasn't nearly as trying as that belonging to other elves they knew — elves like her, elves like Silva. *Elves who aren't constantly ditching their friends every time a guy smiles in their direction.*

"I *do* understand, Dynah," she reminded her friend. She understood, but they'd all been on the receiving end of Dynah's whims, plans broken and calls unanswered, followed by similar stories of heartbreak after a few weeks passed. "I also know that none of these guys are worth your time. They've got you paying their way, driving them around, breaking plans with your friends . . . for what? To disappear by the end of the month? I'm your friend and I love you, but you've got to stop this. How long do we have to be okay with you not showing up to things or canceling on us at the last minute for a stranger? You let your friend go on an out-of-town trip by herself for a *literal* stranger! And it's not even the first time you've done it! I *do* understand because I've been there too, and you're never going to break out of this cycle until you start putting yourself first. Stop screwing your friends over. Stop making these guys a priority when they're only making you a temporary option."

The formerly noisy pub seemed to have gone silent. She hadn't realized how much her voice had risen, her words rising in both pitch and volume, and now Dynah — poor, hapless Dynah — gaped from across the table, blue eyes wide as saucers. The minotaur beside them had turned his head in her direction, eyebrow cocked, and Lurielle watched in horror as a svelte nymph sitting at the bar behind their table raised her glass in a one-sided toast of apparent agreement. *You can never show your face in here again.*

"Like I said," Ris went on cheerfully as though Lurielle's voice wasn't still echoing in the pub's rafters, signing the credit card slip for the tab she'd closed while Lurielle made a spectacle of herself, "you need to come back to yoga and get centered. I'm signing up for ballet classes at that dance studio that just opened next to the nail salon, why don't you join me?"

It was a relief to step out onto the sidewalk a short while later, after enfolding a tearful Dynah in her arms and promising that she wasn't actually mad at her. *The whole clan will be there, it'll be great.* She knew she ought not to take out her stress on her friends, even if she'd meant every word of what she'd said, which she absolutely did. It wasn't the first outburst she'd had over the past few weeks and Lurielle felt as if she were coming apart at the seams.

"Look at it this way," Ris began, slipping her arm through Lurielle's, the serene smile she'd worn for the past several weeks still taking up residence on her angular face. "She needed to hear it. Better from you, and better in a crowded venue where neither of us could be accused of smothering her, right? Are you going to tell me what's going on, or do I need to start inventing stories? That's how rumors get started, you know."

She laughed weakly, leaning into her friend. She reminded herself that they were only work friends, but she'd never had many friends growing up, and she valued the camaraderie from Ris and Silva — and even Dynah — more than she could articulate. "Nothing's going on," she mumbled. "Really. We're going to visit his family and I'm sick over it. It's just . . . everyone acts like my worth in society has suddenly increased. It's insulting, to be honest."

Ris snickered in agreement. "There's nothing more shameful than being a single female elf. Don't worry," she added, "pretty soon no one will care that you're in a committed relationship. They'll only want to know when you're popping out a kid. The wedding isn't even as important. The big visit is coming up, right? Are you all packed?"

"He texted me earlier to let me know they're planning a big party to meet me. And you know how much I love big parties, after all."

"Oh, big parties are your favorite. Hopefully, there will be dancing, and lots and lots of small talk. I know how much you love dancing and small talk."

"Exactly. Small talk with his relatives, and if they don't like me, then what? Am I going to make him pick me over his family? What will happen then? He'll grow resentful and bitter and have an affair with some tall, gorgeous orc woman who doesn't need his help putting dishes away. And what happens if we've already gotten married by then? What happens if we've already had kids? Is he going to take my kids away to be raised by this big amazon and her whole clan? How would I fight for custody? It's not like I can get any elf to take my case, and how's it going to look being represented by an ogre or a goblin? I'll look like someone whose own kind doesn't even want to have anything to do with her, so why should I be put in charge of raising multi-species kids? I'll wind up alone and used up, the stretch marks from carrying orcs will probably go from my chin to my knees. I'll still be a short, chubby elf with no social worth, and I won't have anything to show for it except house I can't reach the top shelf in and an orc-stretched vagina that will never, ever shrink back down to normal size after years of him rearranging my guts. That's it, that's my made-for-streaming movie."

A cluster of sleek-haired selkies turned to look in their direction as

Ris nearly choked on her laughter, each of the waifish young women dressed for a night on the town in towering heels and short dresses beneath their sable-furred coats.

"Wow. WOW. Babe, there is a lot to unpack there. Like, a fucking dump truck worth of unpacking. First of all, I'm sure Khash will not let his family say anything bad about you. That orc is stupid over you. And let's pretend for a moment that they don't like you, which won't be possible because you are brilliant and funny and ballsy as fuck, and *completely* adorable, but let's pretend for a minute that they suck and they don't see that. Khash is a grown-ass man, he's *chosen* to move away from his family, so it's not going to be that much of an ordeal. Your kids would fucking howl to stay with you because you're going to be an amazing mother, and why do you think you would lose custody?! All we have to do is call that werewolf, that one that almost put me in traction, remember? His family owns the whole town! Boom, now you have a lawyer. You live here, so your custody case would happen here, and no one gives a shit about what some out-of-towners think. So now you've got your kids, you've got your house, you take fucking *everything* in the divorce. His girlfriend is going to leave him because he won't have a pot to piss in, and you're going to meet some young boy toy werebear who will keep you warm at night and blow what's left of your back out on the regular. So I'm not sure what exactly you're so worried about, it seems to me like you're going to be fine no matter what."

She was hunched over in laughter by the time Ris finished her diatribe, clinging to the taller elf's arm for support as her shoulders shook. She remembered then why she had become friends with Ris in the first place. At first glance, her tall, slender companion was the exact sort of elf she would have avoided like the plague — pretty, popular, and privileged, too much like the former classmates and clubmates who put her down all her life. But it only took a short time in Ris's presence to learn that she was profane and hilarious, and that even though she had grown up in the same world of Elvish privilege, she wasn't quite a part of it, not truly. She had confessed to not only *not* being a member of the club there in Cambric Creek, but having never been a member of any Elvish club. She'd never come out and said so, but Lurielle suspected that Ris was an accomplished faker, and had skated through her school days on her looks and personality alone.

"I hope you feel better now."

"I do, actually. I do. I should probably stop seeing my therapist and start seeing you."

"Or, better yet — you should keep seeing your therapist and come out with us more. You're not married yet, and even if you were, married doesn't mean dead. I get it, the weather is crappy and it's not as fun to go out, but I've barely seen you in weeks. Don't forget about your friends. And we *are* friends, Lurielle, just because we work together doesn't mean we're only work friends. If we only see each other at work then that's all we are, so we need to put in the effort to be more than that."

"Since when did you get to be the wise one?"

Ris smiled broadly. "I'm sleeping with a smarty-pants, I think that helps."

"What?! You never said you met someone! When? Who is he? Tell me everything!"

"I took your advice and ordered off the menu," Ris shrugged with a cat-that-ate-the canary grin. "It's just a friends-with-benefits thing, but he's really great. And it's just . . . I don't know, like you said. Nothing more worthless in society. And it's bullshit that we should even have to feel that way, because I have been on *so* many fucking terrible dates in the past few months, it's just so not worth it. But he's . . . I don't know. Different. Different for me, at least."

"And he's an orc?" Lurielle demanded.

"He is! I finally met an orc and learned his name. I haven't said anything because I didn't want to make Dynah feel bad, but . . .yeah. He's kinda great? It's gotten me out of my rut, if nothing else."

"And just that fast, I'm annoyed with her all over again. You can't be so worried about tiptoeing around her feelings that you're not able to share happy news! Ugh, whatever. Peak Dynah. I'm happy for you, and I want to hear all about him this week, understand?"

Pulling into her driveway a short while later, she was only marginally surprised to see Khash's car.

"Honey, I'm home," she called out as she entered, hearing the sound of Junie and Ordo's paws across the tiles before they rounded the corner. He was stretched out on the sofa, a takeout container from the noodle place on Main Street on the coffee table before him, looking so relaxed and at home in her space, as if he had always been there, that it almost took her breath away.

They'd already agreed that when the time came, he would move in with her, instead of her moving into his apartment. He had been looking for a house, after all, and hers was already designed for a species his size. They would upgrade into a bigger place when something in Cambric Creek became available. It was a relief to her, for even though he had never done or said anything to make her feel as if she were merely a guest in his space, she couldn't get comfortable in his apartment. She sat at the edge of the furniture and attempted to take up as little space as possible, remnants of disordered thinking from childhood that she still couldn't quite shake off. She tiptoed around the rooms, keeping her belongings tight and close together, easily removable, as if her existence in his life could be packed up in a single bag. Khash had no such insecurities in her own space. Several weeks of his work suits hung in her closet, he had half the drawers in her dresser and more hair products than she had ever owned spread across her bathroom. It was just one of a hundred tiny differences between them, and though he did not always understand her feelings, she was glad for the differences. A partner as neurotic as she was would surely have driven her to drink.

"Mmmm, I didn't think I would see you tonight," she murmured, wrapping her arms around his neck from behind the sofa, pressing her lips to his temple.

"I hadn't intended on it originally, but I don't have any meetings in the morning, no need to rush into the office. And I figured you'd want to talk."

"What makes you think that?" She laughed sardonically, walking around the sofa.

"Well, you know darlin', a nice easy get-together. Good food, nice visit. Nothing to stress out over, just a little ole' gathering . . . But I know my girl better than that."

She laughed again as she dropped into his lap, arms going around his neck, feeling infinitely more secure than she had just a short time ago. *The whole clan. It'll be great.*

"Can you just wake me when it's over?"

"Bluebell—"

"I hate big parties, I *hate* being the center of attention. Can't we just have a video call with everyone from your sister's house?" His pursed lips told her exactly what he thought of that idea. "Can you at least explain to me what the 'whole clan' entails? Your immediate family is already like sixty-three orcs! It is going to be like a receiving line, where I just get to stand there while two-hundred strangers are paraded in front of me? Or am I going to be expected to socialize with every single one of them and learn their names? Because I don't think I'm going to manage that in one weekend trip."

"Darlin', are you done exaggerating?"

"How am I exaggerating?! You have six brothers and sisters, and more than half of them are married with kids of their own. Your oldest sister is already a grandmother! By the time we go back to visit in the spring, there will be 10 more names to memorize!"

"You are being absolutely ridiculous."

She tucked her head against his chest and tried to allow the deep sump of his heartbeat to calm her fraying nerves. He was always so warm, so steady. She wished she had a tenth of his composure, but somehow she would need to manage to get through this with her own shaky foundations. Her therapist had tried talking through the root of why she was so tied up in knots over the upcoming visit, but in Lurielle's opinion, the conversation had only made things worse.

"What if they don't like me?" she'd asked simply. "What if he realizes we just have too many differences and this is the beginning of the end?" The sphinx had tried to get her to examine the roots of why she didn't believe she deserved happiness, but she'd been less than willing to dig into the depths of her psyche. Having a better understanding of herself wasn't going to help in this situation, wasn't going to help her get through the upcoming weekend.

"Relationships end sometimes, Lurielle. That doesn't mean you won't be happy again, and it doesn't have any bearing on your self-worth. All we bring to the table is ourselves, and that means our jealousies and our insecurities, our ability to forgive, and our willingness to work with a partner. There are plenty of people who aren't able to do some of those things. Some of us are only able to do a few of them. Sometimes the jealousies and insecurities overtake everything else. Relationships are a lot of hard work, you already know that. Now, from everything you've told me, your relationship is nowhere near ending. It's only just getting started! So you need to ask yourself *why* you're so concerned over whether or not his family is going to like you, and why you're so certain they won't."

Normally talking through things with the Sphinx helped. But not in this case. She wasn't going to fit in with Khash's family because she didn't fit in *any*where. If the girlfriends and wives at his weekly matches were an indication of her place in Orcish society, the visit was going to be just as grim as she was anticipating.

"Your food is in the refrigerator," he added, nudging her forehead with his nose. "I had a feeling you'd need something to sop up all those fruity little cocktails. Go, heat something up."

He continued to talk as she pushed off his lap, crossing to the kitchen. "Ordo already has a crate for the plane, we'll stop and pick up Junie one this week. You think she'll be happy under your seat, or should we put them together?"

"I already told you, I don't want to take Junie. I already talked to Ghessa across the street, she said she's happy to watch her again. And Violet said she'd love to walk her."

"Darlin', it's no trouble taking them. Ordo is used to the flight. They pull the seats right out and lock them in next to us. I *do* think we need to pick her up a new harness though, I don't know why the two of them got it in their heads that it was a chew toy the other afternoon. She'll be fine."

"I *really* don't want to take her."

"You just let me know if you're going to want to upgrade to a second bag since she'll count as your first. I always under pack when I go home, but I don't expect you to —"

"I don't want to take her!" Her voice had risen once again, rising in volume and pitch as it had at the pub until it echoed shrilly off the light fixture above her head. "You're not listening to me, Khash." She hadn't realized that tears had filled her eyes until she tasted them at the corner of her mouth, realizing that they had already overflowed, spilling down her full cheeks. Khash crossed the room into great strides, his brow furrowed heavily in concern, his huge hands gripping her shoulders as if she were no bigger than a doll before him. "I've already told you I don't want to take her. She's a bad girl! I don't want your family thinking that's how I'm going to raise kids." The Yorkie in question skulked at the corner of the kitchen, Ordo cowering beside her. Raised voices were not a common occurrence in her house and it was clear neither dog knew how to react.

"Lurielle . . ."

"You're not *listening* to me, Khash. You're hearing me, but you're not *listening* to me. I told you I didn't want to talk to my mom, and you wouldn't let it go until I called her. I told you I didn't want your family to make a fuss, and now they've already planned a huge party. I don't want to take Junie. She can stay with the neighbors. If you're not going to hear me on that, you and Ordo can enjoy your visit with your family alone."

The frustration that had been building within her over the last few months seemed to bubble to the surface, as if her emotions were a soda can that had been repeatedly shaken, opened over something as trivial as bringing the dog. She didn't protest when he scooped her up easily, carrying her back across the room to the sofa, cradling her against his chest, murmuring apologies into her hair. For the longest time, she could do nothing but cry. Unable to articulate why she felt so frustrated and furious at her tearful response, the anger only made her cry harder. Lurielle was certain Silva probably cried dainty little tears, her eyes welling up like a cartoon kitten, flowing in attractive rivers down her flawless skin. By contrast, she was an ugly crier. Her ivory skin would blotch red, her eyes puffing up, and her nose pinkening. Her hitching sobs weren't at all attractive, were certainly not dignified, but it was all she could manage at the moment.

After all, Dynah wasn't the first person to bear the brunt of her mood. Her raised voice at the gym the night before still echoed in her head, the mortification she felt over her outburst warring with the fact that she'd *meant* what she said, anger with herself and for everyone else, a resentment that felt at complete odds with the contentment she felt.

"It must be nice not having to worry about arm flab anymore," her gym friend had sighed, waggling her arm like chicken in the mirrored wall before them.

Lurielle had frowned, raising her own not-at-all jiggle-free arm, mirroring the movement. "What are you talking about? I could fly around the neighborhood with these wings."

The petite goblin had giggled at their reflection, a completely absurd sight to anyone who might have been watching, no doubt. "Yeah, but you already bagged that big, gorgeous side of beef. Who cares about a little extra jiggle when you have *that* at home?!"

Her face had flushed, unbecoming splotches of pink coloring her ivory cheeks. "Of course," she'd bit out, unable to stop herself, fire raging through her veins. It wasn't the first time this particular group of friends had made such comments, and she felt at war with herself over the way they made her feel — they were right, after all. Khash loved every inch of her, from the dimples in her thighs and the rounded pooch of her stomach to the aforementioned arm jiggle. It was a sentiment she'd heard on more than one occasion at that point. *Mr. Wonderful. Mr. Perfect. Mr. Gorgeous.* She agreed with her friends, of course — her boyfriend *was* wonderful and gorgeous, even though he was far from perfect . . . but he hadn't changed the way she saw herself, hadn't suddenly silenced the voices in her head she'd lived with for years. *She* was working hard to do that on her own, and it *was* hard work. The assumption that she'd been somehow cured of her negative thoughts overnight, simply by dint of Khash's presence rankled. *What does that make you? The fat girl lucky enough to be with him?* "After all, everyone knows the only path to body acceptance is to find a dick to ride, right?"

The goblin had sputtered and she'd turned on her heel, regretting her words instantly, even if she didn't really. She loved Khash, loved their life, loved their *love* . . . but she loved her house and her job and her dog and her freedom, things she'd achieved on her own which were somehow negated now that she had a partner.

"Bluebell," he murmured against her temple, once her tears had slowed to a snuffle. "Are you gonna tell me what's got you so tied up or—"

"What if they don't like me?" She blurted in a hoarse whisper, an echo of the question she asked in her therapist's office.

Above her, Khash sighed heavily. "Darlin' —"

"You can't pretend that it might not happen. They're your family, and you love them, but you know how orcs are. I know how elves are. What's going to happen when they tell you they don't think I'm good for you? What could happen if they don't like me?"

For a weighted moment he said nothing, just nuzzled her temple with the tip of his nose before gripping her chin and tilting her face up to gently kiss her lips. "Lurielle, they barely like me. Why do you think it would make a bit of difference?"

She gaped as he readjusted her across his lap, both dogs now sitting at their feet. She had noticed the odd dynamic between Khash and his family, picked up on during their biweekly video calls. He was the golden boy and black sheep both, simultaneously doted on by his mother and treated to the odd derisive comments from one of his older sisters; looked up to by both of his brothers, and left out of the camaraderie they shared because of his absence. It was an odd juxtaposition of big expectations and biting disapproval when those expectations were met, at least to her outsider's eyes. He was one of two of his many siblings to have moved away from the clan, he had told her, the other being the youngest, who barely counted, as she was the baby. She had noticed it, noticed it practically from the first week she'd been included on the calls, but her noticing it and Khash voicing it were two very different things.

He sighed heavily again. "They have the party planned for Saturday. We're flying in late Thursday afternoon. That'll give you a chance to get to know mama and the girls before the big shindig, but I promise you it won't be that bad. It might even be easier, with that many people around. It's going to be loud and rowdy, I'll warn your delicate little cupcake sensibilities now. There's going to be music and drinking, and a big ole' fire. You won't have to memorize everyone's name, you probably won't even get a chance to talk to everyone. No one is going to be there to judge you, Lurielle. And it doesn't matter what any a'one of them thinks. Because at the end of the weekend I'm still getting on a plane and flying home with you, away from them, and with or without you darlin', they won't let me forget it. We all have choices to make in life, and I'm happy with the ones I've made. They led me to you."

Tears flooded her eyes anew as she gripped his shirtfront, pulling a fistful of the fabric until he lowered his face to hers, allowing her to sink her fingers into his thick black hair. His kiss was hard, hard enough to leave her lips swollen, the taste of his mouth mingled with her tears. She felt the drag of his thick tusks against the sides of her face, framing her mouth; his blunt teeth nipping at her lower lip and scraping down her jaw. Sucking kisses he placed down the column in her throat had her arching beneath him, tears forgotten, leaving only one thought in her head – *more*.

Her gasp when he surged to his feet, her still aloft in his arms, was swallowed again by his mouth. The bed frame she had moved in with had been sold at a community swap meet, traded for an orc-sized bed, big enough to accommodate the orc *in* her bed. The knit dress she'd worn to work that day was easy to lift and drag up over her arms and head, leaving her in her full-coverage panties and bra. Functional and comfortable and completely unsexy, but he'd never seemed to mind. He dragged her giant panties down her hips, just as easily as he might have done to a strappy little thong. She pushed the T-shirt he wore up his body, her short manicure scraping against his stomach until he assisted, gripping the back hem of the shirt and hauling it over his head in one fluid motion. She'd not appreciated the dark sweatpants he'd worn when she'd come in, and it seemed a waste. His erection pushed out the cotton material, tenting it obscenely, and she gripped his fabric-covered cock, giving it a few pumps before hooking her thumbs in the waistband and yanking the pants down his body.

This didn't solve her problems, didn't quell the panic she felt over the upcoming visit, nor did it reconcile the frustration she felt over the assumption that she was somehow worth more to the world now that she was coupled . . . but it quieted her mind, and that was good enough for now.

She pushed him down onto the bed once he'd deftly unhooked

her bra, tossing it in the direction of her dress, climbing up his body like a tree. She was so much smaller than him, and it made *everything* complicated — except this. Straddling his hips was still like climbing onto a centaur's back, but once she was astride him, her body's low center of gravity worked in her favor, her thighs tightening around him as she fed his cock into her with a backward hand.

"It's going to be fine, darlin'." She dragged her nails through the dark hair on his chest, following the shadowed trail over his abdomen, past his naval, bracing herself against him as she lowered, inch-by-inch, sliding down his rigid girth like she was visiting the Cambric Creek fire station.

She loved this position, she'd discovered in the course of the past half-year. She loved all of the others they'd tried as well, of course; nothing quite compared to his weight above her, covering her like a great shadow, or the way he braced over her as she draped herself over a cushioned platform designed for this exact use, pumping into her from behind. She loved sitting astride his giant head, gingerly lowering herself on his tusks, and of course, she loved being on her knees before him with his legs spread wide, pushing into him with her own unsteady rhythm . . . . She loved all of those, but none quite compared to this — she never felt quite as vulnerable as she did splayed across his hips like this, her entire perfectly imperfect body on display for his hooded eyes. He was the one who made it as enjoyable as it was, of course. His hands, huge and gentle, would grip her hips, able to span them with ease, making her feel dainty for the first time in her life. The drag of him within her made her toes curl at his sides, and she leaned forward until she was able to find just the right angle, every roll of her hips sending a shot of lightning up her back. His hands would slide up her sides, cupping her heavy breasts reverently, as if they were objects of titillation and desire and not another reason she didn't fit into any chic Elvish fashions. His thumbs would roll over the pink of her nipples, catching them between his knuckles as he kneaded the full globes, groaning as he did so. He would cup the side of her face, tracing her lips with his thumb until they parted for him, and she would suck on the broad green pad of his digit, biting down on the meaty center until his breath hitched, his dark eyes locked on hers with a ravenous expression. Finally, their hands would join as she bounced against him, their fingers knitted together as she picked up speed, the rumble coming from his chest just beyond the finish line as she chased her peak, his hands squeezing hers tightly as she fell apart atop him.

Lurielle dropped forward against his chest, her breath coming out in sharp pants, her heartbeat thundering like a runaway horse. One of his hands had dropped to her hip, holding her in place, as the other cradled the back of her head, his thick fingers pushing through the golden highlights in her hair. She was barely able to reach his mouth from this position, the great difference in their size one of many hundreds of tiny differences she counted over the last seven months, but it wasn't one she was willing to let stand in her way just then. She wriggled against his body awkwardly until she was able to grip his chin, plunging a hand into his thick dark hair, begging his lips to chase away the anxiety of the crowded her heart.

"Lurielle, it's going to be okay," he repeated, sucking on her lip as she breathed into him, attempting to steal some of his Orcish bravery. "We can talk about their game plan, if you want, Bluebell. You want me to give you a rundown with a member of my family with notes for you to study? If that'll make you feel better, we'll do it tonight. You want a list of the names of the clan elders so you can address them, if that'll make you feel more confident? I'll make sure you know them. But right now darlin', you got me all hot and bothered, and you're making that face like you're fixin' to start crying again. So I'm going to need to ask you, *very* respectfully, to put your tears away for another few minutes, and let me drain this dragon. You know I love all of your big feelings and how much hard work you've been doing on yourself, and I want to give any topic you want to talk about my utmost attention, but right now all I can think of is filling you up. So why don't you slide off and get on your knees, and let me remind you why it doesn't make a deadly bit of difference what anyone else thinks of us."

She had begun to laugh before he finished his dramatic monologue about the needs of his cock, but she did as he asked, the backward drag of him sliding out of her making her eyes cross. "A list with notes is exactly what I want," she huffed, settling her knees against the padded rocker he slapped down to the mattress.

The curved cushion could have been mistaken for a piece of gym equipment, the only reason why it had wound up moving from its place at the front of her closet to its new home beside one of the bedside tables, always out, easily accessible. Much like her other toy investments, she had done her research online first. It was almost comical, the industry that existed to make multi-species couplings a comfortable possibility. She had been poised to purchase the device online, like her other earlier purchases, but then in her email, a coupon had appeared. It was a locally owned store catering to adult pleasures, and if there was one thing she had learned about her boyfriend over the last half a year, it was that he was extravagant nearly to the point of excess, but he loved a good deal. A petite goblin ran the shop, her friendly and gregarious nature instantly putting Lurielle at ease when she'd hesitantly entered, the bell above the door nearly being enough to send her scampering like a mouse. The goblin had flame-colored hair and trendy, black-rimmed glasses resting on her button nose, and she clearly knew the inventory in the shop inside and out.

"An orc, huh? I know exactly what you want. The liberation rocker. It's super sturdy, and it's better than one of the pillows. You can use it like one of the pillows, which is why it's so versatile, but the rocker side is really where it's at. That way you can move with him instead of just being rammed into, you know?"

She was positive she had been the same color as a plump cherry tomato by the time she'd left the shop, but she knew she would be back. She wasn't sure how her boyfriend managed to put on the veneer of a straight-laced suburbanite when he had so many kinks. Before she'd purchased the strap-on, a leather crop had been added to one of her dresser drawers, and she had become very adept at slapping the flat leather end against the table like-curve of his ass. The goblin was far more knowledgeable and helpful than anything she discovered in her cautious, VPN-protected online bumblings, and if they had regular promos, she knew Khash would not be able to resist.

"The fact that a list with notes was even an option and you've been holding out on me actually makes me really angry," she grumbled leaning forward against the cushioned slope, wrapping her arms around it. "Frankly, I think you should have been putting together a dossier for me two months ago. Names, ages, backgrounds, how you're related to them, including photos. I wouldn't be stressed at all if you had actually done the prep work necessary."

"Bluebell, I cannot emphasize enough how much I don't care to be having this particular conversation at this precise moment in time. I've got one thing on my mind, and paper clipping Polaroids onto detailed descriptions of every single one of my childhood friends is not it."

Her laughter cut off on a gasp when she felt his fat head sliding against her slick folds from behind. It was preposterous how big he was, how thick and long his manhood hung, even in its completely softened state.

"I'm still mad at you," she insisted, twisting her hips back and forth. "Maybe I should only let you put the tip in. What do you think of that?" She pushed back slightly, his head pushing into her, her bravado nearly failing her at the familiar intrusion. She sucked in a sharp breath as she allowed him to penetrate her slightly further, just far enough that her body was able to securely hold his thick cockhead, tightening her muscles around him. She rocked forward on her cushion, letting him slip out, smiling as he growled in frustration. Twice more she took him in that way, just his head, putting her gym work to use in the way she squeezed her pelvic muscles, holding him there for minutes before letting him slide out again.

"Bluebell, you're aiming to have me on my knees. That what you want, darlin'? You want to have me beggin' to bury my cock in you? Well, this is me begging." He'd taken himself in hand, sliding his drooling head up and down her cleft, thrusting forward and letting his thick shaft push through the lips of her sex, dragging against her clit. "This is me begging you to let me empty my balls and pump you full until you're dripping. The longer you keep this dragon snapping, the longer it's going to take to put together your dossier."

She was shaking in laughter by the time he pushed into her slowly, groaning until he'd slid in balls-deep, hilting himself fully within her. "It doesn't matter what we argue about Bluebell, if this is the way we make up, I'll start planning parties for you every weekend."

When he began to pump into her, she was reminded of the goblin girl's words. She rocked forward on every thrust, the backward tip causing a friction she wouldn't have received without the upholstered device. He had planted his feet wide, putting every ounce of his muscle and power into his hips, rutting into her like a freight train, groaning like he had a starring role on one of the multi-species porn sites. Her g-spot was trapped against the thick girth of his shaft, and her clit received a steady bump against the cannily designed rocker, and as she hurled towards her second orgasm of the night, Lurielle thought she might just be *willing* to let him plan a weekly party if this was the way he would fuck her.

When he erupted into her, she felt the pressure of his cock going off like a fire hose, flooding her womb. She understood why orcs had such big families as he grunted, his hips still thrusting erratically as he came. Lurielle imagined her womb expanding like a water balloon, swollen with what felt like a gallon of his release, certain she could push down on her belly and feel it sloshing within her. He'd pressed himself flush to her, an indication he was almost done, like a tiny alarm had gone off and the little workers who lived inside his heavy testicles had slammed the emergency evacuate button. He grunted again, hips continuing to jerk, draining every drop he had. Their hands had come together again, she realized — fingers knitted, her pinky over his, as if she were the one holding *him* in place — as if *she* were the strong one in their relationship.

He groaned, kissing her shoulder before moving his lips to the back of her neck. "I'll make any sort of dossier you want, Lurielle. Whatever happens is going to happen, and it's not gonna make a bit of difference."

She turned her head, catching his lips, his heat, and his steadiness. "It had better not," she said seriously. "I sure hope you grabbed a towel. Otherwise, you're going to have to flip me upside down and carry me to the bathroom. I have a party to pack for, I can't be worried about having the carpet cleaned."

She didn't like the assumption that she was somehow worth more to society now that she was in a relationship, didn't like all of the things she had achieved on her own somehow being negated for the far less impressive skill of opening her legs, but the one thing she knew with absolute certainty was that her therapist was wrong. She was sure she would never be happy again if anything happened to him, happened to *them*, and it didn't matter how many affirmations she said in the mirror.

Silva

The invitation had come in the same vague, roundabout way in which Tate delivered everything that wasn't business-related, she'd come to learn.

Silva had never considered herself especially needy. Selfish, perhaps . . . spoiled, most assuredly, but not *needy* in the way she thought of the word. She didn't expect constant attention; didn't need to be showered with presents or be told she was beautiful several times a day, and she certainly wasn't holding her breath for Tate to show up at her office on a random weekday, insisting on taking her to lunch at the little cafe she loved that had kittens roaming the dining room floor.

If anything, she told herself, she was the *opposite* of needy! She refrained from calling and texting him constantly, knowing he was busy. She almost always alerted him to her incoming presence on the weekends she visited, giving him the opportunity to demure, and she appreciated all of the little things he did. A phone charger had recently appeared on her side of the bed in his apartment, along with a brand of toothpaste designed for delicate Elvish teeth in his bathroom cabinet. The cardigan she'd forgotten one weekend had been neatly hung in the closet beside his own clothes, rather than folded near the front door as a reminder of her temporary, transient presence in his life. Little, inconsequential things that made her feel treasured and valued and seen . . . but none of that changed the fact that if he were posed with a question about a beer delivery or the staff schedule or the most expeditious way to cut ticket times in Clover's kitchen by two and a half minutes, Tate was forthright and unambiguous. Everything else received a willy-nilly wave of the hand with no hint of commitment to be found, and like the needy little kittens at the cafe she loved, the more he withheld his total attention, the more desperately she craved it, her imagination working overtime without a firm hand to ground her.

The first time she'd been on the receiving end of one of his anxiety-inducing texts had been nearly two months prior, when the last leaves of autumn still shivered on the ends of branches, piles of golden and brown and orange, crunching underfoot.

I'm going away for a few days

The text had come on a Thursday afternoon. It had been an aggravating week, full of minor disappointments and small indignities, and she'd been counting the minutes until she left the office on Friday, when she would make the drive from Cambric Creek to the little resort hamlet to feel his sharp teeth at her throat and his hands in her hair. There would be no reason to go home after work, her overnight bag would already be in the backseat, and she would drive straight through, arriving just before dark.

She had slumped in disappointment when she'd read the message at her desk, viciously stabbing at her salad on her lunch break, imagining him at some beachside resort for the weekend, frolicking in the ocean with a scantily-clad cervitaur. When the marketing department had come together for their daily team meeting that afternoon, she'd been dismissively asked to get the coffee, adding to the day's indignation. *You're a junior associate*, Silva reminded herself, silently seething as she bundled up in her quilted winter coat to make the trek to the other side of the parking lot, where the Black Sheep Beanery parked their food truck, half a dozen orders in hand. *This is your first real job out of university, you're supposed to get the grunt work.* By then, her imagination had Tate sitting at some sidewalk bistro, sipping wine with the same giggling cervitaur and enjoying time away from his hectic life, peaceful and content with nary a single thought of her. The buzz of her phone could be felt in the pocket of her cardigan once she'd rejoined the table, but she didn't dare peek at it throughout the meeting and had nearly forgotten about it until she'd returned to her desk.

Fancy coming with me?

It had been nearly two hours since his original message, she'd realized. Two hours of leaving her twisting, two hours of being disappointed and frustrated, two hours of torturing herself over absolutely nothing. Anxiety and jealousy had a way of outracing her common sense and obliterating her good judgment when it came to Tate, but when she forced herself to think rationally, Silva was able to remember the long hours he worked, the way he focused on little outside of his businesses.

He'd probably sent her the first text and then been ambushed by his girls at the bistro, circling him to complain about their schedules or lament their tips. He might have been waylaid by the ancient dishwasher at the Pixie, had probably been standing over Rukh as the grizzled old bartender fixed it for the hundredth time, offering encouragement and threats in equal turn, as she'd witnessed him do several times before. She could easily envision him — pinching the bridge of his slim nose, a wayward pen shoved into his messy bun, which would droop lower and lower throughout the day, pen forgotten; turning away to tap out the rest of his message to her hours after he'd started the thought, no wide-eyed cervitaur in sight, despite her overactive imagination.

The trip had been to another small town, several hours away, where Tate planned to hustle pool for two evenings in a row at a small tournament hosted by a seedy bar that made the Pixie seem like a formal gentlemen's club.

"We should pretend to be strangers, right?" she'd called out from where she'd sat cross-legged in the big upholstered chair in their hotel room, eating vegetarian room-service pizza in her lacy bra and panties as he hogged the bathroom mirror. "I don't want to blow your cover . . . you can buy me a drink and try to pick me up!"

The notion of pretending to be someone she wasn't — someone other than responsible, good little Silva — was wildly exciting, and she'd bounced in her seat in anticipation at the thought.

"I think I should be concerned at how willingly you're embracing this," he'd quipped lightly from the bathroom doorway, pulling his sleek hair into a topknot. "Next you'll be wanting to rob a bank."

She'd sat perched at the end of the bar, after entering alone, and had gigglingly flirted with a blue-eyed goblin who'd bought her a drink. A fast glance back to the pool tables had shown her a tiefling in a low-cut top attempting to win Tate's attention, lacquered nails grazing his bicep, and she'd turned away quickly, cheeks coloring, not needing or wanting to see any more. She could hear his musical voice and lilting laugh, his voice a note higher and his accent a drop heavier than it normally was . . . he'd slipped on a different skin easily, paying her no mind, and rather than be annoyed about it, Silva had decided to follow his example.

He'd been upfront about the nature of the trip, after all, had reminded her that she didn't need to come with him, could stay in the hotel room or avail herself of the small nail bar and spa adjacent to the marble check-in counter. It had been tempting, but the thrill of accompanying him to the seedier bar and slipping on her own new skin had been too great to pass up. *Better to be here instead of going mad wondering.* She'd grit her teeth at the thought of the tiefling, turning back to the goblin with renewed resolve, determined not to let her jealousy derail the weekend.

"Your friend is already halfway to the moon," she whispered conspiratorially to the goblin, giggling as he bent his head to hers. "I'll bet I can outdrink him, though."

"Is that so? That's a bet I'll take, tiny thing like you . . . what are you going to give me when I win, princess?"

"Hmmm . . . a kiss? A kiss against whatever you won at the tables." She straightened on the barstool, preening beneath the unflattering overhead light. "I'm very high maintenance, so you'll be winning even if you lose."

His laugh was a rough rasp, the hand that had been pressed lightly at her shoulder sliding down to rest at the small of her back.

"Oh, I'll bet you are, princess. Your daddy know you're out slumming it in a place like this? I'll bet you like getting just a little dirty every now and then. A kiss from you? I'll take that bet."

It's fine, she reminded herself, feeling her heart rate speed up. *Tate is just over there, and the bartender is probably his friend.* The troll on the other side of the bar had a lilting brogue that nearly matched Tate's, and she'd suspected he was the source of intel for this weekend's little outing, watching the man's smile twitch when she'd called for a bottle of Drarda, the golden Orcish spirit that was so similar to Mirúlvin.

"You know, little girl," the goblin had smarmed into her ear, several drinks in, his breath hot at her neck, "you weren't very specific with this little bet of yours. I think that means I get to pick where I get my kiss . . . how does the tip of my cock sound?"

When Tate finally slithered up to the bar seemingly hours later, asking if he could buy her a drink, she'd declined.

"You're welcome to join me, handsome stranger," she'd giggled, proudly displaying her winnings, "but I can buy my own drink. Maybe *I* should buy *yours*."

He'd almost laughed himself sick as she relayed the story of her bet, clinging to the side of her scuffed stool with his face buried in her neck as the troll clicked his tongue from the other side of the bar. She'd fisted his shirt victoriously as his shoulders shook, feeling his teeth scrape at her neck, incredibly pleased with herself.

"Should'a realized two cutthroats like you would be together," the bartender huffed, earning a fresh peal of laughter from Tate until he was left wiping his eyes. "She played that fucker like a seasoned pro."

"I think she did better than me! She's a regular Aine O'Roisin," Tate wheezed, and the bartender hunched, pounding a fist on the bar as both men howled in laughter before shaking his finger in Silva's direction.

"Careful lad, I heard that one's back in the clinker. Don't go letting this little kitten get into that sort of jam."

"Never," he assured, helping Silva slip into the jacket she'd draped over the back of her stool. "Fucking rich that you let her get up to this, Einan, right under that giant nose of yours. If you'd let that langer hang about any longer—"

"Ahh, enough," the troll interrupted, scowling, although his eyes were still lit in merriment. "This one can handle herself just fine. Away wi'you both," he shooed them from the bar. "If you're back tomorrow, I'll at least know where to expect the trouble."

"Did you think she was pretty?" she'd asked when he'd pinned her to the bed in their surprisingly posh hotel room that night, sliding the short skirt she wore down her hips. "That girl who was talking to you, the tiefling?"

"There was a girl?"

His voice was far too innocent as he lowered his head, kissing just above the waistband of her lace panties, and she scowled unseen. She wondered how he knew the bartender, if he frequented the pub regularly, imagining him meeting the same cervitaur there, far enough away from his own businesses to prevent gossip. The needle-like points of his teeth grazed her skin in a teasing bite, and she squirmed under his ministrations.

"Silva, whatever you're thinking of that has you screwing your nose up that way, why don't you stop."

Her cheeks heated as his long fingers slipped beneath the scalloped lace, ignoring her mental distress, tugging gently until the scrap of fabric followed her skirt. *He's right, you're being ridiculous, you're **always** ridiculous.* She didn't especially want to be placated though, wanted to force him to answer her question; wanted to ask him what they were, what she was supposed to call him, if she was ever going to be anything more than an occasional weekend distraction . . . but the feeling of his nose nudging against her inner thighs, his warm lips kissing over her delicate skin, and the wet heat of his tongue sliding over her cleft completely wiped her mind, and her head dropped back with a breathy sigh as her legs stretched open.

When the sex is so good you let him get away with anything, the sardonic little voice in her head whispered as his tongue dragged against her in wide licks, his lips closing around her clit in small, sucking kisses that alternated with the steady movement of his tongue. Tate knew exactly how to pleasure her, knew just where to angle the two long fingers he pressed into her, stroking her inner walls and making her arch; knew exactly how to lick her, where she needed the undulating pressure to come undone. He knew just how to leave her a needy, panting mess, bringing her ever closer to her climax before slowing, maddeningly, starting the whole process over again, distracting her from the less than pleasant thoughts until she pushed them into a dark corner of her mind where they continued to fester and grow. *You're proving to him that all he needs to do is give you that little smirk and lick your clit, and he can get away with murder*, the voice piped up once again, drowned out by the way she moaned, pushed away by the mounting pressure of his stroking tongue. When he began to suck her steadily, exactly the way she liked, the voice was forgotten and her tentative control broke, her hips lifting to grind against his mouth as she came. She reached out for him as her body pulsed, deftly curling her fingers around his bicep to pull him close . . . just as, she remembered suddenly, the tiefling had at the bar.

"Did she give you her number?"

She shifted, her mound connecting with his face, and he'd pulled back, cursing.

"That was my chin, Silva."

"Did she?" she'd persisted, unable to help herself. She'd never considered herself the jealous type either, but Tate managed to upend something inside of her, forcing her thoughts to the worst of scenarios, her imagination filling in the gaps of his reticence with imaginings of other women and carefree nights without her. She disliked herself when she acted this way, but it was his fault for bringing it out in her, she was sure of it.

"Dove—"

She'd clenched the sheets in irritation, twisting away from his lips as he climbed up her body, unwilling to be placated with his sweet talk.

"Did *you* think she was pretty? Is that why you're asking?" His smile was sharp and glinting as he knelt on the bed, straddling her body and looming over her. The long line of his sternum pulled her eye down, following over the hard plane of his abdomen and the deep cuts of his hipbones, a sharp V that ended where his stiffened cock bobbed, pink head peeking from its green sheath, momentarily distracting her again, until his next words. "Do you want me to call her for us?"

"She *did* give you her number!"

He easily dodged the pillow she swung at him, dropping to cage her beneath him as he laughed, completely ignoring the way she fought, kicking and clawing at his skin as if she really were a furious little kitten.

"I'm a bartender, Silva. Women give me their numbers every single day, have done for longer than I care to admit." Her lungs tightened at his words, a prickle of uncomfortable *knowing* flipping her stomach. *See?* "Why do you think," he went on lightly, pausing to kiss the tip of her nose, "that a single one of them matters?"

"You know why it matters." She hated how pitiful she sounded, cursing her weakness. *You should have let that goblin press his luck, he wouldn't have even noticed. It's not like there was anyone there who cared, certainly no one there who loves you. You don't even have a boyfriend.* Tate eyed her speculatively for a long moment, tracing the shape of her mouth with the tip of a lichen green finger before pushing up to straddle her again, taking himself in hand as he kneed open her thighs.

"The only thing I know, little dove," he murmured in a silky voice, coating his shining cockhead in her wetness before rubbing it against her clit, pulling a sharp gasp from her throat, "is that it's a good thing Einan tossed that blue-eyed cunt out when he did." His shaft was thick between the lips of her sex, small undulations of his hips bumping the head against her clit repeatedly until he pulled back far enough to push the tip into her. "Otherwise I'd have needed to see how far up his arse I could have shoved that wandering hand of his after I ripped his arms off." He fed his cock into her slowly, ignoring the way she scored her nails down his back, urging him to go faster, her needy cunt desperate to swallow him completely. When he bottomed out, at last, he dropped to cage himself around her again, gripping her wrists and pressing his forehead to hers, bumping her nose with his own. "You belong to *me*, Silva."

When he began to move within her, releasing her hands to brace himself against the mattress, she nearly sobbed, whether from the physical relief of being filled by him or from his words and the sentiment behind them, she wasn't sure. Silva fisted his sleek hair, squeezing until she knew it would hurt, *wanting* to hurt him, wrapping her legs around him as tightly as she'd been able. *He'd noticed, after all, had noticed everything.*

Electricity thrummed through her veins as it always did when his mouth met hers roughly, and when he began to hammer into her in earnest, she was seized with a desperate need to mark him as he'd once marked her. The bite he'd left on her skin had taken weeks to fully heal and weeks more to fade, its longevity aided by her own interference, pressing into it constantly with the blunt edges of her nails, keeping the bruise fresh. She wanted to see what color his bruise would be, imagining a dark green stain on his skin; a warning to every tiefling and harpy and cervitaur he might encounter that she existed, that she mattered, and that he was accounted for.

Her unsharp teeth caught at his lips, scraping his neck, biting at the muscle and sinew of his shoulder until he abruptly pushed himself up to his knees, hauling her up with a squeal, flinging her arms around his neck for support until she was flush against him with her legs wrapped around his waist, impaled on his cock.

"Is that what you want to do, Silva?" he hissed, hot tongue at her ear. "Rip me open, bleed me out?" His own teeth had descended, noticeably longer than they had been when he'd pressed into her, and the icy smell of snow-buried pines swirled with the smokey sandalwood smell of his hair, intoxicating her like a drug. "You're already halfway there, dove. May as well finish the job."

She *did*, she wanted to do *exactly* that, and as he began to pump into her again — his upward thrusts dragging against that spongy spot within her repeatedly, making her go nearly boneless in his arms — her small teeth sought out the juncture of his neck and shoulder once more. His hands cupped the curve of her ass, moving her up and down his cock like a toy as a trembling fire started at her toes and moved up her legs. Her clit dragged against his pubic bone as he moved in her, his quickening thrusts making her go nearly cross-eyed as the swell of pleasure rose within her again, and her teeth found their mark, tightening until her body clenched around his cock. A feral cry ripped from her throat as the pleasure flooded her, muffled against his skin, her mouth suddenly flooded with a metallic tang.

Silva couldn't tell if his groan was one of pleasure or pain, but suddenly she was empty, her core clenching around the missing shape of him within her as he jerked against her, his cock spurting white ropes between their bodies. The taste of his blood and the red crescent she knew her mouth would leave behind both thrilled and terrified her, for she realized he was right — she *did* want to rip him open; wanted to crawl inside him and lay claim to his heart, hers and hers alone. The last spasms of his release quivered up his spine as she licked at the wound, simultaneously coating her tongue and her belly, and Silva couldn't help feeling disappointed that he'd not finished inside of her, leaving her dripping in every part of his essence.

She quickly pressed her lips to the small puncture marks in apology, a breath before his mouth crashed into hers in a clash of teeth and heat. She could taste herself still on his lips, mingled with the taste of his blood like something primal and ancient, and it was enough for her body to clench once more, mourning the absence of him within her.

"Are you happy now, dove?" he'd whispered against her temple after — after he'd relocated them both to a gusting shower, washing away the evidence of his release and his smeared blood from her lips, grunting when the water pulsed down on his shoulder. He'd allowed her to fret that she'd actually hurt him for a handful of minutes as he'd toweled her hair, carrying her back to bed and pulling back the duvet.

"Yes," she confirmed. She was in her favorite spot — tucked under his arm, her cheek pressed to his chest, the thump of his heartbeat tugging her eyes closed. It had been late when they'd left the bar, later still when he'd undressed her, hours after her normal bedtime, and the events of the past hour had left her head spinning, the copper tang of his blood lingering at the back of her tongue. "I am. Because it doesn't matter how many cervitaurs or tieflings give you their numbers," she murmured, ignoring his snort at the inclusion of the fantasy cervitaur. The small crescent in his skin would most certainly leave a bruise, maybe even a scar, she thought, gently tracing its shape. "It doesn't matter because you belong to *me*."

His nose dragged against her hair, touching lightly to her crown with a small chuckle.

"Do you hear that, Silva?" The only thing she heard was the solid, percussive thump of his heartbeat beneath her ear, and the warm solid press of his arm, anchoring and surrounding her. He had another scar at the dead center of his throat, silvery and faint, and she'd stretched up to kiss it then. She may have been needy and jealous, may have felt uncertain over the precarious place she occupied in his mind and in his heart, but all of the tumultuous emotions she felt when they were together were stronger and more real than any other she felt through the course of her every day, more real and authentic than anything experienced by bland, mouse-like Silva of the daytime. "Your heartbeat, dove. That's the only thing I hear."

The entire affair had mattered even less the next morning, when she'd woken pressed to him, limbs entwined. He'd groaned as she stirred, hopping out of bed to hobble across the room. From her place on the pillow, she watched the stretch of his thighs and the ripple of his back, muscles pulling in a long line as he leaned around the door, placing the *do not disturb* placard on the handle before slipping back into the sheets with her, rolling her against him. When she'd straddled his face, gripping his hair like the reins of a horse as she ground herself against his mouth and nose, bouncing as he licked her until she came against his tongue, her high moans probably audible through the hotel walls, the girl from the bar the night before had no longer mattered. At all.

They'd stayed in bed until the room was lit with late-morning sunshine, had walked hand-in-hand through the shabby little downtown until she'd determinedly pulled him into a dim little tea shop, the yellowed lace curtains smelling of mothballs and age. She learned that he preferred a strong, golden-colored breakfast tea, that he took it with neither cream nor sugar, that he hated watercress, and was indulgent enough to allow her to steal the strawberry from his plate. It was a far cry from the elegant service at the club, but he was intimately familiar with the entire ritual, a good sign for their future engagement, she thought.

"I'm so glad you've been to tea before," she said cheerfully, sipping daintily from her cup as the old matron who ran the shop checked in on them. His chuckle warmed her as he topped off his own, placing the strainer in its caddy before answering.

"Every day growing up. Sangers and bix. Black tea, and a floral tisane. I've never liked cress, so don't think you're going to go changing my mind about it now."

"Tea at the club is my favorite, I just think food tastes better when it's miniature. We have a black tea, a floral tea, and sometimes a green. Sweets come after the savories, and then our scones. You can wear that dark purple shirt, I'll bet that color makes your eyes pop, with the grey suit, although the jacket might be too formal . . . maybe a vest.

I'll wear that peach dress you like, with the pleated skirt." She sighed, practically able to smell the flowers at the table. "It will be lovely."

"You've thought this all out, haven't you." The tips of her ears heated when she realized she'd gone blurting her daydream out, and that he watched her with an amused smile. She had a panicked moment that she'd shown her hand, ruining everything, when he leaned down to press his lips to hers, catching her lower lip in his teeth for a brief instant. "I'm sure that *would* be lovely. But you ought to be served your scone first, before anything else. You're going to need to go back to your club and teach them a few things, dove."

She'd imagined bringing him to tea more than a dozen times by then — the waitstaff not daring to turn their nose up at him, correcting her grandmother and holding her hand beneath the table. Silva knew without question, as he wound his fingers through her hair, bending to press his lips to her temple once they were on the sidewalk, the entire afternoon would serve as fodder for her daydreams for weeks to come.

She wondered, as she twisted her hair up that night, fastening her earrings in the hotel mirror, what the ramifications would be if she simply didn't return to work on Monday, didn't return home at all. What would happen if she stayed at his side as this other Silva, one who wasn't afraid of not living up to other people's expectations, confident Silva of the nighttime. He'd been made less than an hour after they'd arrived at the shabby little bar, too many of the same players from the previous night turning up as spectators.

He'd inserted himself between her and the smarmy satyr who'd just bought her drink, wrapping a possessive arm around her waist, giving the annoyed satyr a too-wide fae grin that had the smaller man quickly retreating.

"C'mon, dove. We're going to find a very expensive restaurant and be extremely judgemental about everything."

They'd gone antiquing the last day, to spend their ill-gotten gains, and he'd been like a child in a sweets shop, gleefully filling the back of the car with several glass shaded-lamps, a cabriole-legged end table, and several intricately engraved silver serving platters, ones she knew would make the circuit around different rooms in his apartment until they wound up in the bistro. It had been the most fun Silva could remember having in years, and going back to her boring, Tate-less life the next day had been tortuous.

Now, she told herself, things were different. She'd been more overt in the weeks since that little trip, making more and more demands on his time, practically vibrating in victory every time he relented. He'd taken her on a shopping trip to pick out new interiors for the bistro, which had turned into an afternoon strolling in and out of tiny shops and showrooms, a trendy little wine bar in Starling Heights, and her undulating on top of him in his giant bed, doing her best impersonation of a naga as he kissed her breasts. She had persuaded him to meet her for drinks and dessert with Khash and Lurielle on several different occasions, evenings that made her feel so much like they were just another couple, baby steps to introducing him to the rest of her world. There was no doubt in her mind that she was far more significant than an extended fling, that he went out of his way to think of her, that he might even be as in love with her as she was with him . . . except for the times when doubt was all she possessed, of course.

The text this time had come two days prior, once more in the middle of the day.

My friend is having a birthday party this weekend and I can't get out of going.

This time she'd remained calm. Sliding her phone into her purse, she locked it into the bottom drawer of her desk before going to join Ris and Dynah for lunch in the breakroom. Her boss was going to be out of the office until the following Monday, and she'd have ample time to finish her minor assignments and then work on her own portfolio. She'd answered an email from her grandmother, and had agreed to help with a last-minute meeting set-up for the Ladies' Club the following night. Her afternoon was spent in the drafting room, assisting on a branding project for a new pharmaceutical business, and she completed the majority of the meager work her boss had left her. When she'd finally returned to her desk, Silva retrieved the tucked-away phone. Sure enough, his second text had come only fifteen minutes prior. At long last, she thought, rolling her eyes with a smile, she was learning.

It's at a club in the city near your work. Do you want to go with me?

It was not near her work, not at all, but Tate had never heard of Cambric Creek and refused to acknowledge it existed.

You're not supposed to be trying to get out of spending time with your friends! she tapped out with a smile, feeling her heart swelling, inflating like a balloon, in danger of lifting her toes from the ground as she bounced in excitement. She'd met his talkative friend Ainsley several times at that point, always exuberant and cheerful, but being invited to a party seemed significant. A closed gathering, his social circle, a public declaration that she was the elf at his side, a step away from the afternoon tea engagement announcement in her daydreams. *Yes,* she typed. *Just tell me when and where. I'd love to go.*

Ris

When he texted her with the party's invitation, Ris didn't hesitate for a moment.

She had never been to a sex party before, and the thought of crossing the experience off her bucket list — and doing so with him at her side — was too good to pass up. After all, the only way to find out if she was into something was to try it, she thought, and she could think of no one else she would rather experiment with.

The event was invitation-only, hosted by a werewolf couple in a house they kept purely for the purpose of these soirées, which they hosted regularly. She knew there was a swingers club or two in Bridgeton, and knew that Cambric Creek had its own lifestyle scene, but she'd never indulged in either locale. The idea of visiting a sex club in the city by herself made her nervous and did not seem especially safe, and the thought of playing with a married couple right there in her own small town seemed even less so. There would be no way to look her accountant in the eye if she sucked on the ogre's fat testicles; no way to smile and thank the checkout cashier at the grocery store if she'd already watched the girl being double penetrated by the lizard man who ran the hardware store; no way to ever enjoy her dentist's banter before teeth cleanings if she let him lick her cunt in a roomful of strangers. Elves had an adage about not pissing in one's own flower bed, and while she wouldn't say no to those scenarios under different circumstances, she thought it was a very wise sentiment.

This was different. The thought of going on such an adventure with Ainsley felt thrilling, a fun couple's activity with low odds she'd regret it the next morning, and she was eager to put this new kink to the test.

The house was on the far side of Starling Heights, and they agreed to meet in Greenbridge Glen, where the orc resort was located. She would leave her car on the resort grounds and he would pick her up there, driving to the party together; a plan that made her feel safe and secure.

"We need to decide our strategy before we get there," he said decisively that night, moments before shoving a handful of nachos in his mouth. The little cantina was just up the block from his apartment, and she'd grown enamored of the prickly pear margaritas they served, as well as the avocado and salsa-heaped nachos. "Are we only going to watch this time? Are we going to get in on the action?"

"Are we going to play with other people, or just each other?"

He nodded vehemently at her question, gesticulating wildly until he had chewed and swallowed.

"Yes, exactly! Stuff like that. We need to go in with a plan, and then stick to it. It's too easy to feed into the mob mentality when you're there, and then we'll both wind up doing something we regret."

She wondered if that was a good way of thinking about her first experience at the orc resort. The idea of the public orgy had sounded fun in theory, but in practice, the experience had left much to be desired, and she wondered if she had set a game plan for herself beyond the vague notion of getting laid, she might've enjoyed her time at that bonfire party more. *And if he'd been there, but he was too busy jerking off in the bushes.*

"I say we scope the place out for a bit. Let's stick together, no separating. And since this is our very first time, I think I'd feel more comfortable only playing with you. We can leave the door open for something else to happen, but only if we both absolutely consent, and there's no pressure to say no. We don't know these people, we don't owe them anything. So if someone wants to pee on you, you can say no, even if I think that might be kinda hot."

He smiled broadly, that big smile that touched every corner of his face, the one she loved, and she giggled. "I appreciate the permission to say no to being marked by some werewolf. That sounds like a perfect plan to me, Nanaya."

The house was unremarkable. It was the first thing she noticed as they pulled up to the curb, a bit down the block. Brick, with an enormous roof, cascading gables, and a two-story entryway skylight, showing off a giant crystal chandelier, which she understood they were meant to be impressed by. The house matching the address on the scrap of paper in her hand was identical in unremarkableness to those on both its sides, the exact sort of cookie-cutter pretend opulence one expected from the farthest reaches of suburbia.

Cambric Creek may have been small, and the architecture may have been specifically designed to accommodate the wide range of species who lived there, but the homes were at least attractive, she thought. Even the newer developments, like the one Lurielle lived in, were designed to resemble the craftsman style made popular by goblins in the 19th century, with peaked roofs and intricate woodworking. She'd shown Ainsley around town, the weekend he'd stayed with her for the film festival. They'd driven around the subdivisions, and he'd marveled over the adaptive architecture, excitedly telling her about a book he'd read on the history of minotaurs and centaurs creating their own settlement towns at the turn of the previous century, building homes to accommodate their unique physiology.

"They don't have to have their own settlements here," she exclaimed with a smile. "There are special builds adapted to fit different sizes of residents, and then they can get as many specialized add-ons for the interior and exterior as they want. Houses get pretty pricey if they're made to exact specifications, I think most people just get the necessities and then make do with the rest. My friend, she's an elf too, she bought a house designed for an ogre, but it was the only thing on the market that she could afford at the time. She just climbed on ladders for everything."

Next, they'd gone through Oldetowne, and Ainsley had insisted she find someplace to park so they could stroll the block and gawk at the second empire-style manor homes and Queen Anne Victorians with turrets and gingerbread trim, and twee little balconies on tiny third story windows.

"We have neighborhoods like this, I think every old industrial town has neighborhoods like this . . . but it's not like *this*."

"It's a lot of the original families who still live in these houses," she explained. "It's a golden ticket to find a house for sale in this neighborhood. The few times it's happened since I moved here, the entire town showed up for the open house just to snoop."

"I fully expect you to invite me as your plus one the next time that happens," he laughed. "I love snooping."

By contrast, the McMansions lining this out-of-the-way stretch of road were soulless in their identicalness. Ris squinted at the amount of roof the house had, like a mountainside ski slope, oddly-placed dormers popping up like gophers.

"Well, it just goes to show," Ainsley announced, shrugging out of his jacket and tossing it to the car's backseat. "There's no accounting for taste. There's more roof than house!" She put her hand to her face, attempting to hold back her laughter as he came around to the side of the road where she stood. They had dressed for the occasion — she wore a snug, knit camisole, and a short flippy skirt, her thong already discarded on his front seat. Ainsley's white button-down made his green skin glow, sleeves rolled up over his elbows and unbuttoned to the middle of his chest, tucked into snug black jeans which she knew had nothing underneath them. Taking a deep breath, she slipped out of her own fur-lined jacket, adding it to the clothing in the car, unhooking her bra one-handed, and tossing it inside as well.

"We stick to the game plan."

"Game plan," she confirmed, raising her fist to meet his in a bump, giggling again when he gripped her hand, interlocking their fingers and giving her a squeeze before they trekked up the long driveway. "Here goes nothing."

Her heart was thumping in her chest, pressing as tightly as she could to his side for warmth as they rang the doorbell, the door quickly answered by a tall man with piercing eyes. Ainsley already had his cell phone in hand, ready to read off the confirmation code he'd received upon RSVPing, the man cross-checking it on his own handheld device. He squeezed her hand again when they were granted entrance, a petite blonde in a snug red dress standing in the foyer to greet them.

"Oh *my*," she simpered, biting her lip and giving Ainsley a long, lascivious look over. "We don't get many orcs to our little soirées. What a tall drink of water . . . I'll bet you're a *big* boy. There's only one way to measure though." She winked, and Ris felt Ainsley's arm stiffen at her side. "I promise, I give *very* accurate assessments." When neither of them responded, the blonde straightened up, frowning a little. "Well, follow me, I'll give you both the grand tour." The woman turned off the hallway motioning for them to follow, and the instant her back was turned, Ainsley's head swung to Ris, his eyes saucer wide.

"*What. The. Fuck.*"

"*Stop,*" she hissed under her breath, smacking his arm, feeling her laughter rising. "You're going to get us kicked out before we even get to do anything!"

"These are the locker rooms," the blonde announced, cutting her off. "Some people like to dress comfortably on their way in and then change once they get here," the blonde woman explained, "and some people like to strip down to their birthday suits after arriving," she added, glancing back to Ainsley with another little wink. Ris dug her nails into the meat of his palm, biting her lip to keep from laughing until she was sure she was about to break the skin. "Please be advised that playing in the locker room and changing room is not permitted. This is a neutral safe zone. Once you leave the confines of this area, the house rules are in effect . . . And here we have the steam room! It's not kept as hot as in a traditional spa, of course, but it's a nice way to get *steamy,* in more ways than one."

As they stepped around the glass brick wall, Ris made unexpected eye contact with a man sitting on the bench. The room *was,* in fact, steamy, although the woman was right in that it did not have the same high temperature as the steam room at her gym. The man groaned, eyes rolling back, and her gaze dropped to the woman on the floor. She had the green skin and ears of a goblin, but the height of a human. *A halfling*, she thought, unable to tear her eyes away from the way the girl sucked on the man's cock. "As you can see, once you leave the locker rooms, every room is considered full-service."

Ris wondered how much the couple had spent on renovating and plumbing each of the oversized rooms to accommodate the activities within as they were shown from the back of the house to the front, given a tour of a basement dungeon with numerous BDSM props and devices, up to the second-floor bedrooms, where a scene was taking place that reminded her uncomfortably of what she had witnessed at the orc resort's early summer party, when a ring of the hulking bodies had surrounded the two goblins on their knees.

"Well, that's about it! The rest is pretty self-explanatory, the house rules were included in the text you received with your entry code. This is a fully consensual playhouse, that is our main rule and any guest who strays from it will be removed from the premises and banned from all future events. Beyond that, anything goes. I don't like to restrict our guests, we only ask that you respect the property and leave each room in the same condition in which you found it. As I said before, once you leave the locker rooms, every area of the house is full service. That means the hallways connecting each room and every bit in between. Water sports should be confined to an area with a drain. Every guest is expected to clean up after themselves." Another wink in Ainsley's direction, and Ris flattened her mouth, suddenly finding the woman's flirtations not at all appropriate. "Every gentleman knows how much he expels, so we ask that you use good judgment. I *do* ask that you be cautious on the stairwell, by RSVPing yes, you did both sign a waiver of safety. We hope that you both enjoy yourselves and that you'll consider membership. This club was founded because of the exclusionary practices of some members of our community, but we *are* very selective. This is a multi-species club, but we do require humanoid anatomy, and we have some restrictions in place on membership levels. We wouldn't want the whole club overrun with goblins, after all." The woman laughed at her own joke, as Ainsley squeezed her hand fitfully. "If you have any questions, my husband and I are *eager* hosts." The last was said with raised eyes and another lingering look on Ainsley. "And we *do* play, of course. Looking forward to seeing you out there."

As soon as she had left them, heading back toward the foyer to greet the next guest who had arrived, Ainsley turned to Ris, his eyes still wide. "I feel like this is one of those parties where everyone is going to change into tuxedos and those pig-head masks. You heard what she said. I'm going to be the main course." She gripped his sleeve not bothering to hold in her laughter then, pulling him back towards what the woman had called the great room. "I'm not even kidding! These people are speciest. They probably have one of those flags, you know, the one with the bee? It's like 'hey there, I don't care about your species rights, don't step on my bee,' that one."

She pinned him against the wall and slumped against his chest, her shoulders shaking in uncontrolled laughter at his ridiculous monologue. "Do you want to leave? It's totally up to you, you're the one who's going to wind up on a spit, after all. If you want to go, we'll go."

He huffed, rolling his eyes, gripping her hand a little tighter. "No, we'll stay. I don't want to assume the rest of the guests are exactly like the host. Although," he added, "we should probably find out who excluded them in the first place and see what sort of shindigs *they* have."

The majority of the crowd seemed to be werewolves and shifters, humans and nymphs and trolls making up a sizable chunk of the rest. She watched, as at the table nearest them, a smiling woman with two antennae protruding from her forehead allowed the man beside her to pull open her blouse, testing the weight of her breasts in his hands. One by one, each person at the table extended a hand to fondle the woman and tug at her nipples, the original man coming behind her once everyone had a turn, slipping his arms beneath hers to cup her from behind. At another table, two men had pulled out their penises, and much like the first table, everyone standing around it took a turn giving each man a tug..

"Okay," she began, scanning the room slowly, "This is a *lot*. I think we should make a slight amendment to the game plan."

"You're going to give me to the pig-head people, aren't you."

She dropped against his chest again, smacking the front of his shirt in a fit of giggles.

"No! I just think that maybe we should be amenable to letting others touch. Just touch! Rest of the rules still apply. We have to be together, and they can only touch if we both approve. But look around." He looked out at the room, and Ris tracked his gaze as it moved over the tables, lingering over the people on the sofas, nodding his head slowly.

"Yeah, okay fine. I see what you mean. But as soon as they break out the tuxes, I want out of here."

"Deal," she smiled, raising her fist again to bump into his own, when her attention was caught by the action taking place near the wall beyond Ainsley's shoulder, her mouth dropping open. A dryad with fern green skin and long tapered ears was on a backless chaise, her knees tucked tight to her chest, the side of her face pressed into the upholstery. The girl's eyes were squeezed shut and her mouth open in a perfect 'o', sweat beading on her furrowed brow. Behind her was a leanly muscled lagomorph man with long white ears and a fluffy white tail above the swell of his ass, cinched with a black leather strap. He was bent over the girl, his legs tucked over her thighs, his cock jackhammering into her so fast, Ris thought the movement was nearly a blur. The young man's face was splotchy red with exertion, but his pace never slowed, and the girl beneath him was clearly enjoying the treatment, small moans issuing from her open mouth.

"That . . . that, um . . . yeah . . . game plan," she stammered, earning a snort from the tall orc. She would have been lying if she'd pretended she might not like to give the lagomorph a try, particularly when he leaned over the dryad, hooking his arms around her waist, the speed of his hips somehow increasing.

"You're gonna need to get his number," Ainsley shrugged. "My hips can't move that fast. I'd definitely break something. "

She squeezed his hand, grinning up. "Yeah, well . . . your cock is a lot bigger, so it's a trade-off."

Heads had turned in their direction as they moved through the room, a flutter of self-consciousness shivering through her. They were the only two of their species in attendance that she could see, and it was no surprise to her that a tall, handsome orc would stand out like a sore thumb.

"Ready, Nanaya?"

She tugged the front of his shirt until he bent, smiling as she stretched up on her toes to reach his mouth. He tasted like the cinnamon gum he chewed and his clove cigarettes, and she pressed her nose against his jaw for a moment to breathe him in.

"Don't let go of my hand," she whispered.

"Don't let the pig-heads get me," he smiled, kissing the tip of her nose. "Game plan?"

"Game plan."

♥ ♥ ♥

So far, they had watched. Watched and circled and watched some more. The hostess had sidled up to them at one point, running a long, French manicured nail down the center of Ainsley's chest without asking permission to touch him, prompting Ris to insert herself between him and the she-wolf.

"We're actually only watching right now." She had given the woman a sunny smile, but the words had been uttered in her best herd resources voice, and she did not step away until the blonde had moved on. "So much for taking their consent policy very seriously," she muttered. "I guess that's just for other people."

He was still the only orc in attendance that they had seen, and she was the only elf, not in itself a surprise. Still, the scarcity made them a novelty. They'd been approached half a dozen times already by single men and couples both, and even though Ainsley didn't possess the enormous bulk of some of his fellows from the resort town, he was still very muscular, and very, very tall. She would decline demurely for them both, and he would give a tightlipped smile, and that was enough of a deterrent for anyone to push their luck.

"My hand is getting sweaty," she whispered, earning a stifled snort of laughter from him and that big smile that she loved, glancing swiftly down.

"Yeah, I know. I'm the one sliding around on it. I'm not sure which one of us is making it worse at this point. Are you aware this werewolf has your scent?" She looked up sharply, seeing the wolf in question. It was the man from the front door, the blonde's husband, their host. "I guess it's not surprising that neither of them understand boundaries, right? He's been trailing us for the last ten minutes. Either that or he's looking to pee on me. Okay, how about the next person who propositions us, we try a soft yes?"

They had watched and circled and had seen everything there was to see in this main room, and she agreed it was time to either do more than watch, or cut their losses for the night and leave.

She nodded in acquiescence. "Table stuff only."

"Table stuff only," he agreed, grinning.

It didn't take long.

"Can I touch you?" The young man appeared to be some sort of Sylvan sprite, with wide, glossy dark eyes that reminded her of a forest creature, and a graceful bearing. She glanced at Ainsley, who gave her a small shrug and a squeeze of the hand with a smile. *This is it.* Pulling down the straps of her camisole, folding the top hem down to her waist, she gave the young man a nod in the affirmative.

Her eyes fluttered closed at the first touch of his hand, warm and gentle, tracing over the small, firm mounds of her breasts, cupping her in his palms. She let out a soft sigh as his fingertip circled her areola with a whisper-soft touch until her nipple hardened. She didn't need to tug Ainsley's shirtfront for more than a second until he bent, catching her lower lip in his teeth. When the young man asked if he could use his mouth, she nodded again, biting Ainsley's lip when the young man's blunt teeth scraped over her pebbled nipple, reaching down to rub the bulge at the front of the orc's snug jeans.

"Can I touch you?" The young man asked again, his mouth freed from her breast, his breath warm against her throat. At first, Ris wasn't sure what he meant, for he had *been* touching her, the cooler air of the room tightening her nipple further without the heat of his mouth around it. She didn't understand until she felt the drag of his fingers over her cleft, over the material of her thin skirt.

Her hand managed to undo the first several of Ainsley's long button fly, but she wanted him free, wanted him out, wanted him in her hand. She nodded yes to the young man again. The first stroke of his fingertip against the outside of her cleft made her shiver, and he stroked her there for a few long seconds — back and forth, back and forth, before cupping her entire pussy in his palm, feeling the heat of her core, squeezing gently. She had worked Ainsley's cock free by then, her thumb slowly circling over the edge of his foreskin, where a small circle of his shiny cock tip peaked, as the Sylvan man's finger pushed through her lips, sliding through the slick folds of her sex, coming to alight on her clit. Ris gasped when he began to roll the little bud of nerves, the long middle finger of his hand pushing into her until the meat of his palm was flush against her body.

"Can I play with you?" The voice was feminine, and she opened her eyes to find a kitsune in a short skirt similar to her own, three dark red tails pushing out from beneath the hem. The girl's top had been discarded, and her heavy breasts swung with her movements. Ris realized the question had been directed at Ainsley, releasing her hold on his thickened shaft. She had put the cock ring on him herself before they'd left his apartment; a snug, black leather strap she'd fastened at the base. She didn't even have a plan or reason why, she'd simply found it in the drawer of his bedside table, questioning if it was in fact what she thought it was before dropping to her knees gleefully.

She nodded at him, and he in turn gave the Fox girl an affirmative. The Sylvan continued to finger her, and now she had the added pleasure of watching the way Ainsley's cock had begun to swell beyond the black strap, and the way the fox tailed woman skillfully manipulated his foreskin, sliding it up and down the length of his shaft until she released his cock head with a *pop!*

"Can I lick this pretty pussy, pretty girl?"

Her breath hitched and Ainsley's smile stretched, nodding at her. It occurred to her that they had gone way past *table stuff* at that point. *So much for sticking to the game plan,* she thought. The Sylvan man had long, tapered ears, and she ran her fingertips up them as he dropped to his knees, wasting no time before he pushed his chin in between her thighs. She heard a small grunt from her side, the fox girl begining to stroke him in earnest, just as the Sylvan man's tongue pushed through the lips of her sex in a long slow lick, from slit to clit. She enjoyed the way he nibbled and sucked on her, almost as much as she enjoyed the short grunts and groans from the orc beside her. They were facing outward, side-by-side, his long pinky hooking around her fingers as they were pleasured separately, together.

It was then Ris realized: they had a bit of a line forming. There were several men of varying species lined up behind the Sylvan, presumably waiting for their turn to lick her, and two women behind the kitsune waiting for their turn to grip and stroke Ainsley's cock. The long-eared man raised his head, nose and tongue glistening with her slick, grinning sharply.

"I suppose I should let someone else take a turn."

"Don't go far," Ris ordered him. She liked the young man's gracefulness, the way he'd asked permission each time he wanted to progress, and she wouldn't mind him taking another turn.

The next man who knelt before her was some sort of shifter, his tongue wider and wetter than the Sylvan's had been, licking her messily. A human stroked Ainsley, her hands barely able to span his girth. Her clutching fists moved one after another in a continuous stream, twisting as she went, and Ris knew from experience that he liked that particular move, although the girl's grip seemed weak. *Like jerking off with a fish.* She bit back a snort of laughter, and the shifter between her legs raised his head in offense.

The next woman in line had bluish-green skin and ears that resembled fins, and it wasn't long before Ris heard her asking if she could use her mouth. When the girl received her consent, she dropped to her knees, quickly joined by another woman who could have been her twin, were it not for the deeper blue of her skin, and a third a man had taken their place between her thighs, the overeager lashings of his tongue not quite finding their mark. She wondered if it would be rude to say that she had had enough. *We don't owe them anything, right?* The repetitive movement against her without finding that spot that curled her toes was becoming slightly numbing, each mouth a little wetter and sloppier than the next. When she looked over, one of the fin-eared women was attempting to suck one of Ainsley's testicles into her mouth, like swallowing a particularly juicy plum from the vine, tugging on its twin, as the other continued to suck and stroke his cock, and decided she'd let things continue for a few minutes longer, for his sake..

When a fourth man dropped to his knees before her, shouldering open her legs with more dominance than any of the others had up until that point, dipping his head immediately, she didn't realize who he was. His tongue was hot and wet, and he groaned against her as he licked a broad stripe up to her clit, puckering his lips around it and sucking hard. Thrice more he repeated the action, and it very nearly felt good — nearly felt divine — but there was an edge of pain to the way he sucked her, one she did not think was accidental. It made her slightly uncomfortable, and that was enough to make her push on his shoulder. It was the werewolf who'd opened the door for them, the blonde she-wolf's husband, the one Ainsley claimed had been trailing them. The blonde herself was only a few feet away, making her way to take her place behind the blue-skinned girls. Another lick, another suck, just on the edge of feeling good; her head dropped back prepared to quiver in pleasure . . . when once more, he sucked hard enough to make it hurt, and she winced.

"That's enough," she bit out, remembering that they didn't owe these people anything. The man didn't immediately release his grip on her thighs, but before she even had a chance to repeat her rescission of consent, Ainsley had hooked his hands under her arms from behind, lifting her like a doll, out of reach of the werewolf.

"She said enough." His voice was harder than she'd ever heard it, brokering no discussion, and she was reminded that he was, in fact, an orc. He had already tucked himself away as best he could and disentangled himself from the fin-eared duo, swinging her into his arms easily, as he'd done that night at the pub. She thought perhaps in other company she would've wanted to leave; would have wanted to leave straight away, putting the entire evening behind her, but instead, her blood thrilled in excitement — the pleasure that had been sparked by the Sylvan man's tongue was yet unsated, the knowledge that Ainsley was rock hard in his jeans was not something she could ignore, that hard note of command in his voice making her knees shake. Best of all — she had spotted a long bank of mirrors against the upstairs hallway, not something to which she had paid attention during their earlier tour, too aggravated by the she-wolf's attentions and lack of decorum. Ris had never felt so much like Silva as she did at that moment, even thinking such a thing . . . but it was true.

"I want to go upstairs," she murmured into his ear, scraping her teeth against his throat as he carried her away from the wolf couple. "I want to go upstairs and suck you off."

"That's a coincidence," he gritted, "because I want to bend you over one of these tables and empty my balls into you. I suppose we'll have to meet in the middle." She squealed when he hoisted her over his shoulder like a sack of potatoes, rubbing a hand over her bare ass as he ascended the steps two at a time, dodging around the figures loitering there.

One of the backless chaise lounges suited her purposes as she dragged the corner of it to be perpendicular to the mirror, pushing him down to the tufted upholstery. Ris wasted no time dropping to her knees, pulling the solid rod of his cock out once more. He had swelled under the ministrations of the several different women who had been sucking and stroking him, the thick bar of flesh standing rigid, so swollen from the leather cockring it was nearly purple. His sac was just as swollen as his shaft, his testicles pulled painfully tight, hot in her hands as she cupped them, pulsing them lightly.

He groaned at the first stroke of her tongue against his glans, chuckling deeply when she sucked him into her mouth. The sound was intimately familiar, so *impossibly* safe and comfortable, even after such a short amount of time, and she shivered, her stomach flip-flopping. Turning her head to the glass against the wall, she watched the Ris in the mirror sucking that Ainsley's cock, appreciated the way he thrust slightly, and wondered if her mirror twin was able to taste the pre-cum he was seeping. She wondered if *that* Ainsley was able to feel the drag of her nails up the seam of his fat, swollen scrotum; if he enjoyed the pull against his foreskin as much as the Ainsley before her did.

The Sylvan had followed them, she realized, edging in behind her, and she met his glossy dark eyes in the mirror, nodding her consent before he even needed to ask the question, raising her ass high in the air as her head dipped, swallowing Ainsley's cock again. When the smaller man's tongue pressed into her from behind, licking into her determinedly, she moaned, the vibrations moving up Ainsley's shaft until he fisted her hair. It occurred to her, as she hummed, that it was *this* scenario she had been expecting at the orc resort. Sensual and pleasurable for all parties involved. *If only we didn't have an audience.*

She watched the way her mirror twin pushed back against the Sylvan man's face as she came up for air, watched her mouth drop open as his tongue lapped at her clit. She had just curled her tongue around the weeping tip, about to swallow him again when Ainsley pulled her to her feet abruptly, spinning her around. She gasped when he breached her, the thick press of his head catching at her lips, pushing in and stretching her pussy wide. He pulled her slowly down the thick length of his cock until she was straddling his legs on his lap, her thighs stretched open.

"Make her come." His words were directed at the Sylvan man, she realized, squeaking when he pulled the edge of the chaise, tilting them so that she would be able to see the man kneeling between her legs. "I want you to lick her clit until she comes around my cock."

There were *so many* people watching them, Ris realized. A whole ring of onlookers, slowly jerking off as they watched her stretched over Ainsley's lap, pussy on display. On display, at least until the Sylvan man lowered his face to her once more, and began to lick. She reached a hand back to scratch at Ainsley's chest as the long-eared man flicked his tongue back and forth against her, catching at the spikes through his nipples and tugging. Ris had the thought that she would be enjoying herself tenfold more if they were alone. Alone in her condo, or alone in his apartment, no witnesses to the way she was stuffed by him. She wondered if the other man's chin was bumping the root of Ainsley's cock as he ate her, watching as mirror Ris pushed her fingers through the man's head, holding him in place when he landed on the spot that made stars burst behind her eyes, watching mirror Ainsley cup her small breasts and scrape his teeth against her shoulder. *Don't pay attention to them*, she told herself, forcing her thoughts away from the bystanders, closing her eyes. *None of them are real.*

"Are you going to squeeze my cock, Nanaya? Are you going to give this cockring a run for its money?"

Ris knew she was not going to last long. The Sylvan had fastened his lips around her clit, his tongue fluttering around her as he sucked, the fullness of Ainsley's cock leaving her breathless in the exhilaration, and the sight of herself as the long-eared men began to nod his head up and down as he sucked, his tongue catching the side of her clitoral hood as he did so, and Ainsley had begun to thrust himself upwards into her, the barest hint of movement, but just enough to remind her of how big he was and how amazing he felt. She felt the tremors begin around her knees, shaking up her legs and tightening her thighs.

Her clit felt like a live wire, and every sucking pulse sent electricity shooting through her veins; her hands tightening in the young man's hair, squeezing as she held him in place, throbbing against his tongue. Ainsley groaned against her temple, arms encircling her.

"Just like that, Nanaya. You're going to milk it right out of me."

She cried out in disappointment when he pulled out of her,

wanting to do exactly as he suggested. Once again, she became all too aware of the onlookers, the throng of men frantically beating off, watching her orgasm; or else being sucked off by willing partners. She didn't know what he was planning on doing next, not until he produced a foil-wrapped condom which she quickly took from his hands, ripping it open, and rolling it down his swollen shaft.

"Let me get a few good grinds in," he groaned against her neck, pushing to his feet. He walked her to the staircase banister, kicking her feet open as she braced her hands against it, testing its strength. "Otherwise I'm going to look like a two-pump chump in front of these weirdos. Let me at least build a bit of a rhythm before you open the dam." She laughed in spite of herself. She disliked being a spectacle this way, would have enjoyed having him and the Sylvan young man together in a quiet hotel room perhaps, might have even welcomed the kitsune, but this ring of overly horny onlookers left her cold. Even still, there was no one else she'd rather be here with. Ainsley began to pump into her with a slow, steady rhythm, like the rocking of the boat, pulling her back to meet him, his speed slowly increasing until he slammed into her with a steady slap, skin on skin, the sound of carnality. It took a bit of maneuvering, but she was able to reach her hand down to where their bodies were joined, giving his balls a squeeze before she found the end of the leather strap, setting them free. His arm came around her, fingers seeking her heat, knowing exactly what she liked and what it would take to bring her over the edge again. It was unnecessary, for she still felt touch over sensitized from the Sylvan's mouth, but she appreciated his consideration and knew he liked the clench of her. She was still tingling, still sensitive, and he knew right where to press. Quick, tight circles, an upward pull, just the right angle . . . It was a shallow, weak orgasm, but her core still tightened and her muscles still clenched around him, her head lolling. She realized he had been holding himself back, for as soon as she slumped against the banister, he was pulling her tightly against him, his hips jerking as he groaned in her hair. The condom kept her from feeling his heat, but she was able to feel the pressure of being filled, his full balls emptying themselves in rhythmic convulsions, spurt after spurt, until he slumped.

Her head felt impossibly heavy, and the only thing she wanted to do then was curl up beside him beneath the cool sheets in his giant bed, or snuggle against his chest as he attempted to fit in her much smaller one. Instead, she realized, panting, they were still in this ugly house, surrounded by these too eager people and their slightly creepy hosts.

Glancing down the banister that she'd gripped for support, Ris made eye contact with the other half of their host couple, at the same time that Ainsley withdrew himself from her, pulling out carefully. She didn't know what face she'd made at the backward drag and sudden sensation of emptiness, but the werewolf smiled, holding her eye for an interminable moment before his head dropped back, mouth opening in ecstasy as he gripped the hair of the woman kneeling before him.

"Are you alright?" Ainsley's voice was a low purr at her ear, his hand spanning across the bare skin of her stomach beneath her tank. Ris considered the question. *Was* she alright? The public hedonism of the nudist resort was an experience she was glad she'd had, but ultimately not one she was eager to repeat. Was this any different? His breath was hot at her neck, tusks grazing her skin as he pressed his lips to the skin behind her ear. "Ris?" he prodded, soft enough for her ears alone. "I need to hear your words."

"Yes," she answered, turning her head and meeting his mouth. Cinnamon gum and whiskey, tobacco and clove. Familiar and safe. She didn't want to do this again, but she was glad she'd tried it with him. "Yes," she repeated, happy that she meant it. "I'm good."

"Good . . . can we please leave?"

"Please. Right now. I think I saw someone in a tuxedo, it's probably time to put you on the spit."

His hand was tight around hers as they maneuvered down the staircase, once their clothing was restored. He pivoted their positions on the landing, placing himself fully between her and the sharp-eyed werewolf, pulling her quickly down the staircase to follow. She squealed when the icy air hit her bare arms at the front door, but they never slowed, and his fingers stayed tightly knitted with hers until his car came into view.

"I was a woodland scout," he chuckled, pulling two pepwaters from a bag on the backseat, along with a bag of restaurant-style chips. "Always prepared. I'm also starving. I didn't pack the guac though, sorry."

For several long minutes, the only sound was the hum of the engine and their chewing, the heat blasting from the registers warming her skin as the lights of downtown Starling Heights neared. The silence, like everything else about him — like every moment spent in his company — was comfortable.

"So . . . I think I hated that."

"Oh, thank the stars." His head dropped back with his exclamation. "It was terrible, right? Those people were creepy predators, please tell me that wasn't all in my head."

"They were! They didn't respect boundaries at all."

"I'm not going to pretend I didn't like watching you with that Sylvan guy—"

"I liked that too," she agreed quickly. "If it had just been the three of us, that would have been great. And I like watching us in the mirror. But I didn't like all the bystanders, and that werewolf couple was super creepy. I don't think I'm into *any* of that dungeon stuff."

"None of it, or the upstairs stuff, to be honest. I don't want to be peed on, I don't want to be a part of your weird circle jerk, I don't want my asshole licked by some stranger who's simultaneously being plowed by every single member of a k-pop weretiger band, I don't want to take turns on a five-guys-one-girl train. Ris . . . I think I'm vanilla."

She was already doubled over at that point, her eyes streaming, the seatbelt the only thing keeping her in the seat as she laughed.

"Me too! I think I am too!"

Ainsley's face had screwed up in a disgusted scowl, smacking at the steering column and inadvertently honking the horn. The wide body of the ogre in the car ahead of them raised their hands in defense, only making her laugh harder.

"What the fuck?!" he shouted, his voice reverberating in the muscle car's interior as she wheezed in laughter. "How did this happen? We're both too hot for this!"

They were back in Greenbridge Glen by then, she noticed with a pang of disappointment, realizing he'd be letting her off at her car soon. Much like the orc resort parties, she was not interested in a repeat performance of that night's events, but the whole evening had been infinitely more tolerable because of him, and she wasn't quite ready to say goodbye. She was surprised then when he directed the car through the resort town's line of shops, backing into an alley behind the bistro on the corner. His arm linked with hers as they hurried up the street, the narrow lane turning the sharp, early winter breeze into a knife-like windtunnel.

She was unsurprised when they stopped before the window of the black-pricked pub, her stomach flip-flopping at the sight of the slender orc inside, balancing with one foot on the edge of the bar and the other on the shallow counter behind, as he shifted around bottles on the top shelf. He turned sharply when Ainsley rapped on the window, and she held her breath, remembering his terrifying anger the last time she'd been here. Instead, he hopped off the counter with the grace of a gymnast, disappearing from the window's vantage, the pub's front door swinging open a moment later.

Ainsley's strange friend was silent as they entered, locking the door behind them, instinctively wiping his hands on the towel over the top of the short black apron tied around his waist. He said nothing as Ainsley led her to a low table in the center of the room, joining them after a moment with three rocks glasses and a bottle. She watched as he poured two fingers in each glass, adding two more to his own after a moment of hesitation. He pulled out a third chair at the table, taking a seat on the other side of them, and Ris was able to see for the first time that he wasn't quite as young as she had initially assumed that night he'd served them at the bistro.

He had a faint, silvery scar slicing over his forehead that curiously seemed to start somewhere near his eyelid, cutting through his eyebrow, which he had pierced over, and slashing through his hairline, as straight and precise as if he'd ordered his barber to make the mark. His features were fine and delicate, as if he'd been carved from a luminous slab of marble, and she was relieved to note that there was absolutely nothing out of the ordinary about his wide mouth other than the shortness and sharpness of his tusks. Objectively, she thought, he was one of the most handsome orcs she'd ever seen, but she'd never be able to forget the way his mouth had contorted that night, nor the terrifyingly unhinged look on his face.

He took a sip from his glass, eyes fluttering shut as he swallowed, long black lashes fanning out against his cheek before they opened again and he sat back in his chair, leanly muscled arms crossing over his chest.

"Well? Are you orgiasts now?"

Ris felt his words like a solid blow to her chest, her laughter coming out in a staccato burst, Ainsley huffing in aggravation beside her.

"We're not. We're so, *so* not. It was mostly terrible. The hosts were creepy and didn't follow their own boundaries."

"They were *really* creepy," she added, sipping from her glass.

"There were too many gawkers," Ainsley went on. "Too much of an audience."

Tate snorted at his words. "You know, I could have saved you the trouble of the evening. You can't even take a piss if there are too many people around."

She nearly choked on the tiny amount of whiskey sliding down her throat, her chest aching with the force of her laughter. Ainsley slapped the table beside her, his rough rasp of a laugh like a metallic counterpoint to the tinkling bell that poured out of his friend

"That is *not* what I said!

"You said you don't want anyone to be in the room with you."

"You are *mischaracterizing* that conversation. No one talks! There's no background noise! That's what I don't like! You're in a giant room of people and all you can hear are a bunch of strangers taking a leak! So if no one is going to have the decency to have a conversation, I prefer to have the room to myself."

Tate had his head tipped back, laughing so hard that there was no sound coming out of his mouth. "Ah yes, because there's nothing better than being in the jacks, cock in hand, and having the bloke next to you leaning down over your shoulder, asking what you like to do on weekends."

There was a stitch in her side, and she was laughing so hard tears had begun to prick in her eyes and run down her cheeks, her ribs aching. She remembered the story Ainsley had told her about how he'd come to be friends with the man across the table, and the vivid picture Tate painted only reinforced his assertion of harassment.

"This was different! Tonight was different. We found a couple of people we may *actually have been* interested in! But it's hard to really enjoy yourself when there's a circle jerk happening around you".

Tates had slumped over the table, his face buried in his arms, sleek black hair pulling messily from his bun as his shoulders shook. "You're a fucking idiot," he wheezed, raising his head briefly at Ainsley's words, and Ris worried she might actually do herself an injury from laughing as hard as she was. Ainsley pushed up from his chair, huffing as he kicked at the table leg.

"I'm going to the bathroom, so you both had better stay out here if no one wants to talk to me."

Tate continued to laugh as Ainsley stomped across the pub floor, his head dropped back, the high, musical lilt of it ringing in the rafters. "I honestly don't know how I've managed to be friends with him for as long as I've done." He pushed up from the table, crossing back to the bar, returning after a few moments with three bottles from the cooler, beading in condensation.

"He said you used to live in the same apartment building?"

He nodded, pulling a bottle opener from the pockets on the apron he wore, popping open her bottle and setting it on a neat cocktail napkin emblazoned with the same logo from the creaking sign above the door.

"Aye, we did. He'd be waiting for me every weekend night I came home from work, and there was no putting him off. I started coming up the fire escape, and once he caught on, he'd be waiting for me there, and then we had to press against each other to get in the doorway. It was easier to just give in eventually."

Ris snorted, Tate's description of the events matching Ainsley's too closely for it to have been anything but the truth.

"You know, I never apologized to you for that night. I'm sorry you were here to be caught up in all that, and I'm very glad you weren't injured."

Her stomach flip-flopped again at the memory, the spine rattling the terror she'd felt, and the certainty she'd felt that the orc standing in front of her was going to swallow them all whole.

"I'm glad he was here that night, otherwise I might have been."

"He always manages to turn up when you don't think you need him, but you're glad to see him just the same. You'll not be able to keep him out, you know. If that's what you intended. He's a dab hand at getting under the skin. One minute you think you're having a drink with a mate, and next he's chewed his way into your heart, and there's no scraping him out after that. Believe me, I've tried."

She laughed at the mental image of Ainsley as a sort of parasite. The slender orc was right, she was forced to admit, for she'd spent more time thinking of his friend in the past week alone than she had about any other man in her life, and could easily envision him shrunken to bug size, making himself a snug, cozy spot in her heart.

"So if that *is* what you've intended, you'll not be successful."

"I thought he was going to need to call you to bail him out of jail again for a minute tonight," she admitted with a laugh. "Our hosts really did not respect their own rules."

His bark of laughter was sharp, bouncing between the hanging pendants above their heads.

"Absolutely daft, both of you. I'd have let him rot for the night, maybe then a lesson might be learned."

"Oh, you would not have, you big liar." Ainsley returned to the table, giving the other orc his best glare. "Don't let him fool you, Ris. Squishy marshmallow center, this one. Oh good, you brought us something cold to drink. I brought the chips."

She laughed again, somewhat doubting the veracity of Ainsley's claim. The icy bottle was an Elvish spritzer, she realized, in surprise. Imported water from a sacred spring, carbonated with botanicals and floral extracts, and a healthy slug of a high-proof alcohol, the last thing in the world she would've expected to find in an Orcish pub. She listened to the two men chatter and laugh: heard the details of a party taking place in the city the following weekend, to which Ainsley had not been invited, that Tate grumbled he didn't have a choice in attending;

listened to Ainsley's incredibly over-dramatized version of the night's events, implying that there had, in fact, been pig-headed people, and they were not just a figment of his wild imagination. Tate was sharp and funny, and she took the time as they filled the space of the conversation to look him over a bit closer. His ears seemed too long for an orc, tapering to sharp points, and there was nothing in his long jaw or long, slender neck that resembled any of the orcs she had met at the resort previously.

"The rosemary violet is my favorite," she piped up once Ainsley had finished his colorful anecdote, lifting her drink again, taking a long sip. All three bottles were the same flavor of peach and orange blossom, which she also liked, but not quite as much as the rosemary.

"It's my favorite as well, which is why those are all upstairs."

"I would never have expected an orc to be fond of an Elvish drink," she tittered, glad they had stopped in the little black bar. The mirth-filled end to their night was what they needed to sweeten the experience of the house, what *she* needed to be able to look back and only remember the good parts.

"That's because he's an elf? You'd probably not find too many orcs ordering anything with peach blossom and violet."

"It's a violet and rosemary and peach and orange blossom," she corrected, before turning to Ainsley's friend with raised eyebrows. "You're an elf?! That explains . . . well, literally everything I've been thinking for the past half hour. You don't really look like an orc, except for, well . . ." She gestured at his person, feeling her ears heat.

"Except for all the bits that make me look like an orc," He finished for her, smiling briefly, setting her at ease.

"You're from Ireland, right?" Her cheeks darkened as she ducked her head. "I'm sorry, that probably makes me sound so dumb. I have a really bad ear for accents and languages, I struggled so much with Elvish in school. I've met folks before and I've assumed they were from Ireland and they were really from England, so I figure it's not worth assuming."

He chuckled, draining the rest of his bottle before crossing his arms over his chest again. "Well, you can be forgiven for that. There are at least a dozen different places in England who all desperately want to sound Irish. But yes, I'm from Ireland, emigrated nearly two decades ago. My chef at the bistro, I'm sure you'll meet her eventually if you've not already done so, she is as well."

"Do you own the bistro too?!" Ris covered her face with her hands, her shoulders shaking in laughter again. "Well since I'm embarrassing myself, I may as well admit — I thought you were a server there."

Tate raised his hands, shrugging in an expansive gesture of defeat, and she laughed harder.

"Okay, I don't understand how—" Ainsley cocked an eyebrow, hand raised questioningly, his face screwed up in confusion. "Has pop-culture lied to me all these years? Because if movies and television and even songs are to be believed, girls talk to each other about everything? Is that all a big lie? Do you even go to the bathroom together? Do you even *like* lip gloss?! Have you seriously heard nothing about him? How is it even possible that I have been led *this* astray? Was my entire childhood a lie?"

Ris didn't understand Ainsley's words, but she took in the tightening of his friend's eyes, the flattening of his mouth and the slight pull of his posture, as if he were hunching without moving. Less than a heartbeat had passed, Ainsley's words still floating in the air between them, but something had changed, a chill she could tangibly feel, when Tate pushed up from the table, gathering all three glasses and bottles at once.

"You going to be here when my alarm goes off at five in the morning? Shona gets in at six. I like to have the dining room set up and the accounting for the day done before the bank opens."

"The most I am planning to do at five is have a nice horny dream, because that is still practically the middle of the night."

"Then I think it's time for you to get the fuck out so that I can go to bed."

The sharp, hardness she had remembered from his voice that first night in this pub had returned, and Ris felt her stomach twinge, having the uncomfortable feeling that tonight she had inadvertently been the cause of it. She shoved up from the table quickly, pushing in her chair neatly as well as the one Tate had abandoned, not giving Ainsley an opportunity to argue. "It was nice meeting you officially," she called out as cheerfully as she could. "Thank you for the drinks, I'm sure I'll see you again soon."

The smile he gave her was tight, and didn't quite reach his flame-colored eyes.

She pulled her jacket around her tightly as they stepped back out into the black night, the faintest trace of snow beginning to fall from the sky. The lights of the pub went out before they had even stepped off the sidewalk. "I think you hurt his feelings," she murmured as Ainsley gripped her hand, stepping into the empty road.

"Tate only has two feelings, and they're both exceptionally difficult to hurt."

She didn't want to argue the point, but he'd not been watching the way his friend's face had tightened at his confusing words. They were halfway down the block to where his car was parked in the alley when Ainsley stopped short, causing her to jerk to a halt. His head dropped back, his exhalation long and dramatic. She was unsurprised when he spun on his heel, stomping back to the pub. The black brick building was completely black, except for the top floor, above the bar. She'd not realized just how long the building was, noting the pub was far larger than she'd initially observed, and that they likely had a large storage room as well. The upper floor spanned the entire length of the building, its wide windows illuminating the dark night. Ainsley had pulled out his phone, tapping the screen and glaring up to the lit windows.

"It's me—no, I didn't forget anything, I only wanted to—look, I only meant that—" his head dropped back again in exasperation, the arm not holding his cell phone opening wide. "I'm only calling because I thought I might have hurt your feelings. I just wanted to say I'm sorry. You don't need to threaten me with bodily harm."

She could hear Tate's voice, tinny through the phone, sharp and stabby like a switchblade.

"*Fine*, I'm leaving. Don't let that bad mood choke you in your sleep."

He shoved the phone back in his pockets, grumbling under his breath as he took her hand back up, stomping back to his car. "Nanaya, how badly do you want to go back to Cambric Creek tonight? I'm fucking exhausted."

"You technically only have to bring me back to the resort parking lot. That's where I parked."

Ainsley sighed, groaning. "That sounds sooooo far. How about I bring you back there tomorrow, after breakfast instead?"

The drive from his friend's bar to his apartment in Starling Heights was minimal, and she had no complaints once they were both stripped down and curled in the sheets in his giant bed.

"I'm sorry I got you yelled at," she added. "That probably just made things worse."

"He doesn't actually *yell* yell. It's more like a threat from the shadow at the back of your closet. And being threatened is actually an expectation, so don't worry. He really is all bark. Like, I could complain that my arm was useless and that I wanted a new one, and Tate would lecture me about being a spoiled arm hog and that plenty of people live their lives with no arms at all and then somehow manage to turn it into a story about him hiding under his bed for three days when the human and goblin crowns burnt Cork city to the ground and it would all just make me feel terrible, but then a day later there would be a box on my doorstep with perfectly washed and sanitized arm and no note. And then next time I would see him, he would have a bloody stump hanging out of his T-shirt and claim his arm has always looked that way and I'm too much of a cunt to have properly noticed."

She laughed against his chest, his examples as dramatic as ever. "My dad is that way. Generous to a fault. My parents didn't have any money when I was growing up, everything they made went into sending me to Elvish school, they knew it was that important. And the second they managed to scrape a few pennies together, there was my dad, giving it away to someone with a sob story who he claimed needed it more. He had a big heart, but he was taken advantage of more than once."

"Taking advantage of a generous heart is exactly what I'm worried about," he mumbled, his tone a bit more serious than it had been only a moment earlier. "Do you seriously know nothing about him?"

"What am I supposed to know?!" she exclaimed. "He's your friend, he's a switchblade instead of a piece of bread. You claim his bark is worse than his bite, but I've seen a bit of his bite and it's actually terrifying. But he's important to you, clearly. And that's all I need to know."

He huffed out a breath and laid back against the pillows, clearly dissatisfied with her answer. "He *is* important to me. It's hard to find good friends. Do you know what artists and musicians tend to be? Huge flakes. They forget about plans or they break plans at the last second without a thought. I'm an only child, I was a latchkey kid.

I've always had a lot of friends, but very few I could actually count on to be there when it mattered, but he's like having a very grumpy, slightly feral, always reliable brother. I'm just . . . annoyed by the situation. Whatever. It's none of my business, in any case."

She still had no idea what *situation* he referred to, but decided changing the subject might be best.

"I'm glad we went tonight," she murmured, running her palm down his chest, following the trail of dark hair that led to the anaconda she knew lurked beneath the sheets. "I don't think I would ever want to go back again, but the only way to find out if we're into something or not is to try it, right? I don't think we should be kink shamed for not liking something we tried. I do like watching us in the mirror. And if that Sylvan had given us his phone number, I wouldn't say I might not want to call him.

"I might want to call that fox girl. She had an excellent grip."

Ris huffed against his chest, but his words sparked something else that had been floating in her mind. "So . . . what are we, exactly? We're both okay with seeing other people, and that's fine. I don't think I want to change that. But . . . I don't know, it's almost dishonest going out with other guys when I'm half thinking about you."

"What have *you* been calling us?"

She shrugged, smiling. "Friend with benefits?"

He chuckled, a deep rumble against the hand she had over his stomach. He had been cupping her mound as they spoke, a thick finger gently sliding against her cleft, occasionally slipping into her wetness and circling over her clit, before returning to stroke back and forth. "Is that all we are, Nanaya? Friends who fuck?"

An entire kaleidoscope of butterflies took wing in her chest. She didn't want things to change, not really, but he was more than a friend and it felt silly to deny that. "Well . . . I think that's how we started out. I'm not sure if that works anymore though. I don't want anything to change between us, but I just feel like . . ."

"No, you're right. It's dishonest." He thought for a long moment. "We are . . . poly adventurous?"

"A poly adventurous couple?"

"Is that what *you* want?"

"I don't want a boyfriend," she blurted, neck heating. "I don't like the implications of that, and I know that probably sounds really fucking stupid, but I don't want to be responsible for someone else's happiness. I don't want kids, I don't want this big commitment. I like what we have right now, right this minute . . . but I don't know what to call it."

"What does that even mean anyway? 'A girlfriend. A boyfriend.' Who gives a fuck? You can call me your watermelon king, for all I care. Those are just titles for everyone else, right?"

"Yeah," she laughed. "I guess you're right. *I* think of us as a couple. Do you?"

"Oh, we're definitely a couple. If you tell me we're not, it's going to break my heart. Tate will call to yell at *you*, and then he'll be very smug and superior and I honestly can*not* deal with that, so please don't do it to me. An uncommitted, poly adventurous couple."

"That sounds good to me," she whispered against his neck, sucking the pulse points that jumped in his throat. "Are you still horny?" she asked pointedly, as his finger continued to stoke against her.

"Yup. I am, a little. My cock wants to play, but my balls are *very* upset with me, this was not the night to play with the ring. How about you sit on my face and we'll see where things go from there."

"What if I break your tusks?"

He threw back the sheet and blanket that covered them, pulling down the pillow to lie flat against it, giving his cock a few quick tugs. "You seem to forget, Nanaya. I'm a white collar professional. I have excellent dental insurance. If I break a tusk licking your pussy, honestly there's no better way for it to go."

She couldn't argue with that logic, she decided, swinging her leg over his face, sighing in pleasure as she settled her cunt over his open mouth. He hummed against her clit, tongue stroking into her, back and forth until he sucked, with just the right amount of pressure for pleasure to shiver down her spine.

"Mmmmmm . . . this is all I'll ever need again."

She rocked her hips slowly, her head rolling back as he licked her, not holding back her sighs of pleasure every time he suckled on her clit. Stretching her arms, she tugged on the silver spikes through his niples, grinning as he grunted. She would have been satisfied to continue on that way indefinitely, until he gripped her hips urgently.

"I want you to ride my face, then I want you to ride my cock the same way. Then I went to sleep for about a hundred years. Game plan?"

His voice was muffled against her skin, comical when she considered what it was muffled against. A quick glance back showed her his straining cock, flush against his belly, having decided it *did*, in fact, want to play. She'd not planned on winding up coupled, hadn't planned on meeting someone like him at all. She wondered if maybe that was why it happened, because she hadn't actually been looking, not for him.

"Mmmm, game plan," she agreed, gripping his headboard for leverage to give him a ride worthy of the evening's end.

Lurielle

"**Y**ou are just the tiniest little thing I have ever seen! Like a little doll! Khash, do you put her up on a shelf every night?" A chorus of laughter accompanied the question, not the first time she'd heard the sentiment expressed in the last twenty-four hours.

She didn't have any better answer now than she had the first time they'd called her tiny, but she forced a smile, hoping it didn't resemble a grimace. *Tiny! I wish I was recording this.* She wondered, for the umpteenth time since their arrival, if she had actually been permitted to pursue activities and extracurriculars she enjoyed growing up, if she'd actually had a social circle in which she'd fit in, and a group of friends who weren't merely a collection of other misfits, she might have an easier time socializing in a group today.

"I don't know about being put on a shelf, but he *does* have to help me put away the dishes. The house I live in was built for orcs and ogres, and I can't reach anything. I have a whole bunch of step stools all through the house."

Both of his sisters laughed at the image, and she pressed her lips into a smile, understanding his assertion that the big party would be easier. Amongst his siblings, she felt like a bug under a slide: something tiny and strange to be examined. She had never before in her life looked forward to a party as much as she looked forward to the one that would take place the following evening, when food and drink and music and a crowd would take the pressure off of her, leaving her free to escape her microscope prison.

"Why in Va'ghar's name are you living in a house built for orcs and ogres?" his brother Kesst asked with a furrowed brow. He was the one who had taken Ordo hunting, that first week after they'd met. She'd used the knowledge to create a conversational touchpoint, relieved when Kesst unwittingly followed along with her plan, laughingly complaining about the lazy mastiff, giving them all a play-by-play of his lack of hunting prowess through the weekend, much to everyone's amusement, and eating up nearly thirty minutes of the evening, to her relief.

"It was the only thing available in my price range when I moved," she exclaimed with a smile. "The property market in my town is fierce. There's a lot of competition for very few houses, and the prices tend to reflect that."

"So you don't live in the city, Lurielle?" His sister Khel leaned in.

She was the second born, the second of his three sisters, and she was, Lurielle had noticed, the instigator of most of the snide comments about her brother. "You're not a city slicker like Khash?"

Her smile was careful, spotting the obviously loaded question with ease. Elvish society had prepared her well for bitchiness, she reflected, a small wonder. *Years of torment, but at least it was good for something.* "I don't, because that's not where my job is. I live in an inner-ring suburb, it butts right up against Bridgeton. I love the city, though. There's more to do on one block than there was in the entire town I grew up in." That wasn't remotely true, but the lie tripped off her tongue easily enough. She preferred the small-town feel of Cambric Creek; loved the quaintness of the town and the farm festivals and community fairs that didn't exist in Bridgeton, but she wasn't about to admit that to his sisters. "There are three different restaurants on his block alone that I think we spend more time in than his kitchen. So I guess you can say I'm city slicker-adjacent?"

"I suppose that's not surprising to hear. He never was one for simple home cooking."

There was a pit of fire in her belly, and with every small barb his sister lobed, it bubbled. At her sides, her fists balled, nails digging in. Not the direction she'd wanted to lead the conversation, but she supposed his sister Khel would have a retort for everything.

"I want to hear more about these houses built for specific species," his brother continued, not taking his older sister's bait, Lurielle was relieved to hear.

"Cambric Creek is a multi-species community," Khash explained, coming up behind her to sit at the back of the sofa, dropping a huge hand to her back. "Very few humans."

"We don't have any humans here," Khel shot back. "The centaur ranch in Aberdeen doesn't have any humans. Lots of places don't have humans, doesn't make 'em special."

Wow. Wowwowwow. She was going to have *so much* to rehash with Ris and Silva when she got back from her trip. For the space of several heartbeats, Khash said nothing, but she was nearly able to hear his teeth grinding in aggravation, could envision the hard look he sometimes had without needing to turn back.

"Well, I don't think anyone claimed anything about one place being more special than another, and like I said, it's a *multi*-species community. The centaur ranch in Aberdeen doesn't have any ogres living there. Last time I checked — and before you feel the need to point it out, Khel, I know it's been a while — but the clan here doesn't have too many elves. Or minotaurs. Or goblins, or satyrs, or trolls. I think there's at least one each of them on her street. Am I miscountin', darlin'?"

She turned her head up, giving him a smile, feeling it tighten as she faced the room again. "No, I don't think you are." His brother leaned in, eyebrows raising in interest. "My neighbor is a minotaur, he's great. We've been good friends since I moved in. Goblins across the street, the kids grew up together, and actually, I think the teenagers are dating now. There's a valko, she's a local business owner, a moth couple on the corner, Trolls down the block . . . it's a happening development."

Kesst whistled appreciatively. "And all them folks have houses specially designed for their species?"

"Not quite," she explained. "There are special build frames. Ogres, orcs, minotaurs — bigger species with the same sort of sizing needs, they'll all have the same build. The smaller tract is designed for goblins, elves, satyrs — again, all similar sizing requirements. I need the smaller tract, but the bigger one was all that was available when I moved in."

"Kesst, you should see some of these houses," Khash went on, his voice back to its normal warm honeyed tone for his brother. "They have generalized builds, but you can get anything, *anything* added on. Specialized flooring for hooves, accessible showers, the depth of counter and cabinets, sandpits in the front yard, water features for the amphibian folk. It would blow your mind."

His brother grinned hugely, looking so much like Khash that she felt her mouth respond automatically, splitting into a genuine Lurielle smile. "I hope to see it someday. Guess I'll have to come up for a visit."

"You need to," she heard herself saying cheerfully. "We'd love to have you visit. Any of you. All of you!" she added, stabbing herself in the arm with a nail, in an effort to get herself to stop talking before she had given up her house for the week. *Shut up, shut up, shut up! You spent your teenage years hiding behind all your classmates with your nose in a book, and now you want to be the fucking holiday hostess?!*

"How do you raise kids in a place like that?" another sister piped up. "No clan . . . how are they supposed to learn anything about who they are?"

She turned in slow motion towards the sister who had spoken, Keely, the sister right before him in the birth order. Even though she had a brother, a highly uncommon thing for an elf, owing to the fact that one did not have to scratch very deeply on her family tree to find a human, Lurielle still felt as though she'd grown up as an only child. She and her brother had never been particularly close, although she was able to realize now, as an adult, that he had likely felt the strain of their household just as much as she had, escaping after university, moving to the other side of the country and not looking back. Even so, she didn't truly understand sibling hierarchies.

Before arriving, she would have guessed that Khash's eldest sister would have been the one to give him the most grief, rather than it being the middle two. Instead, his eldest sister Kharna had been warm and friendly, setting her at ease when they'd arrived. It was her roof they were staying under, as all four of her own children were out of the house on their own, one having a small child of her own, leaving the house empty, save for her and her husband, a hulking giant of an orc she'd not heard utter more than three words since their arrival, only knowing that Khash liked him enormously. She had not yet met his other brother or youngest sister, but from the way he spoke of them, she knew she didn't have anything to worry about. The source of his familial frustration was before them — Khel, and to a slightly lesser degree, the sister he was closest to in age, Keely.

She felt the press of his thick fingers at her shoulder, digging in with a near uncomfortable pressure, but she did not flinch away. She may have been half the size of every other individual in the room, was dwarfed by these orcs in size and strength, and she was certain some of them probably had tempers . . . but none of *them* had walked away from their families, from their communities. None of them knew the freedom that came from not needing to give a fuck about what anyone else thought, and the strength born from that freedom. She may have been plagued with insecurities, had carried the voice of her douchebag ex and harridan mother in her head for years, letting them chip away at her self-esteem, but when it had mattered, she reminded herself, she had picked up and walked away. Ended her bad relationship and went no contact with her toxic mother. Packed her belongings and moved away from everything and everyone she knew, and started her life over again. She may have still struggled with the voices in her head and the body she saw staring back at her in the mirror, Lurielle thought, the protective lava bubbling in her chest, but after a lifetime of being told what to do and how to look and what to think, her field of fucks to give was barren.

She would be *his* rock this weekend. Not a role she thought she'd be playing, but a partnership meant give and take. She wasn't as proficient in sunny, supercilious smiles as Silva; didn't possess her younger friend's ease at serving up a backhanded compliments to people who were rude or crass, but she had spent most of her life in the same clubs Silva had learned her trade, and had watched her own mother and grandmother in action long enough to be able to hold her own if she had to.

"I can't think of a better environment to raise children in, actually." She fisted the material of her dress, but her smile held firm. *Be Silva.* "Everyone is welcoming and friendly. The folks who run the town don't care where you've come from, only that you're a good neighbor. I haven't been made to feel out of place a single moment since I've lived *there.*" Her voice hung in the center of the room with no opposition until Khash continued a beat later.

"It's a *great* place to raise a family." She could hear the hard smile in his voice again. It was the same smile he reserved for Tate, on the nights she insisted he behave well enough to survive an evening sitting across from Silva's spiky fae boyfriend. She put up with his moaning and groaning every time she announced they would be meeting Silva and Tate for drinks or dessert in the resort's bustling little business district, but she'd never expected to hear that same edge in his voice here, in his beloved and lauded hometown. "It's a family town, and the schools are a big draw. Strong academics, highly inclusive. That's important to us."

"I guess that would have to be important. For you."

It was the first acknowledgment that she was an elf — more importantly, that she was not an orc — and even though she had come here expecting it to be thrown in her face at every turn, Lurielle couldn't deny that the barb stung. She felt Khash draw himself up at

248

her side, but his rebuttal never drew breath. His eldest sister crossed through the room, bustling from end table to end table without raising her head, collecting empty glasses.

"For pity's sake, Khel. You're acting like you've never left the state. Different places are different, how shocking. Just because we're from the south doesn't mean you need to act like a bumpkin just because you have an audience. Lurielle, are you sure I can't get you anything? I don't want you to go wastin' away on us while you're here, suge."

The front door opened as she declined with a smile, his mother and grandmother arriving, accompanied by his two youngest siblings, and the sharp words spoken by his elder sisters were put aside, for the time.

"There's my boy," the old orc crooned, her arms outstretched. He was already on his feet, having stood the moment they heard the door open, and as she watched him being folded in his grandmother's arms, Lurielle understood he'd not been just his grandfather's favorite. His mother was next, both women cooing and simpering, his smile big and open, and more genuine than anything she'd seen on his face since their arrival.

His sisters were jealous, she understood. Understood, because she had spent so many years of her life being jealous of her peers, and to add insult to injury, he had left. They were here to be judged every day, to have their life choices placed under the microscope of their family and clan, their bobbles and mistakes put on display by those closest to them, while he was far away, living his best life in

Bridgeton, wearing expensive suits and eating pricey dinners. None of them needed to see when he was stressed at work or when they had minor arguments at home, none of them were privy to his bad habits and vices. It was easy to maintain his sheen as the golden boy from a distance, his fluffy black sheep wool hidden beneath his tailored suits and buffed nails and genial smile.

"Well, well. Here she is. Like a lovely little flower. Come here, sugar, let an old granny see you proper." She felt the slide of his grandmother's eyes down her figure, appraising her the same way she'd been appraised her whole life, her breath catching, waiting to be told she was too much, took up too much space, was lesser as a result. "Hmm, tiny, tiny thing. You've got some nice hips on you, though. That's good, that's important. Can't carry a strong orc son built like a little twig, he'd tear you in two, but I'll bet you know that already. You'll have to keep your milk up, an orc is going to need to nurse a lot more than one of your little elf babies, but you've got a headstart there. Lovely, just lovely. Khash, you picked the prettiest flower in the field. Can't say I expected anything less."

His grandmother's face crinkled with her smile, lines upon lines in her dark green skin, one for every year she'd been mothering this giant clan, Lurielle thought. She let out the breath she'd not realized she'd been holding, attempting to hold onto her composure, even though her cheeks had warmed, the spreading heat a sign of tears soon to follow.

"I'm very glad to meet you, Buna. I've heard so many stories about you and his granddaddy that I feel like I've known you for years." She could count the gaps in his grandmother's somewhat gummy smile, so very different from her own elder matrons of her species, one more difference between them. She was somewhat stooped, and Lurielle had a feeling she had been shrinking as the years passed, but the old orc was still significantly taller than her. She wondered if she would be the smallest individual in the room the entire weekend, or if perhaps there might be some orc children around her size who she could look in the eye.

"Oh, I don't doubt that. Khash and his granddaddy were thick as thieves. I know he'd be pleased as punch to see you here, celebrating with all of us."

She was unable to push the tears down as her face was cupped in his grandmother's gnarled hands, feeling the heat of her cheeks, at her nose, the pricking at her eyes. She could already tell she would probably never like his two combative sisters, would do her best to get along with the eldest and her family, hoped his parents were as warm and accepting as his grandmother, but she thought, as Kash's giant hand landed at the small of her back just as his grandmother leaned down to kiss her forehead, that she might survive the weekend yet.

♥ ♥ ♥

She decided, once they were pulling up the dark dirt road, surrounded by black trees and nothing else, that giant parties are the only ones she would be willing to attend in the future.

"This is terrifying. Where are you taking me again? This wasn't in the notes and I don't feel prepared. You *do* understand I'm not built for the wilderness, right?"

"Lurielle, hush. I think when we get home, I'm going to put in for some time off this spring. We're going camping, and you're going to love it."

"I have no doubt I will, but this doesn't feel like we're going camping, Khash. This feels like you're either taking me to a pre-dug grave in the woods, or we're going to impose on a woods witch, and I am surprisingly not okay with either scenario."

"I have something more productive you could be doing with that smart mouth, other than running it." One of his huge hands left the steering wheel, gripping her wrist until she was palming the thick bulge at the front of his pants, already thickened and firm. "Now you wanna keep talking? Or do you want to put those pretty little lips to use?"

She laughed, scraping her nails over the shape of him, tracing the shape of his cock. It was pressed against his thigh, and the tight constriction of his pants seemed to her like it would be an enormous discomfort, wondering, not for the first time, how he even managed to get through his days with it always swinging around in the way. At that moment, they rumbled over a root, the carriage of the huge vehicle rocking, and he chuckled.

"On second thought, keep those teeth away from me just yet.

Hold tight, darlin'. We're almost there."

The whole clan had been a noisy, rowdy bunch, and it had been easy to feel invisible amidst the press of huge bodies around the massive fire in the center of the gathering grounds. Lurielle realized, shortly after arriving, that it was not actually a party for her and that she was not the main event. This was a fête thrown for Khash and Khash alone, and she was merely an accessory, ancillary to the events. She had a feeling other elves might have felt miffed over the turn of events, but she was not other elves and all she felt, standing invisible beside the beverage table, was a relief.

The evening proved to be illuminating. If she had hoped she already knew everything there was to know about the orc she loved, she might've been disappointed. Although, if she were being perfectly honest, Lurielle thought she could have guessed most of the facts she learned. He had been a sports star in his youth, playing on the clan's Grumsh'vargh and Ketterling teams, winning trophies and championships and all manner of young adult accolades which she had never achieved. "We would be covered in mud from nose to toes, every day," chuckled one of his childhood best friends, a fern-skinned orc with silver and copper bands stacked on his tusks. "I coach at the school now, and I tell my students about all the shenanigans we got up to every year."

"Smart as a whip," she was told by a brightly smiling orc woman with a waterfall of salt-and-pepper curls cascading down her back who had been his academic advisor in school. She learned that the clan had its own school right there, one of the buildings that created the landscape of their gathering grounds. "I've only had a handful of students in my entire career as smart and ambitious as our Khash," she beamed, and Lurielle had sipped her spiked punch, nodding like a field reporter, filing away every story and anecdote she picked up.

"He was meant to take me to the midsummer formal," griped an orc woman with a dozen piercings on each of her pointed ears, her full breasts barely contained by the low-cut tank she wore. "Canceled two weeks before. I had already bought my promenading shoes and everything."

"Midsummer formal is the last dance before oath swearin'," another woman at her elbow explained cheerfully. They were eating thick slices of a decadent cake, a white sponge filled with layers of crushed pineapple and banana, mixed with chopped nuts and whipped cream.

"It's the easiest recipe, suge, I'll be sure to write it down for you. This is always the one I try to win at the elder's cake throw," another orc woman had interjected when Lurielle's eyes fluttered closed as she took a large bite of the cake. "Bitty little thing like you, you could probably stand to eat a few of 'em."

"Midsummer formal is the last dance before oath swearing," the second orc repeated, shooting a look at the one who'd interrupted her about the cake. "Oath swearing is sort of like our cotillion. You elves have cotillions, right?"

"We have something like that, yes," she answered, hoping her smile was cheery enough to prevent any further questions and that she didn't have any of the shredded coconut from the cake's toppings stuck in her teeth.

"Well, it's our last dance before the big event, so it's pretty significant."

"And he canceled on me two weeks before. Who am I going to find two weeks before the dance?!"

"Melka, are you still goin' on about that? We were seventeen, you plannin' on holding it against me forever? It's not my fault I got asked by someone else." The women all groaned at his words as he materialized behind her, his massive hands spanning her not-at-all bitty waist, telling him off simultaneously in a raucous outburst of voices. He just laughed, stealing a sizable chunk of her cake from the plate.

"Hey, that's mine! Now you have to go get me another piece. And you'd better not take a bite first!" He'd bent with a chuckle, kissing the tip of her pug nose before heading off in the direction of the dessert table. When she turned back to the group, it was to find two of the orc women grinning at her, one being the possessor of the delicious cake recipe, while the other two had looked away, scowling.

He had been a clan heartthrob, sports star, an academic whiz. Everyone liked him, it seemed. More than one of the elders, whom she had been able to greet by name, thanks to the notes she'd studied on the plane, went out of their way to let her know that he was an orc of upstanding character, generous and honorable, a credit to their clan's name. He was handsome and smart and popular, all things she already knew, but the underlying conclusion to every errant conversation she listened in on and took part in, from every clan member she'd spoken with was surprise — and perhaps some small measure of disappointment — that he had left.

He had left, and not come back. Left and not come back, and was now visiting with an elf, the antithesis of all they were.

"Always thought our sons would grow up playing together," his childhood friend chuckled wistfully. "Guess that's not going to happen now."

"He had a full ride to school, did he tell you that? We were all so proud. I never would've imagined he wouldn't come home afterward. I used to tell him when he was in my class that someday he'd be doin' my taxes. Well . . . I hope he's happy with the work he's doing in the city."

"I guess we shouldn't be surprised that he found some pretty little elf. Since he couldn't even follow through on taking me to a dance."

She felt flummoxed as she moved from conversation to conversation, attempting to keep up her smile. She'd spotted his two sisters several times throughout the night, engaged in conversation with tight, pinched faces, their mouths moving quickly, and she hadn't needed to guess what the topic of their fire was. When she finally made it around to a cluster where his eldest sister stood, she gave Lurielle that same big, warm smile that she had when they'd arrived.

"He's making his case to the elders now," she'd murmured, nodding to where Khash was, far beyond the ring of partygoers, sitting on a folding chair before a line of old orcs who all looked to be at least in their 80s. The bonfire's warm orange glow cast him in its halo, making his thick black braid gleam. Even from the distance, and with all these people between them, he was the most handsome man she'd ever seen, regardless of species. His striking profile was outlined in the flames — the broad slope of his features, straight nose and square jaw, ending at his dimpled chin.

She understood his words now, the ones he'd uttered to her that night when she'd had her little break down in the kitchen. These were his people. He loved and revered them, and they did the same in reverse . . . and each of them seemed to resent him, just a little bit. He'd left and not come home, left his clan behind, his traditions behind, and it seemed, to her at least, that they held just a smidgen of a grudge.

She wondered if she'd been lucky, not really fitting in growing up. None of her adolescent peers would look to her today and expect her to be anything other than shy, chubby, bumbling Lurielle. She didn't have the weight of *their* expectations to live up to, other than the expectations every elf had, and she had fled the expectations of her family. Khash was handsome and smart and seemed to have the whole world in his hands, but he'd not done exactly what was expected of him by his community, and even though it had been years since he left, they all seemed to treat the wound as fresh. She was glad they'd come, glad she'd gotten to see a slightly less perfect version of the home he had described her so many times, glad that she would be leaving with a bit of insight on his family's particular dynamic, but she was mostly glad that the weekend was almost over. She still didn't like parties, and more than anything, she wanted to protect him from the passive-aggressive disappointment that seemed to color his interactions with everyone from his clan.

Everyone, that was, except for the elders. "What do you mean, making his case?" She watched as several of the old orcs threw their heads back in laughter at whatever it was he said. Whatever the case he was making, she knew him well enough to know it would come with a healthy side of conversation. She disliked small talk, but small talk was Khash's favorite sport, and he loved nothing better than shooting the breeze with a willing opponent.

"Any oath sworn before the fire needs to be approved by the elders first. There's no walkin' back on it, once it's done."

Lurielle shivered. She wasn't sure what he was asking them, what oath he was contemplating making before the flames of his clan, but she had an idea. Her stomach flip-flopped at the thought, understanding the meaning immediately, for it could mean nothing else. She knew her friends probably thought they were moving too fast, but there was no stopping the trajectory of their relationship, she thought. Them being together seemed to be an indisputable certainty, from the moment she had said yes that night on the sidewalk, that she did, in fact, want to see him again. *Life in the real world.*

Now they were pulling up this dark, dirt road, parking before an equally black cabin. She couldn't help but think it looked a bit derelict, illuminated in the headlights of the rental truck, and she wasn't sure if this was actually an improvement over spending another night at his sister's house. After all, she liked his eldest sister and her house was comfortable, if not a bit outsized for her. Khash had been insistent. He wanted to spend the night on their own, out from everyone's thumb, as he'd said. She'd refrained from pointing out that they would be flying home the following afternoon, where he was as far away from any thumb belonging to his clan as he could be.

"Bluebell, it's not healthy for a man to let the plumbing get backed up this long. A bad humor, I think that's what they called it in the dark ages. And the cure was draining it."

"The cure was draining your blood!" she exclaimed, laughing in outrage, "with leeches, not a blow job!"

"They obviously had the translation wrong, but they had the spirit." His smile was wolfish as he leaned forward, nipping at her lips. "You sit tight, let me make sure I don't have to chase a bear out of our bed."

The cabin belonged to him and his brothers, part of their inheritance from his beloved grandfather. Deep in the woods, set on a glimmering lake, she thought it would be beautiful in the daytime. As it was, she tucked her knees up a little tighter as he left her alone in the truck, surrounded by the black woods. There could be anything out there, she thought. *Maybe even a Bigfoot.* Rationally, she knew there was no such thing, but there were always people who claimed to have seen one while camping deep in the forest range off the Applethorpe Wood. Fortunately, he came back to the truck just a few moments later, no bear in tow, before she had a chance to be molested by anything lurking in the dark trees.

"Good news, our bed is empty. We've got some work to do in it, so let's get a move on there. This bad humor isn't going to drain itself."

The cabin clearly didn't have electricity, but he had lit two oil-burning lanterns, and their flickering flames left shadows across the bedroom as he carried her through the front door, past the small sitting area, and into the single bedroom. She couldn't see any of the amenities the room might've possessed, other than the orc-sized bed in the center of it, which was his only aim.

"It's been a very long day," she pointed out, scratching her nails down his chest. "You had to be *on* for an awfully long time. Aren't you tired? Because I'm fucking exhausted."

"Darlin', you have no idea. I want to sleep for a month. I hope you packed a book to read on the plane tomorrow, because I'm not going to be a conversationalist. I packed my spa mask and my neck massager, your only job on the flight is to make sure I don't snore so loudly it grounds the plane." She laughed against his chest as he tugged on the hem of her dress, huffing when he realized it needed to be unzipped before he could pull it over her head, groaning to find her shapewear beneath. He'd become adept at stripping her from the binding tube, gripping the bottom hem and pulling it straight up her body and over her head. "They all loved you, Lurielle."

It was wintertime, and even though they were in the deep South, the night still had a sharp chill in the air, and she shivered, laughing against his chest at his words. "I'm pretty sure that's not entirely true, but I love you for lying about it." His mouth found hers, despite the darkness, hungry and insistent. "You sure you don't want to just go to bed?"

"Bluebell, that's all I want to do. But watching you all night long in your frilly little dress, making small talk and smilin' like it's your favorite thing on earth was too much. You've got my balls aching. At one point, you were talking to one of the elders and you laughed that little cupcake giggle, and I thought I was going to make a mess in my pants, right there in front of everybody. And it would've been worth it."

"Just watching me almost made you cum in your pants? You're acting like you're on a seven-year dry spell and not three days."

"Three days have felt like thirty, and you're still doing an awful lot of talking for someone who doesn't like socializing. Are you going to let this squirrel bury his nut, or are you going to stand there jabberin' all night?"

She threw up her hands, her whole body shaking in laughter. "Here we go again! In two seconds you're going to be calling him a dragon again. You're the one who still has your pants on. What about you come over here, and get on the bed, and stop shooting orders. Let's get those pants off before you make a mess and have to drive home in it."

She made quick work of his clothes until he was there before her on the bed, his cock already straining and heavy, swollen with arousal. She shook out her chiffon dress, the snug inner lining helping to hold all of her wobbly bits in place, laying it over the back of the single chair in the room, finding his trousers and doing the same. Removing his leather belt from the straps, she had a wicked idea. It was a relief to unclasp the back of her dressy bra, the scalloped straps having dug into her shoulders as the night wore on, and she sighed when her heavy breasts swung free, nipples tightening in the cold air. She wouldn't be cold for long, she knew, for his molten body heat would be more than enough to warm her throughout the night. But for now, the effect of the cold air worked in favor of her plan.

"I think I want to have you up on your knees first. You let me get stuck talking to all your old girlfriends, *and* you stole my cake."

"Bluebell . . ." His voice was lost in the crack of the belt as she snapped leather back on itself. She had never used anything other than her little leather crop at home, and experimenting with a new toy in a pitch-black cabin with no electricity or first aid amenities was probably not the best idea, she would likely admit come morning, but just then she didn't quite care. "You better get on your knees for me so I can put a lil' love bruise on that big ole' biscuit."

The first crack of the leather against him made him jolt, and she thrilled in excitement. She wasn't smacking him hard enough to actually bruise his skin, she wasn't sure if she was even smacking him hard for it to even sting, but the fantasy that she was doing so was enough. The flickering light from the lantern cast the full globes of his in a perfect halo. She pulled his ankles apart, forcing him to spread his knees, the shadow of his heavy scrotum swinging beneath. One crack, two cracks against his skin. On the third, he grunted, as she used a tiny bit more force. On the fifth, he groaned, as the leather caught against his testicles. That was the circuit she kept up for several cycles more — a sharp slap against each cheek of his big biscuits, landing the belt on his balls on the fifth. His hips had begun to thrust against nothing at all, if he were rutting into thin air, and she knew he wasn't going to last long once she was beneath him. He probably wouldn't have lasted long even before she started this little game, but now there was no question.

Finally, she tossed the belt onto the back of the chair with the rest of their clothes, running her hands over each full cheek, cupping his sac gently, and rolling. "You ready to let loose, baby? We've got to help this Dragon drain his bad humors so that a squirrel can bury his nut, or something like that." She cackled in laughter when he snatched her around the waist, swinging her onto the bed with a bounce.

"Lurielle, you and your big ole' panties are going to drive a man to the brink. Bring that sweet pussy over here and let me take a taste before I plug her up."

The first stroke of his hot tongue happened over the mesh of her full-coverage panties, zeroing in on her clit through the fabric. He lapped against her, the wetness from his mouth seeping into the fabric, joining the slick moisture she was producing until the front was a sloppy, soggy mess. It would've been easy for him to pull them aside to suck her properly, but instead, he doubled down, stretching her legs open and pushing her knees back to the mattress, tilting her pelvis up to his mouth as he sucked on her clit through the rough mesh.

"I thought you wanted to take a taste," she panted, wanting to feel his tongue sliding over her with the suction of his lips directly on her skin.

"Oh, I see the way it is. Teasing is fine when you're the one doing it."

He kept up the onslaught through the mesh for several minutes more, hooking his thumbs beneath the waistband and yanking the not insignificantly sized bit of fabric down her hips, pitching them over his shoulder as he attacked her cunt unfettered.

"I want this sweet little honeypot to spill all over my mouth, you understand, Bluebell? Then she's gonna lay back and let me feed her my cock. How does that sound?"

"She's starving," she wheezed, her body arching every time he sucked on her clit in just the right way. "She wants you to shut up and let your tongue do its job so she can eat."

His laughter was a vibration against her, punctuating with a long wide stroke of his tongue, and then he was off. She briefly entertained the thought of stopping him, because she liked to come with him inside of her; like the way her muscles tightened and clenched around him, knew he enjoyed it too, but decided to let him stick to his plan. He was too far gone, and once he climbed on top of her, she wanted him to be able to focus on his own pleasure. His mouth was wide, and his lips were able to pucker around her aching pearl and suck while keeping up the movement of his tongue around it. She'd not started off their arrival at the cabin as horny as he was, but that didn't keep her from quickly falling apart under his ministrations. When she came against his tongue, Lurielle briefly worried that she might crack his skull like a watermelon between her thighs, she squeezed him so hard, her back lifting from the bed.

"That's it, darlin'. Gimme all that honey." When he rose up on his knees, she could tell he wasn't exaggerating about possibly making a mess in his pants. His cock was rock solid, thick veins popped from root to tip. His sac looked especially swollen, enhanced by the paddling she'd given it, and she knew he'd likely not last long at all. Climbing over her, he wasted no time settling between her open thighs, sinking into her heat on the first slow thrust, groaning as he did so, not stopping until the swell of his balls kissed the curve of her ass. "It doesn't make a difference where in the world I am, Bluebell. This is what comin' home is."

She was glad they'd come, she decided, clinging to his back as he began to thump into her with deep, solid thrusts. She understood him a bit better. She understood the dynamic of this place where he was from, understood that he lived with his own heavy expectations and that he too had managed to escape them, even if he didn't quite admit that to himself all time. She thought perhaps that the reason tradition was so important to him was because he felt so removed from it. *And maybe he's just a teensy bit guilty too.* It was ridiculous for them to already be talking about marriage and babies and where they would raise their family when they hadn't even reached their one-year anniversary, ridiculous and stupid and they should probably tap the brakes. But marriage and babies and a family was what he wanted, what she wanted when she thought of her future with him, and as he groaned above her, his hips pressing tightly to her in half a dozen long deep pulses, filling her to the brim, she saw no reason to change anything. They were happy, they were moving in the right direction, and she wanted to give him everything he wanted, which was what she wanted as well, as long as he was at her side. *Life in the real world.*

Silva

Silva checked her lipstick in the car's rearview mirror and took a deep breath, attempting to calm her rapid pulse. *It's fine. It's no big deal and it'll be fine . . . just calm down.* The valet stand was just ahead, car doors opening for sylph-like women in short dresses, dryads and selkies. Just two more cars and then she'd be walking in. She tried to listen to her inner voice, tried to heed its wise words . . . but it was wrong. It was wrong, because it *was* a big deal. It was the first time she'd be meeting her boyfriend's friends, the first time he'd ever invited her to do so, the first time he was *acknowledging* her in the wider world. It was a *huge* deal.

Not your boyfriend, she corrected. That wasn't the kind of mistake she could afford to be making, not tonight. She didn't know what was an acceptable title to call him was, but she'd never once heard him refer to her as his girlfriend. He'd not called her his sweetheart, his paramour, his significant other, nor any of the dozen different words in Elvish and various commons he *could* have called her but hadn't, and therefore he was not, as the unhelpful little voice in her head so often reminded her, her boyfriend.

She didn't know how he would introduce her to these mystery friends, and she didn't want to admit how worried she was over that moment, over what he would call her as aloof eyes flicked in her direction, silently judging. Tate's friends would be as effortlessly cool as he was, she was sure of it — detached and smirking, graceful and poised. Growing up in the country club world of Elvish society meant she was well versed in haughtiness and icy smiles, and Silva was confident she'd be able to hold her own with these people . . . provided she made it past those fraught introductions.

If she was labeled as *my friend Silva*, she would start to cry.

She knew herself well enough to recognize that her disappointment and despair would mix and bubble and overflow, as if her emotions were some ill-fated science experiment; that she'd have a short window in which to push away from him, to escape to a restroom and have her breakdown in private, and that would be the end. No more carefree weekend nights spent at the Pixie, perched on a high stool while he tended bar on Rukh's night off, pressing her face to his strong back once the final patron staggered out the door at closing time, slipping her arms around him; no more waking up on Sunday mornings securely pressed against him, no more soft kisses in the grey morning light and lazy lovemaking, no more freedom and mischief and laughter. No coming back. *Stop it! You're not going to do that, it'll be fine. Just follow his lead.*

The valet gave her a bright smile as she stepped from the car with her heart in her mouth. A minotaur in a tight black shirt stood at the entrance, giving her an appraising once-over as she approached, opening the door before she could even mention that she was with a private party. *Here goes nothing . . . you can do this. It'll be fine.*

The club was low-lit and upscale, with ambient house music and a gleaming bar, populated with dozens of beautiful people. A group of men around a high table near the door, humans from the look of it, turned to watch as she passed, one making a comment too low for her to hear, earning a round of laughter from his fellows. Silva swallowed and pressed on.

She didn't often come to the city alone, and the number of humans here, particularly the men, all too bold and unwilling to acknowledge the notion of personal space, made her nervous.

They crowded the sidewalks, charging along with little heed to anyone else walking, expecting her to dive out of the way upon their approach, and stood too close on public transport. The very first time she'd come to Bridgeton on her own had been during a week-long holiday her second week of university, to illicitly obtain birth control far away from her grandmother's prying eyes, and the catcalls she endured on her walk back to the train nearly had her in tears, running to catch up with a dark-haired werewolf she recognized from Cambric Creek, trailing behind him as closely as she could without gaining his notice, finding a spot on in the train car within a few feet of him. He'd never paused in his phone conversation, but she'd felt safer in his presence, a slight shield from the humans teeming around them like piranhas. Not even the nudist orcs at the resort made her as nervous, and despite Tate's grumbling, she'd found most of *them* to be quite chivalrous once they had clothes on, during the weekends she spent at the Pixie. She edged past another cluster of human men at the front bar, weaving through the press of bodies as invisibly as possible.

She saw him immediately, once she cleared the narrow bottleneck of bodies in front of the bar near the doors, caught the glint of his cocky, crowded smile from across the room on an elevated platform with a dozen other people, as she slid through the crowd. Silva slowed as she neared, her breath catching at his appearance. Tate was slim and short for an orc, lean and strong and graceful like a ballet dancer, possessing none of the bulk of the patrons who crowded around him at the Pixie . . . but seeing him here, surrounded by goblins and nymphs and satyrs made his actual size stand out in a way she'd never really appreciated. There was an cyclops near the bottom of the steps whose height and bulk would surely match his, as well as the minotaur at the door and the assorted other larger species she saw scattered through the crowd, but the vast majority of the club-goers were much smaller in stature, emphasizing his height and broad shoulders. He would dwarf even the tallest elf at the club, she realized with a swallow. *That's going to make it a lot harder to fit in at tea.*

He saw her then, his eyes picking her out of the crowd as she approached the platform, crinkling with his smile. The dress she'd chosen for the night was far different from her normal wardrobe selection. Wine-colored and beaded, the illusion front on the plunging neckline showed off far more cleavage than she normally dared, the spaghetti straps left her arms bare, with a hemline that skimmed her thighs. It was a far cry from her preferred pastel-colored, softer habiliment — frilly, lacey, softly feminine styles that she knew he preferred as well, but she saw immediately it had been the right choice for this coolly sophisticated crowd. She wondered if he'd been shifting nervously, wondering if she'd show, or if he'd not even noticed her absence. Silva did not need to contemplate long to know which side of that equation she herself would have fallen on, but with Tate, it was impossible to tell.

VIP bottle service, she noted, stepping up to the raised platform where the party group was gathered. Silva swallowed her smile, knowing well his opinion of the service and the people who ordered it. There was a small chalkboard in the back hallway of the bistro, a contest for the staff to see who could convince the most orcs to order the exorbitantly expensive amenity, and he and the girls were maniacally competitive about it. As a porter lifted the velvet rope for her, she was unable to name the emotion she saw in Tate's honey-gold eyes, traveling up her legs slowly, but it didn't matter when he tugged her to his side with a firm hand on her hip. She had deduced he was able to alter the perception of his sharp teeth, and as she arrived at his side, the only remarkable thing about his mouth was his slender tusks, ringed in silver and seeming slightly longer than usual in the absence of his normal dagger-like smile.

"You look beautiful." Her cheeks warmed as he whispered in her ear, kissing her lightly before she turned to meet the raised eyebrow of the coffee-skinned djinn he'd been chatting with as she'd come up the stairs. The girl had thick, dark hair, twisted into a fat braid that skimmed her waist, and intricate golden henna around her eyes. She was lovely, Silva noted with a self-conscious gulp, as lovely as the cluster of purple-skinned elves — Silmë elves, like her — and the ivory-skinned Summerland elves with whom they stood. She disliked herself when she acted this way, but she couldn't prevent the traitorous little voice in her heart from wondering, as her eyes traveled over the group, taking in their long legs, graceful necks, and bouncing curls, how many of these beautiful women he'd slept with. She forced a bright smile as he turned, making quick introductions.

The cluster of elves were cousins of the birthday girl, a cool-eyed nymph with expensive-looking hair extensions and designer shoes. The girl looked Silva over with a critical eye as Tate motioned in turn to her boyfriend, a leonine-looking man who crouched at her side, a tiefling couple, two men with flicking, forked tongues, and a leering satyr whose collar was open two buttons too many. Her breath sputtered and stalled as Tate completed the circle of people, his long fingers once more spanning her hip. *Here it comes*, she thought. *My friend, Silva.* The beginning of the end. She thought the restrooms were probably down the hallway past the shiny, stainless steel bar at the back of the main room, and prepared herself to flee.

"This is my Silva," Tate said simply, squeezing her hip lightly. The cat-eyed man smiled with a nod, as did one or two of the elves as she sucked in a shuddering breath, feeling suddenly coltish, as though her legs might not support her for another moment. She melted into his strong side and tried not to appear as though she were going to pass out, as he casually resumed his conversation with the djinn. *His Silva.* Not his friend, not his girlfriend . . . simply his.

Silva fisted the material of his shirt, scratching at his lower back, wanting to wrap her arms and legs around him, to cling to him the way she did in his bed . . . *later,* she thought, straightening. His friends seemed as cool and reserved as she'd imagined they would be, and right now she needed to pull herself together. This wasn't a false skin she needed to wear, she reminded herself, a persona she needed to adopt . . . for all that she complained about her grandmother's control over her life, Nana had left her well-prepared to smile brightly, converse charmingly, and serve up back-handed compliments with the pros. As the nymph continued to scowl, clearly not ready to be friendly with this stranger at her party, Silva gave Tate's hand a final squeeze before releasing him to step away and offer her birthday wishes with a confident smile.

♥ ♥ ♥

If she'd left the house that evening with the assumption that this party would be illuminating, she would've been disappointed.

If she thought she would gain insight into Tate's friendships and social tendencies, perhaps a different facet of his smile, or a member of his inner circle with whom he was particularly close, she might have felt let down. The truth was, of course, she had been hoping for all of those things and more, so the sight of him slipping in and out of conversations like a darting snake, never staying in one spot for long, never revealing anything about himself or sharing with her anecdotes about his relationship with the guests around them left her feeling frustrated and more than just a bit annoyed. He didn't act any differently with this group of people who were his purported friends than he did with the strangers in his businesses. Silva had learned more about him watching his small interactions with his staff than she had in the past hour and a half, although she was still incredibly glad that he had invited her; that he had put his arm around her and called her *his* before these beautiful strangers, but an hour and a half in and she couldn't help but feel that *strangers* were all they were. Strangers to her and strangers to him. Or at least, *he* was the stranger, a notion that left her feeling even more discomfited.

There was something about the way the birthday girl looked at her, her eyes remaining narrowed every time they slid in her direction, her scowl never softening. It left Silva with the distinct impression that she was an unwanted plus one at this little soirée, but rather than react with the eye-crossing jealousy that was, unfortunately, becoming her default state when it came to him, she felt buoyed. He had a history with the woman, that she was certain. *And he brought you anyway!* Brought her and flaunted her at his side, called her his, making it very clear where she stood . . . At least, before this nymph and her other guests. All she needed now, Silva thought, was for him to let her in fully, tell her the contents of his heart and all his secrets, display this sort of steadfastness on a weekly basis and eventually, in front of her family. A small ask, she thought. The bare minimum, even.

Silva found herself sliding in and out of the conversations taking place around her as well, flitting from cluster to cluster, sparkling and charming these lovely strangers who were his friends. When her circuit around the platform brought her back to the cluster of nymphs where the birthday girl held court, she decided it would only be polite to attempt to join their conversation as well. She had spent her entire life cloistered in Elvish society — private clubs, private schools, gated communities and vacation resorts, a breeding ground for petty rivalries and a social hierarchy she had learned to navigate shortly after she'd learned to walk. She knew, immediately upon her approach, when the hushed voices of the whispering elves and nymphs went silent, that she was the topic of their conversation. There was a particular smile she had, broad and beatific, the one her father had always told her would get her anything she wanted, and she pulled it from her arsenal then. She had nothing to feel insecure about before these lovely, lithe strangers. She beamed at the group of them, and beyond where they were sitting, on the other side of the platform, she could see Tate. His dark brows drew together, a slight look of alarm as she approached the circle of nymphs and elves, and her smile stretched wider. He didn't have anything to worry about, for this was *her* world, and she could hold her own with ease.

"So how long have you known Tate?" One of the elves piped up after superficial pleasantries were exchanged, several of the girls giggling nervously and exchanging guarded looks.

"We've been together since the beginning of the summer," she simpered, tossing another smile in his direction, as if she couldn't bear to be parted from his side for more than a few moments. It wasn't a lie, she decided, as the girls exchanged looks. They had never talked over the nature of their relationship, had never had a serious conversation about where they were going and what they were or what the future might hold, but she'd done enough planning for the two of them. Tate had marked her skin and marked her heart that very first weekend. That was more than six months ago now, more than half a year, *more* than high time to assert herself as a fixture in his life. And what better place to start, Silva thought, than with this well-heeled group of his friends.

She continued to chat with the elves, embellishing her answers when necessary when their relationship was the topic, having no shortage of well-thought-out scenarios in which to bolster the truth. The birthday girl remained sullen and slit-eyed throughout, but Silva had decided she wasn't terribly important. Certainly not as important as the cluster of beautiful young women, each of them bearing the mark of professional gossips, none of them being from her own Elvish community, and the tales they took back to whatever social circles he moved in were far more important than this one nymph's personal feelings. Silva knew how to play this game, and she gave the girl her best smile again.

She continued to make her way around the platform, winding up back at his side at last. He gazed down archly, eyebrow raised, one corner of his mouth tugging into a smile.

"Making friends, dove?"

She hummed, grinning up at him. "I don't think I have any friends in that group, but that's okay. I don't get the impression the guest of honor likes me very much." The beautiful nymph was standing at the rail with her boyfriend, who bent nearly in half to speak in her ear. As Silva watched, the girl crossed her arms petulantly rolling her eyes and tossing her long extensions. "But it doesn't seem that she likes much of anything, to be honest. You slept with her, right?" She was proud of how casual she managed to sound, how thoroughly unaffected and confident she seemed. It was all a façade of course, but he didn't need to know that, not just then.

Tate chuckled. "Slept with both of them, actually. Before they were together, of course." She gasped, turning up to him with her mouth dropped open, dissolving into giggles at the sight of his sharp edged smile. "Her father is one of the biggest bottle distributors on the East Coast. I don't want to say that's the reason, because that doesn't make me sound very chivalrous . . . but I did manage to secure a very generous contract with him during our brief entanglement. I'm the one who introduced the two of them," he added. "I thought introducing her to Darvin was a good compromise on walking away."

"I think you're a bit of a rake," she accused primly, feeling a strange bubble of giddiness move through her. It was odd, this ease she felt, so unlike the gut churning jealousy that normally gripped her in all matters where he was concerned, but it was likely owed to the fact that it was evident to all that there was nothing between him and the birthday girl *or* her boyfriend. She thought she probably should have been appalled at the ease of his admission, but the knowledge only made her giggle again. After all, she had read enough books to know that even the most rakish rake could be reformed by the story's end. "You're an absolute cad."

His attention was caught then by a troll on the lower level who had paused at the base of the staircase leading up to the platform, his platinum white hair making his gray skin glow. The troll wore a lanyard identifying him as a part of the security staff. He and Tate seemed well-acquainted, and instantly began an animated conversation. They weren't speaking the common, she realized, leaving her out of being able to listen, but she took note of the way his smile brightened, his voice taking on a warmer tone, one that he hadn't possessed all evening., amongst these beautiful strangers. She wandered a few feet away, not wanting to hover at his side and impede his conversation, not when he actually seemed to *like* this troll. She stared out over the club's expansive main floor, long brightly lit bar at the back, the bottom level's dance floor visible from her vantage point.

It was then that she saw him. He was across the bar, standing at

278

one of the hightops that ringed the open mouth of the dancefloor, a level below. Silva recognized the back of his white-blonde head easily, having miserably stared at it from the corner of his mattress, where she'd been banished for the three months they'd been together.

That first weekend after she'd called Wynn to end things, before blocking his number, when she'd gone back to the little orc resort town with Lurielle and had stood in the middle of the dining room of the bistro with Tate, invisible to the patrons and employees that buzzed around them as he kissed her, she'd decided she would be quite happy to never see her ex again.

They'd left the bistro that day and walked through the little downtown, and she'd sat sideways across his lap on a bench overlooking the fast-moving creek that ran under the bridge.

"Did-did you think about . . . " She'd trailed off, blushing at her blurted question, but still wanting to know, *needing* to know if he'd thought about her at all during those three months. Three months of being miserable with someone else, all the while thinking of him, of being a different person, a freer version of herself at his side.

"I think about a lot of things, Silva," he'd interrupted her thoughts. "What will happen to the girls if it's a bad enough winter that I have to put them on unemployment?" he murmured, his fingers tracing circles over her knees. "Will Cym be able to feed her kids? Is Thessa going to be able to hold on without looking for a new job? I wonder how long we'll be able to get the dishwasher to hold out, or if today's the day she's going to groan her last groan and flood the back room.

I wonder if I'm going to need to fly home this year to check on my mother, or if I can put that off for another decade. I think about a lot of things, Silva, so you're going to need to be a bit more specific. I told you you'd always have somewhere to come, dove, and so you do. And so you're here. If you're concerned about the length of time since last we spoke and things that were done or undone in the interim, that's between you and your calendar."

Her ears heated, neck flushing purple, and she'd been worried her voice would betray how close to tears she was. "You didn't exactly make it easy to contact you, you know. You didn't even give me your number."

His head had cocked, his askance look and knowing grin making it clear he put very little stock into her excuse. "Well, I didn't actually expect to see you again, if I'm being perfectly honest. But I'm very glad that you managed to call the publicly listed business number, and I'm very glad that you're here. Is that what you're asking, Silva? If I'm glad that you managed to find your way back? I am, if you were concerned."

She'd swallowed, feeling foolish, and lowered her eyes. She wanted to hear that he'd been thinking about her, that he'd *missed* her even, that he'd spent a tenth of the time twisting over thoughts of her as she had over him. Tate was busy, had grown-up problems and responsibilities, and was too preoccupied to waste his precious little free time thinking about a weekend fling from several months earlier, she'd reminded herself, feeling herself shrink. She'd jumped when he'd pushed her hair behind her ear, pressing his nose into it and inhaling deeply. For a long, loaded moment, he'd said nothing, simply breathed against her.

"Every day, dove." His voice had been a whisper against her ear, followed by the press of his lips, warm against her skin, and her heart had lifted on beating wings. When they'd finally gone to bed that night, she'd quickly reclaimed her favorite spot from three months prior — pressed to his chest, skin-to-skin, the solid thump of his heartbeat beneath her cheek a percussive lullaby. When she'd woken the next morning to the sound of his too-early alarm, she'd still been spooned against him, his arms around her securely and his fingers tangled in her hair. Silva remembered thinking it had been a far cry from the cold nights she'd spent by herself on the edge of Wynndevar's bed, for three long months.

The sight of the back of his platinum-haired head now made her flush in indignation all over again. She *hated* him. Hated the way he'd made her feel, hated how *mean* he'd been in such a short amount of time, time that should have been colored in the rosy wash of a new relationship, not filled with cutting remarks and barely concealed insults. She thought of the night he'd yanked her wrist as they were exiting a rideshare, annoyed that she was taking too long collecting her bag, hard enough that the aubergine outline of his fingers had been visible on her lavender skin, and of the night he'd shouldered her in the jaw, making her bite her cheek. Most of all, Silva thought, she hated herself for having wasted the time, three months of her life she'd never get back; three months she could have spent wrapped in Tate's arms. She hated that she'd allowed herself to be treated so poorly for so long.

"What's wrong?" Tate's voice was an amused curl around her ear, and she realized how she must have been scowling. She turned from the railing to find his slim black brow arched expectantly, the three small, silver hoops there catching the colored light from the bar.

"Nothing. Just someone I don't like." He followed her gaze, landing slightly short on a table of gnolls who were animatedly conversing with huge gesticulations.

"Do you have something personal against gnolls in general? Or one in particular? Do we need to avenge your family honor?"

"No!" she exclaimed with a laugh, tugging his hand as she turned back to his friends. "I don't have a problem with gnolls." The satyr, she saw, was telling a story, surrounded by several of the giggling elves. Silva wondered if any of these girls knew Tate was Elvish; that he had more in common with them than he did with the orcs who patronized his businesses. She'd been testing her Elvish on him, and he'd laughingly proclaimed it 'a wee bit rusty,' but every time they were together they practiced. She'd never had a particularly strong appreciation for it in school, one of her harder classes, but then again, she'd never had a classroom opportunity to hear it spoken in his lilting accent while she laid against his chest, his fingers gently carding through her hair. She wondered if any of these giggling girls knew him that way at all.

When she'd turned back, it was to see the back of his head. He was facing the bar floor once more, continuing to gaze in the direction in which she'd been scowling. Silva could tell from the tense set of his shoulders that his sharp golden eyes had picked Wynn out of the crowd, as the latter had turned, at last, his lofty brow and fine bone structure visible in profile. For an interminable moment, Tate said nothing. He didn't turn, didn't glance back at her. He continued to stare, stare and stare so hard that across the long, crowded room, Wynn flinched, glancing up in the wrong direction to find the source of his discomfort. When Tate turned at last, his jaw was tight, the smile on his face not reaching his darkened, empty eyes.

"An old friend of yours, dove?" His voice grated, holding an edge that it didn't normally possess, at least, not for her. "By all means, don't let me keep you from going to say hello."

You'll meet and marry some perfect, purple-skinned prat with a respectable, white-collar job and an excellent credit score. She wondered if Wynn was the exact type of elf he'd been picturing when he'd uttered those words to her.

"I don't want to."

"Are you sure? I don't want you to feel like you're being kept away. You don't need to stay here on my account, I'd hate to deprive you of a happy reunion. I don't want to keep you from where you belong, Silva."

She felt his sharply spat words like a fist, her mouth dropping open at the impact. She knew it was jealousy doing the talking for him, knew that all too well, jealousy and perhaps, she thought, a bit of insecurity. He was an elf, like her; like all of these pretty giggling elves around them. He had more in common with her than anyone else around, but at the end of the day, that wasn't what people saw. She already knew that, after all. She'd been lying to her family, lying to her friends, not revealing where it was she disappeared to several weekends a month. She didn't know how to tell her family she was dating an orc, for an orc would be all they saw; the differences between them and Tate, and none of the commonalities. *You'll meet and marry some perfect purple-skinned prat.* It was jealousy and insecurity and nothing more, and no one knew that better than her, one more thing they had in common. She shook her head.

"I don't want to say hello to him. I *hate* him." She moved very close, getting into his space as tightly as she appropriately could, given the surroundings. "I don't want to talk to him at all. Please don't make me." She was mollified when his hand dropped to her hip pulling her a little closer, a bit tighter, skin-to-skin. She wondered if she cut open his chest and climbed inside to be nearer to his heart, if it would ever feel close enough.

"Who is he?" His voice was a breath of against her, for her ears only, and she knew that he already knew. There was no way to play it off as a casual acquaintance, and to do so would destroy whatever trust he had in her, and besides, Silva decided, she had no desire or reason to lie. It was insecurity and jealousy, she reminded herself, and she knew all too well what happened to herself in that double grip.

"We dated for a while, earlier this year. I'm the one who broke it off. He . . . wasn't very nice to me." *If he was jealous,* she told herself, *then he must actually care.*

"Why?" She swallowed at the question, wondering if he hadn't been a part of the equation; if the bruise of his bite hadn't still been a lingering, purple mark on her skin, if she would still be sleeping on the cold, lonely edge of the other man's bed. She and Tate weren't the only party-goers who had slowly edged away from the group, Silva noticed as she thought about how to answer his question, hesitating for a long moment. The tiefling couple was strategically moving towards the staircase leading down the platform, and the djinn was on her phone in the corner, her back to the group.

Because I couldn't stop thinking about you. Because everything that you said would happen was coming true. Because my life is my own to shape. His huge hand cupped her jaw, tilting her face up before his thumb gently moved over the curve of her cheek. It was the same side of her face that Wynn had bashed with his shoulder, the same cheek she'd bitten that night, filling her mouth with blood. She couldn't remember him touching her this gently in the entirety of the three months they'd been together, three months of her life wasted she would never get back. She'd not answered him, but as she gazed up, Silva thought perhaps she didn't need to. After all, he divined her thoughts so easily, pulled words from her mouth before they'd even had a chance to leap off her tongue. Light had returned to his eyes, she was relieved to see, but unlike the warmth that had burned there upon her arrival, as his gaze slid over her in her new dress, a leaping fire burned there now. She thought back to that night in the fall, the jumping flames of the fire that wasn't there, reflected in his eyes as clearly as if he had stood only inches before it. It was *that* fire that had returned, and the blood in her veins thrummed to see it.

"I'll kill him for you, dove, if you want. I just might kill him regardless." His voice was soft and silky, his tone belying the severity of his words, and her eyes widened. She should have been horrified that he'd even make such a joke, should have been frightened that perhaps he meant it, but the excited thump of her heart held only exhilaration, for there was no question that he cared with that sort of threat.

A burst of laughter came from behind them, the ribald satyr demanding his presence in the conversation, an echoing space of heartbeats before he turned back to his friends, Wynndevar's presence momentarily forgotten, and when she looked back out over the sea of people across the club, her ex was gone.

All too soon, she felt a familiar, uncomfortable pressure, the result of the three mixed drinks she'd had from the private beverage cart. The bottle girl had been glancing surreptitiously down to the phone she had nestled between the lemons and the club soda on the chrome-plated cart, and Silva craned her neck over the side railing of the platform, trying to ascertain where the restrooms were. She was an adult, she reminded herself, had lived on her own for several years, had lived away from home for University and had traveled abroad, and the thought of going to the restroom in this unfamiliar club should have not set her nerves jangling. As she looked out over the writhing sea of people though, nothing seemed more overwhelming. She didn't want to push through the crowd on her own again, didn't want to be smirked and whispered at by the throngs of human men who sat in clusters around the bar and at the edge of the dance floor, didn't want to risk catching Wynn's eye . . .

"Tate," she whispered, tugging his sleeve, reluctantly pulling him from a conversation he was on the edge of, between the pretty djinn and the tiefling couple. "I-will you come with me to the ladies' room? I don't know the way."

She wasn't sure if it was her imagination or not, but it seemed as if the sea of people parted before him as he steered her through the crowd, a hand at her lower back, keeping her close. As she'd originally suspected, the restrooms were on the hallway past the long back bar, nowhere near their elevated platform.

The man behind the blue-lit bar was waiting for them as they approached the edge of it, his yellow cat eyes giving him away as some sort of feline were, his long dreadlocks pulled into a high ponytail at the back of his head. Tate chuckled warmly as they approached, and the man exclaimed in greeting. Silva watched them exchange the sort of handshake that she always thought was specific to secret clubs, beaming when Tate introduced her.

"You're doing fine business here, Robbie. It's a good thing someone taught you well."

The man laughed, a big open laugh that made her smile instinctively.

"That's because I haven't changed a fucking thing since you've been gone. Still have your same checklists up in the office. Can't believe it's already been 10 years. We're getting older every minute, and you're aging in reverse. How's Thessa?"

She shifted her weight from foot to foot as the men talked and laughed, Tate's hand landing on her lower back after, what seemed to her bladder, to be an endless amount of time.

"We're headed to the ladies, but I'll be sure to say goodbye before we leave."

There was a line to the bathroom, as there always was in every establishment she had ever been in, regardless of the business type or the species patronizing it, and she sighed as they entered it, shifting on her heels.

"This is where I used to work," he murmured, raising a hand in greeting to another employee who called out to him with a wave. "I was the bar manager here for years."

She tipped her head up to gawk at him, trying to imagine him in this noisy, licentious environment every night of the week. It was the complete opposite of his own establishment, and she squinted trying to imagine him overseeing the crowd here.

"Did – did you live in Bridgeton then?"

"Mhm. For years. An apartment building just up the block, walking distance. I don't miss it, if that's going to be your next question. Well," he smiled wryly, "I *do* miss not being surrounded by orcs day and night, but here it was the humans. So a bit of a trade-off, but one's not much better than the other."

Despite the number of people in line, the queue was moving quickly, the door came into sight only a few minutes later. A group of elves turned out of the bathroom at that moment, not any of the girls from their party, but two Silva instantly recognized from the club. They were younger than her by several years, probably still in university or recently graduated, although the one had an older sister her age. Silva felt as if she were outside of her body, watching the next handful of seconds in slow motion, like a movie or something that was happening to someone else. The hand that had been clutching Tate's wrist released its grip on him of its own accord, her feet moving her a step away without her conscious thought. The group of elves moved on, passing by without hesitation as if she were invisible, but the damage, she realized, was done.

"Careful dove," his voice bit out, taking another small step away from her, "you don't want your pretty friends finding out about your dirty little secret. You're almost in now. I'll be at the bar."

She spun in alarm, her stomach twisting at his words, for she knew his observation of her action was accurate. Heat burned up her face, but he was already several yards away, long legs carrying him back down the hallway and away from her, around the corner to where the bar existed noisily. She berated herself for the next several minutes in line, squeezing out a few self-indulgent tears once the stall door had clicked shut behind her, patting cold water on her face once she stood before the mirror. *You certainly didn't help yourself. Good job making things worse.* Her phone buzzed then, his name on the display increasing her pulse dramatically, her imagination supplying the lines of text before she thumbed open the screen. *Why don't you just leave. Go back to where you belong, dove.* Reality, once she'd open the screen, had her breathing a sigh of relief. *Far left corner on the back bar.* She breathed long and low, trying to center herself and stop her fluttering pulse from lifting her right off her feet in a panic that she bungled the entire evening in one careless movement.

When she turned the corner from the hallway to the bar area, she spotted him instantly, engaged in a laughing, animated conversation with the were he'd called Robbie. She didn't want to interrupt, didn't want to rush him away from an old friend, and certainly didn't want to rush headlong into whatever discomfort awaited her, and so she lingered near the center of the bar, waiting for his conversation to break on its own.

Her phone buzzed as she leaned on the lacquered edge, surprised to see Tate's name again. *He's probably telling you to go home, that he's not interested in being your dirty secret any longer.* Swiping the screen open, she held her breath. *You can go home, dove.* Her heart dropped seeing her worst fear actualized in text. *My destiny just walked through the door.* Her head snapped up, swinging around towards the club's entrance. She saw the girl instantly, for she was hard to miss. There weren't many cervitaurs even in Cambric Creek, and it seemed especially unusual to see one here in the city. She looked delicate and soft, with a tawny hide and a long spill of dark brown hair, making her way through the club floor with two goblins and a dragonborn. Her cheeks flushed as she realized it was a joke, a *mean* joke, of which she was the butt, swinging back around to see Tate doubled over in laughter at the end of the bar. Snatching up her phone, she prepared to tell him off, but she never got the chance.

"You know, if you had dressed like this when we were together, well . . . we might still be together."

Silva recoiled at the sound of his voice, whirling in fury. He was just as handsome and polished as he'd been that first day he'd approached her at the fundraiser's coffee table; all high cheekbones and platinum hair, arrogance oozing from his every pore. Still just as perfect and smug and entirely punchable, she seethed.

"*I* seem to remember being the one to end things with *you*," she spat, hands balling into fists at her side, "and my wardrobe didn't actually have anything to do with it."

There *had*, in fact, been a moment when her wardrobe had been top of mind. There was a high-end lingerie boutique in the city that she'd passed numerous times over the years. Silva had never purchased anything from the shop, preferring to give her patronage to the local salon in Cambric Creek, but she'd always paused in the doorway of the swanky corsetier, wondering if she ought to be extravagant once in a while. She'd been with Wynn on one such occasion, passing by the black pillared boutique as they left dinner. He'd slowed, commenting that he'd need to get her something from the vixenish collection for yuletide that year, *something with some actual sex appeal.* Her cheeks had burned, unsure as always at how she was meant to respond to his less-than-subtle digs, but had only frowned at the time, eyeing the sheer black and red styles — netted and strapped, more tawdry than anything she would ever choose for herself, in a harsh color palette that would not compliment her coloring — saying nothing, knowing the sultry styles would not suit her.

She'd gone back to the lingerie boutique weeks later, after she'd called him to end things, after she'd returned to Greenbridge Glen and Tate's bed, in a fit of vindictive spite. She had always favored twee, old-fashioned styles, and now she went out of her way to wear soft, frilly fashions; dainty jewelry and delicate lace lingerie, especially when she knew Tate would be seeing it. He'd never voiced a preference for these particular styles, but Silva knew it was what he liked as well, using the aesthetic he'd designed for his own restaurant as her guide. She had splurged the styles that *did* appeal to her: floral-print lace in mint green and soft peach, crystal pleated chiffon, and ruffles upon ruffles of frills. She'd treated herself to a chantilly lace set in the palest of pinks—bra and matching thong, garter belt and stockings, a teddy accented with tiny silk ribbons and seed pearls, and a short, ivory silk peignoir with lace frilled cuffs. The first time Tate had peeled her out of her demure dress to discover the softly-colored lace she wore beneath, as delicate as the finely-wrought spoon handles in his dining room, he'd spent a small eternity kissing her, marveling over the smoothness of her skin and the softness of her curves, his mouth paying homage to every inch of her body. The heat of his tongue had pressed into her, with only the pink-colored lace as a barrier; a hot, wet, repetitive stroking, the lace rasping against her clit, preventing his tongue from sliding over it. By the time he was finished and her heartbeat had slowed, the front of the lace thong had been soaked — soaked from his mouth and soaked from her slick.

"Is that how you remember it?"

She felt steam practically pouring out of her ears at Wynn's infuriating rewrite of their history, whipping to the bar to see if there was a drink nearby that she could fling in his face, when his hand landed on her wrist.

"Why don't we go somewhere to talk?" he murmured in a low voice, taking a step closer. "We need to talk about things. We could be so good together if—"

She never got to hear all the rest of his thought; never got to hear what his insinuation would be, for surely it would depend on her changing something about herself, but it didn't matter. She felt the heat of him at her back, a buffeting presence, protecting her from whatever happened next.

"You don't *ever* get to touch her again."

Wynn shrunk back instinctively from the silky menace in Tate's voice, bumping into the troll behind him and bobbing for a moment before he recovered his bravado. The elves who had come out of the restroom ahead of her were at the other corner of the bar, not twenty paces away, and she wondered if he was here with them. She could see them in a cluster, each holding a fruity-looking drink, probably paid for by the three human-looking men that sat to their side. One of them was watching her with wide eyes, the drink in her hand forgotten, but by then Wynn's handsome face was screwed up into a snarl as his head tipped back — and back, and back — to find Tate's eyes. She leaned, feeling the long, solid line of him behind her: broad chest and muscular thighs, his always warm skin, towering over Wynn, just as she'd known he would, obliging the elf to tilt his head back comically. Giving her ex her very best smile, she reached back to wrap her hand around Tate's wrist, where it belonged, where she should have never removed it.

"How rude of me," she said, squeezing the skin below his watchband. "Tate, this is *Wynndevar.*" She exaggerated the pronunciation of the old Elvish name, giggling as if it were the funniest thing she'd ever heard. The whole world seemed to wait then, spinning silently in space as her heart fluttered about her chest. There was no coming back from this now, she thought. "Wynn . . . . this is my Tate." *Hers.* His hand had dropped to her hip, and Silva was positive she could *feel* the hostility he radiated, like a vibration in the air. The elf at the corner of the bar leaned in to whisper to one of her friends, three perfectly coiffed heads swinging in her direction, the human men forgotten, but for the moment, Silva couldn't bring herself to care. *Hers.* The club seemed to buzz around them in slow motion as Wynn blinked his emerald green eyes, lips curling in a sneer.

"Is this why I haven't seen you at any events lately? I'm sure your grandmother is thrilled. I guess the club really does let in any old riff-raff these days."

She took a breath to defend herself, but the words never had a chance to form. Tate's responding chuckle was slow and pitch black.

"Is this what passes for high society, dove? Well beer and a low street watch? Can't imagine why I've been worried. What happened, boyo? Did your daddy not top off your allowance for the month?"

Wynn sputtered in outrage, his face once again screwing up into a scowl. Silva watched his lips moving, and a distant part of her brain was able to process the barrage of ugly things that came tumbling out of his mouth, things he said about her, accusations he made. She saw his lips form the word *whore* but she wasn't quite able to hear it. The room had plunged underwater, the other patrons around the bar moving in slow motion, their voices blurred and indistinct. There was no doubt in her mind now that she had indeed stood unseen in the center of Clover's dining room that day she'd come back to him, existing at his side in some liminal space, for she felt that the same fae magic rippling around her now. *More fae than orc by far.*

Something popped over her shoulder like the cork of a champagne bottle, and she felt the force of the atmosphere shift around her, as if the air itself seemed to jolt, making her wobble on her heels, Tate's firm hand on her hip the only thing anchoring her to the ground. As she watched, Wynn's green eyes widened in fear, the aggressive sneer melting off his face like the slide of wax down a forgotten birthday candle, leaving him slack-jawed. She felt Tate shift behind her, and she didn't need to turn to know that his head was cocked and his smile lethal, having witnessed the motion a dozen times at that point as he presided over the Pixie's weekend crowd. There was something different this time, something more ominous, and the tiny hairs on her neck rose as a heavy pressure clawed at her throat, but she dared not turn around, lest she miss the look of growing terror on Wynndevar's handsome face.

"How many bones do you think you have, lad?" His voice was smooth and lilting, dripping in menace, and Silva shivered in exhilaration. "Do you think it's enough to account for every time you treated her poorly? I'd hate to double back and break them twice, but we all do have to make sacrifices now and again."

The pressure on her chest began to grow uncomfortable, and she clawed at Tate's wrist, desperate for a breath of air she seemed unable to take. In a sudden *whoosh*, sound came flooding back into the room and she gasped, watching her ex-boyfriend slump against the bar, holding himself up on his hands.

"So nice to see you again," she heard a confident voice say. When Tate's hand tightened, she jumped, realizing the voice was her own. "Do send your regards to your mother for me."

The hand at her hip had dug in like claws, but she was able to ease his grip, knitting their fingers together and tugging his arm, not daring to chance a glance back to him until they were pushing through the crowd, pulling him to safety, well away from the slumped form of her ex. His eyes were bright and dangerous when she finally turned, and Silva couldn't immediately discern what, but there was something wrong with his face, his wide mouth seeming strangely off-kilter, but he allowed her to pull him away from trouble and out the front doors, into the frosty black night. Adrenaline raced through her veins and she sucked in a lung full of the sharp, cold air, her lungs burning as though she'd been deprived of oxygen.

When she turned, he was there, bending in half to crash his mouth into hers, lifting her easily as he straightened. It was all going to catch up with her now, she thought, gripping a fistful of his hair with one hand and digging her nails into the back of his neck with the other. Months of lies, of skating around the truth to her mother and grandmother, of pretending, of selfishly wanting to have everything, Silva of the daytime and Silva of the nighttime both. *You don't want your dirty secret getting out to all your pretty little friends.* She felt sick that he thought of their relationship that way, and worse: that he assumed that was how *she* thought of him, and how easily he seemed to accept it. Silva could feel the ground rocking under the precarious house of cards she'd built as he gripped her tightly, holding on to her as if somehow *she* were the tetherline and he was afraid of floating away alone, and not the other way around. He looked as he always did, as she gazed up, breathing hard. Her Tate. *Worth it.*

"I'm sorry," she blurted, tears filling her eyes. Her chest felt full of every emotion she'd been holding back for months, every emotion she'd been holding back for the past year, every time she'd felt invisible in her own life, all of it rising to the surface in a tide of frustrated tears. "I'm sorry that happened, I'm sorry about him. I-I'm sorry I didn't come back sooner." Tears were filling her eyes and overflowing, running down her face, probably taking half her mascara with it. Her shoulders had begun to hitch as every regret she had over the past eight months continued to push against her walls, escaping through her tears. Tate's dark eyebrows knit together, shaking his head, the incident in the club apparently forgotten. "I'm sorry I let go of your hand," she managed to wheeze out before he blurred in front of her; a tall, wavering black outline, completely obscured by her tears. She felt him grip her shoulders, his thumb circling soothingly skin, giving her a gentle shake.

"Silva, you don't have to apologize for anything to anyone, least of all someone like me." There were patrons still in the queue outside, behind the velvet rope, waiting to get in. She knew they were probably watching, and that she was making a spectacle of them, that didn't stop another sob from ripping from her throat at his words. "I'm the only one who should be apologizing, dove. I should've let you enjoy your weekend with your friends. If I wasn't such a selfish bastard, I would've let you go home without ever knowing my name."

His words only made her cry harder. She felt ridiculous; foolish and small, but the knowledge couldn't keep the tears from falling. Too long, too bottled up. She didn't know how to be Silva of the daytime and Silva of the nighttime both, didn't know how to juggle the two sides of herself to make everyone else happy, and the pressure of doing so was wearing a hole in her center, bleeding her dry. All of the lies she told, all of the events she missed, the half-truths to her family and friends . . . . she didn't know how to reconcile all that she wanted, but still didn't want to choose. And even with her lies over the weekends away, she still felt so incredibly far from him.

"Why would you say that," she whimpered, hating how pitiful she sounded. She didn't know how to be the elf he wanted her to be either, one who wasn't so needy and demanding.

"You're the only one playing against the odds here, Silva," he interrupted her thoughts. "You have everything to lose. And if you had an ounce of sense in that beautiful little head of yours, you'd go back into that club right now and ask that perfect purple cunt to take you home. You have *every*thing, dove. Don't throw it away for someone like me." His words left her winded and hollow. Throwing her away, moments after calling her his. Before she could collect herself enough to speak, he raised a shaking hand, jabbing it in the direction of the club with a scowl. "Not him. Don't go running back to him, because I'm still planning on killing him."

The fresh sob that had been brewing in her throat came out as a choked laugh, and then she was in his arms again, his lips following the tracks of her tears, over each eyelid, swallowing her lips. "I think it's my decision on who I should throw my life away for, don't you think so? What's the point of having everything if I'll never be happy?"

She shivered as the adrenaline began to ebb away, goose flesh rising on her bare lavender arms, squealing when the wind caught under the hem of her short dress, melting against him when he held his arms out, always so warm. "Kill him another night. Let's go home. You need to go back in, to say goodbye to your friends."

"No." He took up her hand, shaking his head. "I don't." His lips were light and soft when he bent again, pressing them to her forehead. Sandalwood and snow-covered pines and a wide-open sky, she thought, breathing him in. Free and fresh and home.

"I think that's called an Irish goodbye, right?"

He pulled back sharply, blinking at her, several moments of silence passing before he nearly choked on his laughter, the sharp sound bouncing off the front of the building, and then there was no question the patrons in line were staring as he hunched; manic, musical laughter pouring out of him. It was too cold for him to ride back to Greenbridge Glenn that night, Silva decided at that moment. She loved holding tightly to his waist on the back of his bike, but she was certain the sleek racer was a deathtrap come wintertime. Too cold and too icy, and her bed was much, much closer. She wanted to sleep in his arms that night, wanted to press against his warm skin and feel the thrum of his heartbeat beneath her ear, and put this ugly, emotion-fueled conversation away. She gripped his hand, resolute.

"Come home with me," she insisted, tugging his arm. "It's too late for you to go all the way back to Greenbridge tonight, especially on your bike, that's not safe. *And* you've been drinking." His lips quirked up in a ghost of a smile, and she knew he was likely going to point out that alcohol affected her vastly differently than it did him. "Please? Come home with me tonight." Silva steeled herself for his rejection. After all, hadn't he just told her to go away, opining that he wished he never continued anything with her after that first weekend?

She'd never met his family, didn't even *know* anything about his family, and she'd only tonight been introduced to his social circle, with no promise of a repeat performance. He'd never acknowledged her small overtures before, her murmurings about him coming with her to tea at the little shop she liked in town or restaurants she wanted him to try in Cambric Creek, exhibits she wanted to visit or small local attractions she wanted to show off. He'd never outright said yes or no; had never stopped to make plans or ask more questions, and even after a night like this, deep in her heart she knew it was his way of expressing his disinterest in her as anything more than a temporary diversion. *And he just told you as much.* Good enough when she materialized before him on weekends, but not someone with whom he wanted to make future plans, for anything as trivial as a winery visit or a more permanent designation in his life.

He sighed, peering down on her. She focused on the tooled leather of his well-shined shoes, not wanting to see the *no* take form on his lips, certain her heart couldn't bear it after such a tumultuous evening. His hand gently gripped her chin, raising her face to his, forcing him to meet her eye. "Do I need to drive? I know you can drink a grown ogre under the table, but that doesn't mean I want to get in a car with either of you."

She would have been ashamed of her reaction if her emotions weren't poised on a hair-trigger, but that didn't prevent her from squealing in excitement, flinging her arms around his neck and dragging him down until she could reach his lips.

"I don't need you to drive!" She exclaimed, finding that it took all of her willpower not to dance around like a child. "I only had two or three drinks, and I switched to water forever ago. They were mostly juice anyway, that bottle service was a racket. I'm driving, I want you to enjoy the scenery."

She had never before realized just how small her car was, not until she was forced to watch Tate attempting to fold himself into it, like an accordion. She began to giggle as she buckled her seatbelt, glancing over to him out of the corner of her eye, taking note of the way his knees were practically touching his chin, her shoulders shaking in laughter as she started the ignition.

She decided to disregard his words for now. After all, she herself had said all manner of things she regretted in the heat of the moment. He might've said he wished he hadn't continued on with her, but the heat of his kiss said otherwise. She herself was prone to strong emotions, and she couldn't fault him if he were, in fact, the same. His presence beside her in the car said more than his ill-spoken words. This was it, she thought. *Hers*. The beginning of the rest of her life with him at her side. He would see Cambric Creek, see all of the multi-species couples and neighbors existing there happily and in harmony, couples just like them. She could work on her family, positive that she could turn her grandmother to her side ... but not unless he was on board with her plan for their future. She couldn't fight a war on two fronts, so getting him on the same page as her was paramount at that point. She had a feeling she was in danger of whiplash from her wildly vacillating emotions, but that knowledge didn't stop her from bouncing in her seat excitedly.

The drive from Bridgeton to Cambric Creek was one straight shot, and all too soon the lights of the city were twinkling in the rearview mirror. "Did you live there very long?" She asked, glancing over to where he was cycling through all of her programmed music stations, reading the heading on each as it rolled across the satellite radio's display. "In the city, I mean."

"A fair bit. A friend of mine wanted to invest an inheritance he received from his brother into a pub here. His wife was from Bridgeton, but they were living in London and didn't know anything about the business. I got them up and running, and then ran the place for several years before Efraim came round from the club. Made me an offer I couldn't refuse, and by then I had grown a bit weary with my mate. He and his wife didn't have any interest in learning what it took to run the business, they were happy to have other people do it for them. I suppose that's all well and good for them, but when you're the one doing the running, it gets a bit tiresome. I was still working there when I bought the Pixie."

The knowledge that he had been right there in Bridgeton all along — right under her nose! — took her breath away. She could have gone to that club while he was there tending bar, could have been standing in line at the coffee shop on the corner, or getting her hair done at the fancy nail salon. She could've been shopping at that high-end boutique for lingerie that only he would see several years earlier, if only their ships would have passed.

"You know, Cambric Creek butts up against Bridgeton. Just think, you could have been coming to visit me all those years."

"Silva, I have literally never heard of Kittering Creek, and to be honest I'm still not one hundred percent certain it exists at all. I have a feeling we're going to drive straight on through to Starling Heights and you're going to tell me you live in some fancy development there."

She exclaimed in outrage as he popped open her center console to snoop through her collection of lip balms and receipts.

"We don't have the same sort of nightlife that the city does," she admitted, "but Cambric Creek has its own restaurant and pub culture, you're going to love it. It's nice not having to worry about places being overrun with humans, so people tend to stay close to home when they go out."

"Aye, tell me about it. They all love to tell you how to do whatever it is you're doing, no matter what it is, always think their way is best. Are there no humans that live there then?"

"Oh no," she laughed, "there are some. But for the most part, they're there for work, or they've moved for a partner. It's mostly women, very few human men. I think the men are intimidated to be outnumbered, but the women don't seem to be. Isn't that funny?" Tate chuckled, muttering something under his breath that she didn't quite catch, but it didn't matter because the sign on the side of the highway was looming ahead. *Cambric Creek - Two Miles.* They were almost there, which meant she was almost home. Home to the community she loved, where she knew he would love it too, if he only gave it half a chance.

She had been just about to point out the first waterfall, tumbling over an artificial ledge beside the overpass, when Tate gasped. He hunched in the seat beside her, the seatbelt cutting into the veins that were popping on his neck, big hands scrabbling against her dashboard for purchase. She squealed in panic, asking if he was all right, but he seemed unable to answer, as if the wind had been completely knocked out of him. The gravel on the side of the road crunched beneath her tires when she pulled off onto the berm. There were no headlights coming in either direction, not uncommon for that time of night, but still, it lent the air a bit of spookiness when she opened her car door, coming around to the passenger side where he was gasping, his door already thrown open.

"What in the bleedin' *fuck* was that?" he exclaimed. "Did you hit something? Did you hit a fucking bigfoot?! I asked if you needed me to drive!"

"I didn't hit anything!" she cried, more than a touch offended.

"It felt like you hit a bloody wall!"

"Tate, I didn't hit *any*thing! Look, look back in the road! There's nothing there. Are you okay? I thought you were choking on something! You're not having a stroke, are you?" He shot her a derisive look, still panting slightly, and she slumped, determining that he was fine. "You are the most dramatic elf in the *world*. Are you sure you're okay? I have a bottle of water somewhere on the backseat, if you need it."

He was quiet as she started driving again, leaving the *Welcome to Cambric Creek* sign they'd just passed behind. Silva had already planned out the route in her head, having done so over the course of the last many months, daydreaming about the first time she'd get him to come to visit her. Driving straight to her apartment wouldn't do, wouldn't do at all. She wanted him to see the waterfalls in the center of town, the historic observatory, and the normally teeming businesses on Main Street. She wanted to drive through Oldetowne and let him have a glimpse of the stately Victorians and other turn-of-the-century homes from a more genteel era, where all of his beautiful antique furniture and flatware would fit in so nicely. She wanted him to see the various species living side-by-side and hand-in-hand; wanted to show him how easily they would fit in here together, how their differences wouldn't matter. She would save the visit through Cevanorë for another time. He knew what Elvish communities looked like, after all, and she thought it prudent not to remind him of their differences.

"See, look at how many restaurants and shops there are!" she exclaimed cheerfully as she directed her small car through the business district. "Most people don't even bother going to Bridgeton for a night out, because we have so much here. The businesses all do really well, and the city charter doesn't allow any chain stores or restaurants." She hoped he would see the possibility of the town, wondering if he would ever consider opening a pub here, but he never answered. His nose was pressed to the glass of her passenger window, gawking at something ahead.

"Silva . . . is that an araneaen?" The oddly-proportioned couple were walking along the waterfront, hand-in-hand, up the winding lane that followed the path of the town's titular creek to where it poured over the rockface in a dramatic display. The street was empty, the wide path they walked on theirs alone. Silva had never seen the araneaen man before, but she knew there was another of his kind somewhere in town, an older female who lived close to the Applethorpe Wood. She'd seen the old spider-woman shopping once or twice, late at night when she'd made an impulse grocery run for whatever she happened to be craving. She had to admit, the sight of the araneaen man was disconcerting. He loomed over his companion, his many legs moving over each other in a slow, steady cadence, but the young woman at his side paid no notice. To Silva's eyes, it looked as though he were slouching a bit so that she could hold his hand without reaching, which she found a bit sweet, even if his appearance was jarring.

"Are they allowed to *live* here? Can they be out on the street like that?! Do we need to call the police?"

"What?! No, we don't need to call the police! They *live* here!" The light had turned red, giving her the opportunity to get a better look at the couple. "Oh wow, that's the girl I buy my shampoo from! She's a witch, and she's so sweet and quiet ... I guess it's true that it's always the quiet ones, right?" His head swung to her when the light turned green, still gaping. "This is a multi-species community, Tate, I told you that. Everyone is welcome here. It's not like other places."

"Araneaens *eat* each other. Are you Crackadam Creekers really interested in finding out if that extends to other species as well?"

She pursed her lips, giving him a scowl as they continued, mollified by the way he oohed over and ahhed the Oldetowne Victorians, as she knew he would, and acted appropriately impressed by the old Observatory and the site of the waterfall, lit with colored lights. "It's so pretty in the springtime when all the flowers are blooming. They have them planted on levels on either side of the falls, and there's a cherry blossom festival. In the summertime they fly hot air balloons right over downtown. I like walking in the park in the summer, especially after being cooped up inside all day, and everything is nice and close and convenient." Her ears heated, hoping she didn't sound too much like an overzealous real estate guide, or worse, transparent in her elaborately constructed daydream, starring the two of them. "Oh! In the fall they have a big fall Fest hosted at one of the farms, it's like a big carnival. It's the best apple cider I've ever tasted. And *they* don't use garbage apples."

She expected him to be hesitant; to tiptoe around her apartment uncertainly, the way she'd done in his on that very first night, months earlier. He *had* hesitated, had stood in the threshold of her front door for an interminable moment, as though his feet were stuck, preventing him from taking the next step before she'd tugged on his hand, pulling him through the door and stretching up on her toes to kiss his jaw. Then she'd turned away, determined to be as nonchalant over his presence as he'd been that first night, pulling out extra pillows for her side of the bed.

In contrast to the nervous trepidation she'd displayed in his apartment, Tate had gone exploring. She watched from the corner of her eye as he moved through the small living room, inspecting framed family photos and her small movie collection, opening and closing books, looking over her furniture. In the kitchen he'd pulled open the cupboards, smiling softly at the etched flower design on her glasses, and investigated the contents of her freezer before moving on. Silva pulled two of the glasses from the cupboard as he drifted down the hallway, listening to the sound of the small linen closet being pulled open. When she found him, he was in her bedroom, standing over a mirrored tray that housed a small collection of tiny, velvet-flocked animals, her favorite childhood toys.

"They're old," she murmured, flushing at the worn condition of the small figures, watching the way his brow furrowed. Each was no bigger than a bottlecap, carved in wood, the velvet coating patchy and worn. "They were my great-grandmother's."

"I had this same set." As he spoke, his fingertip moved from animal to animal, alighting on each one like a butterfly, and the tiny hairs on the back of her neck rose, as if she could feel his touch. "When I was a boy."

"Really? I used to play with them at her house when I was little. My grandmother didn't understand why I wanted them when I was older, but they were my favorite thing in the whole world." Tate hadn't yet blinked, his finger poised over the small, dappled fawn. "That one was my favorite," she murmured, feeling a strange twist of nostalgia.

"My favorite was the rabbit." His voice was very soft, his finger moving to the shabby little rabbit, most of its velvet coating rubbed away from four generations of play. One more thing they shared, she thought, moving around the shelf to press her cheek to his back, wrapping her arms around his narrow waist. *Fated mates.*

"Did you get a chance to snoop through my bookshelf already? Are you ready for bed?"

His low laugh was a deep rumble that moved through his back, vibrating against her cheek. He turned in her arms, and she was ready to receive his kiss, her face already tipped up. He made no argument as she walked him backward across the room to sit at the edge of her bed, before dropping to her knees. She had already kicked off her skyscraper heels as soon as they'd entered the apartment, and now she unlaced and removed his oxfords, and carefully unbuckled the front of his belt. She'd not paid enough attention to his accoutrements in the club, she realized, when she reached for the intricate watch on his wrist. The crystal face had a cover, unusual for a wristwatch, overlapping vines with small moths and tiny bees in relief, finely wrought in shimmering gold. There was a turning knob on the side of it, and she raised her head, her brows drawn together in confusion.

"Is this a pocket watch?"

"It was once." His voice was barely a whisper and he offered no further explanation. Silva swallowed, carefully unthreading the band from his wrist and placing the watch on the top of her dresser. She ordered him to stand, peeling the snug black pants down his endless

legs before pushing him back down to unbutton his shirt, very aware
of his warm breath on her arms as she did so. Her hands hesitated
at the unexpected piece of jewelry beneath the dress shirt, her nails
finding purchase against his clavicle, her palms smoothing against
his warmth, down his sternum, and over his hard abdomen, nails
scraping. Around his neck, he wore a chain; a very long chain that
hung nearly to the center of his chest, the pendant it supported
pressed just beside the spot where his heartbeat thumped beneath
her fingers. The chain, she could tell, was newer, but the pendant
itself made her breath catch. A tiny, swooping bird on the edge of
a floral motif, rendered in claret porcelain on an ivory background,
with a faint spider web of nearly translucent crazing. It was a piece
of dinnerware, she thought, filed smooth and placed in a locket-like
setting of mother-of-pearl. It was old and strange and distressingly
lovely, and its presence around his neck made her raise her eyes to
his uncertainly.

"It was a teacup and saucer that I broke when I was a boy. I can't
remember which the chip came from. My nan wanted it set into the
bail, and my grandfather closed it with the filigree." Like the watch,
he offered no further explanation. Not why a fragment of broken
porcelain had been saved, nor why he wore it, but Silva inferred that
it was very important, slipping it over his head, careful not to catch his
hair. She pressed her lips to the center of his chest where the pendant
had rested, before gingerly placing it on the dresser beside the watch.
He rose from the bed, unzipping the back of her dress, sliding it

down her body until she was able to step free of it. Silva watched as he crossed the room, placing the dress on a hanger on the back of her closet door, smoothing out the skirt before crossing back to her. Careful and considerate, she thought, always so careful. Hooking his thumbs in the straps of her thong, he deftly pulled it down her body, and she did the same with his black boxer briefs a moment later until they were both bare, slipping beneath the sheets of her bed.

"Oh! I forgot something." She hopped out of bed, squeaking at the chill air as she crossed the room quickly, pushing up the window and hoping none of her neighbors were awake to see the site of her bare chest outlined in the pane for a brief moment. When she slid back beneath the sheets his arms came around her, pressing her to his front, flush against his warmth.

"Thank you for inviting me," Silva murmured against his throat after a few moments. "It was a fun party. I'm glad I got to meet your friends. Why wasn't Ainsley invited?"

"He doesn't know any of them," he explained, hesitating, his head cocking in thought. "Well, actually I think he does know one or two of them *intimately*, but that doesn't matter. They don't matter." He smiled softly, shaking his head at her protest. "They're people I know, people I've used for one thing or another, who used me for another thing or two in return. That's how this industry works."

Silva was quiet in the wake of his confession, thinking the way he floated from conversation to conversation, not really investing himself in any of the people there. She wondered if he'd ever let her in to meet the people who *did* matter, if this well-heeled group was not it. "What about your actual friends then?"

His eyebrow raised, exaggerated by the way his face pressed into her pillow. "I seem to remember you meeting Shona. Have you met Ainsley? He's hard to forget. Orcish, very tall, never shuts his bleedin' mouth."

"*Yes*, I've met Ainsley," she giggled, "I just mentioned him two seconds ago!"

"You did, but you seem a bit confused and I didn't want to call attention to it."

She pushed on his chest as she laughed, huffing in mock outrage at his response. "He *does* talk a lot," she agreed with a smile. ". . . That's it then? You're not going to introduce me to the rest of your friends?"

"Silva, I like feral cats, very small children, and very old men, and that's about it. I'm not sure where you think I'd find the extra hours in the day to cultivate the habit of being a social butterfly, but I'm sad to have to inform you I've neither the time nor inclination to do so."

She scowled, bumping her nose to his as his low laughter warmed her face. Silva pressed her lips together as he kissed her forehead again, her mind moving on to the next missing piece of the puzzle. Pressing herself a little tighter to his front, she pushed her knee through his legs, gratified by his warmth as he trapped her.

"What about your family? I've never been to Ireland . . . maybe — maybe we could visit? Maybe in the spring? I'm sure your grandmother would like that."

His eyes were sad as he smiled softly, one of his long fingers reaching out to push a lock of her hair back behind her ear, his thumb once again caressing the apple of her cheek. For a long, heavily weighted moment, the only sound was the steady ticking of his watch upon the dresser. *He's going to say no*, the little voice in her head hissed. *He wishes he'd never even told you his name, he doesn't want you to be a part of his life, didn't he say so before?*

"They've been dead for a very long time, dove. But if it makes you feel any better, my nan would have loved you."

"Oh," she whispered in a small voice, her stomach twisting, feeling horrible for even bringing it up. She wanted to ask how they'd died, how old he'd been when he lost them, what he'd done after, but the soft, sad smile had not left his face as he continued to stroke her hair. He'd never mentioned any siblings, neither Orcish nor Elvish, although, she reminded herself, he never actually mentioned much. Passing references to the grandparents who'd raised him, the single statement regarding his mother, that weekend she'd first returned, and that was all. No other family that he brought up, no stories or funny reminiscents, no grievances or gripes. Half mentions without elaboration or explanation, and little else. He worked, morning 'till night, and that was it. "What about your mom?"

"We don't speak." Once again, he offered no further explanation, and his tone brokered no further discussion, but she pushed, not content to let the conversation derail that easily.

"Is she —"

"She lives in the northern part of the country," he cut in, heading off the question taking shape on her lips. "I put her in a care facility before I left, and she has all of the company she might wish to have. She doesn't know me more than half the time, and it's a very long way to travel to have something thrown at my head."

Tears pricked her eyes at the thought. "I'm sorry." She tried to imagine life without her mother, without her grandmother, and her heart seized a bit at the thought. It was easy for other people to tell her she ought to simply walk away from her family; that she ought to tell them all to simply hang and let her live her life anyway she pleased, but those were easy things to say, and much harder to do. She loved her mother, loved her grandmother; couldn't imagine not having their shoulders to cry on or their wisdom over the years. Even though she felt trapped in the carefully constructed roadmap they were laying out for her, she knew all of it was done from a place of love. They only wanted the best for her, misguided as it may have been, and she could not simply walk away from them, walk away from her life, as easily as Lurielle had done. He'd told her that he'd emigrated many years ago, the one time she'd asked, and she tried to picture him doing so alone, moving here with no friends or family. The thought of him growing up not being close to his mother, leaving his homeland all alone without knowing there was someone behind to miss him hurt her heart.

Silva had the sudden realization that his world was actually very small, and he had already shown her every corner of it. The people who were important to him, his daily routine and those who populated it. His business and his home and all of the minutia in between, and she hadn't even told her friends or family his name. Her eyes filled with tears once more, pooling and soaking into the cool, cotton pillowcase beneath her face. She hadn't even let on that she was seeing anyone in the first place.

He sighed heavily, his thumb swiping over her tears. "I'm not worth your tears, dove. Put these away, and save them for something worth crying over."

"You *are*," she insisted, batting away the hand he raised to her face again like an annoyed kitten. "I was worried," she admitted, hesitating for a moment, feeling her ears heat as she sniffled. "I was worried about what you would call me tonight. I was worried sick over it. Isn't that so silly?"

"What do you mean 'what I would call you?'"

"I was worried you were going to call me 'your friend Silva.'"

He huffed, a soft chuff of unvoiced laughter, his thumb smoothing over the apple of her cheek, dragging the moisture of her tears along with it.

"Is that what we are, Silva? Good friends? Is that what you want?"

Her eyes overflowed again, frustrated with herself, how much time she'd let slip by as they sat stagnant over the last months, a situation of her own making.

"*No*, that's not what I want us to be at all. I want to be exactly what you said tonight. *Yours*. We're *barely* friends! I love spending time with

316

you, I love being with you, I love—" She cut herself off, swallowing down the sentiment with a shudder. "You hold me away. You never let me get too close. I don't even know what I am to you." The breath he blew out had enough strength to ruffle her hair as he pressed his forehead to hers saying nothing for a long moment.

"Well, you've never asked, dove, have you? You can call me whatever you'd like. Or don't call me anything at all, it's of no consequence to me. You're the only one with anything to lose here. I told you once before you'll always have a place to come. If that's the place to run away from your family for a few hours, or your husband, or your children, it doesn't make a difference. I'll be there waiting for you. It doesn't matter what you call me, little dove. You have your whole life in your hand, and you're worried if I'm going to call my girlfriend? Do you think a girlfriend is all that you are, Silva?"

Her tears were soaking through to the pillow, and she knew her face was probably splotched purple, but at that moment, it didn't matter. He had her heart in a vice, each word twisting it a bit tighter.

"You're my heartbeat, Silva. You're the pulse in my chest and the blood in my veins. You want to rip me open, dove? Take a bite out of my heart? It already belongs to you, so you can do as you wish, and it doesn't matter what you call me. You're the only reason for breathin', and if you come to your senses and kiss me goodbye in the morning and then put me out of your mind, it won't change a thing. It won't change what you are. You'll always be mine, Silva. That doesn't mean you should want me as yours."

"Well, I *do*," she insisted stubbornly, not bothering to wipe away the tears that ran down her cheeks. "Everyone wants to tell me what I should do, who I should be, who I should marry. What about what I want? What's the point of having everything if I'm never going to be allowed to be happy? Why can't I get everything I want?"

He smiled at her obnoxious words and she pushed on his chest, *refusing* to be placated and pushed aside.

"I would give you the entire world, if I could, Silva. I'd pull the stars from the heavens to lay them at your feet. But I can't give you any of the things you *want*, dove. I can't give you anything beyond this moment, I can't promise you a tomorrow. I won't make promises to you that I'm not able to keep, so please don't ask me to."

"You don't have to promise me tomorrow," she insisted, using the edge of her comforter to wipe away her tears before pressing her face to the center of his chest. His heart thumped beneath her cheek. *His heartbeat. He called you his heartbeat. Nothing else matters.* "I can promise *you* tomorrow." She pushed away his insistence that he couldn't give her all of the things she wanted, knowing he was wrong. "I want to bring you to breakfast tomorrow at the coffee shop in town," she mumbled against his skin. "It's where everyone goes, and it's really good, I think you'll like it." The Black Sheep Beanery was the busiest business in town, the whole of Cambric Creek showing up at least once a day for their caffeine and other assorted beverage fixes. He would see the other couples there, couples just like them, and then maybe he would understand. "Promise me you're not going to leave in the middle of the night. I don't want to wake up tomorrow and you're just gone."

She was able to feel time slowly grinding to a halt; the ticking of the watch on the dresser no longer audible, the world outside of her window falling away as she craned up to look at him when he remained silent. The only thing that existed was his soot-black lashes, fanning over his cheek as his eyes fluttered shut and he sucked in a shuddering breath. The wind had ceased blowing against the pane, and there were no sounds beyond her window, as if the whole world held its breath, waiting for him to answer. She imagined the moon, high above her little apartment, icy white and cold, shivering as she held her breath as well. Time had stopped, and she felt eternity rushing over her like the pull of the tide. His thick eyelashes were able to stop the tears that overflowed when his eyes closed, catching all but one, and she watched it track like a droplet of crystal across his flawless, pale green skin, before his face tipped towards hers, catching her lips. She felt the pull of his teeth and the drag of his tongue, the way he tugged on her lower lip seeming to jolt her into reacting, pushing up to join him in the kiss, attempting to channel every ounce of love and desperation she felt into her lips against his. When his eyes opened, his lips pressed her forehead once more, his arm holding her tightly against him.

"I promise, Silva," he murmured, stroking again at her hair. "I won't leave you without saying goodbye."

Spring

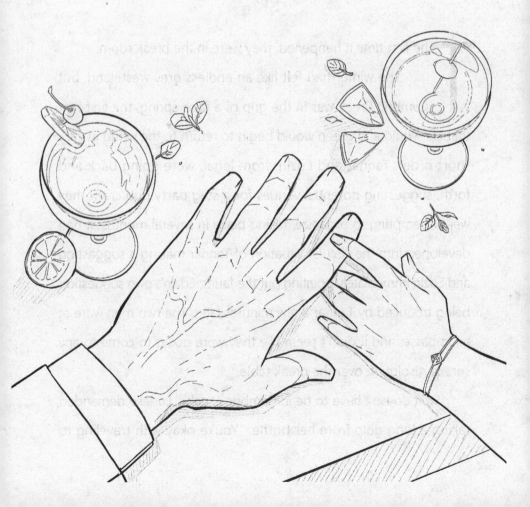

Silva

The first time it happened, they were in the break room.

The winter had felt like an endless grey wasteland, but Cambric Creek was in the grip of a false spring, the first hint that life would and green would begin to return to the world in very short order. Tannar and Edzin, from legal, were going back and forth, suggesting potential venues for a stag party pub crawl they were attempting to organize, taking place in several months. It had developed into the circular situation of Tannar making a suggestion and Edzin immediately pointing out the faults; Edzin's own suggestion being trounced by Tannar a few minutes later. The two men were at an impasse, and it didn't seem like they were going to come to any sort of resolution over the break table.

"So it doesn't have to be in Cambric Creek?" Lurielle demanded, taking a long gulp from her bottle. "You're okay with traveling to

Bridgeton or Starling Heights?"

"Going to either of those places would be fine," Tannar agreed, nodding. "Everyone is meeting at the Pickled Pig, and we're getting a party bus. So traveling a little bit isn't the problem, but we need to pick a direction. Starling Heights has a lot of bars and restaurants, right? They probably won't be as crowded as expensive as the city"

"What about the Plundered Pixie? Have you ever been there? It's in Greenbridge Glen."

Silva's head swung in Ris's direction, her eyes saucer-wide, but Ris never turned, too intent on digging the fruit out of the bottom of her yogurt cup. "It's a billiard pub, you know, shooting pool? It'll be packed with single women come spring."

Tannar cocked his head questioningly. "I've never heard of that one, where's Greenbridge Glen? I don't think I know where that is."

"Yes you do. It's that little town with the nudie resort," Edzin scoffed. "Why in the stars would we want to go there for a stag party?!"

"Didn't you just say you're looking for pubs you've never been to before?" Lurielle shot back, wrinkling her nose. "If you're going to go from Cambric Creek to Starling Heights, this is in the middle." Edzin scowled at her logic, unable to argue.

"You also just said you've got a bunch of single guys coming and they'll all be looking to get laid." Ris shrugged. "Like I said, it's always full of women. I know they have a pool league right now, but I don't know if it's still going on in the spring."

It wasn't, Silva wanted to pipe up. League play only happened in the winter, when Tate shifted his focus from Clover to the Pixie, the menu turning over from the ladies-only drink specials they ran during the tourist season to one more focused on bourbon and whiskey, the action around the pool tables overtaking the normal carnal past times for which the resort town was known. He had told her that some weeks he would only pop into the bistro a few times, finding nothing to do that couldn't be done by one of the girls, and nothing as important as the old girl's needs. She had initially thought that his schedule would free up for her once the cold weather blew into town, but instead, the opposite had proven true. He was a shrewd businessman and knew how to drive traffic through his doors even when the roads were slick with black ice, and had laughingly told her the pub was busier in the off-season than it was during tourist season, dashing her hopes. She didn't know how or why Ris would be mentioning the Pixie with such authority, but her spine quivered in anxiety at her friend's words.

"You probably need to call ahead and reserve some tables if you're interested. The owner can be a little pernicious if you waltz in acting too entitled."

"Pernicious," Lurielle snickered under her breath. "I'm going to tell him you said that."

Ris snorted, and the conversation moved on to a wine bar in Starling Heights, the one Tate had taken her to before, right across the street from the dessert bar whose menu was more than 75% made of chocolate.

She and Tate had met with Lurielle and Khash a handful of times by then, double dates that made her feel as if they were half a foot away from moving in together and planning their futures. The outings had always taken place at Clover, or else, one of the other little establishments in the resort town's business district; never, ever at the Pixie. She got the distinct impression that Khash turned his nose down to the black-bricked pub, a fact she didn't know for sure, but one that raised her hackles nonetheless. She had a feeling if she were to ever make the suggestion for him and Lurielle to meet her there, he would have countered with another venue. She was beyond thrilled for her friend, and she and Ris had begun sending each other photos of bridesmaid dresses they liked, deciding Lurielle would probably leave it up to them, anyway. That she and Khash would be married by the following year was a foregone conclusion, and it was wonderful seeing the bright, radiant light in her Lurielle's eyes, and the way her nose scrunched with her involuntary smile whenever he was mentioned . . . Silva was thrilled for her friend, but that didn't mean she quite understood the attraction. Khash was a little too handsome, a little too perfect, and entirely too pleased with himself. He and Tate had a visceral dislike of each other, which made their occasional double dates an exercise for each orc in controlling their faces. Hearing Lurielle and Ris both inexplicably refer to Tate practically in the same breath felt like something clawing at her insides, and she excused herself from the conversation not long after, desperately needing to get away from the table and get some air.

The bravado she felt having him in her bed for the first time that winter had faded as the snow piled up and the weeks between seeing him grew. It hadn't been particularly snowy that year, a sleety rain replacing the normal accumulation, but it iced over at least twice a week, leaving the roads treacherous. The driving conditions made her nervous, and it was hard to justify making the journey up the rural highway leading to Greenbridge Glen when she barely went anywhere other than work. She packed her lunch each day, and as much as she loved the Black Sheep Beanery, it was a luxury she was easily able to cut out during the inclement weather. She bought a pour-over coffee system for her countertop, a box of Tate's favorite tea, and a pretty new thermos, making herself a cup of his golden breakfast tea each morning, bringing her coffee and lunch to work, glad she had only had a ten-minute commute. It was too easy to come home each evening and snuggle up with a book, the sun already making itself scarce shortly after she arrived in her apartment, feeling like she was on a winter vacation from her actual life. It would've almost been fun, if she would've had him on the phone to keep her company; if they sent each other funny texts and videos throughout the day, and whispered to each other each night before she went to bed, but unless she reached out to him first, her phone remained silent. She despaired each day that passed. He was ridiculous and dramatic, and entirely too pessimistic, and despite the fact that she was *certain* there was a way to get everything she wanted, she could not shake the feeling that he was still trying to let her go.

At first, the absence hurt. He had called her his heartbeat, and she wondered how it was that he could say such a thing and then put her so easily out of his mind. She would wrap her arms around one of her pillows at night, pretending it was him, imagining that she could still smell him in her sheets, despite the fact that a full week would pass without even speaking to him, until she broke down and called or texted, the warm lilt of his voice washing over her like a balm — always happy to hear from her, always quick to respond to her tentative overtures with a cheeky text of his own, content to let her prattle on about the boring minutiae of her days in the cold, and each time she would twist in aggravation that yet again, she had to make the first move. Eventually, though, she simply grew accustomed to the new state of affairs. She imagined that they were in a sort of icicle-encrusted stasis, the world continuing to move around them as the winter grew colder. She began to send him a daily text, reminding him that she was there, of the things he'd said, and that she would be waiting once the ice melted. Until then, in Cambric Creek, a million miles away from him and the solid thump of his heartbeat, life continued as normal.

Her grandmother had been especially maudlin as Yuletide approached, insisting Silva join her for event after event — charity banquets and holiday luncheons for the ladies club, the organizing committee for New Year's fashion show, an event that was touted as a career builder that felt more like a singles mixer. Nana hadn't even bothered showing up for that last one, making Silva's reservation and then dropping her at the door.

Tannar had been there, having recently joined the club. He'd sat at her table, refilled her drink, kept her hostage at the event for longer than she might have stayed on her own, waiting with her for her car to arrive. She'd been peevish the following day at work, dodging the handsome elf in the break room as she put her lunch away, eating at her desk rather than risking more time spent in his company. He had been interested in her since starting at the company earlier that year, Silva was well aware of that fact, as Tannar was hardly discrete in his attentions. Ris had mentioned more than once that he seemed to be everything she was looking for, with the added benefit of actually being a nice guy, and as much as it pained her to admit, Silva was forced to admit she was right. Tannar was friendly, friendlier than most elves tended to be, particularly in mixed-species company. Friendly and mostly kind, casually good-looking, as opposed to Wynn's frosty elegance. He didn't hold a candle to Tate, wasn't nearly as handsome, possessing less than a tenth of her absent lover's sex appeal. More importantly, he did not possess Tate's spark of mischief and wild energy, didn't make her blood thrum in her veins. He wasn't interesting or mysterious or dangerous, all things a good romance hero ought to be. Silva had a feeling if they were characters in a book, Tannar would be the boring, bland betrothed of the female main character, trapped into marrying the bore to save her family's castle, or something similar. Not particularly objectionable, not particularly passionate . . . not particularly anything. Not particularly anything summed up her feelings for him quite well, she thought. Still, as the winter wore on and the time not spent in Tate's company increased, that niggling little voice at the back of her head began to wonder if it would be simply easier to just give in. Give in to what her mother and her grandmother wanted, give in and get everything they thought *she* wanted.

She had pushed away the depressing thoughts, certain that things would get back on track once they broke out of this icy stasis. She would tell her mother she was seeing someone, and announce to her friends she was officially coupled. They would make plans for the spring and she would take him to tea with her grandmother; an entire summer worth of adventures waiting for them. . . . And now here was Ris, mentioning Tate as if she knew him personally, a perplexing scenario if ever there was one. Lurielle's little rejoinder only made Silva feel as if *she* were somehow the odd one out of her own life, and the mere thought left her unsettled.

The breaking point happened just a week later. Tannar had pointedly asked if she was planning to attend the club's social event that weekend, one she had no interest in. He'd not been this forthright since he'd first expressed interest in her months earlier, and Silva found herself ducking around a concrete answer, knowing her grandmother would likely attempt to pressure her into attending. The morning left her nerves frazzled, and she agreed to meet the girls for drinks that night without hesitation, breaking her new homebody routine, desperate for distraction.

When they walked into Gildersnood that night, the place was packed. She understood then why Tate asserted that the Pixie was busiest in the winter months — it was midwinter, and the whole town seemed to be out having a round or three, driven out of doors despite the weather, all possessing the same ich. It happened sometime between the fourth and fifth rounds. It was the weekend, Ris pointed out. None of them had to be up early tomorrow, and it had been weeks since they had indulged in happy hour. Happy hour turned into the dinner hour, and the girls had shared several appetizers from Gildersnood's limited menu before switching from the happy hour specials to the house drink specials, a sweet concoction that nonetheless packed a wallop, and Silva had been eager to lose herself in mild inebriation, putting the stress of the week and the silence from Greenbridge Glen behind her.

Her phone had been face-down with her clutch, silent and forgotten as they laughed at Ris's impersonation of Dynah's most recent ex-boyfriend. When the phone began to buzz across the surface of the table, Silva initially paid it no mind. Even though she spent less and less time with her friends from the club, they still included her in group chats and planning texts, commented on her social media posts, and complained about their own boyfriends and families. She was glad not to be out of the loop entirely, for she had worked hard on achieving her place in the social strata, and it wouldn't do to be forgotten completely, not yet.

When the phone continued to vibrate, she realized it was a

missed call. A missed call from a number she did not recognize, she saw, flipping the phone over quickly and swiping away the notification. When it buzzed again a few minutes later, she picked it up, curiously. It was a text, containing only a video file. She bit her lip, wondering what sort of unsolicited jerk-off video she was going to be subjected to, unsure if she ought to open it. Deciding at worst it would give her something to laugh over with Ris and Dynah, she clicked the triangle in the center of the video icon, her phone screen instantly filled with Tate's face. He was doubled over in laughter, his pupils blown wide like a shark's, a press of bodies visible behind him. As she tried to process where he was, another text came through.

Silva, we need to have a conversation about relationship responsibility.

It was not Tate's phone number, and she couldn't imagine why he would be sending her such a sternly worded message accompanied by such a manic video, but before her tripping thoughts could organize themselves enough to formulate a response, another message came through.

This is Ainsley btw. I probably should have said that first.

Your boyfriend is a sloppy drunk, and you need to come collect him because I'm going to leave him here.

Silva gaped at her phone screen, a twisting tangle of emotions climbing through her like an invasive vine — her anxiety slamming into overdrive over the unexpected message, razor-sharp leaves over the threats that Tate was about to be left wherever he was, and blooming with giddiness that she was thought of as his girlfriend by *his* friend, his important friend. When the phone rang again, buzzing in her hands, she nearly dropped it in her scrambling effort to answer. It was a video call, her stomach French braiding itself when Ainsley and Elshona filled the screen.

The orc woman had seemed uncomfortable with her continued presence on the weekends, and her trips to the kitchen to say hello and goodbye and engage Elshona in conversation had tapered off quickly when Silva realized she herself was the cause of said discomfort. She supposed she understood, for if she had had a weekend fling with someone that she'd not intended to see again, she might not like having their presence forced upon her either, but it still made her feel poorly, and she avoided the kitchen hallway when she went with Tate to the bistro on Sunday mornings, setting up the dining room and preparing for the brunch rush before she left for home.

"It's not our fault, lamby!" Elshona was cackling, all discomfort with Silva apparently forgotten, crowded into the frame next to Ainsley's huge mohawk. "You need to come get yer man, he's completely off the lash." Just behind them, she could see Tate's head, was able to hear his musical laugh, louder than normal with a wild, manic quality. Beside her, Ris gaped.

"Look," Ainsley began raising his hands as if he were about to explain the mysteries of the universe, his shoulders shaking in laughter he was barely able to contain. "First, I just want to say this isn't our fault. Have you ever been to a music festival, lamby-dove? You know you're not supposed to eat the blue pastilles, right? Your boyfriend went face first in a whole pile of them, and I don't think he's eaten today. He's been dancing for like three fucking hours, everyone in this place is now his best friend. I have to work tomorrow, Silva. We both have to work," he gestured to Elshona beside him. "We've been trying to get him to wrap it up for the past forty minutes. I just wanted to let you know where he was, in case he winds up on a missing person's board somewhere, because we need to go home." The music was a raucous Celtic tune, played on traditional instruments and accompanied by a driving drumbeat, faster and more intense than she suspected it was meant to be played. She heard Tate's laughter again, and the braid of her stomach tugged.

"Can't you take him with you? Tell him you're going to another pub!"

Ainsley sighed, rubbing a huge hand over his face. "Humans have this expression I'm rather fond of, maybe you've heard it. 'Like herding cats,' meaning a situation that is aggravatingly impossible. You're just going to go around in circles with this obnoxious cat, right? And everyone knows cats have claws. In this situation, in case you weren't sure, Tate is the cat. I've always been more of a dog person, to be honest."

"These friends of yours, Silva?" There was an odd edge to Ris's voice, but before Silva could respond, Ainsley's face split into a huge smile on her phone screen.

"Well, well. Looks like the gang's all here. Fancy seeing you, Nanaya. You ladies should've joined us tonight."

333

"How do you know him?" Ris demanded, leaning over Silva's shoulder, attempting to see the phone screen. "What does he mean 'your boyfriend'?"

Silva opened her mouth to answer, finding no sound willing to come out. She gaped at Ris like a fish for several moments, coming no closer to an answer than she had when the question had been asked. On the phone screen, Ainsley cocked his head, his eyes narrowing.

"Are you *kidding* me? Do you mean to tell me after all this fucking time that—" he held up a hand cutting himself off, his mouth pressing together in a flat, grim smile, shaking his head. Beside him, Elshona had gone quiet, her eyes widened.

Anger burned in her belly, the urge to defend herself churning at the back of her throat. He didn't get to judge her, she wanted to scream. No one understood what she was juggling, and no one seemed to care. "Ainsley, you can't just leave him there," she pleaded, ignoring his judgmental look. "What if something happens?!" He had called her his heartbeat, his reason for breathing, and then they'd not spoken in nearly three weeks. It was hard to fathom turning her back on her family and her community for someone who seemed perfectly content to not assert himself in her life, to let her go on living without him, to let her follow the tightly prescribed roadmap her family had laid out for her, assigning himself the role of a minor accessory at best. "Please just bring him home."

"Don't worry, Silva. I will absolutely be bringing him home, and when he finally sobers up, I'm going to have a very hard conversation with my friend over pretty things that are a waste of his time."

The screen went black as the call disconnected and Silva bit back a curse.

Ris gaped at her. "'He has his little beauty in this weekend,'" she intoned, her eyes squinting as if she were trying to remember something, her brow furrowing. "You? And *Tate*?!"

"How do you know Ainsley?" Silva demanded, not liking the fact that she was at the center of everyone's apparent ire that evening, that everyone was demanding things of her, and giving nothing in return. "Is that how you know about the Pixie?"

"We've been seeing each other since the fall," Ris shrugged. "It's casual. Only reason I didn't say anything was because I didn't want Dynah going into a tizzy." Across the table, Dynah gasped in offense. "So let me get this straight . . . you . . . and fucking *Tate* . . . and you've been seeing him in secret for . . . how long?"

"It's not been in secret," Silva insisted hotly. "We double date with Lurielle and Khash all the time! And since the end of summer. I met him on our first trip."

Ris 's violet-colored ears darkened. "What the actual fuck nugget?!" She shouted, banging on the table, making their glasses rattle and slosh. "Are you fucking telling me that not only have you been in a secret relationship with that feral fucking *lunatic* since the summer, *I'm* the only one who didn't fucking meet someone on that trip? And Lurielle knows about this? Are you fucking *kidding* me?!"

Ris's expletive-laced tirade seemed to hang in the air over their table, earning the attention of most of the bar patrons in the vicinity. Silence reigned in her wake, and across the table, Dynah still stared slack-jawed. Silva began to giggle, slapping her hand over her mouth, unable to stop herself. Ris' laughter, two beats later, was louder. Her head dropped back, shoulders shaking, the long waterfall of her sleek black hair swinging behind her. "Un-*fucking*-believable."

"I can't believe you're seeing Ainsley," Silva sighed once their laughter had subsided. "He talks *soooo* much! How do you ever get a word into the conversation?"

"I can't believe you're seeing Tate! You know, I think he might actually be part fox. Or like, a really evil rabbit. Something that lives in the forest that bites your ankles." Silva dissolved into laughter again, her chest beginning to hurt from the way it heaved. "And I know about the Pixie because of you, actually, you told us that's where you spent the weekend the first trip." She dropped her head back, throwing a hand up in exclamation. "And I guess now we know why. It's a fun place, too bad it's not closer. He put some of the violet and rosemary Blackfangs in the cooler just for me, so I guess he's a nice rabbit sometimes. What did your family say? Evil rabbit doesn't really seem to fit the whole club aesthetic."

"I haven't told them yet," she whispered, all traces of her laughter extinguished, her head suddenly heavy from the drinks she'd consumed. The thought of Tate going out of his way to accommodate Ris made her lungs seize. It wasn't surprising, she thought, considering the way he adjusted his own home for her comfort. She wondered if he knew Ris was her friend, wondered why he'd never said anything . . . "I don't know how to tell them. And he doesn't want me to. I don't really know what he wants. But he's an elf, did you know that? He was raised in an Elvish community, he went to an Elvish school. We have so much in common . . ."

"But he's an orc," Ris finished, pulling a face. "You have to tell them eventually, Silva. You're not being fair to yourself if you don't. It's really not fair to him, either."

"I'm not being fair to him," she agreed softly. "But he's not very fair to me."

Ris rolled her eyes, sighing. She raised a hand, catching the attention of the slender satyr who was taking care of their table, leaning at the end of the bar. "Well then, it sounds like you two are made for each other. Two evil rabbits who don't know what you want. I think it's time to call it a night, those hurricanes are gonna hit us in about 10 minutes. Dy, you good?"

Silva blushed guiltily, remembering Dynah was still at the table. The satyr made it around with their tab, taking Ris's card as Silva pulled out a fistful of bills for her.

"I've got to hand it to you ladies," he mused, collecting the credit card. "When you four want to make a scene, you really make a fucking scene. And look at that, you're missing one tonight. I hate to hear how loud you're going to scream if all of you are ever here together."

"AJ, just take the damn card," Ris groused at him good-naturedly. "This is why we tip Ruby better."

The rideshare dropped her off first, and she was glad that Dynah had the idea in the first place, before they'd left work. She would call the service again to bring her back to the office the following morning, to collect her car, and treat herself to her long-missed coffeehouse on the way home. Her stomach tensed and tightened when her phone buzzed again, less than 15 minutes after she'd locked her apartment door. It was another unfamiliar number and she answered it tersely, prepared to argue with Ainsley again. She was surprised when a heavily accented voice barked in her ear.

"Corduroy Falls? You live in Corduroy Falls, yes? Can you give me an address?" Silva slumped against her kitchen counter, her jaw working but no sound coming out for a full minute as she attempted to process the words the man spoke. She had no idea what he was going on about, no clue what Corduroy Falls was supposed to be, but she wasn't about to give her address to some rando on the phone.

She was just about to hang up, when she heard the musical lilt of Tate's voice in the background, insisting that he knew what he was talking about, attempting to speak over the person on the phone. When she asked the man who he was and why he was calling her, his response of being another rideshare driver was the last thing she had expected. Tate had evidently been deposited at the Pixie's door, and had immediately ordered himself up another car. Silva pressed her sleeve to her mouth to stanch her laughter, deciding Ainsley didn't need to know this particular detail.

"Corduroy Falls," she repeated, not understanding the words the driver kept repeating.

"Yes!" the harried driver barked, and Silva winced, pulling the phone back a fraction. The man's lightly accented voice was laced with irritation, and she wondered how long he'd been arguing with his insistent, inebriated fare. *Like herding cats*, that's what Ainsley had said. Silva swallowed guiltily. "He said he's trying to get to Corduroy Falls . . . can you just give me some direction? My GPS is coming back empty, and if you're in one of those new developments, it's not going to—"

"Cambric Creek," she interrupted, feeling her cheeks heat, hoping this poor driver hadn't been attempting to herd *this* particular cat for too long. "I live in Cambric Creek, not in—"

It was her turn to be interrupted as the driver let out a stream of what she could only imagine were profanities in what sounded like gnomish. "This is what I asked him 30 minutes ago!"

"I'm so sorry," she implored. "You have the address now, it should be easy to find. I'll be waiting on the sidewalk for you!"

She shivered inside the small foyer of her building, peering out the window light beside the front door, tugging her cardigan around her to scamper outside when the car pulled up. He was curled up on the back seat like a small child, a preposterous site considering the length of his legs and width of his shoulders, beaming up at her when she pulled open the door.

"I curled up and held my breath when we hit the wall," he announced proudly, unfurling himself like some giant winged beast, stepping out of the car with far more coordination than she expected him to have. "We should go dancing, dove. It's midwinter. It's a night for dancing."

"We should go in and go to bed. It's late, and it sounds like you've been dancing all night. I am *so* sorry," she directed the driver, hoping the tip she passed through his partially open window would assuage his aggravation.

"We should run away, dove," he insisted once her apartment door was relocked, and she stripped him of his clothes in her bedroom once more. "We should run away together to the land of always winter, where no one will ever find us. We'll be so happy."

"You are so, *so* drunk."

"I am *not*," he insisted peevishly, tangling his legs with hers beneath the sheets, cupping her bottom and tilting her against him until they were flush. "Why does everyone keep saying that. It's a merry eve. I love the winter."

"Cambric Creek, Tate. I live in *Cambric Creek*."

"Silva," he chided, bumping her nose with his. "There's no such place. You're talking nonsense."

"*I'm* talking nonsense," she mumbled with a grin, biting his lip for a moment. "The land of always winter, that's a real place, but Cambric Creek, the place where we are literally right this second, *that's* made up. Gotcha."

"See, now you're being reasonable. Let's leave tonight. No need to pack, everything I need is right here."

She wondered if he would even remember the conversation

come morning. He might not, she thought, but she would. "I've missed you. You're right, we *should* just run away. Then I wouldn't have to go weeks without seeing you. Why did you come here tonight? I've barely talked to you a handful of times in the past month. Didn't Ainsley bring you home?"

"Home," he agreed. "I wanted to go home. It doesn't matter how long you stay away, dove. You know that."

"But you *were* home," she giggled, pressing her lips to his forehead as he tucked himself against her neck. "Ainsley is going to kill you if he finds out you left again."

"I'm home now."

Her voice stuck, breath hitching, the sudden slackness against her and the steadiness of his breath on her neck an indication that they wouldn't be having any more conversation that night. Instead, she watched him sleep. His brow had smoothed out, the furrow that lived between them gone, for the moment. His features were softer in sleep, not quite as angular, not quite as puckish, and she tried to imagine what he'd been like as a child, as an adolescent, as a young man. When his eyes fluttered open, dim light coming in through the window, she had no idea if it had been hours or minutes that passed.

"Do you know how to play croquet?" Shifting as she asked the question, she turned her body until they were nose-to-nose on the pillow once more. She'd opened her window before putting him into bed and the room was freezing, just the way he liked it. Tate insisted he was unable to sleep in a warm room, and she had grown used to the arctic chill from the central air he'd kept on well into the autumn months; had reconciled herself to sleeping with the windows open in the dead of winter when she shared his bed, and in truth, it wasn't so bad. He was always warm, always held her tightly against him, and unlike her previous partners, Tate never, ever pushed her away. That moment was no exception, and she pressed into his side, sliding her cold toes up his bare leg beneath the duvet until they were sandwiched between his shins, his skin molten as always.

His eyes narrowed to golden slits as he eyed her on the pillow, and Silva was unable to hold in her giggle at his disdainful look. "What kind of question is that? Do you think I was raised by rabbits? Next you'll be asking me if I ever had plum pudding on Fallrite."

She shook against him as she laughed, imagining a family of angry, feral rabbits raising him, giving a bit of credence to Ris's assertion. Silva lifted herself slightly, shifting her hips so that she was able to mold her body to his, tucking the duvet around her to hold herself in place, like a great cotton cocoon. "They're putting in a new field in the community park, they've already broken ground since the weather has been so mild, you should come visit me when it opens and we can play."

She was almost embarrassed by how often she'd daydreamed about that exact scenario, from the moment the banner had gone up announcing the new croquet court. The crew had taken advantage of the relatively mild winter, and she'd watched as the early work was completed: a section of the lawn ripped up for the new sod and turf, where manicured hedges and tournament quality hoops would be installed come spring. The community park was a wide expanse of rolling green lawn, ringed in footpaths and dotted with trees, wrapped by Main Street with its boutiques and restaurants, making it the perfect setting to spend an afternoon together — walking hand in hand up the shaded paths, lunching on the patio of a bistro not unlike Tate's own establishment, browsing through shops and kissing before the waterfall . . .

She'd always had a vivid imagination, but for the last year she had felt as though she lived in an entirely separate world in her head, her rich fantasy life softening the edges of a harsher reality. She wanted Tate to spend quality time with her in Cambric Creek, to see the vast array of couples and blended families who called the town home. She wanted to visit the old observatory and take walks together in front of the town's titular creek, winding through yards and farms until it widened in the center of town where it tumbled down a rocky outcropping in a non-stop deluge. She wanted him to exist in her Monday through Friday reality as more than just a weekend dalliance; wanted her parents to take a picture of her being held by *him* in front of the waterfall. Tate was well-mannered and confident, as handsome and cocky as any elf at her club, and he and his quicksilver smile would easily fit into her world, if only they would let him.

She had chewed over his desire to run away with her as he slept, letting the words tangle through her daydreams and create new visions in her head, the notion leaving her feeling oddly hollow. She didn't *want* to run away. Her parents had always doted on her, setting her up for an easy life of privilege, and her mother and grandmother had penciled in the details . . . and she liked the roadmap they'd laid out, she was forced to admit. There was no reason for them to run away, no reason for her to break with her family as Lurielle had. She could make him fit into the blueprint, she thought stubbornly, certain her fantasy could meld with reality. He could open a bistro in Cambric Creek and fill a stately Oldetowne Victorian with all of his beautiful antiques; could discuss business with her father and the proper care of fine china with her grandmother. They would be just another mixed species couple within the community and her parents would have to learn to live with it. By the time he'd woken that morning, she had worked herself into a state, clenching the sheets and aggravation and mumbling to herself. She wanted a spring wedding with flowers in her hair and a house in Oldetowne, wanted to take *their* child to the community park on Sundays, wanted the exact life her parents had planned for her, albeit with a very different partner at her side than they had in mind . . . but she was willing to start with croquet.

"I'll warn you though," she waggled her eyebrows as he grinned, "I'm very good. I played on our school team and we were undefeated for two years. If you think you're just going to waltz in and teach me a thing or two, you've got another thing coming, Mister."

"Very confident, aren't we, dove."

"Oh, *very*. Don't worry, I'll go easy on you for the first game." In the moonlight that seeped through the sheers on the room's windows, the needle-like points of his teeth looked particularly dramatic as he grinned hugely, and Silva mirrored his wide smile. "Did you play when you were young?"

She wasn't truly expecting an answer, not a real one. His lips were still curled in the barest hint of a smile as he rolled to his back, keeping her pressed to his side. "I did, when I was very young. I was obsessed with beating my grandfather, and we played every evening when he and Nan came home from the shop."

Silva blinked in surprise. The slight inhalation of her lungs suddenly seemed like too much movement, as if any distraction, no matter how slight, might halt his story in its tracks, and she wondered if she would be able to hold her breath for as long as he kept talking.

"I'd have everything set up and would meet him at the lane . . . and I was also very good, so don't go overplayin' your hand just yet, dove."

A million and one thoughts and questions raced and tripped through her mind, the same desire inflating in her that always did — a desperate need to know, to inhale him and absorb everything that he was and had ever been.

"Did-did you play at school too? You said you went to an Elvish school, right?" The quiet that followed her query seemed larger than her bedroom's confines, pushing out the windows and silencing the birds in the bush on the side of her building, silencing the traffic in the street. Her heartbeat had gone mute, the blood that pumped through her veins slowing to a halt, and her breath stilled . . . until

345

Tate sighed, breathing life back into the space, and the sound of the small, inquisitive chickadees who nested in the bush began to chirp once more. His fingers pushed through her hair, scraping over her scalp until he was palming her head, his thumb tracing a lazy arc behind her ear.

"Yes. I did. Go to an Elvish school, that is. For a time. I was going up to the secondary school at the new term and there was a team," he began slowly, his nails dragging lightly against her neck. "My grandfather was so excited. Finally, I'd be good at something normal." His laughter was a short, sharp burst; broken glass replacing polished crystal, and Silva winced. "We played every day that summer, until it was too dark to see the wickets. He was positive there wasn't a single person in the village who'd be able to beat me." His laugh was gentler that time, a soft huff that vibrated against her. "The school's pitch wasn't far from the shops in town, and before the summer was over he'd already made arrangements to close early the day of matches. Had me letter a sign for the door, 'closed for croquet match.' Said he wasn't going to miss a single one."

She hadn't realized his family had owned a shop and wondered what sort of business they'd been in, if Tate had worked there when he was young. Smiling against his skin, she tried to envision him as a lanky youth on a team like the one on which she'd played, a miniature version of his wide smile stretching across a slimmer, boyish face, his green skin glowing against the crisp whites. Her own family had displayed a similar reaction to her participation in the school's club, coming to every match, strolling around the garden pitch afterwards, chatting with the other well-to-do parents and grandparents, an extension of weekends at the club . . .

Her fantasy life bore little resemblance to her current reality though, and she supposed that meant the fantasy life she created for him likely didn't either. For the very first time, Silva tried to imagine what it would have been like if he had been her peer at school, if he had gone to Cevanorë and lived in the community. He would have been shunned by her vicious peers, she knew without question, and his family the source of gossip amongst the well-heeled adults.

She remembered one of her classmates, Dorea Eillis, whose entire existence in school had been upended the year she spent the summer several states away with her mother's kin. Silva had no idea how it had been found out that her classmate's mother was a half-troll, but she vividly remembered listening to her own mother and grandmother discussing the surgical procedure it was discovered the woman had undertaken to shorten the length of her ears and have her tusks removed. By the time Dorea had returned from the summer intersession, her family was the talk of the club, her schoolyard reputation in tatters, children picking up on the animosity of their parents as they listened to the cutting, careless remarks made over Sunday lunch in the club's formal dining room all summer in the Eillis's absence.

It was hard to imagine that the community Tate had grown up in was terribly different, she knew with a heavy heart. He rarely talked about his family, and there must've been a reason *why* he never spoke of them, a reason why he'd walled off his past so completely. There must've been a reason, she thought sadly, why he was the way he was. She wondered if his grandparents had been ashamed of him, the very thought causing a bubble of fiery fury to take up residence in her chest, making it very hard to breathe.

"What happened?" The words had escaped her lips before she had a chance to suck them back, and she tightened the arm around him, as if she'd be able to pull him back from the story's inevitable unhappy end, to protect him from whatever happened next, for although she didn't know any of the details, she was certain his stories of childhood would likely not have the same happy endings as her own. *You shouldn't make him talk about it, what's wrong with you.*

"Well, I shot up that summer. This might be hard to believe, dove, but I was a very small child. 'A wee mite,' is what my grandmother called me. Didn't stay that way for long, though. By the end of the summer that year I was a head and shoulders taller than my grandfather. 'Too tall for the regulation mallets,' that's what they told me. Didn't want to hear that I had my own. I couldn't use anything but the school's equipment, and that was designed for *normal* elves. So my illustrious career as a scholastic croquet star was over before it had a chance to start, I'm afraid."

"Were they mean to you at school? I mean . . . kids are terrible, I already know that. What about your teachers? Did-did they care about you being an orc?"

He snorted against the pillow. "Silva, what kind of daft question is that. Are you still hung over from last night? Of course they bloody cared. How many orcs did you go to school with in your posh little community, hmm? Not many, I reckon. They cared, and they never let me forget it for a minute."

She was certain her chest must have been glowing red from the anger she felt, the bubble in her chest expanding, pressing her lungs until she was sure she'd be able to breathe fire. She tried to imagine the disappointment he must have felt, his childish excitement extinguished, and then having to go home and break the news to his expectant family. If they'd treated him cruelly, she thought, vibrating in fury, she'd combust.

"Was your grandfather very disappointed?"

"Oh, I imagine he was crushed." His hand drifted, the pad of his index finger tracing down her spine before his palm flattened out against her skin, spanning across her back. His voice was casual, as though he were describing a long line at the post office or something similarly trivial, fingers dragging in slow circles against her skin. "Disappeared into his workshop that evening and didn't come out again all night."

The fire had moved up her throat, choking out her words, preventing her from silencing him. Silva was well-acquainted with how cruel and judgemental elves could be in a group, particularly those in positions of privilege within their community, but the notion of him being similarly mistreated in his home was one she couldn't entertain without crying ugly, angry tears. He rarely spoke about himself and thus it was easy for her to forget, easy for her to put him on a shelf on Sunday afternoons and go back to her perfect, glossy life and daydream about him slipping into it with ease; easy to push away the fact that an elf who presented as a different species would never be fully accepted, not truly. *You'll have to be like Lurielle and move away after all,* Silva thought, for she would breathe out her rage and set the entire town ablaze if her own child was ever treated as poorly by her community as Tate had been by his. She didn't want to hear anymore, regretting her infernal need to keep asking questions, forcing him down this unhappy trip down memory lane, needed to stop him before he told her something truly horrifying she'd not be able to forget—

"And then I came home one day later that week, and he was home and the croquet set was gone. There was a billiard table in the parlour, just delivered. We never played croquet again, but we learned billiards and played every night. No need to stop when the sun went in." Abruptly, the fire within her extinguished and she sunk into her too-soft bedding, the arm anchored around his body the only thing keeping her from being sucked out of existence. The edge of his well-trimmed nails skated up her spine once more, fingers pushing into her hair. "Not a lot of money to be made hustling croquet, so I'd say I came out ahead, on the whole."

"He wasn't upset with you?"

She watched the corner of his mouth upturn again at her question.

"No. Not like I'd done anything wrong, at least not that time. This will probably be quite hard for you to believe, but I had an appallingly bad temper that got me into trouble a fair bit. I was rather spoiled at home, though. Only child, of course, no playmates, of course. So ... I got rather everything I wanted. Books, toys, endless attention ... we lived outside of the village and there weren't any children around, so I didn't notice there was anything to be missed until I went to school. Even then, I didn't think anything of it, not for a few years at least. I went to school and I came home, and I assumed that was what all the other children did as well. But no, he wasn't upset with me. He was a good man. Ridiculously kind heart, never had a bad thing to say about anyone." He grinned in remembrance and she bit her lip, overwhelmed by the unprecedented sharing taking place. "He had an absolutely filthy mouth though, and he taught me how to swear. I went into his workshop to learn a new way of telling someone off every week, I only had to promise not to say it in front of Nan, and if I got caught not to say where I'd learned it." She dissolved into giggles at the thought, trying to picture Tate as a miniature version of himself, getting an education in profanity, until his smile faded, his eyes seeming very far away. "He never let it matter that we weren't blood. At least, he never let me feel like it mattered. I was his, as far as he was concerned."

Tears pricked her eyes as his voice trailed off wistfully, and the number of questions his comment raised were too numerous for her to count, so she decided to focus on the questions still rattling in her mind from the last time she'd had him in her bed. "What kind of shop did they have? How did they die? Were you very young?"

He was silent for a yawning stretch of time, and Silva closed her eyes, nuzzling her cheek against his skin, the solid thump of his heartbeat pressed to her lips as she kissed him, knowing she was pushing too much. "I was a teenager, I think? I really don't remember, to be honest. I wasn't there. They had a shop, my grandfather was a goldsmith. Nan would design all of the pieces and he made them . . . but I wasn't there. There was a fire. Half the shops in the village went up. They were in the cellar, that's all I know. I don't know why. There was nothing down there of value, the safe was upstairs, the jewels were kept in the safe. There was nothing but . . ."

"But what?" she echoed softly, not wanting to push too hard.

"A canvas on the wall where we used to draw and paint when I was a boy. That was it. They didn't keep anything of value there, it would take on water sometimes and wasn't worth the risk. I don't know why they were there, but I can guess that she went down first and he went after her. He would've followed her to the ends of the earth. I don't know if the roof caved in, or if the steps had burned away . . . they were together, though. I'm glad for that, because I can't imagine how either of them would've survived without the other. But I wasn't there."

She wanted to ask why, wanted to ask where he was and why it seemed so significant to him that he wasn't there . . . But he had stopped talking as she sniffled against his skin, and she decided the forced trip down memory lane had concluded, for now.

"But none of that takes away from the fact that I was still a *very* good player, and if you think I'll go easy on you, dove, then I regret to say you're very much mistaken. Are you going to wear one of those little white dresses with the pleated skirts? Or the shorts with the grosgrain bits?"

She was unable to breathe through her laughter as his lips moved down her neck, teeth catching at her clavicle, wheezing when his head disappeared beneath the duvet. She was unwilling to compromise, she decided. She didn't *want* to deviate from the blueprint of her life, wanted all of the things her parents had sketched out for her — a handsome husband, a home in Cambric Creek, a child of her own and her community at her back. She liked the roadmap they had set for her, and she loved her family too much to be able to simply walk away from them, unless they forced her to do so. She wanted to have everything; wanted to be Silva of the daytime and Silva of the nighttime both, and she didn't see why she had to choose. She could still get her house in Oldetowne and weekend afternoons in the park. She would make him fit into her world, she thought, or burn it down trying.

♥ ♥ ♥

Ris

"**C**an we talk about the fact that I'm the only sap in this entire friendship who apparently didn't know anything about fucking anything for the last eight months?"

Lurielle cackled at her words, and Ris glared, pulling out a chair from a brick table with a bit more force than necessary. "I don't think it's funny at all! I at least had a reason to keep my situation a little hush-hush, and we're not even serious! You go and meet some perfect orc dreamboat, Silva meets a set of teeth with a heartbeat, and I'm the shnook that comes home and goes on approximately seven hundred bad dates with Dynah before I get suckered into going back to the resort. I literally could have gone there with one of you like, oh I don't know, the next fucking weekend."

Lurielle was nearly choking on her pad Thai by then, dragging her fingers down the condensation on her water bottle before flicking it in Ris's direction. "Look, I'm sorry. I didn't know you were planning on finding your perfect friend with benefits dream man, okay? I didn't say anything about Silva because I honestly don't know what she's doing. I just want her to be careful and stay safe, but she's gotta make her own mistakes and figure it out. I just don't want her to get her heart broken."

"That's exactly what Ainsley says about Tate," Ris scoffed. "He thinks Silva is the heartbreaker. I guess they really are perfect for each other . . . He's a total weirdo though, right?"

"Oh, absolutely, completely. Disturbingly so. But . . . it's kind of funny, the more I spend time with her, I think she is too? Like, she's nothing at all like what we thought a year ago. Either she's changed or we were super wrong. We've done doubles with them a couple of times and Khash absolutely *hates* him, just doesn't have a single nice thing to say." She scowled into her noodles at the thought. "It actually really pisses me off, because I can't tell if he doesn't like him because he's a weirdo who never blinks, or because he's not the 'right kind' of orc. I have to remind him his kids are also going to be half elf, unless he's planning on trading up. But then I can even get mad at him, because Tate practically levitates in his seat with how much he hates Khash, and it's like, *incredibly* obvious he's only there because Silva pulled some adorable little bunny rabbit knife on him or something." Ris had doubled over, laughing so hard that sound had ceased issuing from her mouth. "It's not funny!" Lurielle laughed. "They're like these two giant man-babies just a heartbeat away from throwing food at each other, and then here's me and Silva in the middle just trying to chit chat."

"I think if Ainsley and I were to join you all he and Khash would just talk over each other all night. About absolutely everything and nothing, at increasing volume. If Khash thinks he is a schmoozer, he will have met his match. Tate would probably get up to go to the bathroom and just never come back. At least three of us could have a few cocktails, right? We could probably move to another table and they wouldn't even notice."

Lurielle was wheezing at that point. Someone came in from another department, looking askance at them, hovering with their lunch before thinking better of it and exiting the break room altogether, only making her laugh harder.

"She hasn't even told her family yet? She's been seeing this guy for more than half a year! How has she kept that a secret?! I'll be honest, I didn't give her that much credit, that's an impressive level of subterfuge." Lurielle wiped at her eyes, recovering. "She needs to decide what she's doing now, this is all going to blow up in her face eventually, right? Ainsley doesn't really like her, did I tell you that? He thinks she's self-centered and selfish. Do you think you should talk to her?"

"There's nothing I can say, Ris. And no offense to your boyfriend, but he really doesn't get to have an opinion. No one is telling him he should go no contact with his family. Would you be able to do that? I know you're close with your mom and dad, right? If you had to pick between them and your fuck buddy plus plan, would you be able to? It's real easy to tell someone else that they should cut off their parents. As the only one here who's done it, I can speak with authority: it's really fucking hard. She's gotta decide what to do on her own, and I don't blame her for not knowing how to handle it. It's a fucked up situation where none of us should be put, but here we all are. Look at Dynah. Look at me. Silva's twenty-five. She's figuring this shit out a lot sooner than I ever did, that's for sure. I have my own fucked up family to worry about."

Ris cocked an eyebrow as Lurielle sighed, fishing through her clutch. "This came the other day. I haven't even told him yet. So now the question is: do I suck it up and have him meet my mom beforehand, or let a giant catered party be the first time she meets her potential future son-in-law. Who happens to be a seven-foot-tall orc."

She whistled, reading over the foiled pink invitation Lurielle had produced. "Well, happy birthday to your great-grandma, I guess. That's at least nice. What are you going to do?"

Lurielle shrugged. "Fuck if I know. I can't *not* go to my great grandma's birthday, it's my mom who sucks, she doesn't. Call ahead and find out if there's going to be security? Work on preparing Khash for the reality of someone not thinking he's amazing? It's going to be a serious blow to his ego, he might need to go into seclusion afterward."

"Ugh, that sounds fantastic. I'm so broken up that I have a normal family that doesn't expect me to follow an ancient Elvish fortune cookie's edict on how to live my life. It's such a bummer. I guess I'll go home and contemplate how rough it is that my folks are totally okay with me not having a baby, and then maybe get my back blown out by my poly adventurous playmate. Good luck breaking the bad news to his royal highness."

Ris left the break room laughing as Lurielle shouted at her back.

"You really suck and you're real lucky I love you!"

She found herself curled up in Ainsley's lap that evening, recounting the conversation with Lurielle as she patiently waited for him to remember the name of the documentary he had been so excited over just a few days earlier.

"So she has to decide whether or not she wants to set up a dinner for her mom to meet him before the big party or just hold her breath and hope that the crowd deters her mom for making a scene."

"You elves are fucking wild. If you're this crazy now, I can't imagine what you were like a few centuries ago when you were still kind of scary and feral. Do you think you had claws at one point? Or maybe one of those retractable thumbnails, you know, like the big turkey dinosaurs?"

"I don't know, but isn't it kind of crazy the way we de-evolved like that? Elves were chosen consorts of the high fae! We committed genocides! We were apex predators! Now we're one step up from humans, and all it took was fucking them for a few hundred years. My ancestors were able to disembowel ogres with their bare hands, now I get period cramps and have to take three days off work to lay on a heat pack and cry. What a fucking letdown."

"I'm going to pretend you didn't just say it's a *letdown* that you're not able to commit genocide with your giant turkey dinosaur thumbnails anymore." He tipped his head back consideringly, the documentary forgotten for a moment. "Elves were consorts to the high fae? I didn't know that."

"Mhm. My nana would tell me stories of Elvish women who were abducted by the fae to be their brides, because they were beautiful and strong. They were taken to the otherworld until they produced an heir. It's probably just a story, but it was one of my favorites when I was little. I used to think it was so romantic . . . then I realized how creepy it actually is."

Ainsley's brow was furrowed, his eyes narrowed in thought before he shook it away, shooing the air beside of his face like it was an annoying gnat.

"You okay?"

"Oh yeah, I'm great. Just one of those questions I don't really want answered, I think. If your friends are all so fucked up, how did you turn out so normal?"

Ris sighed, leaning against his chest, shrugging. "I don't know, but I'm grateful. My parents are totally chill. Maybe it's because they're poor?" She laughed at her own answer as he rolled his eyes. "No, I'm totally serious! I told my mom I didn't want to have kids a few years ago and I thought it was going to be this whole big thing."

She sobered, remembering the conversation. It had been at the beach, on their little yearly holiday. They'd been walking along the shoreline, reaching a rocky outcropping where she'd dug for crabs as a child, building elaborate structures behind the protective barrier of the rocks.

"I don't want to have a baby," she'd blurted, her ears heating, despite the wind coming off the waves, breaking in an unending line of whiteheads. "I've thought about it a lot, and I . . . I don't think I'm ever going to change my mind. I don't think I want to get married either."

Her mother had gripped her hand, and they'd walked in silence for several minutes before she spoke.

"Your father and I tried for years," she said finally, smiling as a plover zigzagged before them. "Both of your grandmothers were insufferable. In*suffer*able. The whole time. I had three miscarriages. And all they wanted to know was when we were trying again. They'd pull out birth rate statistics like we didn't know they were declining and it was somehow up to us to reverse natural selection." They'd reached the seaweed-covered legs of the dock above, the spot where they turned around, where they'd been turning since she was a child, hand-in-hand. "It was worth it, sweetheart, because we love you more than anything else in this world . . . but I wouldn't wish that on you for anything. All we want is for you to be happy, Ris."

"Like, maybe they were disappointed in private, but they didn't push," she went on, feeling Ainsley's arm slip around her, curling around her waist. "They never made me do anything I didn't really want to. I won the parental lottery, I think."

"Sounds like it."

"Which is why you don't get to be such an asshole to Silva." When he made a noise in his throat, dismissing her words, Ris frowned, turning. "No, I'm serious. You don't understand the position we're put in. It's not just about having bougie parents who are specist or whatever. And don't get me wrong, most elves are *totally* specist. But correct me if I'm wrong, so are most orcs. At least the ones I've met."

"They are," he agreed reluctantly. "Especially the clan-raised ones."

"This is so much bigger than that. We're literally taught in primary school that our only job in society is to have an Elvish baby so that our bloodline doesn't die out. Elvish populations have been dwindling for more than 100 years. Do you know how much pressure that is? Our grandparents and great-grandparents don't want to hear that we fell in love with a goblin or troll or an orc, because every generation that gets further away from that Elvish bloodline is a generation further away from that stupid turkey claw. None of it makes any sense and it's all completely arbitrary and absolute bullshit, and little girls are the ones who bear the brunt of it. So if I were to tell you right now that it's me or Shu'la, how fair would you feel that is? That's what we deal with. My friend Lurielle went no contact with her mom, and granted, the reasons there are myriad, but the whole 'pressure to get married to the first elf that comes along' was a huge part of it. So be nice to Silva. Your friend isn't exactly unproblematic, you know. I would have an easier job bringing home a rock from your parking lot and telling my parents it's my true love than she has with him, let's be real. He looks like he's going to murder everyone in the room more than fifty percent of time, and you can't even deny that."

"*Fine*. You win! I'll be nicer to your spoiled brat friend, are you happy now? And to be fair, he's only looked that way recently, because all he and Elshona do is fight anymore. We're having a party for him, right at the close of the season. Rukh and I were talking and in all the years the Pixie's been open, we've never thrown a party, isn't that ridiculous? We have a pub! At our disposal! It's such a waste. And in all the years I've known him he's never had a birthday party, so that's our excuse." He chuckled. "I don't even know when his birthday is. But we figured he'd throw a fit if we tried to do anything during tourist season, and once the league starts up, that's it, they're packed. So we have like a two-week window. We'll see if your friend is still around by then." He cocked his head in thought for a moment, a grin spreading on his face until it broke into that big beaming smile. "That'll be our anniversary, Nanaya. Can you believe it? We're the hottest, normalest couple we know, and we're almost one year old. Oh! This is it! It's this one! With the mummies!"

Ris settled back against him, scooping up a handful of the wasabi-flavored popcorn they had in a giant bowl. It didn't feel like a year. It felt like a handful of weeks at most, grains of sand, chafing beneath her skin. A full year of his life, gone in the blink of an eye, the same amount of time it had taken her to wash her hair or blow her nose, or at least, that's how it felt. She needed life to slow down; slow down and let her savor these moments, moments like this.

"We'll have to celebrate that," she murmured, tipping her head back against his shoulder. "One year is a big deal, right? One year closer to putting your brain in a jar."

She tipped her head back as he kissed her, agreeing cheerfully as she leaned against him, settling against his chest.

"Do you know how much neuraltechnology will have advanced by the time I'm ready to croak? You'll probably be able to wear me like a smartwatch!"

She didn't especially want a relationship, she reminded herself as she shushed him, and she certainly had gone looking for love. Ris wasn't still quite sure how both had seemed to find her, but as she made herself comfortable against his warmth, she couldn't quite find it in herself to complain.

♥ ♥ ♥

Summer

Silva

The alarm was a melodic blast, the phone's vibration making it buzz loudly against the polished wood surface of the antique bedside table. Silva jolted awake, lifting her head from the fluffy cloud of softness where she was enveloped, just in time to watch his hand shoot out from the duvet to silence the alarm. The apartment was grey with dim, pre-dawn light, and she felt like she could easily sleep for another hour or four.

She had prepared herself for the early morning wake-up, however, knowing it was coming and actually dragging herself from the bed were two completely different things. Stretching, she forced herself to wakefulness, knowing it would do no good to dawdle, not wanting to throw off his schedule. She was surprised then, when Tate seemed to snuggle deeper into the cocoon of blankets after silencing the alarm, rather than urging her to get up. When the alarm sounded again, nine minutes later, and his pale green hand once more left the confines of the duvet to swipe unseeingly at the screen, she barely managed to suppress a giggle as his head completely disappeared into the white nest of fluffy down.

He'd already been at the bar when she'd arrived the previous evening, having left directly from work. The Pixie's regulars knew who she was at that point — eyes would avert as she passed, no massive green hands would reach out to brush her thighs or grab her ass, and she would make it to her customary stool at the far end of the Pixie's gleaming bar unmolested, a dagger-toothed smile greeting her before she stretched up to kiss his smooth, green cheek.

She'd still been in her work clothes when she'd arrived: a mint green, a-line dress with a scalloped lace hem that brushed the top of her knees, layered with an emerald cardigan, which she knew made her green eyes sparkle. Normally she would have taken a moment to change before leaving the office, but that day she'd been eager to leave, to escape Tannar's too-interested smile and probing questions about her weekend plans. It didn't matter that he was handsome and charming, friendly and eager to impress. His blue eyes were friendly and intelligent and his smile was kind, and Silva knew that he might have been someone she would have been interested in six months earlier, an awareness that tightened her stomach and made her squirm. He had a crush on Silva of the daylight hours, but Silva of the nighttime was no longer happy to be stuffed away, not anymore.

He'd been standing at the end of the bar, lean arms crossed as he surveyed the pool league matches with a sharp eye, listening to the bluster and chatter coming from the huge orcs clustered around the tables. She walked across the pub with purpose, not allowing any of the walking bodies in her way slow her down.

Things had been different since he'd come home to *her*, since the night she'd watched him sleep. She'd memorized the slope and planes of his face, and the rise and fall of his shoulders. The silvery scar that cut through his hairline and eyebrow had a twin at the center of his throat, and she had pressed her lips to it as gently as she'd been able, endeavoring not to wake him. He'd never told her how he'd come to acquire them, but now she wanted to know. She wanted to know *everything*; wanted to climb into his skin, wanted to examine and analyze his memories, and nothing less than all of him would do. She'd brushed her lips to his before tucking back against his front, nestling her cheek against his heart, reveling that she had him there in Cambric Creek, a step away from her daily life.

He'd stood behind her in line at the Black Sheep Beanery the following morning, his hand resting at her lower back, and it had felt more natural and right than anything else in her existence ever had. She'd looked around the coffee shop beaming, *hoping* someone would see her, hoping *everyone* would see her. She was done living a half-life, done with the lies, done pretending. They'd found a table near a side wall, drinking their coffee and picking at a shared pastry as they people watched. She'd pointed out business owners and City Council members, three insectoid sisters who were the proprietors of a darling little plant shop, and Jack Hemming himself, never raising his mirrored aviators as he chatted amiably with the staff as he'd placed his order. It was too cold to spend any length of time out of doors, but she walked him down Main Street, pointing out the shops and restaurants she thought he would be interested in — an occultist's tea shop and an esoteric little bookstore, a stationery shop that pressed their own papers and mixed their own ink, and half a dozen different pubs and restaurants.

He could tell himself that he wasn't able to give her the things she wanted until he was blue in the face — she was no longer happy to sit back and let other people tell her what she could and couldn't have, and Silva had decided she wanted it all. Her family and her community and him, with no concessions.

Honey-gold eyes had climbed up her legs as she moved across the bar the night before, jagged teeth pulling into a smile as she hopped confidently onto her barstool.

"Very pretty, dove . . . . off to someplace special?"

"Yes, actually." Silva had felt her own smile stretch, mirroring the impossible width of his as she gripped a handful of his black shirt, dragging him lower and closer, until she was able to press her nose to his neck, breathing in his freedom before moving her lips to his. "I came straight from work to see someone *very* special."

He'd lifted her with a squeak, placing her on the edge of the bar as soon as he'd locked the door behind the last staggering orc that night. The needle-sharp points of his teeth dragged up her leg, nosing at the trim of her dress as he slipped off her peau de soie slingback, pausing to admire the fabric. "Well I'm terribly sorry, but someone very special is going to have to piss off. You're stuck with me, for now."

She'd huffed, kicking at his shoulder as he pulled up a bar stool. "Stop it. Did you do another double today?" His eyes were tired, she'd noted, wondering if he would want to go straight to bed that night, as he often did. "Have you eaten yet? I can run down the street while you're closing up and grab you someth—"

She'd cut off on a squeal as she was pushed precariously to her back, his long fingers hooking under the sides of her lace panties, dragging them down her hips.

"I haven't . . . but I'm about to."

Now the long line of his body was warm against hers beneath the duvet, and the hard heat of his erection pressed to her belly, and Silva had a mind to give him a taste of his own medicine.

He had been in a particularly wicked mood last night, keeping her on her back with her legs around his shoulders for what had felt like hours, repeatedly bringing her to the edge of her climax before backing off, slowing the movement of his tongue, the points of his teeth dancing over her thighs. She had whined and writhed, pulling on his hair and begging him for release, but all Tate had done, repeatedly, was laugh.

She'd been relocated upstairs at that point, cradled in his arms and carried like a doll, her dress carefully removed and draped over the back of one of his modern-looking chairs, before placing her spread-eagle in the middle of the billiards table. His fingers were long and slender, able to press and slide against that spot inside her that she could never reach herself, making her cry out over and over again, playing her like an instrument, the same as he had that very first night, in the backroom of the bar.

"You are," he'd murmured against her slick center, pausing to press his teeth into the crease of her thigh, "the *whingiest* little princess. Pull my hair one more time and see what it gets you, dove."

His shaft was hard in her hand as she gripped it beneath the duvet, stroking him slowly. A low groan sounded from the mountain of white pillows beside her, and Silva giggled. She loved the heat of him, the slip and slide of his foreskin against her palm, and the softly mumbled curses that fell from his lips as she teased his cock tip with a barely-there pressure of her nail.

"It's time to rise and shine, sleepyhead," she sing-songed softly, smiling when he whimpered in response. The tips of her nails grazed his exposed glans, teasing at the seam, dipping into his slit until he bucked into her hands. "Oh no, that's very rude. It's daytime. *I* get to make the rules now."

The duvet whipped back at her words, and she nearly choked on her laughter at his scrunched nose and narrowed eyes. "Aye, is that so?"

"Mmhm. That's the way it works."

"Just remember, dove, the sun will go down again tonigh—" His words broke off on a groan, his head dropping back as she began to stroke him in earnest, moving with a continuous twist over his shiny, pink-edged head. Silva kept a firm grip, working him steadily until he was weeping pre-cum, his sac beginning to lift and contract from where she cupped it. *It's called a morning stiff, not 'you have all night to do something about it,' isn't that what he said?* He wasn't going to last long, so she intended to have her fun while she could.

His gasp, when she let go, allowing his cock to bob and twitch in the air, shivered up her spine, a thrill of *power* that she'd scarcely experienced before.

"What are you doing, Silva?" His voice was strained with a note of warning and his teeth clenched, and she wondered if the wideness of her smile resembled his own as she gazed down. Tate's hands fisted the bedding as she began to stroke him again, anticipating the moment when she would release him, but it didn't make his growl of frustration any less lovely to her ears when she did.

"You're *very* whiny," she chided, giggling again as he seemed to melt into the duvet, her grip tighter than it had previously been as she resumed, wringing her hand up his engorged shaft. His cock was thick, too thick for her to wrap her hand around completely, so she concentrated on the side that was most tightly riddled with veins. She had never asked him about that weekend back in the fall, when his shaft had developed a deliciously ridged underside, and she wondered when that particular physical attribute might return. She could feel the heat building within him, the quiver in his taut stomach, and knew he was close. "The whiniest sub ever."

"I'm not a sub," Tate gritted, glowering as her hand slowed.

"That's funny," she hummed, keeping her corkscrew motion consistent, even as she slowed. "You seem pretty submissive from up here."

Long, lichen-green fingers locked around her hand before she had a chance to release him again. "Don't. Stop." His lilting accent came out more when his emotions were high, she'd noticed months earlier, mentally adding this moment to her list, biting her lip with a smile.

"You don't want me to stop?" Silva bent as she whispered, kissing his flushed cheek, the tip of his slim nose, before landing on his wide mouth. "Okay . . . . I won't stop."

His thighs quivered and his toes curled as she picked up her pace, his breath coming out in shallow pants. When he came with a long groan, Silva hummed again, silently reveling in the way his release spilled over her knuckles, thick and white and seemingly endless, and it was all she could do to stop herself from reaching for her phone to document the moment, fuel for her fantasies at a later time.

His breath hitched when her hand did not slow. She wondered, as his hips lifted from the bed, a strangled yelp pulling from his throat, if he would remember the way he'd kept her teetering on the edge of relief the night before. The punishment for pulling his hair again had been for him to cease all attention on her aching clit, flipping her to her stomach and entering her in one long, deep glide. He'd alternated between fast, hard thrusts and a slow roll of his hips, and she had thought she might actually start weeping by the time he'd slid his hand down her body, giving her the stimulation she desperately needed.

He yelped again, his hips instinctively pulling to twist away from her, but she merely tightened her grip in response, twisting over his over-sensitized head.

"Si-Silva! Stop!" He gasped her name on a broken, pained laugh before crying out again in a wheeze.

"Tate, you told me not to stop. Ordered me, even. You're very bossy, and I'm only doing what you asked." By the time he'd let her climax atop the green felted table, her clit had been so over-sensitized that her orgasm had nearly been painful, a throbbing that had ripped through her body leaving behind a dull ache in her head, feeling slightly cramped. The high-pitched gasps he was now making were a far cry from his normal confident nonchalance, his breath coming out in shallow, wheezing pants.

She'd been limp as a ragdoll the night before, when he'd eased out of her slowly, gathering her up in his arms. "Are you alright, dove?" Her head had been heavy against his shoulder as he'd carried her through the apartment, pausing in front of the kitchen. "Hungry?" The energy needed to form words had left her, and she'd shook her head weakly, feeling the soft press of his lips against her forehead. "Bed?" His low chuckle vibrated against her as she nodded, and Silva had pressed herself tighter to it, until he'd laid her carefully in the pristine white sheets. Her head had just found his chest when he pulled away, climbing from the bed with a mumbled curse. "Hold on,

I forgot your water."

She loved him, she reminded herself as he jerked beneath her again. She loved him, and she wasn't going to let anyone stop her from getting what she wanted. Not her mother, not her grandmother, and certainly not him. She was his heartbeat, he'd said, his home. That felt far more serious than a simple *I love you*, and she'd not allow him to micromanage himself into a tiny spot on the shelf of her life. She was going to take control . . . just as she did then.

His fresh wheeze of pain broke her from her reverie, and her hand stilled, guilt warming her cheeks. Smoothing her palm over his semen-spattered stomach, Silva braced a hand on the bed and leaned down to kiss him contritely. Tate twisted away from her lips, his brow furrowed in distress, and her insides clenched, worried he was actually mad at her.

"I swear to Danu, Silva, if you don't keep going . . ."

Her eyes widened at his clenched teeth, his long back arching when she gripped his shaft and resumed pumping with steady strokes, avoiding his over sensitized head. He continued to jerk and cry out as though her ministrations were excruciatingly painful, but that didn't prevent him from orgasming once more, coating her hand in a fresh flood of his release as he twitched beneath her.

He was still breathing hard when she returned to the bed with a tall glass of water, after dropping the towel she'd used to wipe them clean into his bathroom hamper.

"I can't feel my back, Silva."

She dissolved into giggles once his arm came around her, pulling her tightly to his side.

"Are you okay? I didn't hurt you, did I?"

"Who, me? I'm grand. That's a kink I didn't know I had until five minutes ago . . . the paralysis is a bit concerning, I suppose. You'd best watch out, dove . . . you are going to pay dearly for that. In the meantime, you can put my cock in your handbag and take it home with you, because it's not going to be able to get hard for at least a month now."

Her laughter was swallowed by his kiss, pulling her back under the balmy warmth of the heavy duvet once more. "Who do you think you're fooling?" she huffed, dragging her nails down his chest. "I'll have your cock hard again by lunchtime." She shrieked as he tackled her, rolling them beneath the bedclothes.

"Well, you can still take it home, because you're the only one who gets it hard."

She preened, stretching like a cat beneath him. "We have to go open the restaurant," she murmured, running her fingers through his silky hair. "You don't want the girls to think you're going soft just because I'm here. I'm going to make you breakfast first though."

"Aye? And what'll that be? You almost burned down my apartment the last time you tried to make me breakfast."

"That was only one time!" Her voice was, by her own admission, extremely whiny, and she hid her face against his chest at the memory of the smoke-filled apartment as he laughed.

"Silva, it was toast."

"That wasn't my fault," she lamented, batting his shoulder with her loosely balled fist. "You have a stupid, old-fashiond toaster."

"That's true, it's not high-tech. There's only one lever. You're really not helping yourself, dove."

His reply was cut short by the ringing of her phone, shrill and insistent—the ringer she had programmed for her grandmother. For as much as she complained about her grandmother's lofty, exacting expectations for her, Silva knew she was adored. It was the reason she found it so hard to simply thumb her nose at her family's expectations, why it would tear her apart to walk away.

"Hi, Nana. Is something wrong?"

Tate's eyes fixed onto her as her face heated, her mind in a panic over her grandmother's words. An event, an all-day fundraiser being put on by the club, one she had not participated in the planning of. An important one, from the sounds of it, which she'd completely forgotten about, too eager and itchy by the end of the workweek to return to the little hamlet and his arms. An important event, that afternoon, all the way in Bridgeton. She heard herself agree, hanging up the phone in a dull panic. It was more than an hour drive to Bridgeton from Greenbridge Glen, not including the time in which she would need to fret over what exactly to wear, to fix her hair and make it to the hotel where the luncheon was being held. She jumped when hands landed on her shoulders, shaking her lightly from her panicked stupor.

"Silva." The musical cadence of his voice grounded her, pulling her back to the room. "Whatever it is, it'll be okay, dove."

"I-I have to go . . . I'm not going to make it on time! I don't know what to wear! I-I don't have—"

"Dove," she jerked at his voice, feeling it ripple through her, grounding her, a resonance she felt in her bones. *Fated mates.* "What kind of party is it?"

"It-it's a luncheon and a dinner, with drinks in between, being put on by two different clubs . . . but I have to look extra nice. Elegant, she said I have to look elegant . . . I don't know what that means! I don't know how to look elegant!"

"Silva," his golden eyes raised in an exaggerated eye roll, "you always look elegant. The dress you came in will do, you just need to faff about with the accessories a bit. Go start your face, then we'll fix your hair."

She sometimes forgot, she realized, as she drifted to the sparkling white bathroom to scrub the sleep from her eyes, that he was from her world, knew the game as well as she did.

Silva wondered, as she smoothed on mattifying moisturizer, if her mother and grandmother would coo and squeal over her handsome entrepreneur boyfriend, if only his skin weren't green.

He appeared behind her as she finished her makeup, brandishing a curling wand, and her mouth dropped open. "What? It came with a blow dryer!"

Silva sat in awe as he brushed her chestnut hair until it shone, winding tendrils around the heated wand until a cascade of long, loose curls spilled down her back. She watched in silence when he crossed to one of his antique bureaus, the one which housed a glass-shaded lamp and the wireless charger for his phone, retrieving an intricate jewelry box from the back of a drawer. Picking through the contents, he returned with a set of hair combs.

Delicate dragonflies, rendered in tourmaline and carnelian, sapphires and emeralds, stretched across a gossamer silver net above tortoiseshell combs. Tate gathered her hair carefully, twisting half of it at her crown, pinning it in place with one of the lovely combs.

"Just the one, I think," he murmured, running the tips of his fingers over her loose curls. "No need for overkill."

Dainty lace gloves and a matching shawl were retrieved from a trunk at the back of his wide closet, smelling of the dried lavender which they were folded around. Silva eyed herself in the full-length mirror, feeling as though she'd stepped through time. She knew Tate had an odd proclivity for antiques, that he spent money on lamps and table linens the way other men spent money on sporting events and electronics, but something told her these were not baubles he'd acquired at an estate sale. Family heirlooms, she was certain. Silva swallowed hard at the implication, wondering what relative to whom they'd belonged.

She'd never felt lovelier.

"There we are. Perfectly elegant, dove."

"I'll come back tonight." She spun to face him, gripping his arm tightly. Nearly forty minutes had passed since they'd left his bed. He should have been at the restaurant over an hour ago, she thought guiltily. "Tate, I-I'll come back after the luncheon. We can—"

"Don't be daft. You've just said it's an all-day affair, and you'd have to turn around and leave again tomorrow afternoon, that's too much back and forth. The Pixie's not going anywhere."

"Next week then. I have to bring back this pretty comb." His eyes were liquid honey as he looked her over slowly, his hand a whisper against her hair.

"I think," he murmured softly, smoothing the wrap on her shoulder, "that you should keep it. It suits you." His lips were a feather-light pressure against her forehead, and she forced herself to breathe. She wouldn't give him up, and no one could make her.

"Go. Fly away, little dove. I'll see you soon."

♥ ♥ ♥

The woman was a huckster. Silva had no experience with such things, had never even had a glimpse of anything unsavory before she'd met Tate, but the excursions she'd taken with him to pubs that were not his own, to pool halls and an empty strip of road where they did illegal drag racing, to the tightly packed urban churn of Starling Heights, had opened her eyes. She would sit on his lap with her back to his chest as he leaned over her, whispering in her ear, pointing out tells and tics that she wouldn't have noted otherwise, behavior and a certain tone of voice that marked a liar. The fae woman had set everyone on edge, and although her grandmother fretfully clutched at her wrist as she coolly conversed with the golden-eyed stranger, Silva remained unaffected. She had done the flowers for the event, a favor to the other club hosting it, and although the room *was* lovely and the floral display sweet smelling and beautiful, Silva could tell immediately that the woman's sly smile was not one that could be trusted. She had learned quite a bit at his side. Unseemly lessons, possibly, but she thought it was a worthwhile education.

"You are just the loveliest little thing. Come sit by me, precious one."

Once more she felt her grandmother's hand fishtailing around her wrist. Silva gave the woman a tightlipped smile, threading her fingers with her grandmothers to quell her soft panic before taking a seat across the table from the uninvited guest.

The flowers were clearly enchanted. They filled the space — ivory and green, petals and leaves on every surface. Lisianthus and ranunculus, roses and hydrangea, bells of ireland and trembling eucalyptus. She had smiled as she followed her grandmother to the dining room, thinking it was exactly the sort of softly-colored, over-the-top display Tate would have loved. The roses had a shimmering sheen, and the colors of everything seemed just a hair too vivid, either the work of enchantment, or something more insidious perhaps, but Silva had no doubt in her mind that this woman alone was responsible for none of it, other than perhaps the procurements, and setting up the room.

The other elves of the club were not seeing it that way, clearly. They saw the breathtaking flowers and were impressed, looking closer and seeing the odd way they sparkled, taking in the wide-smiling florist with her unusual-colored eyes and tinkling bell of a laugh, adding in the odd, deliberate way she spoke, and they were afraid. It was all an affectation, Silva could tell, rolling her eyes slightly as she took her seat.

For the next hour, they were treated to the woman's stories, her shimmering laughter, and her wide smile. She was a bit of a braggart, Silva thought, telling them of weddings for kings and the giant floral arches she'd been commissioned to create for a parade of nymphs, celebrating their centennial.

"And what makes your flower so special, exactly?" Silva asked demurely, sipping her tea. Her grandmother clutched at her skirt.

"Oh well, it wouldn't be good of me to go revealing trade secrets now," the woman laughed, like a glimmering golden bell. Silva smiled again, still unimpressed. She supposed to the elves at her club, the woman's strange, musical laughter was indicative of her to-be-feared status, but Silva heard a shimmering laugh every week, knowing Tate's laughter was genuine, and not the put upon act. "But, as you can see, lovely girl, they are *quite* special."

They had made it through the scones, through the finger sandwiches and petit fours, all the way to the delicate rose-flavoured crème brûlée, when her grandmother and mother left the table, going to greet some friends from their own club before the charity auction began. They rose, her grandmother nervously asking Silva if she wanted to accompany them, glancing meaningfully at the center of the tablecloth, an indication that she should not want to be left alone with the florist interloper, and Silva smiled sunnily, insisting that she wanted to finish her dessert. The moment they had left the table, the woman leaned in with a conspiratorial smile. *Here it comes, she's probably going to try and sell me magical oils to clear your sinuses.*

"Darling, if you're in the market to be kept pet, I *do* have the right connections." She glanced around surreptitiously, making sure there was no one to overhear them. "I have a contact with the Court of Flowers." She raised her eyebrows meaningfully, and Silva got the impression she was meant to be terribly impressed.

"I'm sorry," Silva smiled demurely, before spooning up a teensy bit more of the delicately flavored crème brûlée, "but I don't know what that is."

The woman rolled her eyes, breaking the effect of her being some mystical, ethereal being. "You know, the *otherworld*." Her words came out on hiss, her eyes darting around once more. "I can make some inquiries with my contact, but I'm sure they would pay a fine bride price to keep you. I would take a small finders fee, of course, for setting up the transaction, you understand. All you have to do is tell me what your current cost is, and I can do some negotiating."

"I am, regretfully, not for sale. And dealing with the otherworld is *extremely* illegal."

The woman huffed, her eyes narrowing. "Come off it, princess.

I was able to smell him the minute you walked in the room. He's put his mark all over you. I can get you a *real* position, a very luxurious set up. The Court of Flowers is very generous, and they do love beautiful things. I'm sure they will gladly buy off your bride price, as long as you've not taken up with one of the Court of Night. Have you bound yourself to an unseelie? Because then I can't help you. But," she smiled brightly, "have you ever wanted to be your own boss? One of the other businesses I dabble in is an *exciting* opportunity to leave the daily grind of an office behind and be your own CEO. Would you like to smell this amazing oil?"

♥ ♥ ♥

"Darling, I do hope you're planning on staying for the evening event. There will be plenty of time to refresh before cocktails, and you do look so lovely today. I'm sure that nice young man from your office will be at the dinner, don't you think?"

Her grandmother's words were careless and cheerful, and had they been alone, Silva might have been able to put her off, turning her with distraction until this conversation was forgotten.

It would have been easy to say yes. It would've been easy to agree with her grandmother's words, wouldn't even need to tap out a text to Tate explaining herself or her whereabouts, and that would be that. He would say nothing, and she would go to the club's banquet dinner. She would put on her false smile and laugh a false laugh, socialize with friends who knew nothing about her and didn't care to learn, and her grandmother was likely right – Tannar would be in attendance. He would follow her around the hall, complementing her dress, complementing the work she did with the volunteer society, asking her about her interests and her hobbies, being as charming and genteel as any gentlemen she'd ever known.

Since the early winter when he joined the club, she had upgraded Tannar's standing as a hero in one of her books. She no longer thought of him as the bore, but rather the sweet next-door neighbor, the hero of a friends-to-lovers storyline, her least favorite trope. She could allow him to follow her around the banquet, a repeat performance of the way he followed her around the office, and she could smile and flirt, make dinner plans with him for the week and make her grandmother happy. It would have been easy to do, she knew. Tate, she'd come to understand, truly *didn't* expect her to adjust her life for him. She could cancel on him at the last possible second, and she would feel no repercussions for careless actions, no closed-door upon her return, no cruel words in payment for her cruel actions, content with whatever scraps she threw. Silva had the distinct impression that he viewed their relationship as a clock that was winding down, perpetually braced for the reality that one day she'd simply not come back, constantly attempting to brace her for the same. It would be easy to do, if things were still the same. Unfortunately, she thought to herself, they were not, and she was no longer willing to keep up this charade.

She already knew that her absence on weekends had been

noticed. The first time her mother had mentioned it had been just a few weeks earlier, after the community May Day celebration.

"You've been so busy lately, darling . . . we've missed seeing you, you know." Her mother had a perfectly calm, even-toned voice, but Silva had still clenched in panic at her words. She had made a point of staying home at least one weekend a month, making herself as visible as possible at the club, volunteering with the Ladies Society, attending luncheons and dinners and teas, all in hope that she'd be so visible, people might not actually realize she'd been absent in the preceding weeks, and so far her plan had worked . . . but it was obviously too much to assume that her mother would be so easily fooled.

"We didn't expect you to be running so late this afternoon, darling," she said sharply, in the time Silva was meant to be *refreshing* before inevitably seeing Tannar that night. "Were you even planning on coming at all?"

Silva grit her teeth, forcing herself to keep her composure. It would do no good to act sullen or childish, not for this conversation. "I didn't have the event in my calendar," she admitted. "But I'm glad Nana was able to remind me."

Her mother smiled tightly, not quite reaching her eyes, humming before looking away. "I've heard quite a tale from Vanetta Daerlend. Her youngest daughter says she saw you at a nightclub in Bridgeton, maybe a month or two ago."

Silva breathed slowly through her nose. It had been far longer than that, but she was not about to admit that to her mother. She'd

386

known the tale would catch up with her eventually, and knew the cluster of elves at the bar who had watched her confrontation with Wynn would go back to their friends with the gossip, and that the gossip would slowly circulate its way through siblings and cousins until it reached the club. She straightened in her chair. She was not willing to give him up.

"I'm twenty-six, mother. I'm allowed to go to a nightclub with my friends without permission."

"Silva, I think you and I both know the venue is not what I am referring to. Vanetta's daughter mentioned there was a confrontation. Between Wynndevar and some man . . . whom you appeared to be with."

Breathe. "That's right. He put his *hands* on me. We broke up months ago. He has no business touching me."

"And this friend you were with? Is this the man you've been doing freelancing for?"

Heat burned up her neck. It was one of the more clever lies she had come up with, telling her mother that some of her time away was being spent doing freelance work, bolstering her portfolio since she was given so very little to do at her actual job. Tate had managed to make her lie reality, when she'd shown him some of the designs she'd made for Clover's logo. She received a check made out from his business account, and her design was now printed on the high season menus, the fact that made her giddy each week when she spotted them at Cymbeline's hostess stand.

"It is." She watched her mother's shoulders raise in a sigh. "His name is Tate. He's Elvish, silmë, like us. I think you and Nana would actually really like him. He was raised by his grandparents, very old-fashioned manners."

"And how precisely did you meet him? He's not a member of the club, obviously?"

Her stomach tightened and twisted. She tried to imagine Tate attending an event at her club, imagined how it would *truly* be, not one of her fantasies. She could almost feel the slide of eyes that would be upon them as they moved through the room; could hear the whisper of gossip, of which they would be the only topic. Any children she had with him would be ostracized, as he had been. There would be no lovely afternoons taking tea in the formal dining room, no elegant engagement parties on the garden terrace. She knew her own kind better than that, and she always had. She had been foolish to think otherwise, and she knew, deep in her heart, that she couldn't actually have everything.

"I met him after I did some work for one of his businesses," she murmured, deciding to stick with the lie she had already established. "He owns a very successful bistro and a pub, and he owns the building the pub is in. We've . . . I've been seeing him for a few months, mother. He makes me very happy." It wasn't true, she thought to herself. She was miserable most of the time, but she had come to realize that her misery was a product of her own making. She should have had this conversation nearly a year ago; ought to have ripped off the bandage and saved herself months and months of heartache in the process.

"And he's . . . Elvish, you said?" *Here it is.* She nodded, her lips pressed in a flat smile, already feeling the tears beginning to burn at the corners of her eyes. Her mother sighed again. "Silva—"

"He was raised by his grandparents in a conservative Elvish community," she gritted out through clenched teeth. "He's fluent in Elvish, in several different dialects. He's actually been working with me on mine," she laughed shortly, pushing her tongue into the roof of her mouth to tamp back her tears before she continued. "His father is an orc." She watched her mother's eyes close, watched the elegant hand she raised to pinch the bridge of her nose briefly. "Did I mention that he makes me happy, mother? Does that even *matter* to you?"

"Of course it does, darling. But it's possible for you to be happy with someone else."

She was unable to keep the tears from falling then. She knew she would be splotched purple by the time she had cried out her frustration that day, that her body would be a shriveled, desiccated husk, for she would cry until there was nothing left of her, nothing left of herself to give anyone else if she could not give her entire being to him. She wanted every piece of him – his secrets and his fears, his blood and his viscera, every thought in his head and the essence of his very soul, and she wanted to give herself in return.

"You can't stop me. You know that, right? You can't tell me what I have to do, you can't keep me in a cage and tell me who I have to marry. This is *my* life." She'd not intended for her voice to raise as it had, her voice breaking at the end, but her mother looked shocked for the first time since she'd sat down. Silva of the daytime was a mouse, after all. A perfect, pretty little mouse, who always did as she was told. *Not this time.*

"Silva, darling—"

"No," she insisted, holding up her hand, collecting herself before she pushed off from the chair. "He's not making me choose. *You* are the only one trying to do that. And if I have to choose, you won't be happy with the answer, mother."

"You're going to break your grandmother's heart. Is that what you want?"

"It's not," she choked out, her voice breaking again. "I don't want to hurt anyone, and I don't want to have to choose. If you make me, you're breaking *my* heart, and I don't know if I can forgive you for that."

Her mother's voice followed her out the door, calling her name, but she did not look back. She couldn't continue living this half-life, couldn't continue being Silva of the day time, not when he existed in the night. *It's always night in her majesty's forest.* His odd words from the fall prickled up her spine as she walked away, pulling away from her childhood home, and leaving childhood behind for good.

♥ ♥ ♥

Lurielle

When the invitation had arrived, she'd spent nearly a week fretting over it before she told him. She didn't want to go. She didn't want to see her mother, didn't want to be the source of gossip for the evening, which she undoubtedly would be. She didn't want to see the Elvish club peers she'd left behind, nor the relatives amongst whom she had always been an outsider. She did want to go, would have been more than content to grip the invitation up and toss it in the bin without a second thought . . . But it was her great-grandmother's birthday, and she didn't want to miss that.

Khash, of course, had been ecstatic. He thrived in the spotlight, was excited at the opportunity to meet her relatives, to schmooze for a new crowd, confident in his abilities to charm his way through every situation.

"Bluebell, this'll be as easy as the cake throw at the elder's Grahlak picnic."

"Yeah, that's not a reference I understand," she'd grumbled once she'd finally shown him the invitation. His plan, he'd explained, was simple: charm Nana first, flirt the cousins into submission, captivate the room in general with his genial southern charm, and avoid her mother. She was forced to admit that it was likely a good plan. First, though, she had to get through the torturous affair of introducing him to her parents. That had been her main source of conflict — biting the bullet and getting it over with before the big events, or letting her great-grandmother's party be the very first introduction to the orc with whom she was planning on spending the rest of her life.

Dinner with her parents had gone about as well as she had expected, although, as she'd assured him in bed that night, it could have gone much worse. Her mother hadn't brought an additional date for her, for example, nor had she broken down in noisy sobs over her disappointment in her only daughter's life choices, as Lurielle had expected. The venue selected was a restaurant in the middle of their respective drives, not her childhood home, which was what her mother pushed for, and not at a swanky Elvish restaurant, which had been the second choice selection.

"No. I'm not meeting you at Loterwatra. It's an Elvish restaurant, mother. Exclusively for elves. Maybe you blocked out my earlier phone call when I let you know I am in a relationship with an orc, but he is still actually an orc, so no. I'm going to say 'pass' on the exclusively

Elvish restaurant. We can find a multi-species restaurant in the middle, or we don't need to do this at all."

"I don't understand why you don't want to just drive home, it would be so much simpler—"

"It would be simpler for you, not for me. We can meet in the middle, or we don't have to meet at all."

The voice on the phone was firm and steadfast, and she scarcely recognized it as her own. After all, she had felt ground down under her mother's heel her entire life. She was told she was too big, took up too much space, and was therefore of lesser value, and so she tried to be as invisible as possible for most of her adolescence. Simply doing whatever her mother asked was easier than arguing, because arguing meant she would trot out her best shrill voice and wounded accusations, the absolute opposite of invisibility, and so simply going along had been her MO for years.

Going back to her childhood home, the site of so many arguments that she never even attempted to win, the guilt trips for simply existing, as if her being born with a bigger bone structure was a personal attack that she carried out on her mother daily . . . Lurielle did not want to risk being back in that environment; didn't trust herself not to slip into that old passive, invisible role. When she'd moved out of the Elvish dorms and in with Tev, in university, her reign of invisibility had continued. She wasn't sure how it was that she managed to find someone who managed to be exactly like her mother, didn't like what it said about herself that that's what she attracted and even less — what she was drawn to. She'd done whatever Tev had asked as well, wanting to be agreeable, to take up as little space as possible, even the air she breathed. But that Lurielle was long gone, she reminded herself, and her current iteration had no desire to see her return.

In the end, a restaurant was found off the highway, nearly at the midway point between their respective drives. Her parents had arrived first, and she watched them as they crossed the restaurant's lobby. There were other species in attendance, she was glad to see, lizardfolk and goblins and trolls, but as she and Khash came through the front doors, her mother's mouth dropped open. Lurielle watched in slow motion as her parent's heads tipped back and back, taking him in — every decadently gorgeous inch of him. He'd worn the same jacket he had that first night he took her to the restaurant in the little resort town, fine blue wool, stretched across his back like the sea, his khaki-colored dress slacks a preppy counterpoint. His heavy watch face gleamed goldenly, and his pocket square had been ivory with small burgundy pin dots, matching the wine-colored dress she'd worn.

It was the first occasion in which she'd seen her mother in some time, and Lurielle was only a little ashamed to admit that she had spent hours getting ready. She fussed with her hair that morning, fussed with it again in the early afternoon, deciding she was done fussing sometime around lunch and stopped for a blowout. Her makeup was soft and natural; her shapewear the opposite of soft and natural, displacing her spleen as she wriggled into it before zipping up the wine-toned dress. She'd worn the opal and diamond earrings he bought her for Heart's Day, and the matching bracelet she'd received for her birthday, just a month earlier. She felt put together and pretty, a sentiment Khash had echoed before they'd left, bending to kiss her cheek gently without messing her makeup. And as she crossed the restaurant's waiting area to where her parents sat near the hostess stand, she thought to herself what a fucking shame it was that she was internally clenching, prepared to be picked to pieces by the person who should have loved her more than anyone else in the world.

"Darling, what a nice dress. This color though, Lurielle, it's so harsh! Your palette is too delicate for something this heavy. And you know black is always so slimming . . ."

She'd given her a bright smile, because what could she say? Khash paused, his heavy brow furrowing. Lurielle had gripped his hand, knowing it was just the beginning.

"Well, you're just . . . so big! I can't even imagine how you would fit through the front door."

"Well, it's a good thing I have a big door, isn't it, mom?"

Ordering at a restaurant with her mother was always an ordeal. She would ask a million questions of the server, asking about substitutions to each and every menu item, questioning the caloric intake of everything from the butter sauce served on the side of the baked potato, to a decadent pasta dish, always ordering the same salad of leafy greens and very little taste, watching Lurielle's own menu choice like a hawk, commenting on how she ought to take all the dressings and sauces on the side.

"You don't need those hidden calories, dear."

"The hidden calories are where all the flavor is though," Khash had chimed in genially, but she'd recognized the smile he reserved for Tate. She'd instructed him to eat before they left, in an attempt to stave off his normal two entrées, and to her enormous relief, he'd complied. That didn't stop her from reaching over to his plate with her fork, dragging her beet through the caramelization on his plate, popping it into her mouth cheerfully, as her mother looked on in horror.

Her mother had spent most of the appetizer course grilling Lurielle on her life and her job and her house, trying her best to poke holes in all of the above, questioning how they had met over the entrées, asking Lurielle questions about Khash's job, where he lived, where he was from . . . but never quite addressing him herself, a fact she denied when Lurielle pointed out. She had vacillated wildly between her high, slightly manic party voice, as Khash forced his way into the conversation, attempting to sing Lurielle's praises, and a breathy, accusatory tone, when he announced he was quite serious about their daughter and saw their relationship continuing to move forward, dashing her mother's hopes that it was all a practical joke, acting as if Lurielle had climbed up on the table in the middle of the dining room, lifted her dress, and shat in the soup.

"You don't get it," she'd insisted, pushing and pulling pillows into place in his oversized bed before settling against him, rubbing her hand against his broad chest placatingly. "She was on her best

396

behavior, she's usually *much* worse than that."

His lower lip had been pushed out in a pout, but he'd scowled at her words. Lurielle knew Khash was unused to not being liked, and even though she'd warned him repeatedly over the last several months that her mother would relegate him into the column of daughter's terrible life choices, he'd been confident in his ability to charm. She didn't consider herself a petty person, and it had brought her no joy to be proven right that evening.

"She has no right talking to you that way," he'd seethed, raising a giant hand to enumerate all of her positive attributes again, the third time he'd done so since leaving the restaurant, as though her mother might hear them. "You're smart — no, *brilliant*. You work in a male-dominated field and you ran lead on your department's last big project. That's nothin' to sniff at, Bluebell."

"I improved a jerk-off machine for minotaurs. That's on my resume now."

"For a billion-dollar multinational pharmaceutical company!" he thundered, swatting at her hair. "You are braver than most of the grown orcs I know. You came all the way out here by yourself, no support system, no money, no nothin'."

"Gee, thanks, babe."

"You built a life for yourself, on your own terms, and I don't care what you want to pretend, darlin', that's impressive. You're *beautiful*, the prettiest elf I've ever seen."

"I'm also the fattest elf you've ever seen, which is probably her sticking point."

The noise of disgust he made his throat made her smile. "Pffttgggghhttt, fat. Fat compared to what, my big toe? Compared to one of them little pixies that fly around the gardens? Who are you supposed to look like, one of your little stick figure friends? If I were to try to put this big old dragon in your skinny little friend Silvia, it would come outta her mouth. You think I'd be able to pump you full of strong orc sons if you didn't have them sexy hips?"

"You'd better keep that big ole' dragon away from *any* of my friends, unless you want to be castrated with a toothbrush. And *Silva* has an orc boyfriend, for the record. Despite what both you and he would like to pretend. And you've been doing a lot of talking about pumping sons into me lately. What happens if you pump out a girl?"

He rolled her, pinning her to the mattress as she laughed, nudging her thighs open. Lurielle was forced to admit, no matter how much she teased him, she was certain he had the biggest, fattest cock in the world. He slapped it down on her belly, ridiculously large, even flaccid. "We'll have the prettiest little girl in existence. A dainty lil' cupcake, just like her mama, and her daddy's gonna make sure she can kick someone's ass if they need it kicked. Best of both worlds."

His words sparked a memory, a conversation that had taken place with his brother Kesst and a handful of others, the night of his clan party.

"We're all so excited to have him back once y'all decide to start having little ones." The statement had come from the elder sister of one of his childhood friends, cheerful nods and sentiments of agreement coming from the rest of the circle.

"You won't even have to worry about looking for property down here," Kesst piped up. "You'll probably just want to build something. However big you want it, however many bedrooms you think you'll need for the kids. You can make it like one of those special species houses," he'd beamed at her. He was sweet and friendly, and he and Khash were closer than Khash seemed to be with the rest of his siblings, a fact she understood was important. She'd not brought it up that night, distracted as they'd been with the cabin in the woods, and then breakfast the following morning with his family one last time before heading home, and the conversation had slipped her mind. Now though, it came rushing back.

"Orcs are okay with having kids outside of marriage, right? Or is that frowned on?"

Such a question would have been preposterous to ask, if their positions were reversed. Elves had a hard enough time conceiving as it was, and married couples sometimes tried for years before they managed to have a child. Little girls were indoctrinated young, and Lurielle vividly remembered those mortifying grade school discussions. Tev's mother had been supercilious and cold even during the rosiest part of their relationship, and she had spent more than one sleepless night imagining the guilt and barely disguised insults that would have been heaped on her by both her mother and Tev's alike if she did not produce a baby immediately. Insinuations that she wasn't trying hard enough, hints that her weight was the reason she was unable to conceive — Lurielle had thought through a hundred different scenarios, each more unpleasant than the next. It had been a relief to put that particular anxiety away for good once she'd escaped, and she hadn't given children much thought since then. Now though . . .

She knew Khash wanted children, he'd been clear about that from the start, so she'd diligently made an appointment to discuss the future possibility with the doctor she'd been seeing since her move to Cambric Creek, an eagle-faced woman with a wry sense of humor and a straightforward manner.

"An orc? Interesting! I imagine you'll have considerably less issues with conception . . . carrying might be a challenge with your height, but you have good birthing hips. We'll need to watch the blood pressure, of course, and there's a chance you might need to be on bed rest for the tenth month, but I don't see there to be any underlying health issues that would prevent you from carrying a healthy baby."

She'd left the appointment chewing over the doctor's words, wondering if she'd conceive as easily as the lagomorph girl at the office who worked in reception and seemed to be perpetually swollen with new life. After all, as she liked to say, for all her mother's put-on airs, one needn't scratch the surface of their family tree too deeply to find non-Elvish blood, as evidenced by the fact that her parents had not one, but two children. Her favorite grandfather had been the product of a half-human mother, helping his own progeny pass on their Elvish genes. *You're just following tradition*, she'd told herself leaving the doctor's office with a bounce in her step that day.

"It happens all the time," Khash answered. "Children are raised by the whole community, by the clan. It gives couples a chance to settle into being parents and play at being married for a bit first."

Lurielle frowned, not expecting his answer and not at all sure if she liked it. "What—what does that even mean? So if they decide they don't want to be married, they can just walk away? And then the woman gets stuck with raising a kid on her own?"

"That's exactly what it means, but that's the opposite of what I said. Yes, they can go their separate ways. Things happen, relationships don't work. But the whole clan raises children. Your granny is everyone's granny. Doors are open to all the kids in the neighborhood, there's always room at the table for another mouth. Children are never left behind. That would be a black eye on the whole clan."

"And what of their parents?"

He shrugged. "Free to go their separate way, like I said. You don't have to worry about that, Bluebell, I'm not going anywhere. This is a lot of baby talk, darlin'," he purred, the heft of his enormous member against her belly sitting a bit thicker. "It's enough to make a man *feel* things. I can just imagine how beautiful you'll look carrying our baby, all rosy and ripe . . ." Back and forth against her, Lurielle tilted her hips upwards so that she was able to press up against him, trapping his cock against the heat of her tingling sex. "Is this what you're thinking of, Lurielle? Me filling you with a strong, Orcish son?"

"Again with the strong son business."

"Pumping you full is the point." The first push was always the one that made her breath trip, his foreskin pulled back to reveal the shiny pink-edged glans, spreading open her lips and opening her walls, pressing the air right out of her lungs as he fed his cock into her slowly. "I can just imagine how sweet you'll look. But gettin' there's the fun part."

She wished she could say he was wrong, but she would be a liar. She had often tried imagining what she would look like, swollen with an orc baby, *his* baby, which was the important part, the thought never failing to bring a flush to her cheeks. The weight of his balls slapping into her excited her now, the thought of him draining them inside of her thrilling, regardless of how often it had previously happened or how anatomically incorrect the notion was. Putting her ankles up over his shoulders never failed to make her see stars, and he did it then, making her wheeze.

"Once you say you're ready, darlin', this is what I'll do to you every day. Fill you up with this big cock and pump you full of my seed until you're swollen with me. That what you want me to do? You want me to pump this pussy full until we have a whole brood?"

She had been careening towards a shallow orgasm at that point, the angle at which he bent her shortening the length he had to thrust into her, putting pressure on her g-spot and clit both, but at his words, the moment was broken.

"Tell me you did not just say that like it's supposed to be sexy," she huffed out, laughter overtaking her pleasure, laughing even harder at the way his face screwed up.

"Bluebell, what are you tryna' do. You wanna turn this dragon into a windsock, you keep it up. This ain't the stage for your comedy routine."

She was cackling by then, squealing when he dropped against her, flattening her for a moment under his weight. "I don't ever want to hear you say the words 'seed' and 'brood' together again, unless you really are bringing me home chickens, you understand? Are you gonna want to move back home after we have kids? Because that's not something we talked about before."

"Lurielle, you think we can dill this pickle first? If seeing your mother is going to have you madder than a mule chewing bees, I understand. But this squirrel can't bury this nut alone."

She had begun to laugh again, wrapping her legs around him, using her heels to knead into the swell of his prodigious ass. "Well, you'd better start pumping. This gas tank isn't going to fill itself."

"I'm serious," she murmured once they were finished and cleaned up, back beneath the sheets. "You never said that you wanted to move back home."

"You're right about that, so I'm not sure where you got the notion."

She was quiet for a long moment, listening to this thump of his heart, flattening her cheek to his chest. "It was just something your brother said when we were down there. A few other people were talking about it, and they made it seem like it was a foregone conclusion that we'd move back when we had kids. After all, they had to be raised by the clan."

"And how do you feel about that, Lurielle? You're asking a lot of questions, but you're not giving me any answers."

She thought. "I like Cambric Creek because things like clan don't matter. There's Elvish community here, but they keep to themselves and they don't matter to the rest of the town. I don't want my kids to feel ostracized because of what they are."

"Bluebell —"

"No, don't bluebell me. I know how elves are. You know how orcs are. If had a dollar for every person that said something about how little I was, or how you probably keep me in a box under the bed with the other sex toys, or what a fluffy little novelty I was while we were visiting, we could've taken another vacation. You've met my mom now, you see what I'm talking about. She is *exceptionally* awful, but don't think for a minute that every elf at the club in town wouldn't think the exact same thing." Silva had said something to her about her strange fae boyfriend, a brief anecdote he'd related to her one evening about being turned away from his Orcish clan as a child, never even meeting his father. She knew that every story had two sides and the truth was likely somewhere in the middle, but knowing what she knew of elves and how similar orcs were in their superiority complexes, she didn't doubt the veracity of it.

"Darlin', when my granddaddy died we were all there, all around his bed. One by one everyone got a chance to sit with him alone and say goodbye. I was the last one there with him, and he took my hand with the little bit of strength he had left and he told me to get out of there and go make something of myself. That he didn't want to look back on me from the other side and see me still there, in the same town with the same mine that had killed him. Didn't want to see me working in some low-paying accounting job with all my schooling. Didn't want to see me raising my kids with the same expectations. Now you can think that's putting on airs, I know a lot of the folks at home think I do, some of my own kin included. But I was fortunate enough to have a good start in life, and I didn't intend to squander it. I wouldn't bring our kids back there to grow up thinking they have to stay in the same place their whole lives just because that's the way it is."

"I'm absolutely not continuing the K name dynasty, so you can get that idea right out of your head too, while we're at it."

She wrapped her arm around him as he snorted in laughter, content when he'd folded her in his arms. "I'm glad one of us had a good start in life, because you can see how fucked up I am. Now I just have to get past this party without having a nervous breakdown."

Now they were there, and her breakdown felt imminent.

The ballroom was draped in pink. Pink chiffon swags, pink table linens, pink uplighting. Enormous vases of pink and white flowers graced each table, and the birthday girl herself was dolled up like a poofy pink cupcake. Lurielle loved her great-grandmother dearly, and was thrilled that they were able to celebrate her two hundred and fiftieth birthday at all, but Nana's choice in decor was reminiscent of something a princess-obsessed preschooler might have chosen.

She watched in amusement as one of the waistcoated servers made a wide arc around the table where she sat with her boyfriend, the tray of hors d'oeuvres he carried completely unmolested by disinterested elves. Beside her, Khash grunted in frustration.

"Now you know he's doin' that on purpose," he grumbled, balling up his pink cloth napkin in frustration, as Lurielle snorted into her drink. After all, she had tried to warn him.

"I thought I asked you to order food while I showered?"

Khash had scowled at her in the mirror as he expertly twisted the long ends of his silk tie into a large windsor knot, earlier that evening. "Bluebell, you know we don't have time for that, we need to get ready. You mean to tell me there's not going to be food there? At a *dinner* reception?" He'd rolled his eyes at her reflection as he pulled on his suit jacket, an endless expanse of expensive grey wool, and fussed with his contrasting pocket square.

Lurielle just shrugged. *Fine. If he wanted to be a know-it-all, let him find out the hard way.*

She had yet to determine if all orcs ate as much as Khash did. She'd tried to pay attention when they went out together, would look for other orcs in restaurants, trying to determine if they too had ordered two entrees and an appetizer at dinner. She'd once stalked an orc around the grocery store, surreptitiously peeking into his cart to scan the contents, and had once espied Silva's slender boyfriend through the wide window of his small restaurant one weekend afternoon, sitting in front of a laptop at the end of the bar, eating an apple. Lurielle hadn't noticed a steak dinner hidden beneath his screen, as she'd pointed out to Khash later. His nonchalant rebuttal had been that the other orcs in restaurants were on dates and were clearly holding back as they attempted to woo their intendeds, and that Silva's fae boyfriend didn't count.

Khash had harrumphed when they first entered the cotton candy-hued hall, seeing the fusty servers gliding around the room, bearing trays laden with bite-sized delicacies. He'd glanced down with furrow between his full brows when she hadn't responded with an elbow on her hip and a derisive snort of her own, the anticipated reaction to such a scene. Khash never expected her to be anything but what she was, and the freedom to be a smartass on main, the ability to be her uncensored self was intoxicating, but she didn't dare display anything other than a beatific smile, desperately attempting to channel her inner Silva, keeping all traces of opinions or disagreeableness or personality, anything that might warrant the negative attention of her mother, deeply buried. Being there as herself — short, slightly overweight, unmarried and childless — was enough of a crime. Adding an Orcish boyfriend to the list of offenses was practically unforgivable.

"Oh, I can guarantee he's doing it on purpose," she agreed as the server disappeared into the swinging kitchen doors with his still-full tray, draining her glass before stretching up to kiss her boyfriend's broad cheek. She hated events like this. She'd always been the outcast among her elegant, glamorous relatives and peers — short when they were tall, soft and round where they were concave and willowy.

She'd always been more interested in hiding behind a book than in flirting with the handsome elves at the country club, and now she was surrounded by all of them — aunts and cousins; distant relatives she saw rarely, plus the ones she'd grown up with, all crowding around with knowing smirks and curious glances.

Lurielle was sure it was common knowledge throughout the extended family that she'd had a huge falling-out with her controlling mother several years earlier, that she'd left her fiance and moved away, far from the constrictions and expectations of their Elvish culture and society. Now here she was: stuffed into a body shaper that displaced her internal organs with her huge, orcish boyfriend, attempting to keep her smile from appearing to be a grimace. She had nothing in common with the people who shared her blood, and likely never would. She hated events like this, but having him here, despite increasing the amount of attention she might have received otherwise, was a security she'd not trade for the world.

"My darling girl, let me look at you!" Her great grandmother was an adorable little peanut of an elf, having steadily shrunk since Lurielle was middle school-aged. "Beautiful, just beautiful. It's been too long since I've seen you, too long."

"I know Nana, I'm sorry it's been so long. I should've come for a visit."

Her great-grandmother waved her hand in dismissal. "Last time I checked it was a two-way street. I let myself be too busy with casino trips and bus tours, I'll have to see if there's one going to wherever it is you're living now," she insisted, to Lurielle's delight.

"That would be wonderful. Nana, I have someone for you to meet. You might want to sit down, because I'm not sure if you can look up this high."

That had been over an hour ago, and Khash had thoroughly charmed her Nana, putting his plan into action. She watched, from across the room, as he sat by the wrinkled elf's side, exchanging laughter and confidences for longer than anyone else had bothered, her own mother included. The music that had been selected for the event was upbeat and swinging, without being overly loud, and she watched as several girls she'd grown up with took to the dance floor, dancing with each other until they were spinning in laughter. She watched two older elves around her grandmother's age swaying together at the side of the dance floor as they conversed cheerfully, watched several older women rotate around the floor, taking turns with one member of the party's husband. She watched, sipping her drink, directing one of the maître d''s to her great-grandmother's table when he came around proffering his tray, knowing Khash would appreciate it. She watched, and she watched some more, and when she sipped from her second champagne flute, Lurielle realized something was wrong.

She scanned the ballroom in all its pink finery, taking in the elves who dotted the space. Mothers and aunts and cousins and neighbors, heads of social clubs and teachers at the private Elvish schools. Young girls sitting together and old women sitting on the other side of the tables. She was able to count the number of men in attendance nearly

409

without running out of fingers, almost all of them between her own age and her father's age, and the implications of that eluded her until she drained her glass again.

"Well, how are you holding up, dearest?" She looked up sharply at the sound of her grandmother's voice, smiling guardedly as she pulled out a chair. Her mother had a contentious relationship with her own mother, something her therapist seemed unsurprised to hear. As a result, Lurielle had not spent an enormous amount of her childhood in her grandmother's presence. If she had, she thought that perhaps she might've had an ally . . . An ally or double adversary, which would've made her decision even easier if that had been the case. Now though, she wondered.

"I'm not one for dancing, so as long as no one tries to make me, I'm doing all right." Her grandmother asked about her job, asked about how she liked her town, traded superficial gossip about the garden center where she volunteered and what she was planning on doing with her vegetable patch that year. "Are you not going to ask me about him, Nana?"

Her grandmother smiled, chuckling. "I can see that you're happy, dearest. I don't know if I've actually ever seen you this happy. So I suppose that tells me everything I need to know about him, doesn't it? Would it make a difference what I said either way? You've already shown everyone that you have your own mind, Lurielle."

"Nana, where-where are all the men? I see husbands my age, but . . ."

"That's one of our vases to bury, isn't it? I hope you're granted a child quickly, dearest. The greatest joy is knowing you won't be alone when your husband passes on. What in the stars is your mother squawking about over there? For pity's sake . . . Lurielle, let me see what's happening, I'll be back."

The stone settled in her stomach when she realized the implication of her grandmother's words. She knew, of course, that Elvish men had a considerably shorter lifespan than their female counterparts, she'd known that all her life. Somehow though, in the past year, Lurielle had never quite considered the reality of what being with Khash would mean. She'd only thought of the troubles they might face from each of their own kind, how nice it was being in Cambric Creek, where being a mixed species couple didn't matter. She looked out at the sea of old women in the room, her grandmother and great-grandmother's contemporaries, by and large, already alone in the world. Her grandmother was two hundred and fifty, her grandmother also in her triple-digit years. The average age in the room seemed to be around one hundred and fifty, she thought, a respectable age for an elf. Positively unheard of for an orc.

She pushed up from the table, spinning towards the exit. She needed air, *desperately* needed air, her lungs seemed unable to inflate on their own. Time ground to a halt. She could feel her blood churning in her veins, sounding like an ocean in her ears, feeling her heart beating in her mouth. Eternity was a yawning maw before her, and she wondered how she'd never noticed before. Ris had made comments about time and the way it seemed slow to her, the way superficial milestones grew more and more trivial by the week; the way weeks felt like days, the way months felt like hours. Lurielle hadn't paid it much mind at the time, but she supposed, looking back, that the past year had, in fact, flown by in a way she couldn't quite account for.

She didn't know how she overlooked such a salient fact, how the reality of what her life would look like had somehow escaped her, washed away in the delirium of happiness she felt for the last year, happier than she'd ever been in her life

Overhead, the sky was lit with stars. Burning a hundred million miles away from her, existing in a cold solitary sky. Existing alone. Existing forever. Lurielle didn't know how to explain the way her mind had simply blocked out this reality. She would have to live an entire lifetime without him. She did math all day long, and this was an easy calculation. Orcs aged like humans. He was so big, so strong, so heavy with muscle, and someday his body would wear down under all of that weight and muscle and height, and he would leave her. She understood that reality, understood the simple cycle of life and death, but he would not simply be leaving her for a handful of years to be reunited again. She would live and keep living, would live for another hundred years in this world without his smile, without his voice in her ear, and his hands at her waist. She didn't realize she had begun crying until she was choked by her tears.

As a sob wrenched free from her throat, she wondered if she would simply waste away after he was gone, suspended in a bubble of the past; if the sight of the bed they shared would be a comfort once he no longer warmed it, or if her heart would grieve anew each and every night she returned to it alone. Time stole all things, and as an elf, she had a king's ransom of time. She would forget the petty arguments they had, the disagreements over tiny, inconsequential things. She would forget the way she'd hovered on the edges of groups her entire life, not quite fitting in. None of the minor slings and barbs she'd borne would matter one day — a sign of how little she ought to let them matter now, for time would render them all obsolete. All that would be left was his absence, an empty bed, and a hole in her heart. The stars overhead streamed and Lurielle saw her future, stretching endlessly before her. A life without his smile and his warmth, without his heavy-lidded eyes across the pillow each morning.

"What's wrong, darlin'?"

His voice was a low purr at her ear, his breath hot at her neck. What would she do, without his heat? Without his syrupy drawl in her ear, without his voice in her head every day, to be her affirmation. What would she do without him?

"Lurielle? Did your mother say something to you?"

She would live an entire lifetime without him, which made the life they would have together so much more important. It didn't matter if people thought they were rushing, that they were talking about marriage and kids too soon, if her therapist wanted her to be able to find her own way to happiness without him. It didn't matter what the wives and girlfriends at his matches whispered about her, didn't matter what strangers thought, or his sisters, or her mother. Her weight didn't matter, her inability to style her hair on her, the fact that she hated dancing and parties and small talk. None of the things she let herself focus on truly mattered at all. Every day they weren't together was another day lost, another day wasted, one less day on the shortening balance of their time together.

"I want to get married," she blurted. "I-I want to marry you, Khash. I love you s-*so* much," her voice broke again and she pitched forward against him. "I want to spend the rest of our lives together." Her face crumpled at the end of her words, and he caught her, holding her tightly, shushing her gently, and she thought that he understood.

"Darlin', it's all right. What's all this about? Hush now, it's all fine. We're going to be fine. We can have this conversation at home . . . but do *not*," he emphasized, pinching her lips between his index finger and thumb, "say another word. Lurielle, I *do not care* about all those little things you spend so much time churning over. If you want to raise our kids to eat like rabbits and call them Snowdrop and Daffodil? I'm fine with it. You want me to quit the league and join your fancy lil' club and do basket-weaving and croquet on weekends? I'll be the best Gruvsh-damned basket weaver in your whole cupcake-lovin' community. But if you think you're going to take *this* from me . . ." He trailed off, his handsome face screwing up in an adorable scowl. "*I'm* going to be the one to take you by the hand, and I'm going to build you a bride fire so big it'll burn for a year. Do *not* even *think* about taking that from me. I don't know what's put this bee in your bonnet, but put all your big feelings back in that lil' bag of yours and swallow your teeth for another day. You want to be in charge of everything else? Fine. But *I'm* asking *you*, and that's that."

She was an ugly crier, knew her mother would have something nasty to say, knew she shouldn't wreck her makeup this way, but it no longer mattered. Nothing mattered but the pull of his voice, the warmth of his arms, and the heat of his kiss. His lips were warm against hers, and she breathed in his bravery, stole his steadiness, and pressed her forehead to his. His hand came up to cup the back of her head, holding her to him, and all she felt was the beat of his heart, playing her song. She was going to live a lifetime with him, and that would be the balm on her broken heart when he was gone, to sustain her for a lifetime without him.

"Yes," she whispered against his mouth, cupping his huge face in her tiny hands. "I'm going to say yes."

♥ ♥ ♥

Autumn

Silva

The freedom was intoxicating. She still woke up every day in her own bed; still made her coffee, packed her lunch, and went into the office each day. She still saw her friends, although she avoided the break room these days, preferring to eat alone at her desk with her e-reader propped in front of her. She wasn't interested in seeing Tannar, wasn't interested in making excuses, and wasn't interested in feeding the gossip train, and didn't want to hear entreaties from her mother delivered through him. It was the end of summer, the weather was beautiful, and even though her routine had not changed, she still woke up every day feeling as if the whole world was possible. She would take her tea up to the small area of the accessible roof on her building, where some of her neighbors had strung fairy lights and put up a table and chairs, and admire the sunrise — a swipe of apricot across the fading indigo sky, the sun rising in shades of pink and gold, leaving a cerulean sea in his wake.

Nothing had changed, yet somehow everything had. She still went to Greenbridge Glen every weekend, taking advantage of her office's hybrid policy to work from home up to two days a week, infringing on his space as much as she could.

At first, Silva worried that he would be annoyed having her there, but he'd scooped her up happily the first day she'd arrived on his doorstep and so far her fears had gone unfounded. After the first day, she showed up in the middle of the week — finding his office at Clover impossible to focus in, covered as it was in notes in his handwriting, checklists and order forms, a picture of him drawn by Cymbeline's two small children, and the small yellow thank you note she had sent him after receiving the Heart's Day flowers he'd sent to her office, pinned to the wall with the card inside, but present nonetheless — he had created a small office space for her at his apartment. A lovely, cabriole-legged table and glass shaded lamp, an extra-long charging cord, and a soft cushion for her chair. She had snapped a photo of their entwined legs — slender lavender and long green — on her phone one morning, shortly before his alarm went off, posting it on her social media later that afternoon, fully aware of the scandal it would create, a bubble of giddiness making her float through the rest of the day. She insisted on him taking nights off, exploring the restaurants in Starling Heights, not as nice as Cambric Creek in her opinion, lacking in both atmosphere and quality, but doing things together in public as a couple made up for the inability to do so in the town she loved.

Her mother had evidently decided to treat her emancipation as a temporary phase she was going through. She knew things weren't done; knew she was merely giving her family a taste of what would potentially happen if they pushed her hand. She still lived in her apartment, the rent for which her parents paid. Still drove the car they had bought her when she'd come home from school, still used the credit cards whose bills she'd never once seen. She knew that this was merely a muscle flex, and that her mother was giving her some latitude to get it out of her system. Silva had no doubt there were whispers at the club, no question that her absence at the ladies' club events had been noted, but, she rationalized, she was not the first elf at the club to go dabbling out in the wide world for a time. She supposed at least half of the families who were members could say the same about one of their children, a small-scale scandal that was quickly swept under the rug and forgotten about as soon as the lost lamb was returned to the flock. She was determined to not be included in that number.

She had found it easy to slip into his life, already familiar with most of his routines. It wasn't as satisfying as slipping him into hers, was certainly *not* everything she wanted, but it was good enough for the moment. It broke her heart every day to know that she was likely hurting her grandmother and disappointing her parents, but when she slid into his bed several nights a week, tucked against his chest with his hands in her hair, the trade-off was unthinkable.

It was one of those brilliantly sunny days, when she had put in to work from home, which meant working in his home, that she learned about the party. She'd come downstairs to stretch her legs, expecting to find Rukh leaning on the bar, and instead, finding Ainsley and Elshona sitting at one of the low tops in the back room, whispering conspiratorially. Ainsley looked up sharply when she entered, his eyebrows shooting up in surprise, clearly not expecting to see her.

"Lamby-dove, did you just *teleport* here?!"

Silva forced her mouth into a smile. She knew his friend didn't like her, but she had no idea what she could do to change his mind. She didn't feel that she had ever done anything to specifically offend Ainsley, and if she thought about it long enough, Silva found the whole situation incredibly annoying. Ainsley and Elshona were his friends, his *true* friends, even though Tate and the orc woman seemed at odds most of the time. She had happened upon Thessa and Cymbeline whispering over the increasingly contentious relationship between owner and chef, glad to know that it wasn't merely in her imagination, and slightly panicked that she had anything to do with it all.

"You don't, Silva, don't worry," Cymbeline had assured her quietly one afternoon. "This has been going on long before you came on the scene."

The fact that neither Ainsley or Elshona seemed to care for her presence rankled in her mind, as if it were a mark against her she wasn't able to erase, no matter how friendly she tried to be.

"I'm working from home today," she smiled. "I'm hoping I'll be able to get him out to touch some grass at some point this evening.

Last week I got him to actually take the whole day off, and he worked in the garden all afternoon. It was sort of cheating, because it was still technically work, but at least he was outside getting some fresh air." She had learned of the rooftop garden back in the spring, an ambitious effort he and Elshona had started several years earlier, which they had let slide to the wayside as Clover's business increased. Silva watched as the two orcs exchanged a look, clasping her hands and wishing she had decided to just stay upstairs. She was unused to being disliked, didn't know how to change their opinion of her, and frankly, she was tired of trying.

"Silva, we need your help," Ainsley hissed, motioning her to take a seat at their table. "I don't know why I didn't think of this earlier! You're the perfect person to get him away for the day."

"We're trying to plan a party, lamby," Elshona explained in a low voice. "A surprise party. But that requires him being away so that we can get all the details set up and have people arrive."

Excited butterflies fluttered through her at the thought. "A party for Tate?" Planning parties was, after all, a bit of her specialty. She had been on the planning committees for dozens and dozens of large-scale events over the years at the club, knew the importance of having supplies and food booked early, of how to plan for pitfalls and last-minute changes, and the thought of doing so for him elated her. "I'd love to help! Tell me what I can do!"

"We already have just about everything taken care of," Elshona went on. "The kitchen is taking care of everything, we already have the liquor ordered and paid for so he doesn't blow a gasket. I've got a diversion all set up in the dining room the day of the delivery to keep him occupied while Rukh and that new boy get things to the cellar. Ains is in charge of the guest list."

"All we need is for you to get rid of him for the day. An overnight trip would be ideal."

Silva felt herself deflate, wondering if they could see the air and excitement leaking from her, leaving her small and useless before them. Of course, they had planned the whole thing without her.

"Oh," she said in a small voice. "Oh . . . okay. I'll think of something." She pushed up from the table, feeling her neck heat, wishing she had just stretched her legs upstairs. "You'll have to give me the date, if I'm allowed to at least know that." She turned out of the room without looking back, her hands balling into fists. They wanted her to get him out of town. She had a good mind to take him away, and not bother coming back.

In the end, it had been easy to orchestrate. Silva knew Tate would have followed wherever she led, regardless of her reasoning, even if it was only to collect her and grouse about the drive. She decided to give them both a reason to get away, researching the surrounding areas until she had found the perfect opportunity. An antique shop that specialized in Elvish and Gnomish wares, in close enough proximity to a bar that advertised pool to make it worth their while. He had just come home from the bistro, mumbling about the heat and setting his thermostat to an even more Arctic temperature.

Silva let him shower and change before he headed down to the pub, pushing him back on the bed and straddling his hips, nosing against his damp hair.

"Can we go away again?" she whined, fisting a hand into his black T-shirt. "It doesn't need to be anywhere fancy. We had so much fun that one time, remember?"

He chuckled against her neck. "Did we have fun? I seem to remember you turning into a cannibal at one point, does that happen every time you leave town? I only ask because I'll need to start taking a multivitamin in preparation."

"*Please*," she pleaded, pressing her cheek to his chest, throwing her arms around his neck. "I just want to get away for a day, there's a big dip coming up at work, and I won't have anything to do. We could leave Friday morning and be back by Saturday night. You won't even have to miss the busy night at the bar."

She should have felt more satisfied than she did as she sat in the passenger seat of his car the following month, her GPS set to the hotel she picked out, close to both the antique shop and the pub. It annoyed her that they hadn't even thought of her, that they hadn't included her in the planning at all, but she pushed the frustration away as the highway narrowed down to a rural stretch of nothing but countryside. The trees had already slipped into their autumn coats, brilliant red and gold and orange, blazing across the valley as they sped along. She wondered if they would've been better off planning something back two months ago, that would've been her suggestion if they would've bothered asking. Tate was tetchy in the autumn; his temper shorter and his answers to questions more snappish.

He had picked a fight with her apropos of nothing a few weeks earlier, insinuating that he thought she needed to call and reconcile with her mother. "How much more time are you going to let slide away, dove? The more time that passes, the harder it's going to be to forgive you, harder for your sort to forget. You've had your fun playing house, it's time to go back to your actual life." He'd softened once she was in tears, as he always did. "I'm too selfish to give you up on my own, but it's tearing me apart watching you throw away your future. I can't give you anything you want, Silva."

"Can't," she asked, "or won't?" When she laid against him that night, salty tracks of her dried tears staining her cheeks, he repeated the same line he always gave her — that he couldn't give her the things she wanted. "Why should I have to choose," she demanded hotly. "Why *can't* I get what I want? You're just being stubborn."

His smile stretched again, his nose bumping hers. "And what is that, little dove? Why don't you tell me exactly what it is that you want. Let me guess . . . a summer wedding and a house in your gated community, a perfect little wisp of a daughter. Am I close?"

He needs a wife and at least three children, and a hobby he can only do on Sundays. Her smile was small around the tracks of her tears. "A spring wedding, actually. When all the flowers are in bloom."

"I'm going to have to nix springtime for anything," he cut in. "Spring and autumn are absolutely out of the question, dreadful seasons. Summer would be fine if it weren't for the bleedin' heat. Winter is truly the only acceptable time of year for anything."

Her heart was crowded in her chest by the riot of butterfly wings that fluttered and pushed, pressing against her lungs, a bubble of elation filling her as he played along. "A winter wedding means I could wear one of those long velvet cloaks trimmed and in fur," she mused. "Blue and silver for everything. We have to book a hall, instead of having it outside, but that can be arranged." His laughter was a rich scrape, vibrating against her chest. "You said I was a princess," she reminded him, "so I should be able to get everything I want."

His sigh was deep, and she already knew what was coming. "You shouldn't want me, dove. I was serious before. I can't give you any of the things you want, Silva. You should kiss me goodbye in the morning, and go back to your family before it's too late."

"I'm very tired of having the same argument with you over and over again," she mumbled, rubbing her nose against the dark, crescent-shaped scar on his shoulder. Dark green, nearly black, she'd kept the wound fresh for weeks by digging her nail into it, the same as she'd done to her own after that first time he bit her. Marked as his, marked as hers, meant to be together. If this were one of her books, she thought, she would be close to pitching it across the room. She would be furious with the hero at this point, and aggravated by the heroine's inability to close the deal and get her happily ever after. "I'm just as selfish as you, you know. I'm not leaving. You'll have to throw me out. So I guess we're stuck with each other." His laughter had been a low rumble against her, his lips a soft pressure against her head, and she'd fallen asleep shortly after, putting the same, tired argument to bed once more.

She'd have not chosen autumn for any sort of party at which she wanted him to be truly sociable. She already knew when they arrived back at the Plundered Pixie, he would grit his teeth and endure the night, rather than enjoying it. *That's what they get for not asking me.*

The antique shop proved to be a disappointment for both of them. Mostly Gnomish, the Elvish pieces they did have weren't anything especially impressive, and he only wound up purchasing a few pieces — several teacups that she oohed over, an egg cup she admired, and an intricately designed hourglass that he liked the lines of, mumbling about putting it on Cymbeline's stand to make her aware of how much time she spent chatting with guests. The pool bar had been equally disappointing — populated by a biker gang of ogres, all of whom looked as if they could snap Tate in half like a toothpick. He'd wheezed with laughter against her back the first night they'd arrived, insisting there were easier ways for her to have him killed. It was the hotel room where they wound up spending the bulk of their time, and not even that was as nice as the pictures she'd looked at.

"I'm terrible at planning anything," she moaned against him as he laughed.

"Oh no, Silva, we're trapped in a hotel room together. How ever shall we pass the time, dove?"

She supposed she should have done better planning the trip; should have investigated the hotel room more and read a larger selection of reviews, should have checked out the species populations of the town to have an idea of who might patronize the little bar . . . But she couldn't quite find it in her to complain a short while later, when she knelt in the center of the bed, holding herself up on her elbows and knees, keening as he pumped into her from behind. Her options for this trip had been limited, and she'd not had time to do a thorough casing of the neighborhood for diversions, so they had created their own diversions. She could feel the rub of that delicious ridge within her, not as pronounced as she knew it would become, but enough to make her press her face to the mattress and moan, every slide of it over her G spot feeling like a jackhammer to her brain. When he pushed her flat to the mattress, grinding into her from a tighter angle, she was lost. He might hate autumn, for whatever nonsense reason he gave, but if *this* was what happened to him every year, Silva vowed she would live for this season for the rest of her life. She wanted him to come inside her, was determined that she would not let the weekend end until he both came in her mouth and flooded her womb in his seed, uncaring how crass that made her seem.

Now they were back, her little diversion executed, her part played. Whatever happened next would have nothing to do with her.

The collection of voices within the pub was a cacophony, exploding the instant the Pixie's door groaned out their arrival. Tate froze, stiffening at the threshold, the sudden rigor of his long fingers causing her hand to slip from his. They were meant to be coming back to a quiet night in the off-season — the Pixie's Orcish regulars crowded around the pool tables and a few at the bar, gossiping with Rukh before settling their tabs and disappearing into the chilly autumn night, the air still damp from an earlier storm. Instead, the pub was packed with trolls and werecats, lithe nymphs and laughing satyrs, the exact same sort of crowd that had populated the birthday party at the club in the city, months earlier. For what felt like a small eternity, he stood mute in the Pixie's doorway, too shocked to even blink, a statue beside her, and Silva was certain he'd stopped breathing.

They'd actually done it, she realized with a sinking heart. Months of careful planning, none of it involving her, and it had gone off without a hitch. She had served her only purpose: distract him with her neediness and her body and her tears while Ainsley and Elshona did the rest, and to her great shock and slight dismay, it had actually worked.

They shouldn't have come back, she thought for the millionth time. It was an impractical daydream she'd had on the journey home, moving from town to town, living in hotels, leaving their judgment and responsibility-laden lives behind, but for the last several months, she'd felt whole. Silva of the daytime hadn't existed, and the freedom to be, without splintering herself into tiny shards, was intoxicating. She watched how the hand that had slipped from her tightened around the wood of the interior jamb, as if the pub had betrayed him, and gulped. *You can deny having anything to do with it. Ainsley and Elshona are responsible for all of this.*

Silva followed the line of his sight, golden eyes boring into Elshona's, and she couldn't help but notice that the latter looked as though she were ready to flee if necessary. She kept her hand wrapped around his wrist when Tate moved, at last, ignoring the well-wishers and pushing through the tight press of bodies with a single-minded focus, dragging her along until they stood before the orc. Elshona sucked in a shaky breath, pressing her lips in a firm line, and jutted her chin out defiantly. Her eyes gave away her panic though, and Silva tightened her grip around his wrist. Why they thought throwing a surprise party for a control freak like Tate was a good idea, she'd never know, and from the look in the orc woman's eyes, Elshona was realizing the folly.

"You have the bald fucking audacity to pull one over the minute I'm out of town." It was a statement, not a question, her nostrils flaring as he continued before she could draw breath. "Who's footing the bill for this? Who invited this crowd? Do you think for a minute I'll not pack you up and ship you back to that sheep pasture that spat you out if I have to socialize all bleedin' night?"

She would never understand their relationship. Silva bit her lip as Tate's fists balled and Elshona smiled, evidently deciding the danger had passed, mirth replacing the look of fear as she beamed at Tate's words.

"You don't need to worry about footing the bill for a thing, we took care of all that, right under your meddlin' nose. Ains invited everyone, said these are your friends. It's your party, you can do whatever you please, I suppose. If you want to stomp upstairs like the miserable cunt you are, no one'll stop you. As for pulling one over... Scarlet on your mam for raising the eejit that fell for it."

The air in Silva's lungs dissolved, for though she knew practically nothing about the man she professed to love, she had knowledge enough to know all mention of his mother was verboten.

She would never, ever, *ever* understand the relationship Tate and Elshona shared, she realized when a choked laugh escaped Tate's throat, his shoulders shaking as he leaned forward to press his lips to the orc woman's temple.

"Fair play, Culchie."

Silva slumped against him, relieved that the danger had passed, if only for the moment.

"And you!" He spun in a blur, trapping her in the cage of his arms. Silva squeaked when she was lifted, the sharp glint of his teeth catching her collar bone. "In on this whole time? Lead me off by the nose to act like we're a couple of runaway fucking children? Little minx."

She was an integral part of the plan, Silva reminded herself when his lips met hers, the pulse in his neck jackrabbit quick as her mouth drifted. It didn't matter if they had forgotten about her or discounted her importance or assumed their relationship would have run its temporary course. *They never could have managed this without you.*

"I was," she agreed, yipping when the hand around her thigh squeezed. No one would ever discount her again, she'd make sure of it; from now on if Tate was thought of at all, she'd damn well better be imagined at his side. "I was the glue that held it all together."

"And *you*. It's not my birthday," he hissed, making Ainsley laugh again.

"Does it make a difference?" Ainsley pointed out. "It's not like you're ever going to tell us when your birthday is. I bought this for you like three fucking years ago, and have you had a single birthday party since? Have you had a single birthday party in all the time I've known you? No. We both know the answer is no." The box he handed Tate was long and narrow, the blade inside very old-looking, and very odd. "I knew I had to get this for you the second I found it," he exclaimed excitedly. "The owner of the shop and I have been looking for provenance for literally over a year. He's insisting that it can't be Elvish and Orcish, that there would never be an Elvish orc. I happen to know better."

The antique dagger had a solid-looking construction, designed to fit in a big hand. The shape of the blade was Orcish, as was the handle, all things she knew from watching more episodes of Attic Wanderers than she ever thought she would in a lifetime. The overlay, however, and the design on the blade was clearly Elvish. Delicate lines, intertwining vine, perplexing and incongruous. It was, Silva had to admit, a perfect present for Tate.

He smiled, a genuine smile that lit his eyes. "I love it."

"Elvish and Orcish. And look at how lovely it is, how functional. Two things that can coexist. Just some food for thought, Tate. Happy birthday-ish. "

432

"I'm so glad you're here," Ris whispered a short while later. "I hate not knowing anyone."

Silva beamed, linking arms with her friend. "I know, I hate it. These are all their friends. But at least we have each other . . . you should have made him invite Dynah, she might have met someone." Ris wheezed in laughter as Silva reached into the cooler, pulling out two of the Elvish spritzers for them.

She managed to corner Elshona a short while later, a rare moment of the orc woman being alone, and Silva decided she could not wait any longer.

"I don't know what I did to make you so mad at me," she blurted out, knitting her fingers together nervously. "I don't plan on going anywhere though. I already told him he has to throw me out, I'm not breaking up with him," she laughed awkwardly. "So I'd like it if we could be friends again . . . but I understand if that's not something you want."

He was being passed around, from cluster to cluster, friend group to different group. Silva recognized several of the people from the party he'd taken her to in Bridgeton, the rest of the crowd being a little more casual — the sort he hustled pool with and raised cars with, a far cry from the sleek haired nymphs of the birthday party, but he'd fit in there as well. He was a chameleon, she thought, able to slip on and off false skins to fit in anywhere he needed to at the moment. She could only hope that the version he showed her was his true self. The cacophony of the bar around them had not decreased since Tate's arrival, and she was obliged to take a step closer to hear Elshona's low voice.

"Lamby," the bigger woman began, her brow furrowing, eyes turning down, "I'm sorry if I've made you feel that way, love. It . . . It doesn't have anything to do with you. I mean . . . . It does but it's not *you* you. He and I have been together for a long, long time. We've dated a lot of the same girls. We've fucked a lot of the same girls. But at the end of the day, it was still always just the two of us. You're the only one who's stuck around. It's not you I'm mad at, it's myself. I'm too dependent on him. I hope you believe that. This is my own issue, and I'm sorry that I've made it yours. I am happy for you, both of you. Honestly. Sometimes I dream about murdering your boyfriend in his sleep, it's true, and other times I dream about murdering him while he's awake, which is exponentially more satisfying, that's also true. But again, those are our issues. Not yours."

By the time the crowd had begun to dwindle, he was gripping her hand. "I'm going to kill all of them if they're not gone in five fucking minutes."

Silva wrapped her arms around him and breathed him in, smoke and wet leaves, dark times and black earth. The same bonfire he'd smelled like a year ago, she realized.

"You're so cranky. You're such a grump. Grumpy and sunshine, that's us. I've always liked that trope."

"Silva, what the fuck are you going on about?" She collapsed in giggles against him, as eager for the crowd to leave as he was. It was gray sweatpants weather, she realized, bouncing excitedly on her toes. She wanted to get him upstairs and peel him out of his jeans, wanted to feel that hard, textured ridge again and fall asleep in his arms.

She had just managed to get him across the apartment to the bedroom, the last of the partygoers finally disappearing into the night, when she stopped, stamping her foot.

"We left my weekender in the car. Both of the phone chargers are in there, and your laptop. What if the car gets broken into?"

The barricade said still been up on the road, preventing them from being able to drive through town, necessitating him to park on the other side of the lake. It wasn't a far walk, simply through the little business district and over the cute little bridge, up a footpath to where the lake's parking lot sat. There was very little crime in the hamlet, although cars were regularly rifled through, petty crimes of opportunity.

"Let's just get them now, you're going to be extra cranky in the morning when your phone is dead." She could already hear him grumbling, slipping her shoes back on with a grin. It wasn't fated mates, but grumpy/sunshine was a trope she could live with. "I'm going to beat you," she called out in a sing-song. They were going to be fine, she decided. She was going to be Silva of the nighttime without splintering, and if that meant giving up her Elvish community, so be it. Her mother and grandmother would forgive her eventually, she hoped. Happily ever after wasn't going to find her without her doing a bit of hard work she'd come to realize, and she was ready to get to the end, and start a new chapter . . . with him. They would be together, and together they could weather whatever storm faced them. "Tate, I'm going to beat you!" she called over her shoulder once more, racing down the staircase and up the short, pitch-black hallway. Silva crashed into the back door, anticipating the bite of the cool evening air on her bare legs and shoulders, but the door unexpectedly refused to yield.

The building seemed to shudder around her, the old wood of the Pixie groaning as she struggled to push the crashbar open, but his old girl held fast, thoroughly stuck. She had begun to laugh, squealing as he approached, knowing he was going to come swooping around the hallway like a giant bat, no matter how slowly he thudded down the staircase; would swoop around the corner and scoop her up, announcing himself as the winner. It took several hard shoves, Tate's footsteps on the stairway echoing down the hallway, before the latch finally gave, spilling her with a stumble into the night. She was running towards the future, she thought, excited to face it with him, unchartered territory, new adventures. The whole world felt possible.

Silva stumbled out the door, spilling into the alley in the cool autumn darkness . . . but the alley behind the bar was gone.

♥ ♥ ♥

The Girls will return in Girls Weekend Book 3

♥ ♥ ♥

Small Talk

A Girls Weekend
supplemental short story

"S o . . . sports?"

Khash eyed the smaller man hopefully. They'd been sitting in silence for what had felt like several eternities, even though he knew it had likely only been a few minutes.

The restaurant was quiet for a weekend, quieter than he'd been expecting, and the lack of background noise only served to amplify the heavy, tangible silence sitting between the two orcs. It was a stark difference from the bustle of that first night he'd met Lurielle here for dessert, months earlier, and he wished — not for the first time — that they were here alone, just the two of them, nestled into a booth in the shadowed corner of the nearly-empty dining room. He could envision the way her hair would shine like burnished gold beneath the low lighting; the way her sapphire eyes would sparkle as he tilted her chin up to steal a kiss . . . his mind's eye might have been focused on the delectable thought of the plump lips belonging to his beloved, but as his gaze shifted, his actual eyes landed on his companion at the table and the effervescent champagne bubble of warmth that had been rising within him popped, leaving behind the acrid reality.

Bluebell's friend had demurely mentioned going to powder her nose shortly after the dessert plates had been cleared away, and the next thing he knew, Lurielle was rising from the table to join her, leaving him alone.

With Tate.

It wasn't the first time he had been forced to endure the smaller man's unsettling company. There had been several occasions when Lurielle had insisted on him joining her in meeting her friend Silva at the, admittedly, excellent bistro that Tate owned in the small resort community's downtown. He'd enjoyed his visits to the restaurant during his resort stays in years past, but now . . . Khash felt his stomach muscles clench the instant his feet left the safety of the crosswalk, stepping onto the distinctive and controversial herringbone brick that surrounded the bistro, felt his hackles raise each time he was forced to step through the ornate doorway, and he would be obliged to swallow down his defensiveness and paranoia.

The sidewalk had been filled and sealed the previous month, several days before he and Lurielle had driven up for their monthly stay. The restoration work was done at the owner's expense, so he'd heard in line at the bakery that morning, and he'd learned the whole hamlet had grumbled and squawked when an unfamiliar work truck and crew had rolled into town.

"Maybe he makes a point to hire other immigrants, did you think of that?" Lurielle had shot back, as he spread their hot coffee and fragrant pastries on the cabin's small kitchen table.

She'd only just pulled herself from bed, her hair an adorable bird's nest as she blew on the coffee as he'd relayed the gossip that The Plundered Pixie's proprietor had eschewed the hamlet's custom of hiring one of the construction companies owned by the local residents. The troll and his work crew had not spoken a lick of the common, he'd learned as he picked out an almond-studded croissant for Bluebell, knowing it was her favorite, but the foreman had babbled away in an incomprehensible language with Tate, who'd apparently stood sentinel in Clover's doorway the entire day the work was being done, arms crossed over his chest, daring anyone from the council to drop by and impede the work.

"You guys are like clucking old women, do you know that? You don't like the people he hires, you don't like the way he runs his business, you don't like the way he wears his hair, you think his pants are too tight . . . the elves at my mom's club aren't half as bitchy as the orcs around here are!"

Khash had silenced her with his lips, scooping her up and carrying her back to the bedroom, annoyed that he was allowing that smug faerie to occupy even a single moment of his thoughts. They were meant to be relaxing, to be reveling in each other's love and attention, and he would remind her of that. "We'll see who's an old woman," he'd grumbled, covering her body with his and pulling up the edge of her t-shirt as she laughed. The coffee had gone cold by the time they'd returned to it, but it had been a worthy sacrifice, he had thought.

Besides, he thought privately, it wasn't as if the commune residents were the only gossips. He liked the hostess at Tate's restaurant, a talkative mothwoman who looked as though she ought to be gracing the covers of high fashion magazines rather than toiling away in the service industry, but the rest of the staff — the servers and bussers, the overly-friendly tiefling who seemed to always be there and the reedy troll who tended bar when Tate himself was not holding court behind the polished dark wood — was just a hair *too* attentive, too watchful. Khash was unable to shake the suspicion each time that every eye in the place was on him from the instant he entered until the moment he left on the few occasions they met Silva there and was certain their table was the source of staff gossip.

The man himself would join their party briefly each time, although Khash had the distinct impression Tate was only placating the pretty young elf who, for reasons he was completely unable to discern, no matter how many times he and Lurielle discussed it, seemed completely besotted with the smug bastard. Silva was a wide-eyed innocent, greener'n a baby's switch, and clearly too naive to see the sort of two-bit snake oil salesman with whom she'd gotten involved, but Khash saw him plain.

Coming here tonight had been Lurielle's idea, a compromise of neutral ground, one he appreciated, even if it was still aggravating to even be forced to spend a moment in the smarmy fae's company. Still . . . he hadn't been raised up to sit with company in silence, no matter how odious he found said company to be; prided himself on his southern charm and ability to find common ground with everyone he met, and he'd promised the woman he loved that he would play nicely. He wasn't about to disappoint Bluebell by sitting sullenly.

♥ ♥ ♥

Tate wrinkled his nose in response to Khash's question. He tried to imagine the kind of sports this big lout would be interested in, no doubt something barbaric and violent.

It was comical, he sometimes thought, how rarely he had real conversations with orcs like this, despite living amid a clutch of them, and how very little he had in common with them. Oh, he knew all manner of sordid details about his patrons — their habits and vices, who owed money to whom and who had more than a passing fancy with the bottle — the same particulars he made sure to learn no matter the patron or their species, the mark of a good barkeep, always useful information to have . . . but he was certain he likely had more parallel life experience with the linen napkins than he did with his companion across the table, despite sharing a species . . . at least, in part. A most unfortunate part.

One of the last visits Silva had paid to Clover with Khash and Lurielle still chewed at the edge of his mind, a sharp reminder of how he was perceived, even to the people who thought they knew him well. Cymbeline had been buzzing as she followed him to the office that night, once Silva and her friends had left, cooing how happy she was to see him in a relationship, how cute it was that they were able to have double dates right here, how adorable it was that Silva brought them.

"And it's another orc-elf couple, just like you! That's so precious!"

Her voice had been an annoying hum as she continued and his knuckles had been white as he'd gripped the sleeve of his jacket, digging his nails into the black leather and reminding himself that he liked Cym, that she was a single mother and if he locked her into the walk-in overnight, he'd likely be responsible for her kids when she was frozen solid come morning.

"I'm cracking off," he'd interrupted her cheerful obliviousness, and there had obviously been something in his tone, a sharpness he typically saved for the Pixie's patrons, rarely used on the staff here, and her mouth had snapped shut, her feathery pink antennae bobbing as she nodded with a swallow. "Call if you need anything," he added in a gentler tone, leaving out the back door. He'd been able to feel her eyes on his back as he moved up the street towards the Pixie, already knowing that every orc in the pub that night would get a piece of his bad mood as a parting gift for the evening.

An orc, just like him. Despite the fact that he'd been raised as an elf and knew next to nothing about Orcish culture and possessed less than zero desire to learn. Ignoring that he spoke several different

Elvish languages in three different dialects, that he'd grown up in a conservative community, observing the sabbaths and ritual days, sang the ancient hymns to the old ones, rituals that were unknown to this new crop of elves. The scent of dried flowers and incense of those iaun-nights with his grandparents still pulled at his nose, the sound of soft lutes and harps and a melancholy flute, delicate details these lumbering brutes could never understand . . . but he was an orc, no different than the cunt across the table, it was how the world saw him, what they saw first. He had tried once, as a boy, he'd tried. He'd gone stomping away from his home, tired of being unwanted, tired of being a constant source of conflict, tired of never fitting in. If the elves didn't want him, he'd thought with a child's fury and logic, he'd go where he *was* wanted. He'd simply learn to be an orc, and live with his father's kin, but he'd been turned away by the clan at the village gates, not even granted entrance to plead his case. The two orcs who'd stopped him had exchanged a loaded look, and he'd known that they knew his story was true, that his father lived in this village . . . but they'd turned him away just the same. *There's nothing here for you boy. Go on home now.* A good reminder that even if he didn't have his own excellent reasons for staying unattached, Silva's family would see tall, green, and tusks, and that would be the end.

Eyeing the larger orc speculatively, Tate presumed there would be grunting and rolling in the mud involved in any sport he played. "Not really," he answered lightly, examining the stemware critically. He didn't like the weight of the glasses, too clunky and cumbersome.

Purchased with the orcish clientele in mind, no doubt, but he'd watched the awkward way Silva's tiny hand had struggled to span her water glass. Poor planning, he thought. A successful business put the needs and wants of its female clientele first. Make the women happy and the menfolk would follow. "Billiards." He refrained from pointing out it was a game that required actual skill and not merely brute strength, as Khash pressed his lips together flatly.

The knowledge that Silva and her friend would be returning to the table momentarily made him exhale sharply through his nose, knowing that she'd be displeased to find him and the big orc sitting in a standoff of soundlessness. He'd already been treated to her full lower lip pushed out in a pout, eyes wide as saucers when he'd initially balked at accompanying her to meet her friends for drinks that evening. It was a weekend, he'd pointed out, ignoring the fact that they were at the thick of the off-season, adding that he'd not built extra hands into the schedule to account for an unexpected absence.

He still wasn't sure how she'd managed to make herself appear so small at that moment, as he'd turned with a *no* already leaving his mouth. She'd gazed up with pleading in her wide, emerald eyes, tiny and lovely and beseeching, and he knew he'd already lost. It was stupid to allow her to grow attached, stupid and selfish and cruel . . . but he hated seeing her lovely mouth turned down in a frown, particularly knowing that he'd been the one to put it there. Her recovery when he'd relented had been suspiciously swift — squealing with a delighted clap, pulling his shirtfront until he bent in half to meet her lips. The satisfied smile that had replaced her frown had left Tate with the certainty that he'd been hustled. She'd be unhappy to find them sitting in uncomfortable silence, he thought as he blew out the hard breath.

"Music?"

Khash could tell immediately that his answer had not been satisfactory, as the smaller man gave another world-weary sigh in response. He could only imagine the type of music Tate would find acceptable . . . something loud and piercing no doubt, that would make the nerve behind his eye pulse, like a personally engraved migraine invitation. He wondered what the smug bastard would think of the music he'd grown up with — fiddlers and skilled banjo players, and the smoky, soulful voice of the clan's elderwife; songs of sacrifice and tradition and clan, things Tate would never understand.

The smaller man's attention turned to the empty place setting before him, evidently deciding Khash was no longer worth his effort: examining the water and wine glasses with what Khash thought was an overly-critical eye, rubbing the table linen and napkin between his thumb and forefinger, flipping over the fork to inspect the stamp on the back. Khash had the distinct impression that Tate would immediately root through his medicine cabinet, were he ever to be granted access to Khash's home, a nightmare of a scenario. *That's never, ever going to happen.*

He was saved by the reappearance of the smiling server, the unnatural shine of her eyes giving her away as some sort of shifter.

"Can I interest you gentlemen in a specialty menu? Maybe one of our house flights?"

Tate was a barman, Khash reminded himself, returning the shifter woman's bright smile. Surely they could find common ground here.

"Bourbon?" He turned his head to find the fae had also returned the server's big smile, too-wide and completely unnerving, and he was unable to prevent his automatic shudder. Khash swallowed hard when those strange golden eyes moved to him, squinting slightly.

"Whisky."

The server departed and silence reigned.

Khash huffed in frustration as the moments ticked steadily by. This was *not* his fault, he wouldn't let it be. He'd known orcs like Tate his whole life, for every family in the clan seemed to have one: dissolutes with no respect for tradition or clan, black eyes on their family names . . . but this shifty-eyed fae was infinitely worse.

The Pixie had a reputation. He'd not purchased his cabin until the resort had opened, building around the existing nudist commune, but Khash had heard rumors. The old business had been a gathering place for the commune, a reliable community haunt, named for the orc who'd owned it; an orc who'd, allegedly, been strong-armed into selling, with the Pixie and her bar business opening in its place. Ladies-only drink specials and its desirable location in the shopping district made it reasonably popular with the tourists who came into town, but everyone in the village knew the pool tables and the illicit gambling that took place around them was the main attraction. The proprietor, it was rumored, ran odds, kept a book, hawkishly kept tabs on the sums owed, and Khash was flummoxed by how many of his fellows had willingly allowed their names to be placed in said book, to allow a faerie even an ounce of control over them . . . but the lure of vice was too strong, evidently. *Weak-minded. A sign of poor upbringing.*

"They really overpaid for this place, you know." Tate wasn't sure why he'd voiced the thought, it wasn't as though this big orc would be interested in the subtle politicking that encompassed business ownership in the small community, the back-scratching and favors granted by the council. He actually liked the owner here, a rangy shapeshifter who cared more about profitability than he did about rubbing elbows and playing the game with his orcish neighbors, and recognized their table's smiling server as one of the man's daughters, having exchanged change with her on more than one occasion.

He had witnessed the shifter receiving similar treatment as he himself had, back when he'd fought the uphill battle to open the Pixie. The council had learned their lesson thrice over, reaping what they'd sown with him over the years and Clover's launch had been a walk in the park by comparison, but he still hadn't liked to see another non-Orcish owner receiving the poor treatment, and had been as helpful as he could, passing on the name of his own distributors and vendors, offering insight and resolutions to the council's ludicrous demands. His new neighbor's success would only help his own, after all, a thriving business district meant more patrons for all . . . but it had been too late to offer council on the purchase, and he'd been grateful for his years of experience behind the bar hearing tales, as his features had not betrayed the shock he'd felt when the shifter had confided the shockingly high price tag attached to the business he'd purchased.

Tate was nosy, always had been, ever since he'd been a wee thing trying to peek into the handbags of the elves coming into his grandparents' shop, and after the conversation with his new neighbor, he'd made it his business to know more about the other shops and restaurants that had steadily popped up around town in the years after the resort had opened, finding similar stories of poor decision-making, leading him to believe he might actually be one of the only owners in the hamlet whose business ledgers operated completely in the black. . . . not that the strutting, puffed-up peacock across the table would be interested in any of that.

"Oh? Well, they seem to do a good amount of business, right? It's a good location . . . not as good as yours, but still . . . what's too much?" *You're like an old woman!* He could almost hear Bluebell's admonishment, but Khash couldn't help it. He was southern, gossip was a part of his culture. Tate was not someone he'd choose to chew the cud with, but then again, he was playing nicely, doing as he was asked. He watched the younger-looking man glance around the room before leaning in conspiratorially, hoping whatever he was about to disclose would be enough to keep them talking until the girls returned.

♥ ♥ ♥

She thought the evening had gone well so far, all things considered. Khash had done his normal moaning and carrying on at the thought of having to spend any time in the company of Silva's friend, but after her outburst that morning, he'd buttoned his lip and had kept his complaints to a minimum as they made the short walk from the cabin to the town's small downtown.

She understood, she'd told herself in the bathroom mirror as she got ready that evening. She understood and was overreacting. The two orcs weren't fond of each other, and that was fine. She understood. Lurielle didn't dislike Silva's boyfriend, not the way Khash did. He had a bone-dry sense of humor and a biting sarcasm that she, as a fellow smart ass, appreciated, and from what she could tell, he treated Silva like a fine porcelain doll, with care and indulgence.

She didn't dislike him, but that didn't mean she trusted him, not entirely. He'd joined them a handful of times by that point, but Lurielle didn't feel she'd managed to learn anything about him, beyond hazy half-answers and vague roundabouts. His unsettling smile never quite touched his eyes; eyes that seemed to dance around the room, as though he were constantly assessing the potential to cause trouble, a personality trait that seemed completely at odds with her sweet co-worker. Silva said he was Elvish, a claim that checked out in Lurielle's opinion, for Tate certainly carried himself with as much arrogance as any elf she'd ever known, even if he did possess an odd intensity that made her nervous, ridiculous considering he'd be doing nothing more menacing than sitting quietly across the table, his long fingers threaded with Silva's smaller ones.

The two men had next to nothing in common, other than an almost palpable dislike for each other, despite the friendship of their partners ... but she didn't like the way Khash spoke of Tate's unorcish behavior and mannerisms, as though that alone were an indictment of some deep, personal failing.

"So you don't trust any orc who has mixed blood?" she'd countered that morning, feeling her cheeks heat in the midst of his complaining and carping.

"Bluebell, he's as slippery as a pocketful of last night's pudding!"

"Well, that's good to know for the future. You do remember I'm an elf, right? I guess I should make sure my birth control is up to date when I get home." He'd sobered instantly, swinging around to face her, his mouth dropping open in shock as she left him in the kitchen. She'd been unsurprised when he'd followed her into the bedroom, dropping to his knees before her as she perched on the edge of the bed to put lotion on her legs.

"Lurielle, you know that's not what I meant."

"Are you sure, Khash? Because you've got a lot to say about being the wrong kind of orc, and I should keep that in mind before we ever think about having — "

"That's not what I meant," he repeated, taking the bottle from her hands. "I love you, I love everything about you. I don't care that you're not Orcish, and neither will my family."

She'd sucked in a shuddering breath as he warmed the lotion

between his palms before dragging them over her calves, not exhaling until she was certain the wave of emotions his words churned up were firmly tamped down. They were traveling south later that month to visit his family, and the date of their departure seemed to loom on the calendar like a growing shadow, her nerves increasing each hour as the date grew nearer. Introducing her to his family was the only reason for the trip, a fact that tightened her lungs and made the room spin, but he'd assured her it would be a low-stress visit and would make subsequent clan events easier to bear.

"The whole clan can be . . . a lot," he'd admitted grudgingly when he'd first proposed the trip south. "You'll feel better already knowing Mama and the girls."

Lurielle was certain she'd feel better *never* having to meet them, wishing, not for the first time, that she'd fallen in love with an orphan, or at least, another self-made orphan, like her.

His big hands moved slowly down her leg, thumb rolling over her ankle bone before pressing over her heel, moving with steady pressure up the center of her foot until her head dropped back.

"I'm sorry," he said in a low voice, as steady as the movement of his fingers over her skin. "I don't like him. That's all, just him. I shouldn't attribute it to anything else."

She said nothing as he lifted her other leg, giving it the same slow treatment. Her head was buzzing when he finally slipped her strappy sandals onto her wide feet, her pulse a dull thump behind her ears. "I don't care if you don't like him. Suck it up. Silva is my friend,

453

and you're going to be nice."

Lurielle had been certain, as Khash grumbled under his breath one last time when they'd crossed the street before the restaurant that night, that the same sort of complaints had been levied at Silva from wherever it was that Tate lived in town.

Her young co-worker had certainly seemed happier since the first time she'd rode shotgun beside Lurielle on the way to the resort hamlet. After that first week, Silva had apparently plucked up the courage to make the trip on her own, for she'd not driven with Lurielle again, although it was always easy to tell by the brightness of her eyes and the unconscious way she smiled on Monday mornings when she'd spent the weekend outside of Cambric Creek. Lurielle was curious to know what Silva had told her family and how they'd taken the news that she was seeing an elf with Orcish blood, but didn't want to pry. *Not every family is as over the top as yours.* Despite her slight misgivings, she remembered what it was like being newly independent and wouldn't be the one to tell Silva what to do. She only hoped Khash was behaving himself . . .

♥ ♥ ♥

Silva met Lurielle's eye in the mirror, smiling brightly. Getting to know her wiser co-worker better over the past few months had done wonders for her confidence in their friendship, and she no longer felt as though she existed at the periphery of the office clique. Seeing Lurielle on nights like this — outside of work, far away from Cambric

Creek and the same spots around town where they regularly dropped in for happy hour with Ris and Dynah — was nice. Adult, as ridiculous as that was, but Silva couldn't help it: she felt like a proper grown-up when she and Tate met Lurielle and Khash for dessert or for drinks, in a way that she rarely did at home, surrounded as she was by elves who'd known her since birth.

Tate was a proper grown-up, after all. He owned property, owned businesses, had moved across the sea completely on his own. The comfortable bubble of her reality seemed to grow thinner and shift every time she spent the weekend at his side in the little hamlet, and she felt ignorant and small and horribly spoiled by her easy existence in the face of the people she met there . . . but then Cambric Creek would seem pitifully provincial upon her return, her friends from the club circulating the same boring gossip and complaints, her life too easy and candy-colored and dull. The edges of her rigid world were stretching and expanding, the freedom Tate offered pushing back the boundaries, and she had no idea what to do with the extra space.

She'd been finishing her makeup at the mirror above the antique bureau in his room when he'd come home from Clover that evening; watched him change clothes and brush out his sleek black hair before returning it to its artfully messy bun. Her friends would think he was just as handsome and trendy-looking as any uppity elf they might meet in the city, she thought as he crossed to the tall chest of drawers on the opposite wall, removing a box from the back of the top drawer. It was a jewelry box, a very old one from the look of it, and she watched in fascination as he removed the top shelf, revealing a row of men's watches beneath. He chose one from the center before replacing the top, palming and slipping a pendant on a long chain over his head and into his collar in such a quick, practiced movement that Silva would have missed it if she'd blinked at that moment, before returning the box to its home in the drawer.

"Are you ready to leave?"

His skin was always warm, and that moment had been no exception as she clamoured onto the bed behind him, wrapping her arms around his neck. "Are you going to be cranky with me all night?"

"I'm not being cranky. I'm getting ready." Tate never paused his movement to look back at her, bending to adjust the laces on his oxfords.

"You're being *so* cranky!" she moaned into his neck, feeling his huff of laughter against her. She wondered if he was wishing she would have just stayed in Cambric Creek that weekend, leaving him and his routine in peace. *Don't be stupid, he's glad you're here. Stop being so insecure.* "Lurielle is my friend," she reminded him in a small voice, looking up from beneath her lashes as pitifully as she could when he lifted her chin with a curled finger, turning to face her at last.

He had tried to claim he couldn't possibly pull away from work for the night when she'd told him about the plans she and Lurielle had made, had insisted he was needed. Silva would never say so, lest she hurt his feelings, but she wasn't entirely sure Tate was *ever* actually needed at either of his businesses — Thessa was terrifyingly efficient, a constant presence, having worked for Tate for years prior to coming to Clover to run the front of house with Cymbeline, and she had seen with her own two eyes that Rukh was more than capable of handling the Pixie alone. His excuse had been too quick, too well-crafted, and she knew that he simply didn't want to endure the company of Lurielle's boyfriend, but she'd effectively changed his mind, giving him her best abandoned kitten look, one that always worked on her parents. Tate had proven equally susceptible, relenting just a moment later.

"I know she is," he agreed, leaning in to kiss the tip of her nose, "which is why I'm willing to risk having to throw these clothes away once I sit across from that orc. Don't worry, dove. I'm the most charming person I know."

She wasn't worried about him being charming, she thought, lathering up her hands as Lurielle inspected her lip stain in the mirror beside her. She was worried about him being *nice*, which was entirely different. Tate was nice to her, was nice to his girls at work and always had a smile for Clover's patrons, but she saw how he was with the orcs at the Pixie. Nice was outside his wheelhouse, she understood. She knew he had nothing in common with Khash, knew the way he felt about orcs in general. He'd snorted in laughter when she'd pointed out that his best friend was an orc, responding that she herself might have been more Orcish than Ainsley.

Once they'd been seated by the smiling shifter, Silva had felt the buzz of Tate's phone in his pocket pressed to her leg, a non-stop barrage of messages, until he'd pulled it out to turn it off completely. She'd stayed his hand briefly, seeing the endless line of messages from his punkish friend, positing hilarious worst-case scenarios for the evening, coupled with questions about ancient Orcish culture he demanded Tate ask. She'd first met Ainsley at the Pixie, when he'd come breezing in on a Saturday night when she'd been visiting, and had been mortified to realize he was the mohawked orc she'd ogled the night she'd met Elshona. He talked more than anyone she'd ever met, was taller than almost every other orc in the room, and Silva thought, as she met Lurielle's eye in the mirror once more, that Tate was right — she was probably more of an orc than him and his friend combined.

Khash was very nice, was charming and polite, and most importantly, was head over heels for her friend. Still . . . there was something about him. He was too perfect, too handsome and charming and entirely pleased with himself. She was thrilled for Lurielle, and had agreed with Ris and Dynah, when the two had opined that Lurielle would be engaged by the time summer returned, but still . . . he lacked any sort of edge, and Silva had discovered that she liked a bit of an edge. *There's no accounting for taste . . .*

"Do you think they've killed each other yet?"

She was startled from her thoughts by Lurielle, dissolving into giggles when her mind caught up to her friend's words.

"Tate's probably setting something on fire as we speak," she laughed. "The sprinklers are going to go off any minute."

"I'm sure Khash is holding the server hostage at the table so he has someone to charm." Lurielle rolled her eyes at her reflection before turning to Silva with a smile. "Big giant men, and they're the biggest babies the second they have to do something they don't want to."

"That's the truth," Silva agreed. "I guess we've punished them enough, let's rescue them from each other before the building needs to be evacuated."

♥ ♥ ♥

"Mortgage rates. Are you kidding me?!"

She'd lost track of how many times the exclamation had left her mouth since leaving the restaurant, hand-in-hand with Khash. Silva and Tate had turned in the opposite direction on the sidewalk, towards his black-bricked pub, and as she watched, the slender orc stooped, allowing Silva to hoist herself onto his back with a delighted squeal. The temperature had dropped considerably since the sun went in, and she shivered against the cold, not complaining when Khash scooped her up halfway back to the cabin.

When she and Silva had arrived back at the table, Khash and Tate had been talking animatedly, their conversation not ceasing until the server had dropped the check on the table. She had met Silva's eye, the smaller elve's green eyes wide with surprise, a pleased-looking smile on her face. Their chatter had been too fast, too technical for the girls to jump in, numbers and percentages, talking over each other and finishing each other's sentences, Khash dropping his head into his massive hands and groaning as Tate's silvery laughter glimmered around their corner of the dining room, and the server had waved brightly as they departed, the evening ending on a much different note than it had started.

"Mortgage rates!"

"Subprime on the whole block! Bluebell, these people are up to their eye teeth in debt! It doesn't sound like a single one of them went in with a financial advisor, and I have a good mind to go to the council and offer to host a class on — "

"Mortgage rates?!" Khash scowled as she cut him off, turning to spit her toothpaste in the sink. "Khash, this is like the fourth time we've gotten together with them and I think you've exchanged maybe three words with him *in total* before tonight. The two of you were literally talking over each other for an hour! Over . . . mortgage rates?!"

He shrugged as she climbed into bed. "The man knows his business. He was speakin' my language . . . he's still a smug, shifty-eyed faerie, and I've officially reached my Tate quota for the fiscal quarter, so don't go makin' any more plans for us . . . can you explain why you put so many clothes on? I believe I was promised a reward for good behavior."

"I said I was going to make you breakfast tomorrow!"

Lurielle squeaked as she was pulled astride her boyfriend's hips, stretching her thighs wide as her knees came to rest on either side of him. Her t-shirt was dragged over her head as she laughed protestingly.

"If you think that's what I'm hungry for" — Khash pulled her forward against his broad chest as he shimmied her sleep shorts down her hips, one of his massive hands squeezing a palmful of her equally massive ass — "then I can't even begin to explain how wrong you are, darlin'."

"So does that mean you're making *me* breakfast?"

He scowled and she laughed, sliding her palms down his broad chest.

"That's the thanks I get for spending the night with that sanctimonious little . . . you know, Bluebell, he's so crooked, if he swallowed a nail, he'd spit up a corkscrew. I oughta check to make sure my wallet's not missing . . . "

"Stop!" she yelled, dropping against him, shaking in laughter. "You are ridiculous. Fine, I'll make breakfast."

"Tate. Quota. Reached."

Lurielle leaned forward, shutting him up the most effective way she knew how, with lips and tongue, dragging her teeth down his jaw until he was groaning against her, all talk of their companions for the night forgotten, as he pressed upwards against her, the hard evidence of his distraction pressing into her.

It had been, she thought with a satisfied smile, a very nice night.

♥ ♥ ♥

Silva breathed deeply, willing her heartbeat to slow. Beneath her cheek, Tate's thunderous heartbeat had begun to even out, and the hand he had curled in her hair cupped her head, holding her in place against him.

"I think you broke my back."

She giggled against his molten skin, arching when that same hand moved down her neck to trace her spine. "You're the one who wanted me on top."

It had turned out to be a very nice night. When she and Lurielle had arrived back at the table, Tate and Khash had actually been engaged in conversation, something about the neighbors and their cost of operation, the little bakery she liked and the restaurant across from Clover. He'd carried her back to the Pixie afterward when she'd whined that her shoes pinched her toes, where Tate had announced to Rukh that he was leaving him to close up alone. League play wasn't until the following night, and she'd laughed at the old orc's eye roll as he surveyed the nearly-empty bar, before tightening her arms around Tate's neck as he carried her piggy-back up the staircase to the apartment.

"Silva." His voice was a low drone; a deep, pleasant buzz around her ear, and she inhaled deeply filling her lungs with the smell of his skin. He used Sandalwood-scented products, soap and shampoo and assorted other sundries, enticingly warm and smooth smelling, but Silva had come to determine it was something else — the smell of the wide-open sky and a towering forest, as free as the wind — that made her go slightly cross-eyed in desire. Curiously, it changed subtly with the passing weeks. Every time she buried her nose in his hair or against his bare skin in his bed, or pressed her face to his back after the last patron left the bar on Saturday nights, Silva inhaled deeply, mentally tracking the shift of warm air and piney greens to the bonfire smell of cooler nights, the breath of frost mingling with fir needles. *More fae than orc by far.*

"Dove, it defeats the point of the condom if you're not going to move."

"That's your problem," she sighed, feeling deliciously languorous and drowsy. Her head was leaden and sleep beckoned. "You put it on, I didn't tell you that you had to." The wild smell of freedom was steeped in cold, but his skin was warm, so warm, and Silva felt herself slip beneath the surface of lucidity, letting the world fall away.

Sleep seemed like a distant memory when he rolled, flipping their positions, his honeyed eyes narrowed as he glared down at her before withdrawing himself carefully. "Lazy little imp." Her shoulders shook with laughter as he slid his long leg back, staggering off the bed. "I was sitting very close to that orc, I probably smell like a wet dog now," he grumbled. "That shirt is ruined for sure. Don't go makin' any plans for me for the rest of the season, I've met my quota of playing nice."

Silva sat up and bounced from the bed, sleep forgotten as she pushed past him. "You're right," she announced, pausing in the bedroom doorway, "you do smell like a wet dog. But you were very nice tonight, so tomorrow you get to make me breakfast . . . race you to the shower!"

She had the water on by the time he entered the bathroom, shaking his head at her antics. She would leave tomorrow afternoon, back to Cambric Creek and Daytime Silva and the lies she told. She wanted to believe her family would welcome him with open arms, that her happiness would matter more to them than status or family name or the color of his skin, that her friends would not make her the subject of every hushed whisper and cruel joke; she desperately wanted to be brave like Lurielle and walk away from it all . . . but Daytime Silva was a mouse, and she couldn't bring herself to have the conversations that needed to be had. She wasn't so much as playing at being a proper adult than playing make-believe.

His hair was silky in her hands and his lips hot against hers as he lifted her, pressing her back to the cool tiles as the hot water cascaded down, and she pushed reality away once more. *Tomorrow. You leave tomorrow, you can think about it then.*

"I was very nice to that orc. The nicest anyone's ever been. Nicer than he deserved."

"The nicest boy in Nicetown," she agreed, gasping when he lifted her higher, his slim nose pressing to her jaw.

"It's going to be fine, Silva. You're going to be alright."

His words were soft enough that she was nearly able to convince herself she'd imagined them, but she nodded as he kissed the shell of her ear. She wished she had his confidence, wished she had Lurielle's bravery . . . but it would be fine. He'd said so, and she needed to believe him. She'd not let her anxiety and fear ruin the weekend.

After all, she reminded herself, as Tate pulled her leg to wrap around his waist, it *had* been a very nice night.

(To read The Trouble with Leprechauns, another GW short,

subscribe to my newsletter!)

Moon Blooded
Breeding Clinic

Coming Summer 2022

He'd been still chewing over the idea that morning when he saw the flier.

The silhouette of a happy family, a mother cradling an infant to her chest and smiling beatifically beneath the intriguing text which caught his eye.

Are you a healthy werewolf aged 25-40?

We need you! Help families achieve their dreams

-Call us for information today

Lowell read and reread the flier several times, not gleaning any better idea of what service it advertised on the fifth reading than he had on the first, before snapping a photo with his phone.

It was several hours before he got around to calling the number, having finished the arduous task of winterizing the pool with his brother, retreating to the small guesthouse at last to video call his office for a status update, only to be told there was still no change: his travel visa was virtually worthless in the current state of things, he would be stranded stateside for the foreseeable future. *Volunteer work it is.*

He was unprepared for the conversation which resulted.

"What we offer is a revolutionary new way for families to achieve their goal of natural childbirth, particularly those interspecies couples unable to have a child together due to reproductive incompatibility." The doctor to whom his call had been transferred—once he'd answered a brief survey of questions confirming that he was, in fact, a healthy werewolf within the desired age bracket—had an impassioned manner of speaking, and Lowell leaned forward on his elbows, eyebrows drawn as he wondered if this actually constituted as "volunteer" work.

"Our donors are not just contributing genetic material, they are providing the opportunity for these families to end months of frustration and money wasted. Interspecies adoption is cost-prohibitive for most families, as you may know, and the viability of in vitro fertilization is very low for so many people...in contrast, we are not another dead end. Due to the uniqueness of our service, our success rate is unparalleled, I assure you."

Contributing genetic material. "It's sperm donation," Lowell cut in, attempting to find the straightest path forward, as he always did. "Why do you specifically need werewolves?"

"Ah, that is where you're wrong. The service we provide is far more than merely donating sperm in a specimen cup. The success rate depends on actual copulatory practices, and the unique physiology of the lupine male provides the most effective method to ensure successful insemination."

"On actual..." His cock twitched as he considered the meaning behind the doctor's words. "Actual *intercourse*?" Being trapped in a succession of his brother's homes had been challenging in more ways than one, and he'd not had sex since arriving in Cambric Creek months earlier. Grayson's poolhouse afforded a bit more privacy, but being a Hemming in Cambric Creek was a handicap in and of itself.

"That's correct. You see, a lunar estrus cycle is triggered in each patient..."

The doctor's words fell away as Lowell mentally slotted the final piece of the puzzle together. Lunar estrus was just a fancy term for a heat, and if the copulation would be taking place at the full moon... *the unique physiology of the lupine male.*

"I'd be *knotting* someone?!" His cock twitched again, thickening at the thought. It was an act rarely indulged in; the danger of the turn, the reproductive ramifications, outing oneself as a werewolf—there was much that could go wrong in such a scenario. It was a lecture they'd all received from their father once puberty hit, and from the notes compared with his brother's Jack's speech remained the same from son-to-son: you do *not* knot your partners. The risk of injury was present, the risk of an unwanted pregnancy substantial, and life as a werewolf outside of Cambric Creek's well-sheltered borders was not always a picnic. It was mortifying and he clearly remembered holding his breath, trying to disappear into the cushions of the sofa as his father paced agitatedly before him and Owen, but the lecture had stuck. He'd had more partners than he could count who'd been disappointed he'd *not* knotted them, not understanding that the *unique physiology* was something that came with the turn. *And these people are willing to pay for it!*

On the other end of the line, the doctor cleared his throat. "We don't like to use that term, but yes, essentially. The breeding instinct triggered by the smell of a receptive female coupled with the reproductive advantage of the bulbus glandis is quite sufficient to—"

The breeding instinct. Completely animalistic, mindless rutting, over and over into a woman in heat who would be writhing and begging for his cock, for his knot; tightening around him as he filled her repeatedly, again and again until he was spent and she was full of his seed. Lowell shifted, his erection practically scraping the table's underside. *It's been a very long summer...*

"The process is completely safe. Everything happens in our clinic, and the safety of both the donor and recipient is our utmost concern. If you are worried about being unduly othered, let me put your fears to rest—the clinic founders and all its doctors are of the lupine persuasion, and we take the privacy of our donors very seriously. You will be in good hands with us."

Lowell thought about Jackson's little boy again, the overwhelming joy of watching him learn new things and explore the world...he could give that gift to another family. He was a Hemming, a highly sought-after bloodline, and he had no plans to tie himself down to a mortgage and family in Cambric Creek, not anytime soon, despite his mother's wishes. The donor werewolves were compensated, and he could donate those funds back to the clinic, or to another charity.

The clinic itself was in Starling Heights, a decent enough distance from Cambric Creek to ensure he'd not likely run into anyone who would know him. Devotion to family, loyalty to pack, service to community, that's what his parents were always going on about. There seemed no better service to the community than to help a family achieve their desire for a child...and the fact that he would actually get to enjoy the process was all the better.

"I'll do it," he blurted, knuckles tightening on the table. He was going stir crazy, the open road normally before him abruptly curtailed, and he needed something to break up the monotony of his new non-routine. He could help a family, could do something worthwhile with his time for as long as he was stuck here. And it won't be so terrible for you either, he thought, an end to the hometown dry spell. "Where do I sign?"

About the Author ·

C.M. Nascosta is an author and professional procrastinator from Cleveland, Ohio. As a child, she thought that living on Lake Erie meant one was eerie by nature, and her corresponding love of all things strange and unusual started young. She's always preferred beasts to boys, the macabre to the milquetoast, the unknown darkness in the shadows to the Chad next door. She lives in a crumbling old Victorian with a scaredy-cat dachshund, where she writes nontraditional romances featuring beastly boys with equal parts heart and heat, and is waiting for the Hallmark Channel to get with the program and start a paranormal lovers series.

Do you love exclusive short stories and character art? Consider supporting me on Patreon! https://www.patreon.com/Monster_Bait

Visit C.M. Nascosta's website for Content Warnings, blog posts, and newsletter signup: cmnascosta.com

Stay in touch on social media!

facebook.com/authorcmnascosta

twitter.com/cmnascosta

instagram.com/cmnascosta

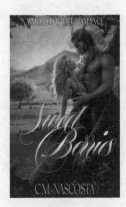

Grace has a job she loves, a community she adores, and plenty of friends . . . but her lack of bedroom action has left this event planner too horny to think.

When one ill-advised night at the bar leads to her giving an exhibitionistic show to an unknown presence outside her bedroom window, she thinks she's hit a new low. When her voyeur turns out to be a nebbishly charming mothman, Grace needs to decide if she can trust her body — and her heart — with this garnet-eyed stranger before he flys out of her life for good.

Sweet Berries is a monster/human romance featuring high heat and a lot of heart, with a guaranteed HEA. It is the second book in the Cambric Creek Steamy Sweet Monster Romance series.

COMING MAY 31ST, 2022